T0115489

THE
GETAWAY
GOD

A SANDMAN SLIM NOVEL

RICHARD KADREY

HARPER Voyager
An Imprint of HarperCollinsPublishers

Harper Voyager and design is a trademark of HCP LLC.

THE GETAWAY GOD. Copyright © 2014 by Richard Kadrey. Excerpt from KILLING PRETTY copyright © 2015 by Richard Kadrey. All rights reserved. Printed in the United States of America. No part of this book may be used or reproduced in any manner whatsoever without written permission except in the case of brief quotations embodied in critical articles and reviews. For information address HarperCollins Publishers, 195 Broadway, New York, New York 10007.

HarperCollins books may be purchased for educational, business, or sales promotional use. For information please e-mail the Special Markets Department at SPsales@harpercollins.com.

A hardcover edition of this book was published in 2014 by Harper Voyager, an imprint of HarperCollins Publishers.

FIRST HARPER VOYAGER PAPERBACK EDITION PUBLISHED 2015.

Designed by Paula Russell Szafranski

Library of Congress Cataloging-in-Publication Data
Kadrey, Richard.
  The getaway god : a Sandman Slim novel / Richard Kadrey. — First edition.
    pages cm
  ISBN 978-0-06-209461-2 (hardback) — ISBN 978-0-06-219762-7 (paperback) 1. Imaginary wars and battles—Fiction. I. Title.
  PS3561.A3616G48 2014
  813'.54—dc23
                            2014007995

HB 01.09.2024

They stood on the far shore of a river and called to him. Tattered gods slouching in their rags across the waste.

—CORMAC MCCARTHY, *THE ROAD*

"I'm very brave generally," he went on in a low voice: "only to-day I happen to have a headache."

—LEWIS CARROLL, *THROUGH THE LOOKING-GLASS*

This book was finished on William S. Burroughs's one-hundredth birthday. This one is for you, Bill.

ACKNOWLEDGMENTS

Thanks to my agent, Ginger Clark, and my editor, Diana Gill. Thanks also to Pamela Spengler-Jaffee, Kelly O'Connor, Caroline Perny, Shawn Nicholls, Dana Trombley, Emma Coode, and the rest of the team at Harper Voyager. Thanks also to Dave Barbor, Sarah LaPolla, and Holly Frederick. Big thanks to Martha and Lorenzo in L.A. And thanks to Suzanne Stefanac, Pat Murphy, Paul Goat Allen, and Lustmord for the sound track to Hell. As always, thanks to Nicola for everything else.

THE
GETAWAY
GOD

YOU'D THINK THE end of the world would be exciting, but this apocalypse is about as much fun as dental surgery.

Take the current situation. Sitting at a dead stop in traffic, as lively as a stone angel over a tomb. Not one car has moved in ten minutes. It's bumper to bumper on Sunset Boulevard, which is nothing new, but this kind of traffic is 24/7 these days, as it seems like half the city is hightailing it out of Dodge all at once. And the rain. It's been coming down nonstop for two weeks. It's like L.A. lost a bet with God and the old bastard is pissing his Happy Hour whiskey all over the city. Which, when you get down to it, isn't far from the truth. This isn't how I figured I'd ring in the apocalypse.

"Any time now, Jeff Gordon," says Candy from the passenger seat. "I thought this was supposed to be a car chase."

"By current L.A. standards, this *is* a car chase."

"Current L.A. seriously blows. And I think my boots are starting to grow gills."

We're in an Escalade I stole in Westwood. I hate these showboats, but it can handle the flooded streets and gets me high enough over the other cars that I can keep an eye on a cherry black '69 Charger up ahead. There's a guy inside that U.S. Marshal Wells, grand high shitbird boss of the Golden Vigil, wants to talk to.

"I should go up there, rip the fucker's door off, and stuff him in the back of the van."

"And you could take a brass band so no one misses the show. Your boss would love that."

"He wants discreet, but he knows I'm not good at discreet. I swear he did this to me on purpose."

I reach for the Maledictions in my coat pocket. Drop them and the lighter on the floor on Candy's side. She picks them up and taps out a cigarette.

"Marshal Wells is a man of God," says Candy, grinning. "He only has your best interests at heart."

"Abraham was a man of God and he almost did a Jack the Ripper on his kid to prove it."

"See? You get off light. Your father figure just sends you out in the rain to drown."

Candy flicks the lighter and sparks a cigarette. Hands it to me and rolls down her window to let out the smoke.

I say, "Wells is a father figure like I'm one of Santa's elves."

"There you go. You're getting into the Christmas spirit. I'll have to get you a pointy hat with a bell so you feel like a real elf."

"You already gave me the Colt. I thought that was my present. And I gave you the guitar."

"That was different. Those were 'We might die tonight' presents. And it was November, so they don't count."

"This is just you angling to get another present."

"It's the end of the world, sweetheart. Crack open the piggy bank."

"We spent the piggy bank on Max Overdrive."

She shrugs.

"That's your problem. I already have something picked out for you, so don't try to weasel out of this. I want a real damned present on real damned Christmas morning."

I puff the Malediction. Brake lights go dark in the distance.

"Yes, ma'am. Anything else? Eight maids a-milking maybe?"

"Are they hot maids? 'Cause I never had a nine-way before, so, yeah."

Somewhere far away a car moves. More brake lights go off ahead of us. In the distance, I actually see a truck inch forward.

"It's a Christmas miracle," shouts Candy. "God bless us every one."

Like some great wheezing machine no one has fired up since D-Day, cars around us begin to creep tentatively forward. I take my foot off the brake and let the Escalade roll.

At that moment the sky opens up. I hit the windshield wipers, but a second after the glass goes clear, it's drenched again. I roll down my window and stick my head out. The Malediction is instantly soggy. I spit it out. The sky has gone dark gray, dulling the colors on all the cars. In the downpour I lose sight of the Charger.

"Do you see it?"

Candy has her head out her window.

"It's about a block ahead," she says. Then, "Wait. It's got its signal on. I think it's turning. Yeah, there it goes."

Traffic lurches to a stop. Horns honk. People shout at each other.

"Wait. He's gone?"

"Yeah, around the first corner."

It's a sea of brake lights again. No one is going anywhere.

"Know what?"

"What?" says Candy.

"I'm about to call in that brass band. Get your head back inside the car."

"Now you're talking."

Traffic is ass to nose again. I put the Escalade in reverse and ram the car behind me. Put it in drive and ram the car ahead. Reverse again, then drive the van up onto the sidewalk. I hit the horn and floor it.

Angelinos are used to desert heat and chocolate-colored smog skies. Rain is kryptonite to these people, so there's hardly anyone outside. The few rain birds hear me coming and jump out of the way. The only casualty of my sidewalk Le Mans is a sign outside a café and a bench outside a Chinese restaurant. No one's used the damned thing in weeks and no one will until the world ends, which means it shouldn't even be there, so fuck it.

I turn hard at the corner. The rear end of the van fishtails and hits a mailbox. Letters explode like New Year's confetti over the stalled cars.

"Jerk," says Candy. "Now people's Christmas cards are getting wet."

"Will you shut up about Christmas and help me look for the car?"

Traffic is a little lighter on the side street, so the Charger could still be ahead. Or have pulled off into a parking lot or another side street.

"Shit. Shit. Shit."

On the next block is a row of warehouses. Distribution points. The kind of places that get goods from big warehouses and parcel them out to regular stores.

"There," says Candy. "By the open loading dock."

I look to where she's pointing and spot the Charger. It's sideways to the dock and the driver-side door is open; not parked, but abandoned. I stop the Escalade and get out. Instantly, I'm soaked. My frock coat, motorcycle pants, and boots weren't made for this Noah's ark bullshit. It feels like I've gained twenty pounds before I take a step.

Candy comes around the van. I start across the street.

"You got your gun?"

She holds up her Swiss folding pistol. Unopened, it looks kind of like a skinny lunch box. She's covered it with stickers from some of her favorite animes. *FLCL. Ghost in the Shell. Blood. Appleseed.* She pushes a button and the lunch box unfolds like a matte-black Transformer into an extended 9mm pistol with a shoulder stock. She grins. She always grins when she gets to use her gun because she thinks she's Modesty Blaise and who am I to tell her she's not?

"I'm going in the front. Go around the side and see if there's a back way in. If you can't get through it, make sure no one gets out."

As she starts away she says, "Be careful."

"I'm always careful."

"Right. That's how you got all those scars. From being careful."

I wait for her to disappear around the side of the building before I go in. I jump up onto the Charger's hood and from there onto the dock platform.

It's at least twenty degrees colder inside the warehouse. I spot maybe fifteen people working. Carrying boxes and driving forklifts. It's a meat-packing plant, prepping orders to take to butcher shops. I can see my breath in front of my face.

Wells gave me a photo of the man I'm supposed to follow but I don't see him among the faces up front. I head into the back of the plant to the big freezer. The entrance is covered with a thick plastic curtain with slits every couple of feet so forklifts can pass in and out. I grab a clipboard off a nail on the wall and stroll past a forklift coming the other way.

Inside the freezer the real cold hits me. This isn't muggy L.A. showers weather. This is penguin country. I swear my wet clothes start freezing to my body.

They must be doing good business at the warehouse. The freezer stretches away in both directions, full of sides of beef on nasty-looking meat hooks. I don't want to go in unarmed, but I might as well try the discretion thing as long as I can. I take out the na'at instead of my gun. The na'at is a weapon I picked up in the arena in Hell. It collapses to no longer than a cop's riot baton, but can extend like a spear or a whip. It isn't always a quiet weapon because of all the screaming, but it's more subtle than a Colt pistol.

I snap open the na'at into a spear shape and move through the meat forest as quietly as I can. This might be a mistake. Maybe I should have checked the office first. But Wells didn't say anything about the guy working here and most people when they're scared head as far from the front door as possible. That's back here. Still, after staring at row after row of dead cow, I'm getting bored and hungry. Then I spot a different kind of light a few rows ahead. It's softer and more diffuse than in the rest of the freezer, and tinged in pink. I head for it and find Mr. Charger. He's not alone.

Thirteen of them stand in a circle in an open area in the back of the freezer. By open area, I mean there aren't any sides of beef hanging back here, but there's a hell of a lot of meat. They've made a whole cathedral of the stuff. Arches made from ribs, livers, hearts, and leg bones all frozen together. A vaulted ceiling from muscle trimmed from sides of beef hanging on high hooks. Their flesh church even has nave windows made of stitched-together sheets of pig caul. The light back here is a milky crimson.

All thirteen of them, six men and seven women, smile at me. Big and toothy.

"It took you long enough to find us," says Mr. Charger.

"Sorry. I took a wrong turn at the pork chops."

"No worries. You're here. That's all that matters."

I know I should watch the crazies, but I can't take my eyes off the meat Notre-Dame.

"I love what you've done with the place. Ed Gein chic."

"Thank you. It took some time to get it just right."

"Who's your decorator? We're finishing my new place and there's all this leftover chorizo. Maybe we could use it for a rumpus room."

Mr. Charger doesn't say anything because he's watching me as I see it.

Not all the meat in the church is animal. There's a human body cut into six pieces—arms, legs, torso, and head—hanging like nightmare piñatas over the smiling circle of freaks.

Mr. Charger says, "Do you understand why you're here?"

"If you think I'm going to be the next one hanging from those hooks, you're extremely mistaken."

Normally, I could probably handle a flock of unarmed fruit bats. Hell, the freezer is big enough that I could just run away if I broke a nail. But these particular fruit bats are all armed. Each holds a wicked-looking motorized meat saw, like an oversize electric knife. Outwardly they all look calm, but they're sweating, even in this cold. They smell of fear and adrenaline. The sweat steams from their bodies and collects at the ceiling like incense in their mad church.

Mr. Charger shakes his head.

"We're not here to hurt you. You're here to help us."

"How did you know I was coming?"

Mr. Charger looks around at his friends.

"God told us."

I shake my head.

"I'm kind of acquainted with God and I don't think he told you dick."

A thin redhead from the back says, "We mean the true God."

"Oh hell. You're Angra worshipers, aren't you? Is that what this is all about? I don't mean to cramp your little chautauqua, but my boss wants a word with you. How about you put down the saws and you can come and be crazy where it's warm?"

A chuckle goes around the circle.

"I'm not going with you because I'm not here for you. You're here for us," says Mr. Charger.

"If you're selling candy bars to go to summer camp, I'm tapped out right now."

Mr. Charger raises his meat saw. I move my weight onto my back leg, ready to move when he tells them to rush me.

"We don't want anything from you except to be our witness."

"To what?"

"The sacrifice."

Without another word or a signal, all thirteen of them raise their meat saws to their throats.

Mr. Charger is the first to shove the buzzing saw into his neck. He screams, but just for a second before the blade rips through his larynx and his throat fills with blood. He goes down twitching as the others fire up their own saws, following their leader's example. It's the same for all of them. A small scream as the blade tears into them. A gurgling as their voice box goes, the blood fills their throat and jets from their severed arteries. It only takes a few seconds and all thirteen are on the floor, their blood steaming on the cold metal. Their saws rattle and buzz where they dropped them.

I've seen some cold moves in my time, I've fought and killed in Hell and on earth, but I've never seen anything quite like this before.

Over the sound of the saws I hear voices. All the screaming got someone's attention. That's all I need. A warehouse of hysterical meat packers with big knives and cell phones. Imagine explaining this to a 911 operator. It might take awhile to get a patrol car. But still, it's the principle of the thing. I'm not in the mood to deal with another crazed mob right now.

They're getting near me now and I let them. When the first few tough guys emerge from the rows of beef and see me in the meat cathedral surrounded by freezing corpses, they stop. Good. They're not going to rush me but they're still between me and the door. I pull the Colt and shoot three rounds into the floor by their feet. That alters their mood and sends them scurrying like sensible rats out of there.

Only one person is still coming in my direction. Candy shoulders her way between the beef rows, her gun up, sweeping the room. But when she sees me, even she stops. For a second I can see it in her eyes. She wonders if I did this. Then she sees the meat saws and relaxes. She lowers her gun and comes over to me.

"Oh man," she says. "I mean. Oh man."

I go from saw to saw and turn them off. The sound is giving me a headache.

"Yeah."

"What were they . . . ?"

"It was a sacrifice to one of their idiot Angra gods."

"Couldn't they have just had a bake sale?"

I walk over and put my hand on her gun, lowering it to her side. I put my arm around her. I haven't seen her this freaked out before. She presses against me.

I say, "Wells is going to be pissed."

She nods.

"He can't blame you for this insanity."

"Wells blames me for tooth decay. He can sure blame me for this. But maybe there's something I can do. Help me find a cooler and some dry ice."

There's a stack of Styrofoam coolers just outside the freezer. I grab one and Candy gets plastic packets of dry ice. We go back into the cooler. I have to work fast. Someone's called the cops by now. For all I know, one of the workers has a pistol in the back of their truck. There's a lot of that going around these days. When we get back to the suicide circle, I tell Candy to go back and guard the door.

"You just don't want me to see you do it," she says.

"You're right. But I also want you to guard the door."

"Okay."

She runs back to the freezer entrance. I turn on one of the meat saws and get to work. It doesn't take long. Mr. Charger did the hard part himself. All I have to do is get through some gristle and the spinal cord so I can twist his head all the way off.

When I do, I put it in the cooler and pack ice around it.

Candy shakes her head when she sees me with the container.

"I've dated some messed-up people in my time."

"Write 'Dear Abby.' Let's get out of here."

"Let's."

There's a nice dark shadow by a stack of boxes on the loading dock. I start to pull Candy through and stop.

"What you said before. Eight maids and you. That's a nine-way. Where am I in all this?"

"That's your present. You get to watch."

"I can see it for free on the Web."

"I'm better than the Web."

"I'll give you that. But you're still coming out ahead on this deal. Better get me that pointy hat so I won't feel cheated."

She takes my hand.

"You got it, Jingles."

We step into a shadow and come out in the Golden Vigil's

new L.A. headquarters, right off the eight hole of the Wilshire Golf Club. They eminent-domained the place right out from under the blue bloods, paying ten cents on the dollar, for what it's worth. It's the first time I ever really respected the Vigil. Marshals and Vigil witch doctors still dress up in pricy sports clothes and play round after round of existential golf on the grounds. No one keeps score, but someone has to be out on the greens keeping up the appearance that the club is still just a place for rich morons to blow an afternoon. Like maybe none of the locals noticed the surplus Iraq War ASVs, enough lab gear to restart the Manhattan Project, and about a hundred blacked-out bulletproof vans sneaking into the club.

A man is waiting for me inside the clubhouse. He's wearing a black suit and skinny tie, with a flag pin on the lapel. He looks like a mortician's idea of a high school principal.

U.S. Marshal Larson Wells is God's own Pinkerton on Earth. The Golden Vigil is Homeland Security's dirty little secret—an investigation and law enforcement operation for supernatural activity. Which is a nice way of saying they're dedicated to harassing people like me and pretty much everyone I know. They're thorough and obsessive. From what I've heard, they still have Lucifer on a terrorist watch list with a price on his head.

Wells is a charming piece of work. A Nevada Holy Roller marshal who hates working with me as much as I hate working for him. But we both have a vested interest in stopping the old gods, the Angra Om Ya, from returning and eating the world. Wells has a habit of calling all Sub Rosa and Lurkers "pixies," which isn't so bad on its own. It's just that he says it the way a backwoods redneck says "faggot." He used to run the Vigil with an angel named Aelita. She's dead. I didn't do it, but I would have been happy to.

I've been back on the Vigil payroll for a couple of weeks and things are going swell.

"Where is he?" says Wells when he sees me and Candy.

"There was a problem," I say.

"What kind of problem?"

I hold out the ice chest. Wells's eyes narrow and he opens the lid an inch before dropping it down again.

"What in all of God's creation is wrong with you? I sent you on a simple snatch-and-grab. I wanted to question this man. Where's the rest of him?"

"In a meat locker near Sunset and Echo Park, along with a dozen other dead Angra fans. They built a Sistine Chapel out of body parts in one of the freezers. You might want to send a team over before the cops haul away all the evidence. You can get the GPS off my phone."

"Don't move," says Wells. He pulls out his BlackBerry and thumbs in a text like he wants to punch the keys in the face. When he's done he sighs and peeks in the cooler again.

"Why did you even bring that thing here? I'm not paying you by the scalp."

"He didn't do it," says Candy. "Well, not all of it. Just the last part to get his head off. The guy did the rest himself."

Wells turns to Candy. It's the first time he's acknowledged her presence.

"It's truly a comfort knowing that your paramour only partly cut off the head on a key witness in our investigation."

"Just 'cause he's dead doesn't mean we can't still question him. That's why he's on ice," I say.

"Go on."

"There's this ritual I know. It's messy, but if I do it right, I can catch his soul before he goes into the afterlife."

"And how pray tell does the ritual work?"

"First I have to die a little."

Wells puts up his hands and claps once.

"Well, isn't that peachy? Another death today? And a suicide? Right here in Vigil headquarters? I can't see Washington minding that at all. Please go ahead."

"It isn't technically suicide because I'm only partway dead and only for a little while."

"Good, because suicide is a sin, this is consecrated ground, and I've already broken enough commandments just letting you in here."

I hand Candy the cooler and go up to Wells.

"You came to me for help, remember? You know what I do and how I work. Anytime you don't want me around I'm gone. But when I leave, the Magic 8 Ball comes with me."

"So you can lose the weapon again? How about you clean up this mess before you go causing another?"

"Fine. Get me a room where I can do the ritual. Preferably somewhere quiet and private. There's going to be some blood."

"More good news," he says. "Come with me. I wanted you to see this anyway. It's one of the old club offices. We've turned it into a kind of lab so you pixies can do magic or whatever without contaminating or scaring the bejesus out of the newer agents."

"They sound a little too sensitive to be cops."

"Don't bad-mouth my people. None of them's ever come back with a head in a box."

"Maybe you didn't ask nice enough."

Wells leads us through the place. The building is swarming with agents. Some in dark suits like Wells's. Some in lab coats.

The building doesn't resemble much of a country club anymore. They've knocked down walls and torn out floors and ceilings to bring in their special tech. I never had much use for the stuff, but I guess it suits whatever most of them do. The tech is a mix of hush-hush black budget science-fiction toys crossed with angelic hoodoo they used to get from Aelita. I don't know what they're doing for it now. Maybe they have another angel on the payroll. They sure can't ask me for help. I'm a nephilim. Half human, half angel. And I worked hard to get the angel part of me under control. The little prick is a boy scout and a bore. I'm not bringing him out again just to sup up some laptops and ray guns.

Wells leads us into what used to be one of the business offices. Now the windows have been blacked out and it's been turned into an occult space. A place where disreputable pixies like me can perform forbidden rites and magical high jinks.

Candy sets the cooler down on a worktable piled high with old books and manuscripts.

"What do you think? Looks like you finally got your hoodoo man-cave."

"I've seen the Vigil do worse. At least they're admitting that they need something more than angelic halo polishers on their side."

Candy flips through the old books, looking for wood prints of medieval monsters, one of her favorite things. I look around.

There are lab coats, aprons, gloves, and eye protection by the door. Dry-erase boards mounted along one wall covered in English and angelic script. A few Angra runes too. There's what looks like an alchemy setup in the corner, with test tubes, burners, alembics, and enough herbs, elixirs, and powders to build a hedge maze. Some clever boots has installed a silver magic circle in the floor. A massive crucifix is bolted to the back of the door. A rube's talisman designed to keep our unholy magic from contaminating the rest of the Vigil's headquarters. Same as always. They need us hoodoo types, but they never let us forget that we belong in the back of the bus.

"What's that?" says Candy.

Back by the plants and lab gear is a broken-down Japanese shrine, just big enough to hold a wizened old body. The coffin-size shrine and mummy look hundreds of years old. The body sits cross-legged in a meditation pose. It's dressed in gold ceremonial robes and a conical monk's hat, so someone is looking after it. Paper-thin flesh stretches over delicate bones. It almost looks polished. Like the body isn't a mummy at all, but a statue carved from lacquered wood. There are offerings of *mochi*, an orange, and incense at the foot of the shrine.

I go over and touch the dried, worm-eaten word on the top of the shrine.

"Don't know. It looks like Norman Bates's prom date."

Wells comes in and sees me.

"Don't touch that," he barks.

"What's the deal with Skeletor here?"

With a creak, the mummy turns its head.

"Me? What's the deal with you, fatty?"

Slowly, the mummy monk unfolds its arms and legs. It's so slow and delicate, it looks like a giant stick insect waking up.

I take a few steps back. Candy comes around the table and stands beside me, holding on to my arm. Not out of fright but in a "Holy shit can you believe this shit?" way.

Finally, the mummy is standing. The golden robes hang off him like a layer of extra flesh. He stands up straight, puts out his arms, and stretches.

"Nice nap," he says, then looks back at me. "You're the one I've heard so much about. You been running around shooting more people, fatso?"

Dead man or not, Candy steps up.

"Don't call him names, you bony bastard. He's skinny as a rail."

The mummy waves a dismissive hand at her.

"You need glasses."

"That's a holy man, young lady," says Wells. "You do not speak to him like that."

"Then he shouldn't call people names," she says.

"Stark, let me introduce you to Ishiro Shonin."

Before Candy can start arguing with Wells, I go over to the mummy, hoping this is all some kind of hazing ritual.

"What's your story, dead man? I hear you speaking English, but your mouth is doing something else."

He shuffles to the table with the herbs and lab equipment. Drinks something green from an Erlenmeyer flask.

"Ah," he says when he's done. "You have good eyes for a fool. I speak how I like and you hear how you like. Same thing for me. I hear you, so you make sense. Not that someone like you makes much sense."

"I bet you wow them on talent night at the morgue. Do you do balloon animals too?"

"Fat, and ugly too. Not much for someone like you out in the world, is there? You have to hide and consort with the dead like me."

"Speaking of the dead, why don't you get more shut-eye? I need to talk to a dead man before he's gone completely. You have any crow feathers around here?"

Ishiro Shonin glances over at the ice chest. I don't have to tell him what's in there.

"How are you going to talk to him?"

"A messy ritual. But effective. It's the Metatron's Cube Communion."

The Shonin nods.

"That's why you want crow feathers. You lie down with the dead man and slash your wrists. Lots of blood and all that? Of course you'd choose that one."

"I've used it before. It's goddamn effective."

"Watch the blasphemy," says Wells.

"You like the Cube Communion because you're in love with death," says the Shonin. "You die a little and come back. Cheat death over and over like a bad boyfriend kissing another girl." He looks at Candy. "Is he a bad boyfriend?"

"No. He's great."

"Then you shouldn't let him be so stupid."

I say, "So what do you suggest?"

The Shonin pokes around the table of herbs with the black bony fingers. Picks up a furry twig dotted with small yellow blossoms.

"Dream tea. I learned it from a moon spirit. You probably don't believe that kind of thing, but it's true."

"Me? I believe in everything. How does it work?"

"You make a tea. You meditate. You enter the spirit realm and find your man before he drifts away. That okay with you, fatty?"

"Great. Brew some up. I'll try it."

"You know how to meditate?"

"Everyone in L.A. knows how to meditate."

The Shonin looks as doubtful as a skeleton can. He puts water on a small flame to boil. Drops the twig into the pot.

"I should do it. I have more experience," says the Shonin.

"And I have trust issues. I'll do it."

"If you get lost and can't come back, don't blame me."

"If I get stuck because of your hoodoo juice, my ghost is going to come back and shit in your skull."

The Shonin shakes his head. It sounds like twigs cracking.

"No reasoning with some people."

"Amen to that," says Wells.

Candy says, "You're really going to drink that stuff?"

I take off my wet coat and throw it over the back of a chair.

"If I don't have to slice and dice myself, I'm willing to try it. Wells won't let him kill me, will you, Wells? I'm the only one with experience handling the 8 Ball."

"So far," says Wells. "But there's always tomorrow."

"Maybe not too many," says Candy. "You might want to remember that."

The Shonin takes the tea off the burner and pours a brown mess into a small ceramic cup.

"The girl . . ."

"Candy," she says.

The Shonin looks at her.

"Your name is food? How about I call you Banana Split or Hot Dog?"

Candy turns Jade for a second. Her eyes go black, with pinpoints of red at the center. Her teeth are as sharp as a shark with a switchblade.

"Why don't you just do that?"

The Shonin looks at Wells.

"What the hell kind of a place do you run here? You bring me a fatty and a demon to work with? I didn't meditate in a hole in the ground for four hundred years for this crap."

Candy goes back to her human face and I touch her shoulder on the way to the cooler. She doesn't take shit from anyone. It's one of the reasons we get along.

I take the dead man's head from the cooler and sit facing it in the silver circle on the floor. I take the Colt from my waistband and hand it to Candy. She snatches the tea out of the Shonin's hand and brings it to me.

"Thanks."

"Now I have both of our guns. If anything weird happens here, I'm shooting these two first."

"Please do."

I look at the Shonin.

"I'd still like that crow feather."

He goes to the herb table and pulls a feather from a bundle wrapped in twine. Candy takes it from him and brings it to me. This isn't like the old days. I'm still getting used to having someone watch my back. It's an okay feeling.

"Thanks, baby."

I throw back the cup of tea. It tastes like hot swamp water filtered through a baboon's ass.

"Okay," the Shonin says. "Now you meditate. You need a *zafu* to sit on? What kind of meditation do you do?"

I pull a flask from my back pocket.

"The liquid kind," I say, unscrewing the top and downing a long drink of Aqua Regia, the number one booze in Hell. It goes down like gasoline and hot pepper and washes the taste of baboon out of my mouth.

The Shonin says, "Drink all you want, dummy. You won't find God in a bottle."

"I already found God," I say. "That's why I drink."

I hand Candy the flask and she takes a quick gulp before putting it in her pocket. I'm used to Aqua Regia's kick, but down enough at once and it's going to turn anyone's cerebral cortex into chocolate pudding. I let it and the tea do their work. They fight it out in my stomach. The Hellion hoodoo wrestling whatever kind of magic Mr. Bones uses. My stomach cramps and for a few seconds I want to throw up. But I hold on and the feeling passes. The room gets thin, like it's made of black gauze. I put the crow feather between my teeth just as I fall out of myself.

I'm standing on an alkali plain stretching out flat and cracked in all directions. In the far distance is a shaft of light, but it never moves. The sky is dim, like just before sunrise or after sunset. Flip a coin to decide. The air is thick and hard to breathe. I wouldn't want to have to run a marathon here.

The dead man wanders around shivering. Probably from being on ice for so long. I'm glad it worked and I didn't have to come halfway to Hell for nothing.

The dead man stumbles back a couple of steps when he sees me. A second later he recognizes me and starts over, a little cautious.

I say, "Joseph Hobaica."

He stops.

"How do you know my name?"

"We're standing in fuckall limbo and that's your first question? It's just a little trick I can do."

He looks around, hands across his chest, holding on to his shoulders, shaking.

"Where are we?"

"I just told you. Limbo. Halfway between Hell and Heaven. You're dead. Remember?"

His face changes. Things start coming back to him. Death can be a real kick in the ass, especially a death like Hobaica's. Sometimes it takes awhile for spirits to come back to themselves.

"This isn't right," he says. "This isn't where I should be. Where's the Flayed Heart?"

Now we're getting somewhere.

"I know that name. It's a nickname for one of the Angra Om Ya. A big goddamn carnivorous flower. Her real name is Zhuyigdanatha, right?"

He drops his hands to his sides. Narrows his eyes at me.

"You know nothing about the Flayed Heart."

"I know it's easier to say than Zhuyig-fucking-danatha."

"Don't blaspheme her name."

"You can knock that off right now. I've already got one schoolmarm worrying about my language. I don't need two."

Hobaica turns in a dazed circle.

"I don't understand. Where's the fire? Why is my body still intact?"

"Maybe you blew your ritual. Remember that? It's where we met."

"You were the witness to our sacrifice. An ordinary, mortal man shattered by such a holy rite was our way to paradise."

"And yet here you are. Downtown Nowheresville. Like the view?"

Hobaica comes at me.

"You did this."

He tries to grab me. I sidestep, give him a little shove to throw him off balance, and stomp on the back of his knee. He goes down on his face, hurt but in one piece.

"You got that out of your system and now you're going to be smart, right? Good. First off, who told you I was following you?"

Hobaica nurses his hurt knee, but manages a smile.

"A little birdie. *Der Zorn Götter* has friends in many places."

I've heard of them. An upper-crust Angra sect. They have connections in money and politics all over the Sub Rosa and civilian world. Could they have connections to the Vigil?

"You made a mistake asking me to be your witness, genius. First, I'm not exactly mortal, and second, I spent eleven years in Hell. You think a bunch of nitwits sawing their own heads off is going to shatter me? In Hell we called that 'Wednesday.'"

I go over and pull Hobaica to his feet.

"This is a trick," he says.

"Show me what's in your head. I want to see what you expected when you died. Show me the Flayed Heart."

"Never."

"Listen, man. I know you don't mind a little pain, but you're dead now. You don't need to have to do that anymore. Show me what I want or it's going to hurt."

He stands up straight. A moron with scruples.

"I won't tell you a thing."

I nod.

"No matter what the old mummy said, I knew I wasn't getting through this without losing some blood."

"What?"

"Hold still," I say, and pull my knife.

Hobaica tries to run, but his gimpy leg collapses and he goes down on his face. I kneel on his chest, pinning his arms to the ground.

"I should probably feel worse about this, but you hack up people to decorate your playpen, so I don't."

I grab his chin with my free hand and cut a sigil into his forehead. The mark of Nybbas, the Seer. He stops thrashing for a second when the blood flows into the eyes. I take that moment to run the knife over my own forehead, making a deep gash. Grabbing Hobaica's face, I push my forehead to his until our wounds touch. As our blood flows together, I get a dirty, low-res image of his mind.

This is what Hobaica expected. What he wanted.

An endless sea of fire and bones, and floating there, as big as the sky, is a lotus made of rotting human teeth. Bodies pour into the flower's fanged maw and are ripped apart. Zhuyigdanatha swallows some of the bodies, but there's so much falling into its stinking gob that limbs, heads, torsos, and feet cascade down the side. They crawl together in the fire, forming new, weird creatures. A couple of arms merge at the shoulder with an eye attached under each armpit. Torsos with six, eight, ten legs bob along on the flames, swimming in one direction and then another as the legs compete with each other. A few piles of limbs have pulled together enough pieces to form a complete body. These climb up the sides of the tooth lotus, pushing back bodies that miss the Flayed Heart's mouth and try to get away. Others swim through the fire into caverns at the base of the lotus.

Since he's dead, I can't gauge Hobaica's mood by the smell of his sweat or the sound of his heartbeat, but being in his head, I can feel his excitement. This is what Hobaica hoped for when he cut his head off. To be one of those bodies falling into Zhuyigdanatha's mouth, feeding his master.

The old Angra moves as it chews its lunch, twisting this way and that to catch the choicest bodies. If you see it from different angles, Zhuyigdanatha changes. It becomes a slimy lizard, snaring falling bodies with a prehensile tongue a thousand miles long. A baobab tree, with razor foliage and a trunk made of rheumy eyes. A crawling fungal mass plucking bloating corpses from a sea of sewage. At least I know this really is an Angra I'm seeing. Zhuyigdanatha isn't really changing. It's a transdimensional being. We ordinary slobs can only see one dimensional aspect of the God at once, so it seems to change as it moves and dreams.

From inside Hobaica's head, I can feel the man wilt as it finally comes to him that he'll never be saved by his God. His sacrifice was a joke. The Angras are in another dimension. The other God, the God of this dimension, isn't wild about people deity shopping. It starts to dawn on Hobaica that he's not only lost his personal Jesus, but killing himself as a sacrifice to the Flayed Heart means he's pissed off the other God. With his frequent asshole miles he's earned himself a window seat on the big coal cart to Hell. He's not even scared. He's beyond fear or even despair. He knows he's lost. That he lost the first day he drew his or anyone else's blood for Zhuyigdanatha.

There's a mountain range off to the side of where we lie. I climb off Hobaica and he struggles to his feet.

"Where did those mountains come from? I swear they weren't here before."

An opening appears in the side of one mountain. Pale light shines out onto the dim plain.

"That's for me, isn't it? I'm going to Hell."

"Don't feel so bad. It beats Fresno."

Hobaica drags his arm over his forehead, wiping away the blood.

"I'm a fool."

"You bet on the wrong horse, yeah. But you're not the first one, so don't beat yourself up."

I sort of feel bad for the sucker. I mean, his life has been a joke from day one. But Hobaica's current attitude isn't a bad way to enter Hell. There's not much the Hellions can do to him that he isn't already doing.

He says, "What do I do now?"

"You can stay where you are for the rest of eternity, which, the way things are going, might not be that long. Or you can go inside."

"To Hell."

"Yes."

"So, I can be somewhere awful or nowhere at all."

"It's a lousy choice, I know."

He looks at me. His clothes are speckled with his blood. He looks a little like what he looked like back in the meat locker. It's pathetic.

"Which would you choose?" he says.

"I didn't get to make a choice when I went. But if I were you, I'd choose to be someplace. All they can do in Hell is hurt you. Out here with nothing but yourself to talk to, you're going to destroy your mind. Being alone is worse than being somewhere bad."

He nods. Even manages the faintest smile in human history.

"Thank you," he says, and starts for the mountains.

"Vaya con Dios."

He stops.

"Is that a joke?"

"Yeah. Not one of my best."

"A bad joke isn't much of a send-off before an eternity in Hell."

"I could tell you the one about the one-eyed priest and the bowlegged nun."

"I'll be going now."

He walks to the mountain and goes into the tunnel without looking back. It closes behind him. Alone on the alkali plain, I sit down with my legs crossed. I wipe the blood off my face with my hand and the alkali burns the cut in my forehead. The drunken feeling comes over me again. My shoulders sag. My head falls forward and my mouth opens. Something light drifts out and settles on my leg.

I wake up in the circle across from the severed head. There's a puddle underneath it where it's starting to defrost. Candy takes my arm and helps me up. I run my fingers over my forehead. No blood. Score one for the bag of bones. I didn't have to bleed in real life after all.

I put Hobaica's head back in the cooler and hand it to Wells.

"I'm done with this. It's your problem now."

He sets it on the floor. Goes to a sink and washes his hands.

"Did it work? Did you see anything?"

"Some bad dental work. And fire. And bodies being ripped apart. The meat locker where I found ice-chest man was feng-shuied with body parts."

"You think the man cut up the bodies?" says the Shonin.

"Him and his friends, yeah. My guess is those meat piñatas were volunteers. More Angra zealots."

"They wanted to be cut up like meat?" says Candy.

I nod.

"Yeah, but they didn't see it that way. The feeling I got from Hobaica—that's your dead man—is that he and his pals wanted to be hacked up like those bodies. They thought if they sacrificed themselves right they'd be reborn as bouncing baby Angras."

The Shonin laughs at that.

"They're even dumber than you."

"Did he actually tell you he cut up those bodies?" says Wells.

"I wasn't taking a deposition. These are all just impressions I got from a shell-shocked dead man on his way to Hell."

"Is that all?"

"Some of the body parts clumped together and made new bodies. There were caves they might have drifted into. Everything was on fire."

"It sounds like the realm of the Flayed Heart," says Shonin.

"It was."

"Zhuyigdanatha likes underground places," says Shonin to Wells. "If there's a larger Angra group, you might find them there."

Wells shifts his weight from one foot to the other.

"What caves are we talking about? Carlsbad Caverns? A salt mine in Louisiana? Lascaux?"

The Shonin pours out the muck he gave me. Puts water and green tea into the pot and places it back on the burner.

"These were California boys, so it will be a California cave that connects, at least on a spirit level, with the Flayed Heart's dwelling place."

I start to say something, but don't. I know some caves nearby, but if the Vigil doesn't know about them I'm not going to tell them yet. I need to check with someone first.

Candy is slumped on a metal stool on the other of the room, away from everyone. She's pale and fidgety. I go over to her.

"You all right?"

"I'm fine," she says. "Just let me sit here."

"I can take you home if you want."

"I'm fine. Okay?"

I nod.

"Okay."

"Stark," says Wells. "You know lowlifes. Any of your pixie friends like to spend their time underground?"

"What makes you think the Sub Rosa or Lurkers have anything to do with this? Angra worshipers are mostly lily-white civilians."

"You didn't answer my question."

I look at the Shonin.

"You want to know about underground dwellers? Why don't you ask the jabber over there?"

Jabbers are ghosts so scared of the afterlife that they won't even leave their dead bodies. They claw their way through the soil under the city, dried-out bones living in dirt.

"Don't you dare talk about Ishiro Shonin that way. This is a holy man. Jabbers are cowards. What this man did took years of dedicated training and preparation. Successful self-mummification is incredibly rare."

I fish around in my coat pocket for a pack of Maledictions. I find them but they're soggy with rainwater. I crumple up the pack and throw it in a wastebasket.

I look at the Shonin.

"You're what successful looks like? I've met Buddhist monks before. None of them looked like Johann Schmidt's foreskin."

"It took a thousand days to purify my body and mind before I could inter myself, preparing to come back when the world needed me. Of course," he says, looking around, "I didn't think I was coming back to a world of *gaijin,* urban *yôkai,* and whatever it is you are."

"Angels call me Abomination, but looking at you, I don't feel so bad about it."

"What's 'urban *yôkai*'?" says Candy. Her voice is shaky.

"He means Lurkers. Don't you, *muertita*?"

The Shonin says, "I knew, for instance, respectable *tengu* back home. You Los Angeles people—humans, and monsters—you are lost beings."

"Speaking for all the *yôkai* in L.A., go fuck yourself," says Candy.

"Watch the profanity," says Wells.

I go over to him.

"Exactly what is Mr. Bones doing here?"

"He was a *yamabushi* back in Japan. A lone mountain monk in Sennizawa. They called them Swamp Wizards. He has a deep background in the mystical arts. He's going to figure out how to make the Qomrama Om Ya work."

"I'm supposed to be lab partners with this guy?"

The Vigil has the 8 Ball locked up in a secure clean room all by itself, suspended in a magnetic field. It floats in the air and changes shape as you walk around it.

"Not supposed to," says Wells. "You are. It's done and settled. He'll figure out the Qomrama and you'll use it."

"Why don't you clue me in on these things from time to time so I know what to expect?"

Wells pushes the cooler against the wall with the toe of his highly polished shoe.

"Fine. Here's your clue for today. I want you to write down everything that happened before the man you brought in died and everything you saw and heard when you went inside his head. Make sure Ishiro Shonin gets a copy and so do I."

"Now I'm your secretary."

"For the kind of money we're paying you, you're whatever I need. Today you weren't much of anything at all."

"Speaking of money, I still don't have my first check."

Wells squares his shoulders.

"I wanted a man to question and you bring me back a horror show. This isn't a good time to complain to management about your salary."

I look over at Candy. She's leaning her elbows on the table.

"I'll write your report, but I'm doing it at home."

"I want it by nine A.M."

"Noon, it is."

Wells is tense. His heart rate is up a little. His pupils are narrow. I head over to Candy.

"Is there something else you have to say? Something you're not telling me?"

"Yes. Up your game, Stark. These might be the End Times. I don't want you half-assing your way through them."

It's a good party-line statement, but it's not what he's thinking about. There's something else.

"Sure," I say. Then to the Shonin, "See you around the watercooler, King Tut."

"Don't eat too much tonight, fatty. Salads are your friend."

I grab my coat and Candy and I follow Wells outside. The Shonin stays behind and pours himself some tea.

"What an asshole," she says.

"He's just trying to get under my skin. Sounds like he's getting under yours."

She shakes her head.

"Maybe. I don't feel well. I'm going to see Allegra."

I touch her cheek. It's cold, but Jades always run a little cool.

"You feel a little colder than usual. Want me to come along?"

"I'll be fine. I'll see you at home."

"At least let me take you through a shadow. It'll take you forever on the street."

"I'm fine," she says. For a second she flashes her Jade face. It's almost subliminal, like she wasn't in control. "Stop getting all over me."

I say, "I'll see you at home."

Candy doesn't say anything. Just walks away.

I remember that she still has my gun and I almost go after her. But I don't. Maybe some space is what she needs right now. Anyway, whatever's wrong, Allegra's clinic will fix her up.

I find a good shadow by the lab door and go through, coming out at home. Maximum Overdrive. The video store I run with a not-quite-dead man named Kasabian.

MAX OVERDRIVE IS located on Las Palmas, right off Hollywood Boulevard. It sits midway between Donut Universe and Bamboo House of Dolls, the only junk-food place and bar that matters in L.A.

Kasabian used to run the store. When I came back from Hell I cut off his head. I might have been a little hasty, but he'd just shot me and I wasn't feeling entirely reasonable at the time.

The trick with the black blade I used on him is that if you hold it just right it cuts, but it doesn't kill. And that's what I did to Kasabian. He's spent most of the last year as a disembodied head and he hasn't shut up about it.

Lately I started feeling sorry for him, so I had a Tick Tock Man called Manimal Mike attach Kas to a mechanical hellhound. Now he sort of has a body, even if it's a little wobbly and whirs like a toy train when he moves.

Some Lurkers are in the store. A young Lyph whose denim jacket looks like it was mugged by a Bedazzler. All rhinestones and shiny bits on the back. Jim Morrison's face in flames. Underneath it says LIGHT MY FIRE. Lyph have horns and hooves and tails just like Halloween devils, but they're as sweet as peach ice cream when you get to know them.

A couple of Tykho Moon's boys are in the shop, dressed to the nines in the best leather and latex you can steal off a dead model.

Tykho is the boss of the Dark Eternal, the biggest, baddest vampire clan in L.A. Yeah, Dark Eternal sounds kind of like an eighties Goth band, but Tykho assures me the name is a lot scarier in Latin. The Eternal have been around for a long time. Tykho's boys are arguing, bumping shoulders like a couple of young pups, and whispering to each other.

Kasabian isn't anywhere in sight, which isn't a big deal. It isn't like anyone is going to shoplift any of what we carry. Max Overdrive used to be a regular video store. We rented movies, sold new and used discs. In other words, a money pit. BitTorrent and movie streaming were killing us. Thanks to Kasabian's obsessive collecting, our impressive porn and horror collections kept us afloat for a while, but we were going down fast. Now we're a boutique shop catering to a select clientele of Sub Rosas, Lurkers, and a few civilians with money and a taste for something special. Mainly, movies that don't exist.

The taller of Tykho's boys turns and spots me. He wears a patch over one eye. Sucks for him. He must have lost it while he was still alive and couldn't regenerate it when he turned. He gives me a toothy smile and comes over. Leans on the counter, hooking his thumb at the rack of our specialty movies.

"Don't get me wrong, Stark. I appreciate all the artsy stuff, but don't you have anything that's actually fun?"

What we rent mostly now are lost movies. Movies cut to pieces by the studios or lost in fires or time. Movies that literally don't or shouldn't exist anymore in this dimension of reality.

"*London After Midnight* is fun. It's a murder mystery. Lon Chaney plays a creepy guy with a giant set of fangs and a weird beaver hat, who might be a vampire."

Eye Patch leans back, frowning.

"Silent movies? Those are as scary as a damp sponge."

"That means you wouldn't like *Metropolis.* I have the only totally complete copy in the world with the original score, you know."

He shakes his head.

"Not interested."

This isn't the first time this has happened. We only have one rack of special discs. We're still building up inventory. You think it's easy conjuring video and film from other dimensions? It's not. And the young *curandera* I contracted with to get them charges a fortune for each one.

"What is it you want?"

"Action. Guns. Explosions."

"Go home, crack open a light beer, turn on your TV, and find some Michael Bay shit."

"Come on, man. You have any Clint Eastwood?"

"No special ones. You like his spaghetti westerns?"

The shorter vampire comes over when I mention westerns.

"Who doesn't?" he says.

I point to an old poster on the wall.

"You know that gangster flicks are the natural descendants of those Italian westerns, right? Action. Crime. Lawless loners and gangs riding the range, only in cars, not on horseback. Antiheroes and ambiguous heroes who aren't all good or all evil. You follow me?"

Eye Patch says, "Look at you. The philosopher."

"*Once Upon a Time in America* is what you want. Leone shot it to run five hours. The studio cut it to ninety minutes. Later there was a three-hour version, but it still wasn't the whole thing. If you like cowboys, you'll like it."

"Who's in it?" says Eye Patch. His buddy goes over to the poster and reads off names.

"Robert De Niro. James Woods. Joe Pesci. Tuesday Weld. William Forsythe . . ."

"Sold," says Eye Patch.

"Good choice," I say, taking a disc from under the counter. I put it in a couple of plastic bags to keep it from getting wet.

"Your turn to pay," says Eye Patch. His friend sighs, which always hits me as slightly creepy. I mean, vampires don't breathe, so sighing is something they have to practice. Willing their diaphragms to move, sucking air in and pushing it out again. It's a lot of work just to sound disgusted.

Short guy slaps a hundred-dollar bill on the counter.

"Your prices are highway robbery."

"You can find any of our movies somewhere cheaper, go rent from them."

Eye Patch puts the disc in the pocket of his PVC jacket.

"I always wondered about that. How do you keep people from bootlegging your wares?"

I get out another disc, an original cut of *The Magnificent Ambersons,* and show him the runes inscribed around the edge.

"The discs are hexed. They know when they're being copied and melt down like a nuke plant, killing themselves and whatever machine they're in. We have an alarm rigged up that goes off when it happens. Store policy is that you kill my disc, well, you know."

"You kill them?"

"Don't be stupid. I can't kill off my customer base. No, I just cut off their fingers and feed them to Kasabian."

From the back room Kasabian yells, "I heard that. Fuck you."

"See? A barely controlled beast."

"Take it easy, Stark," says Eye Patch. "How long do we have the movie?"

"Three days. After that, it's a hundred-dollar-a-day late fee."

The short vampire gets their umbrellas from the bin up front.

"You're a fucking thief, you know that?" he says.

"Wrong. I'm P. T. Barnum. You want to see the Fiji mermaid, I'm the only one in town who has one and no one gets in free."

"This movie better be fucking great."

"If you don't like it, come back and you can exchange it for one of these."

I hold up my middle finger.

Eye Patch laughs. When his friend takes a step toward me, he puts a hand on his shoulder and he backs down. Yeah, the short one is new to the bloodsucker game. Anxious to show off his power. Good thing he's got Eye Patch looking out for him. He might actually make it to New Year's.

The Lyph comes over and asks for Eisenstein's *Ivan the Terrible Part 3*.

"You have good taste," I say.

She lays down a hundred.

"You too," she says. Her horns are still a little damp. Rain beads on them like she's glued rhinestones there too.

"You okay getting home with your radar showing?"

She realizes I mean her horns and grins.

"I'm fine. The umbrella has a glamour on it."

She picks it up and instantly looks like the kind of sweet old lady who spends her days baking apple pies for orphans.

"Nice trick."

"Thanks," she says, setting the umbrella against the wall. "Can I ask you a question?"

"Shoot."

"Why do you wear that one glove?"

I hold up my left hand. The prosthetic one. Flex the fingers.

"I paid good money for this manicure. I'm not messing up my cuticles around here."

She hesitates.

"People call you Michael Jackson behind your back, you know."

"I've been called worse."

She purses her lips in embarrassment.

"Sorry. I didn't mean to pry. It's just, you hear stories."

I hand her the disc.

"No problem. For a hundred dollars a movie, I guess you're entitled to a question or two."

She glances around the store.

"You have some really nice stuff, but you ought to expand into BBC shows."

"Which ones?"

"In the early sixties they used to erase a lot of TV to save on videotape. They lost old *Doctor Who*s. *The Avengers*. Cool shows like that. I have friends who'd kill for those."

"Tell you what, make me a list of what you want and I'll see what I can do."

From the back, Kasabian yells, "That's TV. We don't do TV."

I shake my head.

"Ignore him. He's a snob. Bring me the list and your next rental is free."

"Awesome," she says. She gets her umbrella, does her old lady trick, and heads out. Stopping by the door she says, "Merry Christmas."

"Same to you, Mrs. Cratchit."

She opens the door and a blast of wind blows rain inside. It's coming down hard enough that the street out front is flooding again. I lock the door behind her.

"Cute girl," says Kasabian, coming out of the back. His mechanical legs click with each step. He wears a loose knock-off Nike tracksuit. It makes him look like the movie version of a Russian mobster, if Russian mobsters were robots.

"Nice salesmanship with her," he says. "Not so much with the guys you threatened."

"The little guy annoyed me. Anyway, we need signs or warning labels or something on the discs. I don't want to keep having that conversation."

"If it'll calm you down I'll print out something."

"Yeah, it would."

Kasabian has lost more hair in the year since I've been

back. His face is still as round as it ever was. Must be the hoodoo keeping him alive. He eats plenty, but the food drops right through a tube in his mechanical body, so it's not like he's taking in any calories.

"You're in a mood," he says. "You and the other Johnny Laws have a busy day arresting jaywalkers?"

"It was a funny day, now that you ask. I cut off a guy's head, and when he died I followed him into limbo. Sound familiar?"

Kasabian touches his throat.

"You and cutting people's heads off," he says. "You're like an alcoholic, only with a guillotine."

I think about getting a drink, but the moment has passed. I don't want it anymore. I'm worried about Candy.

"You notice anything about Candy recently?" I say. "She wasn't feeling well at work."

"Was she there when you started lopping heads off, because regular people aren't exactly used to that?"

"Candy isn't regular people. She's seen a little blood in her time."

Candy is a Lurker. A Jade. They're kind of like vampires, only scarier. More like spiders, really. They don't drink their victims' blood. They dissolve them from the inside and drink them dry. Candy has been clean for years. Doc Kinski came up with a potion that curbs her appetite for human milk shakes. After he died, Allegra stepped in and took over his practice and has been giving Candy all the Jade methadone she needs.

"How's the swami biz?" I say, wanting to change the subject.

"This is how it is," says Kasabian, dropping a pile of print-outs on the counter.

"What are these?"

"Requests from potential clients."

Kasabian started a little side business a few weeks back and it's taken off like a bottle rocket out of a carny's ass. He can't go to Hell like I can, but he can see into the place. He set himself up as an online seer. For a fee, he'll tell you how the dearly departed are getting on in the Abyss. Seeing as how most people seem to end up down there, he doesn't lack for clients.

Kasabian riffles the pages with his pointy hellhound claws.

"All these people have family or friends Downtown. And all want more than I can give them. Paying clients don't want to hear about sweet Aunt Suzy up to her eyeballs in a river of shit."

"And this concerns me how?"

"Most of these people want to, you know, talk to the departed. Hear a story about redemption, maybe. Mostly, they want to know where they hid the good silver or did they really love them. You know. Normal family bullshit."

"And you want me to go Downtown and play twenty questions with damned souls because they don't have enough problems."

"Yes. That's what I always want. Come on, man. Look at the streets. This city is going to be empty soon. Empty and underwater. It's no-shit Ragnarök. People want to know what to expect on the other side."

I shake my head. Push the papers back across the counter.

"Not my problem. And I told you. Mr. Muninn is still pissed at me for stealing Father Traven's soul. He doesn't want me back in his petting zoo playing with the animals."

"It doesn't have to be all of them," says Kasabian. "Just for a few of the high rollers. We need the money."

That much is right. We are severely on the rocks. Kasabian squirreled away a few grand from a payoff I got from the Dark Eternal when I put down some pain-in-the-ass zombies. But we blew the last of that fixing up Max Overdrive so we could live here and reopen the store. The special video section is bringing in cash, but barely enough to pay for beer and utilities.

"Okay. Cash is a good incentive, but seriously, Hell is kind of off-limits for me right now."

"What about Samael? Would he do it if you asked nice?"

"You think you're going to bribe Samael with money? He's a fucking angel. He doesn't carry a lot of pocket change."

Kasabian picks up the paper. Taps it on the counter to straighten the edges.

"Maybe Muninn would be happier to see you than you think. Hell isn't looking too pretty right now."

"What's going on?"

"Nothing, that's the problem. All the public-works projects, fixing the place up after you broke it . . ."

"That wasn't my fault. Samael fucked it up when he was still Lucifer. I just let it get a little worse when I was running the place."

"Whatever you say, man. Well, it's all stopped. They're not even pretending to put the place back together again."

"That doesn't sound like Muninn."

"You so sure he's still in charge?"

"I'd know if anything changed."

"How?"

"I just would."

"Okay, Cassandra, there's something else. Did it rain much when you were down there?"

"No. I don't remember it raining at all."

"Well, it is now. Raining cats and dogs and little imps with pitchforks. I mean, there's doomed. There's screwed. And there's monsoons-in-Hell fucked. And we're at fucked o'clock."

Suddenly I want a cigarette. I take out the Maledictions. I go to the back door and open it, blowing the smoke outside. Candy doesn't like me stinking the place up with cigarettes that smell like a tire fire.

"I don't get it. Could the Angra be doing it?"

"Who cares? It's happening and whoever's in charge down there can't stop it. What makes you think I can?"

"You were the Devil," says Kasabian.

It's true. I got stuck with Lucifer's job for three miserable months. And what do you know? I wasn't good at being a bureaucrat or a diplomat. I fucked Hell up worse than it was when I got there, and barely made it out with my hide intact.

"You know God," Kasabian says. "Get him off his backside. Or better yet, hide us in your magic room. You've always said that nothing can get in there. It's the perfect fallout shelter."

I puff the Malediction, cupping it in my hand so the rain doesn't put it out.

"So your solution to the end of the universe is to hide for the next billion years in the Room of Thirteen Doors? A room with nothing in it and nowhere to go."

"Okay. It doesn't sound great when you say it like that.

But we could fill it up with food and water and movies. Everything we need."

"There's no electric outlets in the Room, and more important, no toilets. Get the picture?"

Kasabian comes over to the door and sticks his fat face into the rain, looking up into the black sky like maybe if he stares long enough God will part the clouds and give him a thumbs-up.

"If we can't hide, then fix this shit. My business is going to fall apart when people realize they don't need me to find their relatives because they're going to be Downtown soon enough themselves."

He wipes the rain off his face with his sleeve and heads to the back of the shop where his rooms are.

"If anyone wants me I'll be having a Béla Tarr festival in my boudoir."

"Bullshit. You don't watch gloomy Hungarians when you're depressed. You'll be watching porn all night."

He gives me the finger without turning around and closes the door to his Batcave. I head upstairs.

Yeah, we're broke now, but it was money well spent. We got Max Overdrive up and running again, at least on a small scale. And we fixed the place up so it's less like a crash pad for a crazy person and a dead man and more like a place where actual people might live.

Kasabian has the ground floor, in three small rooms built behind the video racks. Candy and I have the upstairs. Three rooms like he has, with a little kitchen area. When we were building the place, all I insisted on was a bed with an extra-strong frame, the largest flat screen humanly possible, and a dishwasher. I would have been happy eating off paper plates with plastic forks for the rest of my life, but Candy said I should stop pretending that the world is a squat and that I'm just passing through. I've stuck around for almost a year, so maybe she's right. After losing room service and our cushy life at the Chateau Marmont, there was nowhere else for us to go but Max Overdrive. I don't think Candy ever lived anywhere very long before Doc Kinski took her in. She doesn't talk about her life before that. If playing *Ozzie and Harriet* makes her happy, then it's all right with me. But I'm still not folding fucking pillowcases. Good thing for everyone there's a laundry down the block.

Why has she been moody and off her feed lately? Today wasn't the first time she's been mad enough to snap. What if she feels like she got in too deep with the domestic bliss stuff? She dumped me once before, back when I disappeared for three months in Hell. Wouldn't it be a hoot if after getting sheets and plates and all kinds of kitchen trinkets, she decides she can't handle it? It wouldn't exactly surprise me. Most of my luck revolves around breaking things. If every day was car chases and sawing people's heads off, I'd be the Pope of Lucky Town.

CANDY COMES HOME about an hour later. I have *Spirited Away* going on the big screen. Her favorite movie when she's feeling down. She sticks her head around the door and raps on it with her knuckles.

"Knock, knock," she says. "I brought a peace offering. Burritos from Bamboo House of Dolls."

"Then you may enter."

"Thank you, sir."

She puts the burritos on the table. She left her jacket downstairs, but her jeans are soaked through. She's even given up her Chuck Taylor sneakers for shin-high rubber boots with skulls and stars. She takes them off and tosses them in the tub, then comes over and flops down next to me on the secondhand sofa.

"What are we watching?"

"If you don't remember it, Allegra needs to check you for a brain tumor."

She pushes up against me and gives me a little elbow in the ribs.

"I'm sorry. Was that your side, Mr. Sarcastic?"

"You're dripping on the linoleum and getting the couch wet, wino."

Candy unbuckles and slips off her jeans, leaving them in a heap on the floor. She sits beside me and shivers. Pulls my arm around her. My left arm. She doesn't mind the prosthetic. I think she kind of likes it. I pull her closer.

I say, "So, Allegra fixed you up?"

Her head moves against me as she nods.

"She said it was probably the stress of getting the new place together and doing stuff with you and the Vigil, knowing no one at the Vigil wants me there."

"Fuck 'em," I say. "They're paying me to be there. They're getting you for free. If you don't want to come in you don't have to. Take it easy and settle into the place."

She looks up at me.

"And let you have all the fun? Besides, what would I do here while you're gone? We only get a few customers, and unlike Kasabian, I can only jerk off so many times a day."

"What do other domestic ladies do? You could take up needlepoint or do crossword puzzles. Maybe get into Valium and martinis."

"I like the sound of the last part. But seriously, Allegra has all the help she needs at the clinic and I like being Robin to your Batman. That and my Duo-Sonic are about the only things I give a shit about right now."

I gave Candy a cherry-red electric guitar a few weeks back. She got herself a little used Roland CUBE amp and bashes away every moment she can. She only knows about three chords, but she plays them with great conviction. Sometimes Fairuza, a Ludere who works with Allegra at the clinic, jams with her on drums. They're talking about starting a band, calling it the Bad Touch Sugar Cookies because it sounds like one of the *idoru* bands they like. Supposedly, Fairuza's old band once opened for Shonen Knife at the Whiskey. I think Candy about dumped me for her when she heard that, but I have a better movie collection, so she stayed.

I take a blanket off the back of the couch and wrap it around Candy and we watch the rest of the movie. After that, I write the report I promised Wells, and e-mail it to him. I still can't figure out what the mess in Hobaica's demented head meant. Tooth flowers. Seas of fire. Hacked-up bodies. It's like a Texas Chain Saw wet dream. Maybe it doesn't mean anything at all. Maybe I just left him on ice too long and Hobaica's soul was all screwed up from his brain getting frozen and oxygen deprived. Anyway, it's not my job to figure out. That's for the bag of Shonin bones.

Later, Candy reheats the burritos and we eat them while watching *Hausu,* a funny Japanese haunted-house flick.

Candy cackles the whole way through it. I don't pay much attention. She goes downstairs when we're done eating.

I'm still wondering if I should take a chance and go see Mr. Muninn in Hell. Maybe it would be smarter to check in with Samael first. He's living in the palace with Muninn and would know if it's all right for me to go down. Your holy roller types are talking about God sending a new flood to cleanse the world. I've got news for them. God's got his hands full right now. The parts of him that aren't already dead.

A rhythmic thumping and buzz comes up through the floor, from the storeroom we soundproofed with egg cartons and blankets. Candy and Fairuza are thrashing through a ragged version of "Rock 'n' Roll High School" because what else is there to do at the end of the world?

A FEW GLASSES of Aqua Regia later, I remember something I promised to do. I put on a hoodie and one of my frock coats and dig around under the bed for a dusty sack of bones that I took out of Kill City, a cursed shopping mall at the beach in Santa Monica. There was a pack of ghosts in the basement that wanted me dead, but we cut a deal. They let me go and I promised I'd bury their bones in the ground outside the mall. With fixing up Max Overdrive and starting back with the Vigil, I'd put it off a dozen times. All this talk of the apocalypse, I think maybe I should do it now just in case. I don't want to die having lied to a bunch of poor slobs buried under a thousand tons of concrete, corn dogs, and panty hose.

I put a little LED flashlight in my pocket and step through a shadow. Go through the Room of Thirteen Doors and come out under the Hollywood sign in the hills overlooking L.A.

From up here, through the air that's been washed clean by the rain, the city is beautiful. L.A. always looks best in the dark, when it's just lights and the ugly hulks of the buildings have been softened to vague night shapes. Even from up here, I can see the traffic snarling the main streets and spilling out onto the Hollywood Freeway. People are leaving town and they don't even know why. They're running just to run. Some animal part of their brain knows something bad is coming and they want to get as far from it as possible. Who can blame them? But if the Angra come stomping back to the world, there won't be anywhere too remote to hide. In the meantime, they run like lemmings.

Idiot that I am, I didn't bring a shovel, so I have to dig with my hands. I put the bones in the ground between the H and the O in HOLLYWOOD. I don't know if being in soil will help those ghosts rest easier, but I'll sleep better knowing I'm not just another liar in a city built on slick pitchmen who'd sell you their mother's kidneys if it got them salesman of the month.

It's dark up here and there isn't a shadow in sight. I turn on the LED flashlight and bury one end in the ground. I get in front of the beam and step into my own shadow, soaked and cold, heading home.

Later, Candy comes upstairs. Her T-shirt is soaked through with sweat.

"Having a little drink?"

"I went out. I'm trying to get the chill out of my bones."

She takes off her shirt and tosses it on the back of a chair. She comes over and straddles me on the couch, presses her warm body into mine.

"Better?" she says.

"Much."

She leans down and kisses me. I set my glass on the floor. She pushes me down on my back and starts pulling my pants off.

I should have insisted we get a sturdier couch. We break one of the legs and have to prop up the end on a pile of ancient VHS tapes from the bargain bin downstairs. Broken furniture rescued by forgotten movies. The place is starting to feel like home after all.

THE FLAYED HEART is all over my dreams. Grinding teeth. Pulped bodies in flames. Zhuyigdanatha is in the freezing locker where I found Hobaica. Fire licks the meat-hooked body parts in the flesh cathedral. Chars the sides of beef. Fills the locker with a dense, oily smoke that settles on the walls and floor like a slick skin. Hot blood bubbles from the broiling meat. It pools on the locker floor like wounds. I double up in pain, maybe just in my dream or maybe for real.

I'm stuck somewhere dark. Bound to a wall underground in Kill City. Besides ghosts, the place is full of addled Lurkers and Sub Rosa families so far down the food chain they haven't seen daylight in years. Ferox, the head of the Shoggot clan, is there with his giggling relatives. They've filed their teeth to points and let maggots clean the places where they've carved up their own bodies. Ferox wants to see what makes a being like me tick. He shoves a scalpel low into my belly and drags the blade north. He wants to open me up. Pull me apart like those bodies falling into the abyss of the Flayed Heart's gullet. I've never felt anything like this, even in Hell. It's not just the pain. It's the idea of being gutted like a trout and left a hollow husk. After all I've been through, here I am, dying at the hands of a freak in the basement of a goddamn department store. I cramp again. This time I'm sure it's real.

The dream changes. I'm back in Vigil headquarters. Their first one, down south of L.A. Aelita is there. She's an angel. One of God's most hard-core. Pure Old Testament rage. She runs the Vigil with Wells. Only she's crazy, or maybe I make her crazy. The knowledge of my existence does. I'm Abomination. Nephilim. I shouldn't exist and yet God lets me live. She does Ferox's trick. Pig-sticks me with a flaming angelic sword. Kills me good. My first death. But I got over it and stabbed her right back. Still, I can feel her sticking me more than I can feel any satisfaction in getting revenge.

My stomach burns like it's filled with fire and metal.

All these scars. The road map of my life. My armor. Sometimes being hard to kill isn't exactly a blessing. Maybe that's the point. Maybe it's my punishment for being born a freak. I don't think even God knows at this point. He's broken up enough these days I don't know if I'd trust any answers he gave me.

Aelita declared war on God before she died. Wanted nothing more than to murder him. Here I am with her former friends trying to do the same thing to the Angra Om Ya. Who's right and who's wrong doesn't matter anymore. Maybe God did trick the old gods out of this universe and steal it for himself. But here's the scary question: which God is worse? The Angra, who might be competent, but want to wipe us out, or our God, who isn't good at his job, but if not benign, is at least indifferent to us? Parental neglect is starting to look pretty good right now, isn't it?

Maybe the Angra are entirely in the right to want back in, but if they're coming back means wiping us out, then fuck 'em. This isn't Metaphysics 101. This is self-defense. Anyway, what else am I going to do? Where else am I going to go? Hell is boring and Heaven sounds like a Disneyland fireworks parade forever.

My Shoggot scar burns and I feel mountain-size teeth crunching my bones.

But why be a Gloomy Gus about Armageddon? I survived Hell and Hollywood and the 1989 remake of *Godzilla*. I can survive this. The pain in my gut eases up.

Besides, I still have the Mithras and the Singularity. I can burn the universe to the ground or I can start it over brand-new. True, I'll be toast, but when I make that last big fuckup at least Wells won't be anywhere around to say "I told you so."

IN THE MORNING, Candy is feeling sick again.

"What's it feel like?"

She shrugs.

"Anxious. My stomach hurts like I haven't eaten for days. I have a headache like there's thunder in my head."

"You're not . . ."

"Pregnant?"

She gives me a soft kick.

"Allegra's a doctor, asshole. That's the first thing she checked. Besides, the pregnancy thing isn't really an issue for Jades. We only make babies when we want and that's only when we're told."

"What do you mean when you're told? You never said anything about that before."

"It's not a big deal. There's a council in charge of things like how many of us there are in the world and when we need more. Don't worry about it. They're not going to ask me to pop out little Jadelets."

"How do you know?"

"Because I'm fucking a monster. The biggest monster on Earth. You've polluted my precious bodily fluids."

She says it like it's a big joke, but she's never talked much about Jade life before.

"Tell me the truth," I say. "Did I fuck up some big deal for you? Get you on the outs with the other Jades?"

She sits up and puts her hand on my arm.

"You didn't fuck up anything. I chose to be here with you, remember? If any of the Jade Ommahs have a problem with that, they can take away my cookies and my merit badges and I won't care."

"Thanks. If that ever changes you better tell me."

She gives me a push.

"Shut up and go to work, drama queen."

I lean against the bedroom door and pull on my boots.

"I have to spend the day with cops and you get to hang out in bed."

"Sucks to be you," she says.

"Maybe I should call in sick."

"Maybe you should go and get us some money and find out more about what was going on in that meat locker. Don't you sort of wonder about that?"

"Not really."

"Well, I do. Don't come back without some answers and ice cream."

"Yes, ma'am."

She turns the light off and I shut the bedroom door. I'm going to have to trust that she isn't bullshitting me when it comes to the Jade stuff. I want to know more about it now, but if I ask her about that she'll want to talk to me about Doc Kinski, my real father, and I'm not ready to do that. Maybe if I can get her talking first she'll forget about my crap.

And what the hell is an Ommah? The Shonin is supposed to be Mr. Wizard. Maybe he'll know.

I step through a shadow and come out in the Vigil HQ across town.

I HEAD INTO the Shonin's room, but the place is empty. There's a note taped to the door with a map and a red X over a nearby room. I find it around the first corner. There are heavy curtains over the window in the door. Someone has left a drawing on the clipboard attached to it. It's a clipping from a newspaper. A butcher-shop ad with a cow sectioned into the different cuts of meat. Someone has drawn a little headstone and Xs over the cow's eyes. I never knew feds had a sense of humor.

The inside of the morgue is almost as cold as the meat-locker freezer. Wells and the Shonin are there. Wells is reading aloud from the report I sent in last night. Both men look at me and Wells stops reading.

"You took your sweet time getting in today."

"But it looks like I haven't missed brunch."

The room smells of incense. All thirteen bodies from the meat locker are laid out on stainless-steel tables, with their heads propped up next to them. The top of each head has been sawn off, revealing the gray brain matter. Each brain sports three incense sticks jammed right into the head meat.

I look at Wells.

"You give me a hard time and this guy's one step away from turning these people into bongs."

"Very funny. This man has been doing real work while you've been lying around at home."

I walk between the tables, checking out the bodies. It's like a weird corpse maze. Each head has a sigil painted with a brush a little below the hairline. Over their third eye. My guess is that the Shonin has been poking around in some of these dead people's memories.

I say, "How did you get the bodies? You scoop them up before the cops get there?"

"No such luck. Local law enforcement arrived just as we were removing the physical evidence."

"Dead people, you mean."

"Among other pieces of evidence, yes. I'm afraid there was an ugly scene. I don't enjoy territorial clashes, but I suppose with a crime this large local authorities are bound to be . . ."

"Emotional?"

"Clingy. However, when I explained the gravity of the situation to the commanding officer, he was happy to allow us to assist in the investigation."

"You pulled rank, didn't you? Got all federal. Maybe threatened to bring in Homeland Security."

"I didn't have to. As I said, the commander was a reasonable man."

"LAPD is a lot of things, but I don't remember reasonable."

"The chief is Sub Rosa, so he understands how important our investigation is."

"Having fun, fatty?" says the Shonin. "Does he always waste time like this?"

"He's a child," says Wells. "A misbehaving child. That's why I'm so reluctant to give him this."

The Shonin laughs a grumbling laugh. Like rocks in a tumbler. I hope I don't hear him do it again.

"We're getting early Christmas gifts? Are you my Secret Santa?"

Wells reaches into a jacket pocket and takes out a folded piece of leather. Hands it to me. Inside is a card with my name on it and the Golden Vigil insignia.

"This is official Vigil ID. If a situation develops with local law enforcement, show it to them. It won't work in little Podunk towns, but it will in L.A. and you're not going anywhere anytime soon, are you?"

"Not with a 'Get Out of Jail Free' card, I'm not."

"Do not even begin to think about abusing the authority afforded to you by this identification."

"I wouldn't dream of it. But LAPD does know that I'm a car thief, so the thing might actually come in handy."

Wells takes back the ID.

"Speaking of your previous criminal activities, understand this. This identification is only good while you work for this organization. My organization. You get cute, you go off the reservation, and I'll throw you to the wolves. Do you understand me?"

"I'm a team player, sir. I won't let you down."

"See that you don't," he says, and hands me back the ID. I put it in my pocket before Wells can take it away again.

The Shonin crooks his finger at me and says, "Come over here and see what real mystical forensics looks like."

I go over. He waits on the other side of a table holding Hobaica's body.

"The man's name is Joseph Hobaica. He's thirty-eight years old, and by the cross around his neck, a good Catholic boy."

"Wow. You and your mystical powers found his driver's license and a first communion present. You're goddamn Kreskin."

"Language. He runs the distribution company where you witnessed the ceremony," says Wells.

"Was that even a ceremony? It just looked like some kind of elaborate suicide pact to me."

"You know damned well it was an Angra offering ritual. Stop being a smartass."

"What I'm saying is, the all-beef church aside, the whole thing looked kind of thrown together. There weren't any ritual objects. They didn't have time to do an invocation before I got there. They didn't even have decent suicide instruments. What kind of Gods want a life offering made with something you can get at a hardware store?"

"Do you have any brilliant theories?"

"I think they were freaked out and desperate. I could smell it on them. Maybe they were offering themselves to their freaky God, but they were also splitting town. Just like all the other suckers clogging the freeways."

Wells nods.

"You might actually have a point there."

"But you're wrong about there being no ritual objects. Did you see the amputated limbs hanging among the circle?"

"They were a little hard to miss."

The Shonin goes to a table nearby and throws back a blue hospital sheet revealing arms, legs, hands, a whole buffet of body parts.

"These are what Marshal Wells's men brought back from the scene. Four arms. Four legs. Four hands. Four feet. You get the idea."

"Yeah, they butchered two poor slobs or two of them committed suicide before and let themselves be cut up."

The Shonin shakes his head.

"You were closer to right on your first guess. The marshal and his men saw this collection of wretched humanity and logically assumed that with this particular inventory of parts, they were the remains of two bodies."

"But there're more, aren't there?"

Wells goes to the table and pulls the sheet back over the limbs.

"The Shonin expressed some doubts after examining the remains, so we ran DNA from each limb. There are parts of twelve bodies here. I seriously doubt they butchered twelve of their own members just so that thirteen more could commit suicide."

"So, what are you saying? They're part of some kill-crazy Charlie Manson gang?"

"You'd like it to be that simple, wouldn't you, lazy boy?" says the Shonin.

Wells picks up a manila envelope from a nearby desk.

"This isn't the first time we've seen this kind of corpse desecration. Limbs severed and mixed together."

"I saw something like that in Hobaica's head. Body parts in the fire."

Wells opens the manila envelope. Looks at a couple of pages.

He says, "Have you heard of a killer called Saint Nick?"

"I think maybe I saw something when Kasabian was channel-surfing. A killer running around in the rain. So what? L.A. cranks out more serial killers than shitty sitcoms. He sounds like cop business to me."

"To me too until yesterday," says Wells. "Do you know why they call him Saint Nick?"

"Because it's close to Christmas?"

"Half right," the Shonin says. "He's Saint Nick because he likes to give his victims a little cut." He laughs.

"You mean he chops them up?"

Wells nods.

"And removes some of the parts. Different combinations of limbs and organs with each killing."

"Why?"

"We don't have a motive yet," says Wells. He tosses the manila envelope back on the desk. "But we found some notes and coded e-mails that lead us to think that this Angra bunch wanted to die by his hand. They thought they'd draw him out by imitating him."

"That explains all the mystery bodies."

"Right."

"But he never showed up," says the Shonin. "Hobaica was afraid that they'd been rejected by their God."

"So, this Saint Nick guy is an Angra worshiper?"

"Who knows?" says Wells. "But this bunch thought he was, and when they felt rejected they did the only thing that made sense to them."

"To prove their loyalty to the Flayed One, they sacrificed themselves imitating Saint Nick as best as they could," the Shonin says.

I say, "Hobaica told me he was waiting for me. How did he know I was following him?"

"You're so fat he saw you coming a mile away," says the Shonin.

"I saw that in your report. You're certain he said that?" asks Wells.

"He saw me standing in a slaughterhouse with a knife to his throat. Yeah, the moment is pretty well imprinted in my brain," I say.

"That's bad. It means at least this one Angra cult is working with a psychic. And if one has a practicing psychic, it probably means they all do."

"I have a slightly different theory."

"What's that?"

"You have a mole in the Vigil."

Wells comes over to me.

"Are you trying to be offensive? This isn't just a law enforcement organization. It's a holy calling."

"What this bunch did was a holy calling too. To them. You think you're immune to bad influences in the ranks? Stop a moment and think who you're talking to. I'm a bad influence on bad influences, but at least I'm up front about it. If an asshole like me has Vigil credentials, who else does?"

"I do not believe one word of this malarkey," says Wells. He doesn't say anything for a minute. "But it can't hurt to get new security clearances on all the personnel."

"I left my résumé in a hole in the ground in Yamagata

four hundred years ago," says the Shonin. "Happy hunting for that."

Wells looks at me like he's thinking of taking the ID back.

"Get out of here for now," he says. "But keep your phone on. I might need you later. I want to sort this Saint Nick thing out fast."

"What about the 8 Ball?" I say. "Shouldn't the bag of bones be working on that instead of playing medical examiner?"

"Unlike some people, I can multitask," says the Shonin. "So fuck you, round boy."

"Please," says Wells. "The profanity. You're a holy man."

"Your nephilim is right about himself. He's a bad influence. Go home and infect your friends."

"Don't leave yet," says Wells. "I need you to go and see Marshal Sola."

"Julie Sola is back in the Vigil?"

"Marshal Sola is with us again. And she has some papers to go over with you."

"What kind of papers?"

Wells smiles.

"Part one of your psych evaluation."

"Excuse me?"

"Everybody goes through it. I did it. Marshal Sola—"

"How about Aelita?"

That stops him cold.

He says, "You will go to Marshal Sola, do her paperwork, and pass the evaluation or you don't get paid."

"This is bullshit."

"Watch your language. And this is nonnegotiable."

I start out but stop and look back at the Shonin.

"Hey, *muertita*. You know what an Ommah is? I heard a Jade say it."

"You're involved with a Jade and you don't know what an Ommah is?"

"I lost my library card. Just tell me what it means."

"It's an old word. Arabic. It means 'mother.' The Ommahs are the Jade matriarchs. They control the whole Jade world. Set the rules. Tell them where to go and what to do."

"When to have kids?"

"Especially that. Breeding is very important to Jades. They like to keep their lineage clean and controlled. It's why they go for such a high price."

"What do you mean a high price?"

"At market. When they're sold. There are few Jades in the world. They live short, exciting lives and are gone. That's why they're so expensive." The Shonin laughs. "How do you not know these things?"

"Thanks," I say, and leave. As the door closes I can hear the Shonin.

"Seriously. How dumb is that boy?"

Apparently, dumber than even I thought.

To hell with Wells and his inkblots. I need a drink.

I go outside and call Candy. No one answers, so I leave a message that I'm going to Bamboo House of Dolls and that she should meet me there if she's feeling better.

The rain still pounds down. A couple of agents under an awning palm their cigarettes when I come out. They whisper to each other and quietly laugh. Yes, I'm a commander of men.

Six Vigil agents in expensive golf clothes play a round under oversize umbrellas. Disguised spooks playing a fake round of a brain-dead game in a billionaire's playpen in a monsoon while around them, the city reaches population zero. If the Angra have a sense of humor they won't be able to invade. They'll laugh themselves stupid and wait for us to die off pretending that nothing is wrong.

I STEP THROUGH a shadow and come out in front of Bamboo House of Dolls. It's my Sistine Chapel. My home away from home. The best bar in L.A. The first bar I walked into after escaping from Hell. It's a punk tiki joint. Old Germs, Circle Jerks, Iggy and the Stooges posters on the wall. Plastic palm trees and hula girls around the liquor bottles. And there's Carlos, the bartender, mixing drinks in a Hawaiian shirt. On the jukebox, Martin Denny is playing an exotic palm-tree version of "Winter Wonderland."

It's a small, damp afternoon crowd in the place. Smaller than usual. Few civilians. Mostly Lurkers. Three gloomy necromancers play bridge with a Hand of Glory filling the fourth seat. A couple of blue-skinned schoolgirl Luderes play their favorite scorpion-and-cup game. A table of excited Goth kids throw D&D dice and cop discreet glances at the crowd from the back of the room. Games for everyone. A necessary distraction when the sky is falling. Still, it's Christmas and the mood isn't bad. *It's a Wonderful Life* crossed with *Night of the Living Dead*.

Carlos serves drinks wearing a Santa hat.

"The salaryman returns," he says when I sit down at the bar. "How's life behind a desk?"

"If anyone ever actually gets me to sit at a desk you have my permission to shoot me."

Carlos pours me a shot of Aqua Regia from my private supply.

"It's not so bad," he says. "Take me. The bar is sort of my desk. I come in at pretty much the same time each day. Do my prep. Serve my bosses—you ungodly things—and go home tired and satisfied knowing that I've kept America watered and prosperous for one more day."

"You're a saint. When you die they'll name a junior high after you and your reliquary will be full of shot glasses and lime wedges."

"Don't forget a boom box. I need my tunes."

"The difference between us is one, you're the boss. Two, you can throw out anyone you want anytime you want. And three, you have a jukebox by your desk. Me, all I have is a dead man in Liberace robes and a cowboy with a stick the size of a redwood up his ass."

Carlos pours himself a shot and leans on the bar.

"Why don't you have a drink and listen to the carols? That always makes me feel better."

Someone comes in and Carlos stands, looking serious.

"Be cool," he says, and goes to the end of the bar, where two uniformed cops have come in. The three of them speak quietly. Too quietly for me to hear over the jukebox. After a minute of chatter, Carlos hands one of the cops a Christmas card. The card is misshapen. Bulging. There's something inside it. The three of them nod to each other and shake hands. One of them glances at me and stops like he thinks we might have gone to high school together. A second later, he turns and heads out with his partner.

"What was that?"

Carlos says, "Exactly what it looked like. Protection. But for real. Do you know how many cops are left in the city? They're splitting town just like everybody else. The cops that are left, they need a little extra motivation to answer the phone if there's trouble."

"A nice racket."

Carlos shakes his head and throws back his drink.

"The price of doing business in L.A."

He pours us both another round and holds up his glass for a toast.

"Merry Christmas."

We clink glasses and drink. I shake my head.

"I can't believe it's Christmas again. How do you people stand having the same holidays over and over? In Hell they only have holidays when Lucifer feels like it, so it's always a surprise and all the little goblins are giddy as kindergartners."

"You going back to the old country for the holidays?"

"Yeah, I'm Hell's Secret Santa, bringing all the good little imps coal and fruitcake."

"How do you tell the difference?" says someone behind me.

I turn and find Eugène Vidocq, besides Candy probably my best friend on this stupid planet. He doesn't like talking about his age and swears he isn't a day over a hundred and fifty, but I know he's well over two hundred. He's also immortal. And a thief. And after being in the States for more than a hundred years, he still has a French accent thick enough to slice Brie, a last remnant of his home that he won't ever let go of.

He claps me on the back and nods to Carlos. Orders a couple of drinks. He isn't alone. Brigitte Bardo is with him. She gives me a quick peck on the cheek. Brigitte is Czech. She was a skilled zombie hunter back in the day and used to do porn to support her hunting habit. These days she's working her way into regular Hollywood films. But it's slow. She still has an accent and it's, you know, the end of the world, so there's fewer films in production. When she's not auditioning, she helps out at Allegra's Lurker clinic.

Carlos brings Vidocq whiskey and Brigitte red wine.

"Where's Candy?" she says.

"She wasn't feeling well. Did you find anything wrong with her when she stopped by yesterday?"

"Nothing that I know of. She just took her Jade potion and left. She seemed fine."

"Maybe I should call her again."

"Leave her alone. This time of year can put people into odd moods."

"Don't I know it," says Carlos. "It was just about a year ago that you wandered in here the first time. You were looking a little bleary, Mr. Stark."

"As I recall, I'd just crawled out of a cemetery and was wearing stolen clothes."

"You always make an impressive entrance," says Vidocq. "As I recall, after your return you were going to shoot me the first time we saw each other."

"Total misunderstanding. And sorry."

He holds up his glass.

"Whiskey under the bridge."

"You kicked a bunch of skinheads' asses for me, remember?" says Carlos. "I didn't know about any of you Sub Rosas or Lurkers back then. If those fuckers came in here these days, I'd give them a faceful of this."

He holds up a potion from behind the bar.

I look at Vidocq.

"One of yours?"

"You're not the only one who barters for drinks," he says.

"Rumor has it you're doing some freelance work for the Vigil these days too. How does it feel to be back?"

Vidocq shakes his head. Regards his drink.

"Strange. As strange as I bet it is for you."

"I'm still not sure it's the right thing to be doing, but if I wasn't working for them I don't know if I'd be doing anything at all."

"Confusion. Strange alliances. God's new deluge. These are the things the world has been reduced to. Apocalypse. *Le merdier*. So let's drink to the void."

Brigitte sighs and picks up her wine.

"You boys are too grim for me. I'm going to find more congenial company."

I say, "Sorry. I didn't mean to be a drag."

"You're never a drag, Jimmy, but I see a studio friend I met when I first came here. A girl must maintain her connections, mustn't she? Maybe I can be in the last movie before the world ends."

"Now who's the drag?"

She shrugs extravagantly.

"Knock 'em dead," I tell her.

I turn back to the bar and pick up my drink. I haven't had a cigarette in hours. My lungs are aching for abuse.

"Tell me the truth. Are we good enough for this? Look at us. What a bunch of fuckups."

"What choice do we have?" says Vidocq. "Who else will do this if not us?"

"The government."

"Save us from our saviors."

I sip my Aqua Regia and Carlos moves off to serve other customers.

"I don't trust the Vigil much more than the Angra. What's more important to them, saving the world or controlling whatever's left when this is over?"

Vidocq looks at his hands. Flexes his fingers. He looks good for two hundred. Not more than his forties.

"I was twenty-five when I faced my first apocalypse. When the bloated corpse of the eighteenth century rolled into its grave, making way for the wonders of the nineteenth. You should have seen Paris. Half the city praying, flagellating, and prostrating themselves before Notre-Dame and images of the Madonna. The other half whoring and drunk while fireworks burned brighter than all of Heaven."

"I wonder which group you were with?"

"The Madonna and I had parted ways many years before that, I'm afraid."

I look around the room and spot Brigitte sitting at a table with a group of network executives decked out in designer faux-military gear and safari vests like they're running off to a Brentwood *Red Dawn* key party. But like a few million others, they're just headed out of town with the family jewels sewn into the lining of their bulletproof trench coats. Brigitte laughs as the gray-haired alpha wolf exec lays some of his survival gear on the table. Lengths of paracord. Sapper gloves. A multicaliber pistol. Condoms in Bubble Wrap. A multitool with more moving parts than a Stealth bomber. Watching her smile, I wonder if Brigitte is pulling out of her depression or if she's just an actress playing at being all right.

"There were suicides and riots. Fury and ecstatic joy, and all for the same reason. The world would end or be transformed, and unlike now, in this age of science and desperate rationality, there was nothing we could do about it. So each of us did what made sense. Drink. Pray. Stay with loved ones or sail off to the ends of the earth."

"And here you are."

"And here I am. Alive and not quite yet mad."

He finishes his drink and holds up the empty glass for another.

"The point is that I believe we will survive. Or enough of us will to make the world worth fighting for."

"It better be. I'm not kickboxing monsters so the Vigil and Homeland Security can turn L.A. into one big It's a Small World ride."

One of the Luderes gives a little shriek. She's been stung by one of the scorpions. The shrieker gives the room a little wave.

"Sorry. Everyone's fine. Carry on."

She and her friend crack up.

I turn back to Vidocq, but there's someone in the way. One of the Goth boys from the table in the back has joined us. He's dressed in a long high-collared coat and has wild Robert Smith hair. He looks vaguely like a mad scientist disguised as a priest. There's something funny about his eyes. I glance over at his friends. They look as surprised as I am.

"No autographs today, kid," I say. "I'm with friends."

The kid takes a step. Stumbles and slams into the bar. I have to grab his arm to keep him from falling over.

He says, "It's not going to stop. No matter what you do."

"What are you talking about?"

"That's my message to you. It's never going to stop."

I know what's wrong with his eyes. He's possessed. In Hell there's a key. If you know how to use it, and not many down there do, you can temporarily take possession of a body up here. Someone is riding this kid like he's a carousel pony.

"He isn't Death. Or God or the Devil. He is the Hand. Cut one off and another takes his place. He is many-bodied. Many-handed. A hand for each soul on Earth."

I slap the kid. Shake him. His eyes stay vacant and dead.

"Who are you? Who gave you the message?"

"Come out and see," he says.

Vidocq puts a hand on my arm.

"Don't you dare go anywhere with this boy. He is dangerous."

"I know. But if there's something out there I can't stay here."

"Don't be stupid," says Carlos. "Let me call the cops. This is why I pay the fuckers."

I nod.

"Maybe calling them isn't a bad idea."

I turn to Vidocq.

"Keep everyone else inside."

The kid is still holding on to me.

"Let's go," I say.

I get up and the kid lets go of me, leading the way outside. I put my hand under the coat and slip out my na'at.

We go out into the rain. Smokers huddle under the awning. A few of the regulars nod and wave. I don't wave back.

The kid walks all the way to the curb. I stay a couple of steps behind him. We stand there in the rain like a couple of assholes. He steps into the street between two cars, looking around like he's waiting for a cab.

"You saw a golden woman in the water. There," he says, pointing west to the Pacific.

"I remember."

When Kill City collapsed into the ocean a few weeks ago, I was in it. Something that looked like a woman covered in gold swam up from the wreckage and tried to pull me down.

"She served the Hand. She was beautiful."

"Except for the part where half her face was missing."

He nods. His long hair is plastered to his head, covering one eye.

"She was incomplete. That won't happen again."

"You couldn't tell me this inside, where it's dry?"

He holds his hands out wide.

"You don't understand what's happening and even if you did you can't stop it. The old ones are coming. They will bless us with annihilation."

A delivery truck speeds up the street. It swerves toward the curb. Hits the cars the kid is standing between. The impact drives both cars up onto the sidewalk. The kid is still between them, but now he's in two pieces. A girl screams and keeps on screaming.

The kid's friends must have followed us outside. A couple of the other Goth kids run to the curb like maybe they can put their friend back together again. I climb over the trunk of one of the wrecked cars. Go to the truck and pull the driver-side door open. The driver half falls out, held in place by his seat belt. His head is pulped from smashing into the windshield. I test his seat belt. It's locked right across his body. It doesn't make sense that he could have hit the inside of the windshield. Unless someone else belted him in after his head was in pieces and he was dead. I step up onto the running board to check out his body. His right arm is gone. Cut off neatly at the shoulder. Another Angra groupie? I can see why he'd sacrifice himself, but why take out the kid? No way he was looking to die.

I start back into the bar. The kid's phone rings. He had it in his hand the whole time.

"Don't touch it," I say.

I kneel down and pry it from his hand. One of the boys vomits into the street. I go back inside the bar and head straight for the men's room, where it's quieter. No one is inside. I shove a trash can under the doorknob so no one can get in. Where the number of the caller should be displayed it says BLOCKED. I thumb the phone on.

"He's right, you know. You can't stop it."

There's static on the line, but I know the voice. This isn't the first time he's crank-called me from Hell.

"Fuck you, Merihim."

Merihim is head of the Hell's one official church. But it was all a ruse. He's also in a Hellion Angra cult. A lot of the fallen angels want the old gods back so that they'll destroy the universe, hoping it will relieve them of the torments of Hell. It's the biggest suicide pact in the history of creation.

"Try again. Do you think there's only one who can speak through mortals?"

The line static clears up.

"Deumos?"

She's another fallen angel. She ran another underground, radical church in Hell. Except it was all a con job. She was working with Merihim to bring the Angra back. I guess you can't trust Hellions or preachers. Who would have guessed?

"The who doesn't matter. The what matters. Return the Qomrama Om Ya. That's the only way the killing will end."

"So you can summon the Angra? I know how you want things to end."

"Admit it. You're as exhausted by existence as we are. Help us end it."

"Hello? Say that again. It's hard to hear you over the bullshit."

There's a pause. I start to think that the line has gone dead.

"Hello?"

"You'll find each other sooner or later, and when you do, you'll see how pointless your cowboy antics really are."

I hear a click and the call is over. I drop the kid's phone in my pocket and take out my own. I hit redial and call Candy.

It rings twice and she picks up.

"You all right?" I say.

"Yeah. Why wouldn't I be?"

"No reason. You weren't feeling well earlier."

"Where are you?"

"Bamboo House."

"I'll be there soon."

"Don't bother. Cops are on the way."

"Are you okay?"

I switch the phone to my left hand. There must have been blood on the kid's phone. I wipe my right hand on my coat.

"I'm fine," I say. "You stay put, lock up the store, and I'll bring home some donuts."

"Yum."

I try to slip out the front of the bar, but the cops are already there. It's the two that were in the bar earlier. When they try the bully-boy routine, I use the only weapon I can think of. One that might backfire in my face. I flash my Vigil credentials at them. They back off. Reluctantly, but they back off.

"I understand you removed evidence from the accident scene," says one. The one who looked at me funny before. He's still looking at me kind of like I'm a talking lobster.

"I'm taking in a cell phone to the Vigil's labs."

"You don't think this was a traffic accident?"

"I don't know what it is, but I know the kid is a person of interest in a Vigil investigation, so I'm keeping the phone."

"Let me see that ID again."

I pull it out but keep it close enough that he can't grab it from me.

He writes down my ID number and closes his notebook.

"We'll be in touch," he says.

"I'll count the seconds."

I walk around the corner into the alley next to Bamboo House. The headlights of the cop car throw a nice shadow on the wall. As I step through I catch the cop with the notebook watching me. I keep going. This is Hollywood. Fuck him if he can't deal with a little street magic.

I'M HOME MAYBE twenty minutes when someone pounds on the front door of Max Overdrive. I grab my Colt and head downstairs. The front of the store is all glass, so if someone really wanted to get in they could. Still, I'd like to know who I'm dealing with. I flip on the outside light and go behind the counter. We installed a surveillance camera over the door when Kasabian and I had the place fixed up. Except tonight all I can see is the outline of a body outside and heavy rain. More pounding on the door.

"Stark. I know you're in there. Open up, dammit."

It's a woman's voice.

I take a chance and look around the shade that covers the door and recognize Marshal Julie Sola. I stuff the Colt in my waistband and unlock the door. She brushes past me to get out of the rain. She's in a long slicker raincoat with the hood pulled up over her head. Still, she's drenched and making a puddle on the floor. I point to the peg on the wall where people can hang their raincoats. She gives a soft "Ah," takes off her coat, and hangs it up.

Her hair is long and dark, pulled up high and pinned in place. It was, at least. Now it's a wet rat's nest. She's dressed in light, loose-fitting sportswear, a kind of idiot camouflage the Vigil makes many agents wear to try and blend in with their country-club location. She looks vaguely embarrassed, but quickly shakes it off.

"Thanks," she says. "I thought I'd find you here."

"You're half drowned. Why didn't you wait till I came in tomorrow?"

"Would you have really come to see me?"

"Maybe not first thing, but sure. I like you fine."

"That isn't what I mean," she says. "This is what I mean."

She hands me the manila envelope she's been holding. She had it under the jacket, but the front is still damp.

I open the envelope and find official Vigil stationery and forms. Many pages of forms. It's my psych evaluation.

"I have to do all this?"

"Ah no. This is just part one. There are three parts."

"Fuck me," I say. The pages are full of word problems, shapes I'm supposed to group together, drawings, and questions about my parents.

"I can help you," she says. "I know the right answers to give so Washington won't ask any questions."

"You think Washington is going to buy it if I come off like Mike Brady?"

She smiles and rubs her hands together to get the circulation going.

"So we'll leave some rough edges on. The point is you'll pass. We need you."

I drop the envelope on the counter.

"Why are you back working with them? Last I saw you, you were happy in the Mike Hammer PI biz."

She shrugs.

"Look at things. The world is too crazy to want one more inexperienced private investigator. Don't get me wrong, I was good at my job, but I was slowly starving to death. Eating through my savings and playing a lot of Tetris waiting for the phone to ring."

"Bad timing, I guess."

"To say the least. When Marshal Wells called and offered me my old job back, it wasn't hard to say yes. What about you?"

"Not so different. But he told me he knew how to work a weapon, something to fight the Angra with. Turns out it was a fib. He has a bag of bones working on it. Maybe he'll figure it out."

"I met him once. Creepy guy. He called me 'tubby.' I don't look fat to you, do I?"

"I don't know. He called me 'lardass' last time I saw him."

Candy comes down the stairs.

"Is this where the party is?"

"Candy, this is Julie Sola. Marshal Sola these days. Julie, this is Candy."

Candy comes down and they shake hands. She has powdered sugar on her fingers and it rubs off on Julie.

"Sorry," she says, and holds out the bag she's holding. "Want a donut?"

"No thanks. I was just dropping off some paperwork."

Candy says, "You're the private eye he talked about. You got him onto the zombie case."

Julie nods.

"Yeah. We thought it was a simple demon possession at the time. He saved us."

"Yeah, he does that."

"I've seen you around Vigil headquarters."

"Don't bring me any paperwork. I'm just this one's unofficial assistant."

"Don't worry. If you're not on the payroll you don't have to take the psych evaluation."

Candy looks at me and laughs.

"You're supposed to pass a government psych evaluation? Oh man, I hope you like the smell of a rubber room because that's where you're headed, pal."

"I can pass for normal if I have to."

"Yeah, and I'm Nancy Reagan's wrestling coach."

Julie puts her hand out and I shake it.

"Listen," she says. "If we make it through this maybe we can work together again. Believe it or not, I still have a few clients. And I don't think you're going to want to stay in the Vigil forever."

"Sounds good. If the world doesn't end, let's talk."

She starts to put on her raincoat.

"Don't forget about those papers."

"I'll get on them first thing in the morning."

Candy holds out the bag again.

"One for the road? I have plastic wrap upstairs."

"No thanks," Julie says. Then, "Shit. I almost forgot the real reason I came. Marshal Wells gave this to me to give to you. It looked important."

It's an envelope. Nice, crisp, expensive paper. On the inside, it's lined with a molecule's thickness of gold. The thing is uncomfortably familiar. I open the note inside. It's from Saragossa Blackburn, the pope of the whole Sub Rosa kingdom in California.

The note says, *Come see me tomorrow. At noon. I know you're not an early riser.* His signature is under that, signed with a fine pen using ink that probably cost as much as a lung transplant.

"Thanks," I say, and drop the note on the counter with the papers.

"Good night," says Julie. To Candy she says, "Nice meeting you."

Candy gives me a look.

"Offer the lady a ride home, Sir Galahad."

I turn to Julie.

"Want me to get you home the fast way?"

She shakes her head.

"No thanks. I have my car."

"Drive safe."

"Thanks."

"She seems nice," says Candy, biting into a jelly donut. "What else did she bring you?"

I pick up the note from Blackburn and drop it again.

"I have to go and see one of the few guys in town who can call in a hit on me. I saw a kid get crushed today. I got a phone call from Downtown. And now this."

I look at Candy. She's already headed for the stairs.

"These are really good donuts."

"Thank you for your concern."

"Don't whine to me. You forgot the coffee. Now I have to go make some. Forget those papers for tonight. Come upstairs and have something to eat, fatty."

I can tell by her tone she's going to be calling me that for a long time.

Before we fall asleep I almost ask her why she never told me about the Ommahs. Almost. Maybe I'll ask later when we're not so tired. Yeah, then.

I CAN'T SLEEP, so I get up at the crack of eleven. Candy is still asleep, so I pull on my clothes quietly and go into the bathroom to brush the taste of lard and sugar out of my mouth. We killed most of the bag watching *Barbarella* and *Danger: Diabolik* last night. I don't need to experience the wonders of fried dough again for a year.

I'm sick of hiding from the world, moving through the Room all the time. When I'm ready to leave I go around to the alley beside Max Overdrive and uncover the Hellion hog. It's a little something I picked up in Hell, back when I was playing Lucifer. I wanted a motorcycle so I could get around by myself and not always in a clown-car presidential motorcade. I asked the local demon techs to throw together a 1965-style Electra Glide. They did their best. In fact they did a great job, but what they came up with was a lot more Hellion than Harley. The bike is built like a motorized rhino with handlebars that taper to points like they came off a longhorn's head. The pipes belch dragon fire and when I kick the bike hard, the engine glows cherry red like it wants to shoot off into the sky, a panhead Space Shuttle.

But it's not just kicks I want right now. The overcast skies mean there aren't many good shadows to move through. Plus, I don't want to spook any of Saragossa Blackburn's guard dogs by appearing out of nowhere. When I get to his place, I want them to hear me coming.

I kick the bike into gear and it roars like a hungry Tyrannosaurus. At the curb, the water comes up almost to the tire hubs, but the bike doesn't slow. The engine boils the water around us and every time I stop I'm enveloped in a cloud of steam.

The streets through Hollywood in the direction of the 101 are as snarled as ever, though some of the side streets are starting to be passable. People running for their lives 24/7—hell, even L.A. has to start emptying out sometime. I'd love to collar one of the runners and ask them why they're going, but I know what the answer would be. Aunt Tilly is sick in Nebraska. There's a vegan lute hoedown in Portland. Skull Valley Sheep Kill is headlining a nonexistent music festival in

Houston. Lies, all lies, and they know it, but do they understand it? It's animal stuff. Zebras don't hang around a watering hole when the lions show up.

Maybe this parade of chickenshit civilians knows more than the rest of us Vigil and Sub Rosa types determined to tough it out until the end. I mean, why should the Angra pick L.A. to be their launching pad? Then again, why not? Maybe Zhuyigdanatha wants to do an open-mic night at the Comedy Store. Maybe the Angra want to have a drink at the Rainbow Bar & Grill like real old-time rock-and-rollers. Maybe they want to stomp us into the dirt because L.A. defines reality for three-quarters of the world. Or maybe because Mr. Muninn used to live here and they fucking hate him and the rest of the God brothers.

The brothers make up what's left of God. See, he had a little nervous breakdown a few millennia back and split into five pieces. He's weak, and one part of him, the brother called Neshemah, is dead. Murdered by Aelita and cheered on by big brother Ruach. Like the Ramones said, we're a happy family.

Maybe I'm making too much of it all. L.A. is turning into Atlantis, slowly sinking beneath the waves. If the rain keeps up, those Brentwood blue bloods will be chain-sawing their mansions into arks, loading up the kids, the Pekingese, their favorite Bentleys, and heading for warmer climes. Trust-fund pirates and showbiz buccaneers, sailing the briny to Palm Springs and Vegas, where it never rains and Armageddon can't get through the guards at the gated communities without an engraved invitation.

WHEN IT COMES to showing off, the Sub Rosa aren't like the civilian big-money crowd. They like anonymity more than kittens and cotton candy. While civilians compete for *House Beautiful* trophies, wealthy Sub Rosas like their places to come across as the most miserable shitboxes outside of the town dump. If they could live in a greasy Big Mac wrapper they'd do it.

Blackburn's mansion is downtown, in an abandoned residency hotel on South Main Street. The bottom floor is boarded up, covered in aeons of graffiti and posters for bands and clubs that haven't existed for a decade or more. The second and third floors have been gutted by fire. There's something heroic about the utter devastation of the place. It probably says more about what the Sub Rosa have become than Blackburn ever intended.

The mansion is protected by more hoodoo than the gates of Heaven. So much that Blackburn didn't have guards for years. Then I broke in that one time, and ever since, he's stationed a private army outside. To fit in with the look of the street, his mercs are covered in grime and sporting the latest haute couture rags from Bums "R" Us.

Blackburn's security chief, Audsley Ishii, and a dozen of his crustiest compadres surround me as I pull up outside the mansion. It takes me a second to recognize him under the moth-eaten wool cap and stage-makeup stubble. His raincoat is a plastic trash bag, which he's cut open at the bottom for his head and the sides for his arms. He doesn't pull a weapon. Neither does any of his crew, but if I sneeze I'll have enough bullets and hoodoo thrown at me to knock loose one of Saturn's moons.

Ishii says, "Stark. Don't you even know enough to get out of the rain?"

"I like it. Makes this neighborhood smell less like a piss factory."

"Well, you'd know all about living like a pig, would you?"

"Are you trying to insult me? 'Cause I can't hear you over the sound of your garbage-bag tuxedo."

One or two of his crew smile, but sober up when he throws them a look.

"What do you want here?"

"Don't fuck around, man. You know I'm here to see Blackburn."

He looks me and the bike over.

"I couldn't help noticing you weren't wearing a helmet when you drove up. You're aware that the state of California has clearly spelled out helmet laws, aren't you?"

He takes a couple of steps back and spreads his arms wide.

"And there's no way this, whatever the hell this thing is, is street legal. It doesn't even have a license plate."

"So, write me a ticket, Eliot Ness. Just get out of my way."

Ishii holds up a finger.

"Before I maybe let you in, I'm going to have to search you for weapons."

"Try it and the last thing you'll see is me pulling your skull out by the eye sockets."

That does it. Ishii's goons go on high alert, guns, hexes, and potions at the ready. It's kind of fun really. Like a scene from some kind of hobo Power Rangers movie.

"Not smart," says Ishii. "You know I can have you arrested this fast for making a terrorist threat."

He snaps his fingers like maybe I don't get it.

He says, "All Mr. Blackburn has to do is nod and you'll be buried so far underground you'll be sleeping on lava."

"Yeah, but you still won't have a skull. Your head's going to look like a jack-o'-lantern a week after Halloween."

He shakes his head in mock sorrow.

"I'm afraid under the circumstances I can't allow you to see the Augur. And I'm forwarding your name to the local police watch list."

"Do it. What are there, like a hundred cops left in L.A.? And they don't want to be out in the rain any more than you do."

"Maybe I won't have to do anything if you turn this circus act of yours around and go home."

"I'd love to, but I have an invitation from Blackburn himself."

I reach into my pocket and Ishii's crew goes rigid. With my fingertips, I slowly pull out Blackburn's note and hand it to Ishii. He looks it over and crumples it up. Tosses it into a puddle.

"With your criminal associations it's probably a forgery. Go home, Stark, before you fall on a bullet."

Ishii's phone rings. He has to fumble under his trash bag to pull it from inside his tattered coat. He puts it to his ear and listens intently for a few seconds.

"Yes, sir. He's here now, but he's not behaving rationally. He's made threats."

Ishii listens.

"No. Not to you personally, but this is a highly unstable individual, with a history of violence. As head of security, I have to take these things seriously."

He abruptly stops talking.

"Yes, sir. No, sir. I understand."

He purses his lips as he fumbles the phone back into his coat. Waves his arm in my direction.

"Let him through, boys."

His crew gets out of the way so I can roll the bike to the curb and heel down the kickstand.

Getting off, I say, "Your problem, Ishii, is that you like playing protector of the realm for the Augur because it gives you a power hard-on. But you really don't respect the man. I mean, he peeks into the future. He probably knew exactly what you were going to do before you did. The only reason he waited this long to do anything about it is he wanted to give you a chance to pull your head out of your ass."

Ishii looks at his watch, waves his people back to their posts. He doesn't want to look at me.

"Stop talking, Stark. And go inside before my gun goes off by accident."

"Have fun with the fishes, Noah."

The door is open for me when I reach the hotel.

The outside of Blackburn's house might be a wreck, but the inside is something else. The inner sanctum is a Victorian fever dream of potted palms, gaslights, silk settees, and arsenic-green walls. You half expect to see Dickens and Queen Victoria sipping laudanum in the living room. I know the layout, so I stroll through the place to the parlor, where Blackburn has his office.

The Augur is a scryer. A seer. All Augurs are scryers and Blackburn is supposed to be a good one. He's an okay guy in an executive kind of way. His suit looks like it was cut by

God's tailor. His graying temples make him look like he's in his late forties, but I know that he's well over a hundred. The rich are different. He comes around from his desk and puts out his hand. I shake it.

"Thank you for coming," he says, and gestures to a chair before going back to the iron throne.

"I don't know why I'm here, so I'll say 'you're welcome.' For the moment."

Blackburn's heart beats faster than a powerful politician's heart ought to. He's nervous, but good at not showing it. He picks up a pen and sets it at a right angle to his papers.

"I asked you here in hopes of clearing up any differences there might be between us. In times like this, I don't want us to be enemies."

"I didn't know we were enemies."

"You know what I mean."

"No. I don't. I saved your wife's soul and got treated like a rabid dog."

"You did break in here and terrorize my guests during your time as Lucifer."

"I was just back from Hell and having a bad day."

"You have a lot of those," he says.

"You try coming back from Hell feeling springtime fresh."

Blackburn pours himself a drink of something brown and whiskey-smelling from a crystal decanter. Holds up the bottle toward me and raises his eyebrows.

"Sure," I say, figuring he has easier ways of killing me than poison. I take a sip and it takes me a minute to recognize it. A kind of rye called Angel's Envy. There are whiskey-colored wings on the bottle and everything. The stuff is aged in rum barrels and has about twelve different tastes going down. It's not Aqua Regia, but it will do.

I say, "Nasrudin Hodja sent a car full of punks after me a while back. They shot up the street and nearly killed a friend of mine. Were you in on that?"

He sets down his drink.

"No. I give you my word."

His heartbeat doesn't change. He's not sweating. He's telling the truth.

Tuatha Fortune, his wife, comes in. Perches on the edge of Blackburn's desk. She's in a white silk blouse and black pants. Old-money modest.

"He's not lying," she says. "I was there during the discussion."

"He didn't try to have me killed. He just talked about it. I'm all relieved now."

"Nasrudin came to me and asked permission to right the insult after you tortured his nephews in that bar."

A few weeks back, while looking for the Qomrama, I hassled some Cold Case soul merchants at Bamboo House of Dolls. Stripped them and made them think I was skinning one of them. It was just a spell, a Hellion hoodoo trick. Nothing bad happened except to their egos. Some people can't take a joke.

"I didn't torture anyone. They were as safe as baby chickens under mom's wings. I scared them a little and sent them to bed without their supper. That's it."

Blackburn pours his wife a drink. It's a little early in the day for whiskey, even for me. They really don't like having me in their house.

I hardly know Tuatha at all. When I first met her she

wasn't much more than a walking corpse. I thought she might be on chemotherapy, but why would a high-class Sub Rosa be using civilian doctors? Turns out Aelita had hidden her soul somewhere in order to blackmail Blackburn. I convinced Mr. Muninn to find it and return it to her. However much she might be one of L.A.'s pampered rich elite, she didn't deserve to get ripped apart by a lunatic like Aelita.

"You have a madcap definition of safe, Mr. Stark," she says.

I raise my drink in her direction.

"It's just Stark. And yeah, I'm all about the merry pranks."

"Physical torture or not," says Blackburn, "Nasrudin took what you did as an attack on the entire soul-merchant clan. He demanded satisfaction and I didn't have any choice but to say yes. It was politics, pure and simple. As an ex-Lucifer, surely you understand that."

Tuatha says, "Don't tell me you didn't see it coming. You understand revenge, if nothing else."

"I understand fine. I just get testy when it's aimed at me."

Blackburn waves his hand, dismissing everything that's been said.

"Let's put that behind us. I've made it clear to Nasrudin that he overstepped when he tried to gun you down. It won't happen again."

"And he's such a reasonable guy. I'm sure he keeps his promises."

"To me he does."

I can believe that, actually. Sounds like I'm clear of one source of immense bullshit for a while.

Tuatha says, "You know, you did a lot of people a lot of

good when you dispatched Norris Quay. I can tell you truth-fully, he won't be missed."

Old, decrepit Norris Quay was the richest man in Califor-nia, but not anymore. He's severely dead.

"I bet. But I didn't dispatch him. He was killed by crazies in the basement of Kill City."

"Naturally," says Blackburn, humoring me but not believ-ing a word of it. He opens a desk drawer and pulls out an old book. It's battered, like one of the heretical books in Father Traven's library.

"However it happened, it's given us access to his con-siderable collection of occult objects and texts. My great-grandfather wrote this one. One of the first set of bylaws and family trees for the American Sub Rosa. Would you like to see it?"

"Thanks. But I'm afraid I'll spill my drink on it."

"Of course," he says, disappointed I didn't want to be daz-zled by his family roots.

"In any case," he says, "I've sent a particularly interesting book to the Golden Vigil. I understand they have an actual Buddhist priest helping with them with research."

"They do."

"You could have knocked me over with a feather when I heard that those old fundamentalists were consorting with Eastern heathens," says Tuatha. When she smiles there are lines at the corners of her eyes. I like that unlike a lot of Sub Rosa elite, she's not trying to glamour away her age. "Have you met him? What's he like? I've heard those old monks can be quite the pranksters. Fun workmates."

" 'Fun' isn't the word I'd use. And I haven't worked with

him much, so I don't know how good he is. Wells seems to think he's the bees' knees."

"You must tell me more about him the next time you come by," says Tuatha.

"I'm coming back?"

"I hope so," says Blackburn. "I offered you the job of my security chief before and I'd hoped that since then you'd reconsidered it."

"Actually, I hadn't. Listen, I was bodyguard for the first Lucifer and was lousy at it. I'm not being modest. I got us ambushed and him cut up. I'm good at hitting things, not keeping things from getting hit."

"I'm sorry to hear that."

I finish my whiskey and start to set down the glass. Blackburn smoothly slides a coaster under it before it touches down.

"You're a scryer. Shouldn't you know I was going to say no?"

He shakes his head.

"It doesn't work like that. I see probabilities, some more likely and some less. In a case like you, where someone has to make a yes-or-no choice, I see both outcomes and some of the consequences of each decision."

"So, no lottery numbers, then?"

"Actually, he's very good at lottery numbers," says Tuatha.

"But I'm not going to give you any," he adds.

"See? The rich are no fun. They get everything and then wag their fingers at us proles for wanting a taste."

"Is that why you won't take the job? I never took you for a Marxist. A Situationist, perhaps."

"I don't know what any of those words mean. And I'm not

going to argue about it. A politician like you, you'll have me convinced I wanted the job, that it was my idea, and that I wanted to be paid in candy corn."

"There's nothing I can offer you to change your mind?"

"It's nothing personal. I have a job to do, even if I have to do it with the Vigil. A friend died looking for the Qomrama. I'm not going to let that happen again."

Tuatha stands up and goes around to the back of the desk.

"My husband is afraid, Mr. Stark. He won't say it. He's seen dark days ahead, for the Sub Rosa and for us personally. Please reconsider."

"You have a whole army outside and you can get a bigger one. Talk to Wells. He doesn't like us pixies, but I bet he'd send people to protect the Augur."

Tuatha looks at Blackburn.

"That might not be a bad idea. And it will give Mr. Stark—excuse me, Stark, a chance to think things over."

To Tuatha I say, "Can I ask you something?"

"Of course."

"All this rain. Do you have something to do with it?"

She cocks her head to the side like she's telling a kid there are no monsters under the bed.

"That's a common misconception about the art of brontomancy. I'm a thunder worker," she says, and looks up as a monstrous clap of thunder rattles the windows. "I use thunder and even lightning for purposes of divination and spell casting. Brontomancers don't have anything to do with rain."

Her heart and breathing are steady. She's telling the truth too. These people are no fun.

"Do you know any rain workers who might be doing this?"

"Believe me, I've asked," she says. "I've even offered a reward to anyone who can tell me who or what is causing it."

"Okay. You'll let me know if you hear anything?"

"Of course."

"If you won't work for me now, maybe you will when this matter is settled?" says Blackburn.

"If we make it, I'll think about it."

Blackburn stands. He and Tuatha come around the desk.

He says, "I have every confidence that you and Marshal Wells will get us through this."

"I wouldn't put too much money on that horse."

"You don't think Marshal Wells is confident?"

We start walking to the front door.

"Wells is a believer. In God and the feds. He's morally obligated to believe that we can win. But I don't think he's any more confident than I am."

Tuatha says, "You saved me once. You can do it again."

"Why not? There's not much else to do in L.A. these days."

Blackburn and Tuatha shake my hand and a second later I'm back in front of the ruined building with the moist, surly guards.

I head for the bike, but Ishii gets in front and stops me.

"Just a minute," he says, and we stand there in the rain like a couple of dummies.

"Are we waiting for something?"

"A phone call," he says. "Telling me you misbehaved."

"I was a perfect gentleman. Freddie Bartholomew in *Little Lord Fauntleroy*."

He keeps his hand up between us.

"We'll know in a few seconds," he says.

His crew stays put, trying to keep out of the rain, but ready to move when the ringmaster says "jump."

Ishii's phone doesn't ring. He looks more disappointed than a tiger at a vegan luau.

He hooks a thumb over his shoulder.

"You know, one of these times you're going to show up and there's going to be an accident," he says. "It won't be anyone's fault. Shit just happens sometimes, right?"

I get on the Hellion hog and kick it into life. It roars and the water around us steams.

"You're right," I say. "Here's some shit that just happened. Your boss offered me your job."

I pop the clutch and haul out of there before Ishii can say or, more importantly, do, anything.

It's nice to be wanted, but it's unsettling to see the boss of bosses rattled. As much as the mansion-on-the-hill crowd bugs me, it's weird seeing them actually scared. You want them dumb and arrogant. When they're scared it means that however bad you thought things were, they're worse.

I TAKE BACK streets all the way home. A lot of street- and stoplights are out, drowned in the endless rain. Whole neighborhoods—almost the entire length of Franklin Street— are dark. No lights on in the houses. No cars on the street or in driveways. The city really is emptying its guts onto the freeways. I wonder how many of us there will be left in the end. And who's going to be top of the food chain? Civilians, Sub Rosas, or Lurkers? I can deal with any kind of supernatural asshole playing King of the Hill, but civilians make me nervous. In times of stress they tend to grab pitchforks and torches. I don't know how many staying behind even know about L.A.'s hoodoo world, but based on history, I hope it's not many.

When I get to Max Overdrive, I park the Hellion hog around the side and let it sit for a while to cool off. If I throw the cover on now, it's likely to melt.

As I walk inside, I'm hit with a blast of noise that makes my ears ring. It's like a 747 having rough sex with a skyscraper on a pile of exploding transformers. The sound doesn't let up, but settles into a steady beat. Steady enough that I can identify it as a warped version of a song. "Ace of Spades." Candy is practicing guitar again.

"Tell me again why we built her a soundproof practice room?" says Kasabian. He'd like to stick his fingers in his ears, but they're modified hellhound paws and ungraceful enough he'd probably put an eye out if he got them near his head.

"The practice room is to make us grateful for all the times she doesn't do this."

I go upstairs and open the door to our rooms. The sound is like getting punched in the chest. I hold up my hands in a T time-out signal. She smiles at me like a demented eight-year-old.

"It sounds great up here, doesn't it?" she says.

"It's beautiful. Angel choirs and demon songs. Now please go and play in the practice room. If I hear much more of this gorgeousness it will spoil me for all other music forever."

She screws up her mouth into a half sneer.

"You're weak, old man. And you're dripping all over the floor."

"I'm glad you're feeling better," I say.

She unplugs her guitar and amp. Picks up both.

"You're off the guest list for our first show."

"Then it won't be the first show I've crashed. I know all the back exits and kitchen doors on the Strip."

She comes over and stands on her toes.

"Kiss me and I won't hate you forever for being such a noise wimp."

I lean down and we kiss. She head-butts me lightly when we stop.

"Nope. I still hate you. You'll have to make it up to me later."

"How?"

"Be sure to lock the door tonight. We're going to play the Cowboy and the Duchess."

"I don't even know what that is."

"You will," she says. "And I make no promises that you'll be the cowboy."

"I wouldn't expect you to."

I get out of my wet clothes and leave them to dry in the bathtub. Pull on some dry jeans and a moth-eaten Max Overdrive T-shirt and go downstairs.

"Thank you," says Kasabian.

"If I'm the Duchess later, you're going to owe me."

"What?"

"Nothing. What's that you've got?"

He holds up a disc and wiggles it.

"Your witch stopped by with a new movie. The full eight-hour version of von Stroheim's *Greed*. Before us, only twelve people ever saw the uncut film. We can be the thirteenth and fourteenth."

"I like a lot of odd stuff, but even I think eight hours of Teutonic existential grimness sounds awful."

Kasabian shakes his head.

"Pussy."

"Everyone is calling me names tonight."

Kasabian sets down the disc and puts a copy of Hitchcock's lost flick, *The Mountain Eagle,* back on the shelf.

"People keep asking about buying copies of the discs," Kasabian says.

"Selling isn't part of the business plan. We're strictly a rental operation."

"That's what I keep telling them. But those vampires can get scary insistent."

"Tell them to come and talk to me," I say. "Besides, what can a vampire do to you? I mean, do you even have blood anymore?"

He looks hurt.

"Watch the language. I'm just starting to feel good about this body and you go and bring that up."

"Relax. We've both been dead. It's no big deal."

"Says the guy with the hot girlfriend and a body still made of meat. You think sweat stains are hard to get out of clothes? Try machine oil."

"Anytime you want to go back on your magic skateboard, I've got it for you in a closet upstairs."

"No, you don't."

"Candy uses it to do her paper rounds."

Kasabian pulls a beer from behind the counter and twists the cap off. I've talked to him about drinking in front of customers, but he's just one more person around here who doesn't listen to me.

"You two are so domestic these days it's sickening."

"You should get out more, or at all," I say. "You'll meet someone nice and we'll have little puppy hellhounds running around the place."

"Speaking of shit that's never going to happen, guess who just showed up in Hell?"

"Who?"

"Chaya, the long lost God brother. He doesn't look too good. Like he booked a long weekend in an ass-kicking machine. You should go down and check it out."

"You just want me to do your swami work for you."

"We need the money, genius."

"I'm sick of talking about money."

"That's what people with no money say."

I want to say something. About an incident that's bothered me for almost a year. Even thinking about it makes me angry and ashamed. Angry she got killed and ashamed I couldn't do anything about it.

"I'll make you a deal," I say. "There's a green-haired girl in Hell somewhere. Find her for me."

"A green-haired girl? Sure. There can't be more than a million of those."

"She used to work at Donut Universe. I never told anyone, but I found her name in an online obit. Cindil Ashley. Find her and I'll do your job."

Kasabian waggles an eyebrow at me.

"An old love? You sly thing."

"You do not even want to begin joking about this," I say. "She was murdered by the Kissi right in front of me. If they weren't dead, I'd kill them all over again for it."

The Kissi were a race of mad, malformed angels that lived in the chaos at the edge of the universe. They're gone now, but before they went, they killed a lot of innocent civilians. When I lost an arm in Hell, the Kissi marked me by replacing my normal arm with a Kissi one. Now I wear a glove on my left hand to hide it from people.

Kasabian holds up his metal hellhound hands in a "calm down" gesture.

"It's cool. Sorry. I didn't know."

"Now you do. Find her for me."

"I'll do what I can."

There's a knock at the front door. I open it. A blond Ludere girl comes in. She's all wet and all smiles. It's Fairuza, Candy's drummer.

"Hey, Stark. Hey, Kasabian," she says.

Kasabian hides his beer. I've never seen him do that before. But I've never seen him around Fairuza.

"How are you doing?" he says.

"Great. Thanks for the movie. It was cool. I never thought I'd like a silent flick."

She hands him a copy of *Metropolis*.

"You said you liked sci-fi, so I figured."

"Good choice. You have anything more like it?"

"Are you kidding? We specialize in shit . . . stuff . . . no one's seen. Let me dig around and see what I can come up with."

"Cool. Thanks."

"I don't know how you watch your movies. Lots of people do it on computers these days . . ."

"Yeah. That's me."

"Well, if you ever want to see something like it's supposed

to be seen, a good screen and sound," he says. Then stops. When he starts up again he speaks in a rush. "I have a real good setup in my place. If you ever, you know."

She hesitates.

"I like to eat Chinese food when I watch movies. Do you, I don't mean this in a bad way, eat?"

"Sure. All the time. Ask him," he says.

I nod.

"He's a great white shark. Nature's perfect eating machine."

Fairuza shrugs.

"Sure. Why not? Find me something good and it's a date."

"Okay. Great," he says.

Candy starts torturing "Ace of Spades" again in the practice room. Fairuza points.

"That's my cue," she says.

"I'll have something for you when you're done," says Kasabian.

She smiles.

"Impress me."

He nods and she goes into the room.

I say, "I believe you have a date."

"Now all I have to do is find something dazzling."

"I don't think you know her well enough for *2001* or *Zardoz*. One's too weird and one's too slow."

"Yeah. Those are second-date movies."

"Third."

"You think?"

"At least."

"She means it, right? Like, you don't think she just said that to make fun of me?"

"I don't think Candy hangs out with people like that. She knows killers, but not mean girls."

"Okay. Now I just have to find something. *The Fifth Element?*"

"That could be a first-date movie."

"Okay," he says, taking out his beer and finishing it in one go.

"You keep saying 'okay.' "

"Do I?"

"Yeah."

"Okay."

Drums come through the wall, mixing with the wailing guitar.

"Good luck," I say. "I'm going to Bamboo House."

"Okay."

A LITTLE HUNG over, I head to the Vigil the next afternoon.

Outside, I stop with the other smoking fed delinquents and light up a Malediction. A grounds-keeping crew is running an industrial mower over the golf course, convincing absolutely no one that life goes as usual in the country club. How are they trying to fool with this shit? Is there anyone left in the neighborhood? These were high-toned families. Old money on the skids and new money on the way up, but all with enough resources to be among the first to blow town when the skies opened up.

Maybe the Vigil is keeping up the charade in case they get buzzed by enemy drones. Only who's using drones over L.A. anymore? Not the Angra. Maybe al-Qaeda is in cahoots with the old Gods. Why not? We don't look much like winners down here.

Inside Vigil headquarters is like the outside. Busy. Busy. Busy. Feds in suits and others in their golf togs disguises hustle from meetings with tablets under their arms. Others unpack and test angelic Vigil tech freshly shipped in from Washington. Maintenance crews swab the walls and floors. In the constant damp, mildew turns up here like anywhere else and the wet fouls some of the gear.

A group of Dreamers sits around a long plastic table in a break room. There's a crèche and a little aluminum Christmas tree by the microwave. The Dreamers seem tired and a little hung over themselves. Looks like holding reality together is a bad career choice these days. Keitu Brown is there with her parents. Ten years old, she's the leader of the bunch. Kids are always the strongest Dreamers. I met her once through Patty Templeton, a dead Dreamer I didn't do a very good job of protecting. Keitu gives me a little wave. I wave back. Dad gives me a look and puts his arm around his daughter's shoulder. I keep moving.

The door to the Shonin's magic room is locked and there's something new on the wall. A key pad and a box the size of an old PC, with a glass plate on the front.

There's a shade over the door to the Shonin's room, so I can't see if anyone is in there. I bang on the glass. A few seconds later an intercom crackles.

"Put your hand on the scanner, fatso."

I push the key on the intercom.

"The glass plate on the front?"

"No. The one sticking out of my ass, stupid."

I touch the plate and the panel lights up. I feel a gentle vibration as a light inside runs across my hand. A second later, a panel above the scanner lights up.

ENTRY.

The door buzzes. I push and it opens. I'm pissed off until I get inside and see why they put on the extra security.

The Qomrama Om Ya sits in the far corner of the room. It floats, suspended in a magnetic field, spinning slowly, changing shape as it moves.

"You're in the big time now," says the Shonin.

"I wasn't before?"

"Bigger. You get to play with the expensive toys."

"I found the damned toy."

"Yeah, but you gave it to the Vigil, so it's here's now, isn't it?"

The fucker is right. I did give it to them. And I guess it's as safe here as anywhere on Earth. And if I hid it in the Room, where no one could get at it, we'd never figure out how to use it.

The Shonin comes over to where I'm standing and looks at the 8 Ball.

I say, "How did the Vigil get my prints?"

"Have you ever touched anything?"

"Here?"

"Anywhere."

"I see your point."

The Shonin goes back to his worktable, piled high musty books marked with highlighters and Post-its. There's an old box on the table with about a hundred little cubbyholes, each holding a potion in a small vial. If Vidocq was here he could probably tell me what they were. Maybe the bag of bones gets tuckered out and needs mummy Adderall to study for his finals.

"I have a present for you," I say, and hand the Shonin the dead Goth kid's phone.

"I already have an iPhone. And this piece of shit is cracked," he says.

"Fuck you. I got this off a dead kid. He was possessed and I got a call from some really annoying people in Hell on it. I thought maybe you could do some hoodoo on it and learn something."

He looks at the phone. Presses it to his chest like he's listening for something.

"I hate this kind of technology. Old stuff. Wood. Fabric. Stone. Metal. It holds pieces of the spirits that move through it. This stuff," he says, tossing the phone onto the table with his books. "This stuff is empty. It beeps. It plays music. But it has no life."

"Can you do anything with it?"

"Me? No. But maybe one of Wells's machine fuckers. Boys and girls love staring at the screens. They think I don't see them jerking around, playing World of Warcraft. Planning attacks when they should be saving the world."

"Everyone needs to blow off steam."

I can't believe I have to defend federal geeks to a dead man.

"Tell it to Lamia or Zhuyigdanatha. Think they're blowing off steam?"

The Shonin stops for a second. Stares off into space, then grabs a pen and scribbles something on a yellow legal pad.

"That reminds me. The kid said something about the 'Hand.' He said something like he's many-handed. A hand for every soul on Earth."

The Shonin nods and goes to a whiteboard. The names of the thirteen Angra are written there. He puts a check mark next to a name I've never seen before.

"His name is Akkadu. The Hand. Dumb as monkey shit. An enforcer."

"It was just the kid talking. I didn't see any Angra and the kid wasn't any more or less powerful than other possessed people. He was just a vessel for whoever has the possession key in Hell."

The Shonin writes *Hellions* on one corner of the whiteboard.

"What did the phone caller say?"

"Just what you think. Give us the 8 Ball. Resistance is futile. Help us destroy the universe because we're bummed and daddy's a drunk."

"Your God really fucked things up when he came up with Hell."

"My God? You don't believe in him?"

"I'm Buddhist, stupid. I believe in the God in each man and woman. I respect that you believe in your God, but he isn't my concern."

"Yeah, but he exists. You just admitted that when you said he fucked things up."

"Oh, he exists. I just don't care," he says. "But don't tell Wells I said that. His metaphysics are as simple as your brain."

The Shonin takes one of the potion vials from the box, pops the cork, and drinks, shuddering as it goes down. The shuddering sounds like someone shaking shrubbery in a paper bag. When he's done he scribbles more notes on the pad. I start to say something, but he holds up a finger for silence. When he's finished writing he looks up.

"You're still here? Go out and do something useful. Get attacked again so you can bring me more useless junk."

"Funny you should use the word 'useless.' I'm starting to think of it when I think of you. You talk big about magic and studying the 8 Ball, but what have you got to show for it? Can you use the thing yet?"

"You think I'd be standing here talking to you if I could?" he says.

The Shonin stumbles and sits on a wooden stool next to the table with his books.

"It's not so simple, understanding the Qomrama. Remember, it's two things."

"It's a weapon. The Godeater."

"Yes, but it's also a summoning object. The Angra can pound on the door to our universe. They can stick a finger or toe in, but they can't enter without being summoned with it."

"I guess that helps us a little. But even a little piece of an Angra is trouble. Have you ever fought a demon? They're just tiny brainless fragments of the Angra. The dandruff of the old Gods that fell off when they were kicked out of here. But they can kill you as dead as a bullet."

"Seen a few. Never fought one," says the Shonin. "Of course, you have. You'd fight your own shadow if you got the chance."

"So, what does knowing it's a killer and a dinner bell get us?"

The Shonin shrugs.

"I don't know yet. That's why I have my books. And this new one your friend Blackburn gave us."

I go over to his desk.

"He told me he sent something over. Which book is it?"

The Shonin puts his hand on the box of glass vials.

"This one. Great stuff. Fascinating old magic. One of the rarest grimoires in the world."

"It looks like a medieval juice bar. How is that a book?"

The Shonin smiles. It cracks his dry cheeks.

"Magic, dummy. You don't read it. You drink it. Each potion is a page of powerful old knowledge. The right bastard could kill the world with what's in here. Good thing it's a trap."

"What does that mean?"

The Shonin puts his hand back on the wooden box.

"Each potion is a page. And each page is a different poison. See the trap? You gain vast power and knowledge from a book like this, but when you have all of it, it kills you. It's genius, don't you think? It keeps deep, world-altering magic out of the hands of people like you."

That's what the Shonin has been scribbling. Poison wisdom from a killer book.

"I get it. That's why Wells wanted you on this case. He knew about the book or knew about something like it. Something that would kill a regular magician. So he hired himself a dead one so it wouldn't work on him."

The Shonin sits down again.

"But it *is* working. I told you, this is old magic. Stuff from when the world was young. Not like the flashy stuff you magicians do today. This is the magic of continents dividing and life moving from the sea onto land. Powerful enough to kill even a dead man."

"Then why is Wells letting you read it? Drink it? Whatever the hell you're doing with it."

"Because it's necessary. Why do you think I worry, working with such a fathead? I won't be here for the end. But you will be, and all these poor fools will rely on someone who'd rather be eating pork chops."

"And all you do is make fat jokes when you should be teaching me about these things. Like, if the Angra can't get through to us, what about Lamia? I talked to her. She appeared as a demented little kid, but she still managed to murder a lot of people."

The Shonin nods impatiently.

"Her real name is Aswangana. What you saw was like a demon version of the goddess. Not all of her broke through to this dimension, but enough so she was smarter and more powerful than ordinary Qliphoth. What you defeated was a fragment of her essence. Do you believe you could do that to a full Angra?"

"I'm not stupid enough to think that."

"Good. You know something after all."

"The Angra sound a little like Hellions. They can't break out of Hell into this world, but they can influence the world through their worshipers and using the possession key. But they're no closer to bringing the Angra back than anyone on Earth."

"I'm trying to learn how to destroy the Qomrama. If it can be destroyed," says the Shonin. "I don't have much more faith in the Vigil than I have in you. If things go badly, destroying it might be the only way to save the universe."

"Have you found anything?"

He gets up and goes to the magnetic chamber holding the 8 Ball.

"No. I don't think it can be destroyed. Gods made it. Only a God can unmake it."

"What about Mr. Muninn? He's a piece of God. Maybe I should take it to him."

The Shonin laughs his rattling laugh.

"Your God is so broken up he can barely wipe his own ass. You think he can destroy this?"

He's probably right. If Muninn or any of the other God brothers could kill the 8 Ball or the Angra, they would have done it by now. Especially Ruach, the only part of God left in Heaven. Blind and half deaf, he has it in for all the other brothers.

"Maybe I should take it to him. Just to see."

"No," says the Shonin. "It doesn't leave here. There's something to be done with it and I'll find it out."

I stand next to him at the magnetic chamber.

"What about the Tears of Gihon? That's a potion that's supposed to cure all poisons."

"I know what it is," says the Shonin quietly. "It won't work. I'll drink a hundred different poisons by the end. I'll be too weak for any cure, from this world or Heaven."

"Seems like a waste of four hundred years to just die."

"You're telling me."

"How did you do it?"

"Do what?"

"The only interesting thing about you. Self-mummification. How does it work?"

"Everybody asks that sooner or later," he says, and walks away. "It's boring. Monk stuff. You're a monster in love with another monster. You wouldn't understand."

"Maybe I will and that won't make you so special anymore."

The Shonin stands and pulls his robes around him in mock outrage.

"Ooo, psychology," he says. "You took me down a peg, didn't you, you sly dog? Here's the truth. I didn't want to talk about it because I think all you want to do is compare it to your time in Hell and see who suffered the most. Think about it. What if I suffered more? Then you're the one who won't be so special anymore."

"I'm willing to take that chance."

The Shonin looks at me with his empty eye sockets. The bone around the edges is the color of dirty tea. He opens and closes his mouth. Thin lips stretched across rotten teeth.

"It begins with a thousand days," he says. "Fat rots the body, so you have to get rid of it. Even rice can make you fat. I ate only nuts and seeds, with a little tea, but mostly just water. I worked hard. Manual labor. It burns the body down to its essence. Want to hear more?"

"Right now it doesn't sound much worse than what an Olympic runner goes through."

The Shonin shakes his head.

"In the next thousand days there's nothing but bark and pine roots to eat. You'll find this part funny. To prepare my body I had to drink a kind of poison mixed with tea. Not strong, but it will ruin you if you drink enough. You puke your guts out. Maggots hate it. I drank plenty. I loved it more than you love tacos.

"When there is so little of us left in this world we're barely ghosts, monks like me, we enter our tombs. There's a tiny breathing hole and a bell. We sit and meditate. Clear our minds and let eternity enter us. Once a day I rang the bell to let other monks know I'm alive. Soon I can't even do that. I'm not sure if I'm dead or dreaming I'm alive. I've stopped ringing the bell, so the other monks seal my tomb. I stay there for another thousand days before the tomb is opened. They took my body, placed me in robes, and put me in a place of reverence. There are not so many like me who made the journey intact."

"So, you're dead. What happened next? I mean what was the point of the whole thing?"

"I preserved myself to come back with wisdom to help the world when I'm needed."

"Why you?"

"Why not?"

"Who woke you up?"

"No one woke me up. I woke myself when I sensed it was time. A young attendant came in one day to brush the dust off and I said 'Boo.' Not only was I awake, but the boy attained enlightenment the moment I spoke to him."

"One soul saved. Only six billion to go. That's a lot of 'Boos.'"

The Shonin gets up and puts a kettle on for tea.

"What do you say, fatty? You heard my story. I already know yours from Wells. Tell me. Who suffered more?"

I feel in my pocket for a Malediction, then remember I can't smoke in here, like maybe I'm going to give a dead man lung cancer.

"You suffered plenty. I'll give you that," I say. "But if we're going to get along you've got to give me something. The difference between us isn't who suffered more. It's who chose it. You chose to suffer. Me, I was just standing there and Hell opened up and swallowed me. Eleven years of torture, rape, slavery, and fighting monsters, that's not the nothing you want to make it out to be."

"I never said it was nothing. I'm saying you don't carry your suffering with grace."

"And you get to decide what grace is?"

"I've been dead, remember?"

"So have I. Think about this. Maybe what you're claiming is grace is you just wanting me to be more like you. You never knew me before and you don't know me now. Maybe I'm what grace looks like when God forgot you and you crawled out of Hell on your own."

"See? You're still complaining."

"And you're still bragging. You had four hundred years to sit around and think about how you were going to save the human race, and you fucking loved it. Every minute of suffering. You're no better than Lucifer at his worst. You're up to your eyeballs in the sin of pride."

"You're going to talk to me about sin, Abomination?"

"I'm talking to you about ego. You poisoned yourself once and now you're doing it again, you show-off. In L.A., you're what we call a one-hit wonder."

"And you have the grace of a three-legged elephant."

"That's the best you can come up with? My mom used to call me that."

The Shonin's kettle boils.

"Your mother sounds smart."

"She had her moments."

He nods and stirs his tea.

"Are you ladies done?"

We both turn to the door. Wells is standing there.

"I don't know whether I should send you to your corners for the next round or take away your toys and put you in a time-out."

"No harm done," says the Shonin. "We were just discussing ontology."

I look at him.

"We were?"

"I was," he says.

"You were slapping each other like a couple of biddies at the old folks' home fighting over the last dish of banana pudding. You're done. Kiddie time is over. Grown-up time starts now. Understood?"

"Sure," says the Shonin.

"Whatever."

Wells comes over and glances at the Shonin's notes. They're in Japanese. He frowns.

I say, "What did the Dreamers want?"

"What do any of us want?" says Wells. "Order. The little one, Brown, says it's getting harder to hold reality together. Poor kid. She barely eats. Her sleep is abysmal. Her parents want to pull her out of the Dreamer program."

"That would be a disaster right now," the Shonin says.

"That's what I told them. Mom listened. I don't know about dad."

Stark goes to the whiteboard. Stops when he sees a check mark next to Akkadu's name. He looks at me. I don't like it.

"What happens if they take her out?"

Wells shakes his head and walks around the room.

"Brown said they're barely holding reality together as it is. Without her . . ."

He shrugs.

"We've had reality rips here before, but it sounds like the next one could be like a dam bursting."

"Why L.A.?" I say. "I mean, why is the shit coming down here?"

"We're sitting on a major power spot," says the Shonin. "A great part of the imagination of the world is attached to this city. Also, the Qomrama Om Ya is here. And you."

"Me?"

"You do seem to attract these things," says Wells.

I've wondered about that myself a few times. Do I have the bad luck to show up at the right time and place for Armageddons or am I a shit magnet that brings the monsters down on anyone in my general vicinity?

"And you love it," I say. "You secretly want it all to end 'cause you think you're going to get Raptured and that idea gives you a salvation hard-on."

"Language," Wells says.

But he doesn't deny it.

"I have something for both of you to do besides standing around catfighting and playing Marian the Librarian. There's been another Saint Nick killing. At least it looks like Saint Nick. You two are coming with me to check it out."

"Shouldn't we stay here and study the Qomrama?" says the Shonin.

"That would be nice, if you have time between rounds. But this isn't an ordinary killing. From the first reports, the scene sounds something like what Stark found in the meat locker. I want Stark there to see how well it matches and I want you there," he says, looking at the Shonin, "to keep an eye on him."

"You won't be coming?" I say.

"Of course I'll be coming. But I'll be busy doing actual forensic work. I'll leave the pixie stuff to you two. But I'll want a basic assessment on the scene. Is this another Angra-related killing?"

This time I take out the Maledictions. Smoking is a good way to get away from these two for a minute.

"Another thirteen dead? That sounds like the Angra right there."

Wells shake his head. Gives me a grim smile.

"Not thirteen this time. Last number I heard was eighty plus. It's hard to tell, what with all the body parts mixed together."

I'm glad Candy didn't come with me today.

"When are we leaving?"

"Go out and have your cigarette. We'll be done packing by the time you finish it."

Wells starts out of the room, then turns back to us.

"The killing took place at Greendale House, an upscale funny farm. Where the rich tuck away their embarrassing relations. We're going to be meeting the head of the facility. Is there any chance of you wearing a suit?"

"Not much."

"Silly of me to ask."

"Kind of."

WE HEAD OUT in a caravan of three Vigil SUVs modified to cut through the flooded streets like icebreakers. Candy didn't answer when I called to tell her I might not be home for a while. I probably didn't even need to call, but I can't tell time anymore. With the constantly dark skies it feels like midnight all the time, even though I know it's the middle of the afternoon. I've heard that it's becoming a problem for some people, the ones susceptible to light. Seasonal affective disorder. Without sunlight, some people go into hibernation mode. Depression is up. The Vigil has its own stockpiles of drugs because L.A. is running out of every upper, mood stabilizer, and antidepressant known to man. Smack chic is a thing of the past. Who need drugs to stare at your shoe all day? Living half asleep all the time, it's easy. Meth is the new drug of choice, or coke for those with money to burn. And prices are going up, up, up. I should have invested that money the Dark Eternal gave me in coca-leaf futures and the plastic surgeons who are going to have to repair all the septums movie stars are burning out trying to stay awake.

We head north on the 110 toward Pasadena. Pull off on a side road and head onto a winding private road not far from Huntington Hospital. It's one of those funny places you find in even the poshest towns. Sort of a secret street backstage behind the world. Not quite an industrial district, but where deliveries and the help arrive for all the shiny places you see on the street.

We pull into a parking lot beside what looks like a two-story office building. Poured concrete exterior. Big mirrored windows. There's no name on the front. Not even an address. It looks like just the kind of discreet place you'd want to store crazy Aunt Sadie when the attic got full.

Our three vans pull up in a line. Wells gets out first in a clear plastic raincoat.

"You too," he says to me. "But keep your mouth shut. You're here to observe."

We splash through the rain to the hospital's front door under a concrete overhang. The guy waiting for us doesn't look like the head of a hospital. More like an accountant who found out that his boss has been embezzling money and investing it in porn and nuclear weapons. His coat and shoes are expensive, but it doesn't look like he's combed his hair since Halloween.

"You're the people?" he says when he sees us.

"We are indeed," says Wells. "I'm Marshal Larson Wells and this is one of my associates." He doesn't introduce me. "You just leave everything to us from here on out."

The guy looks so relieved I think he's going to cry. Even through his suit, his raincoat, and the rain I can smell his fear sweat.

"I'm Huston Aldridge. The head of the facility. I don't have to go back inside with you, do I? I don't want to go back in there," he says.

"No, sir. You don't."

Aldridge nods.

"The board has already decided to close the hospital. There's no earthly way to make it habitable again."

"Is your staff out of the building?"

"Staff? What staff? There are the ones on holiday. The rest are in there. No. There's no one alive inside, if that's what you mean."

"I'm very sorry for your loss," says Wells with all the sincerity of a Hummer salesman. He wants to ditch this sniveling civilian and get his mitts on the place.

I say, "What kind of security does the place have?"

Wells gives me a look, but lets the question pass.

"Ample. I thought. Not many people in the city know it, but years ago this was a holding facility for prisoners on their way to or from county jail. We kept some of the old gates and cells in place."

"Sounds homey."

Wells steps in front of me.

"Do you know how many people are inside?"

"It was a holiday weekend, so, thankfully, the number of staff was low. Some patients who could went home with their families for Christmas. The last count I'm aware of was sixty-six patients plus twenty-four staff."

Wells nods, keeping up the good-cop routine.

"Right. Any unusual incidents lately? Hirings? Firings?"

"Magic?" I say. "Evidence of a haunting?"

"What?" says Aldridge.

Wells says, "What my associate means is did anyone, patients or staff, see anything unusual, anything they couldn't explain?"

"Nothing that I know about. It's usually quiet this time of year. Visits are down. People have other things on their mind."

"Do we need keys to get around inside?"

Aldridge shakes his head.

"What's the point? Everything is wide open."

"Thank you, sir. We'll be in touch," says Wells.

Aldridge says, "How did they do it?"

"They?"

"Of course. No one person could have done what's inside. It would take a large surgical team. More than one, probably. A dozen people working at once."

"Thank you, Doctor. You understand that the facility will be on total lockdown once we're inside. Is that all right with you?"

He looks out at the vans in the pouring rain.

"I'm not going back in there," he says. Then, "Why aren't the police handling this? Why federal agents?"

"The police have their hands full keeping rubber ducks from blocking the sewers," I say. "Besides, eighty bodies inside? I don't think cops can count that high."

Wells grabs my arm hard enough to leave a mark.

"Go over there and wait by the door."

I go. Wells and Aldridge shake hands. The doctor glances at me over his shoulder then heads for his car and drives out of there as fast as he can.

Wells comes over, but won't look at me because maybe he'll strangle me if he does.

"I wanted you there with your mouth closed because you're supposed to have a good sense of these things. Was Aldridge telling the truth?"

"If you mean was he scared shitless, yeah. If you mean did he do the deed inside, I doubt it. You don't think he's Saint Nick, do you?"

"At this point, I'm open to any possibility."

Shit.

"No. That guy stank of PTSD. He couldn't kill anything bigger than a housefly."

"All right," he says.

"Why did you want me to read the guy for lies? Don't you have your own supercharged lie detectors?"

"Yes. I just wanted to hear what you had to say."

"If I implicated him."

"Right."

"Then I'm on your list of suspects."

"Not necessarily," says Wells. "Though you do have a history of decapitation."

"Meaning I'd be in the clear if I shot more people. I'll have to remember that."

"I'm not accusing you of anything."

"You're just open to possibilities."

"I want this chaos ended," he says. Without turning around, he waves his arm and the side doors on all three vans slide open. Vigil agents in transparent raincoats pile out and start unpacking gear. Two other agents wheel a crate on a dolly.

I open the front doors and let them in. Wells follows us. Once we're inside, one of the agents takes a crowbar from the side of the dolly and pries open the crate. Surrounded by a plush interior, like a piece of prized family porcelain, is the Shonin. He puts out a bony hand to me.

"Help me out of here, fatty. I'm an old man."

I want to yank the prick to his feet, but I'm afraid of pulling off his arm. I give him a hand and let him pull himself upright. He adjusts his conical headdress and looks around the lobby.

"Not bad," he says. "In my day, some families took their unstable relatives deep into the woods and left them there to die. Some became *tengu*. Most were just fox food."

"Can you smell?" I say.

He nods.

"I can smell this place."

The stink of the place is like a kick in the face. Shit, sweat, piss, and the disinfectant they used to try and mask it all. But riding on top of it all is the sweet reek of bad meat and the coppery aroma of blood. Wells pulls a surgical mask from his pocket and slips it on over his head.

"You don't deserve it, but do you want one of these?"

I shake my head.

"It's too late for that. I'm going to be smelling this place until New Year's."

He nods in something that actually looks like sympathy.

The Vigil boys and girls start piling in around us. Each new wave puts on surgical masks and respirators as they hit the lobby.

Wells talks to what looks like some team leaders and splits his crew into three squads. They fan out through the building carrying their ridiculous Vigil forensic gadgets. The mix of Pentagon high tech and angelic add-ons gives them a look like fifties science fiction crossed with eighties video games. Some devices float down the hall in front of the operator, while others hang around agents' necks. Others they wear like exoskeletons. They look like they're off to a *Forbidden Planet* masquerade ball.

Wells's cell phone rings. The Shonin and I start inside without him.

The place looks like a regular hospital reception area if you don't know what to look for. There are holes in the ceiling above the intake counter where bulletproof glass covered it back in its prisoner incarnation. Pull up the beige carpet and you'll find scratch marks from the metal detector and two sets of gates. You go to the first and have to be buzzed through the second into the prison area. Once you're past that first gate, if the guard on the second gate doesn't like your look, he can lock down his side and you'll be trapped in a steel cage.

There's a long hall beyond reception that leads past the old prison cafeteria. They've transformed it into a homey dayroom with better furniture than any agent in this building has. Past that is a lockdown ward where the old prison doors have been left in place.

All the other doors have ten-key pads and card readers, including the employee restrooms. The real giveaway that the place used to be a prison is the other restrooms. Pure jailbird stuff. Clear plastic doors with a clear view of the toilet so the orderlies can make sure the patients aren't using drugs or each other. Maybe this place helped its patients, but I bet it made its staff a little crazy.

Wells comes up behind us with a piece of paper he must have picked up in reception. It's a sketchy map of the hospital layout. So far, nothing looks out of place.

"The initial report was that all the rodeo was down in the chapel," he says, and consults the map. "This way."

We find it around another corner. Like a lot of hospitals, it's a quiet nondenominational place. Back before the fun and games it might have been pretty. It's big enough to hold a congregation of maybe a hundred people. Not anymore. Someone pulled all the pews out of the floor and tossed them into the hall. All that's left of the original chapel are the stained glass windows and the altar. The rest is slaughterhouse chic by way of the Sistine Chapel.

Half finished, maybe rejected chop-shop bodies lie in piles

on either side of the chapel doors. Body parts—arms, legs, internal organs, and more—are grouped together around the walls like some kind of cannibal food court. A worn gurney crusted with dried blood sits in the center of the room, a discarded woman's arm and a heart tossed on top.

Like the meat locker, the chapel has been transformed into Angra party central. The place has thirteen naves. In each hangs a naked chop-shop body crucified upside down. The cover on the altar is gone. In its place is a stitched-together sheet of human skin. Here and there you can see moles. Old scars. Tattoos.

Aldridge said there were around ninety people inside the building, but there's no way there are ninety bodies now. There aren't enough parts left to make twenty. Saint Nick didn't just play butcher boy here, he took some of his trophies home with him. Worse, from the look of the bodies' decomposition, they weren't all killed at the same time. It's been maybe a day or a day and a half since the slaughter was really rolling along. Enough time for fresh bodies to enter and pass through rigor mortis and for the fresh meat to turn greenish-blue. Those are fresh kills. The patients and staff. But some of the bodies are swollen and the flesh raw and blistered. That takes around three days of decomp, which means Saint Nick didn't just kill this bunch. He stockpiled bodies from another kill and brought them here. This is a busy, organized boy. I bet his record collection isn't alphabetical. It's a freaky, obsessive system by year and genre and probably color. Something only he understands. God help you if you put the Dead Kennedys near the Dictators. East Coast goes here. West Coast there.

But it's not the corpses Saint Nick dragged here from his playpen that get to me. I keep wondering about the staff and patients. What would it be like to be the last person to go under the knife? To see almost ninety other people killed, gutted, and sewn back together again. I saw a few things during my years in Hell, but nothing like that. Maybe they party like that in one of the really shitty regions where guys like Stalin end up. The House of Knives, maybe.

In a weird way, I guess I was kind of lucky when torture time rolled around. I was never the last to get beaten or cut or spun around a Catherine wheel. The Hellions wanted to make an example of me, so I always went first. I never thought about that before. I didn't have to wait and piss myself watching everyone else get hammered. I guess if you can get lucky being tortured, I was lucky.

The Shonin and I walk around the room, checking out the piles, trying to make sense of things. Wells stands in the doorway, arms crossed. The poor sap can't come in. He's a God-fearing guy, and if there's any place I've seen in this world that says God's away on business, this is it. At least when Aelita went batshit, she was just one angel and he could imagine a Heaven full of other good and true halo polishers. But this is a bad, bad place. Wells got the Vigil back together, circling the wagons of true believers, and this is what he finds. The wagons are burning. Everyone is wounded and the cavalry isn't coming. Maybe that's why he put on the surgical mask. He didn't want his people to see him reciting Hail Marys.

I go over to the Shonin.

"Old dead mixed with new," I say.

He nods his tea-colored skull.

"Yes."

"What do think, could one man have done this over a long weekend?"

"Why do you say 'man'? Everyone keeps saying man like it's a fact."

"You think Saint Nick is a woman?"

He shrugs.

"You think Saint Nick isn't?"

We stop by a pile of naked torsos. Arms, legs, and heads cut off. Ribs spread where someone pulled out the organs. It's like some kind of old Aztec sacrifice. I'm starting to wish I had a surgical mask, but I'm not about to ask Wells for one.

"What I'm saying is that moving this many bodies, and hauling more in from somewhere else fast enough to get all this done over a long weekend, is hard physical labor."

"Not if she had help. Or if she used magic to move them and perform the surgery."

"She would have to be a pretty powerful witch."

"Yes."

"So, you think Saint Nick is a woman."

We walk back to the altar. The wet ceiling of the meat chapel extends from the back wall over to where we're standing, turning the light pink.

"I doubt it," he says. "I just object to assumptions."

I look back to the door. Wells has taken a few tentative steps into the room.

The Shonin is probably right about one thing. If Saint Nick didn't have help, he or she would be a world-class magician. I suppose an ordinary person could have gutted the bodies over a long weekend or could have made the meat church. But not both. That means using a crew or hoodoo. I hope to hell that Saint Nick had a crew. Worst-case scenario is someone with powerful hoodoo but with a crew too. That would put a Hulk Hogan–powerful magician right in the middle of an Angra sect. Why can't nutcase killers get their orders from talking dogs anymore? Life was so much simpler when crazy meant crazy.

The Shonin says, "Why does Saint Nick cut up the bodies?"

"Because he's an asshole with a Jack the Ripper complex."

"Don't talk like that. You know better."

"I don't know. He's making offerings maybe. Killing people isn't enough, so he cuts them up and puts pieces together 'cause the Angra prefer turducken to steak."

The Shonin walks back to Wells, who's come into the room. He's walking from pile to gory pile, as stunned as Aldridge was.

"All you all right?" says the Shonin.

"Are you?" Wells says.

"This is a bad place. There's an aura of malevolence. You and your people shouldn't remain here long."

Wells nods.

"I'll pull them out after they sweep the building."

The Shonin looks at me.

"These aren't sacrifices," he says. He points at the naves with the thirteen inverted bodies. "Those are sacrifices. The rest of these bodies, they are machines. Parts of machines. Do you see?"

"Not even a little."

"Saint Nick is creating empty vessels. Inhabiting an intact human body would be difficult for a God. But by using specific parts of different bodies, someone could make something more suitable."

"He's making meat vacation homes for the Angra to move into?"

"The other Saint Nick murders and corpse defilements could have been experiments. Beta tests. Saint Nick was honing his talents."

Wells says, "He's never killed on this scale before. Why does he need so many bodies now?"

"Remember that the Angra aren't just thirteen primary Gods. There are smaller pieces of the old ones on Earth."

I look at Wells and back to the Shonin.

"You mean demons? Qliphoth?"

The Shonin wipes a spot of blood from his robe.

"The Angra will want an army. One that can move and interact with the human world. Bodies built specifically to hold Gods or Qliphoth would make good vehicles for that."

"But we talked about this once. About Lamia," I say. "She had a body and lost it. But she could still kill as a ghost."

"Yes. But when she lost her body she was just a fragment of a fragment of a God. Like a demon. If Lamia had access to one of the empty vessels when she was alive, humanity might be gone by now."

"If Saint Nick is making an army, where is it?" says Wells.

The Shonin leads us out of the chapel and back into the hall. He closes the door behind us.

"That's a very good question. And having succeeded in a mass killing like this, will he try more?"

I say, "Could Saint Nick's chop-shop people do what he did and make more vessels?"

The Shonin leans on one of the broken church pews in the hall.

"I doubt it. This is very powerful magic. Qliphoth wouldn't have the skill or knowledge for it."

"What about another Lamia? A smarter piece of the Gods?"

"We would have heard about something like that by now," says Wells. "The Vigil is always on the alert for reports of possible Angra infiltration."

The Shonin puts his hand on my arm, steadying himself on the pew. If a dead man can look unwell, that's how he looks.

"You got all this from that book you're drinking?"

"Most of it. Why?"

"Think there might be another copy lying around somewhere?"

"It's doubtful, but anything is possible. Do you know someone who might have one?"

There's blood on the bottom of my boots. I scrape the soles on the side of a pew.

"I don't know. You're the expert. I'm just trying to keep up."

Wells says, "If you know something, Stark, speak up."

"It's not anyone here. Some Hellions I know are awfully anxious for the Angra to come home. I was wondering if you could do something like what we saw in there to fallen angels."

Wells shakes his head and checks his own shoes for blood. He doesn't care about Hell's problems. I can't say I blame him.

"It's an interesting question," says the Shonin. "If you find the answer let me know."

"What about *Der Zorn Götter*?" says Wells. "Your dead friend Hobaica said they were involved with the scene in the meat locker. This could be their work too."

Julie Sola comes around a corner holding a computer tablet. She stops for a second and without thinking puts her hand to her face. Even though she's wearing a respirator, this close to the chapel the smell is getting through.

"Yes? You have something?" says Wells.

She hands him the tablet. Then reluctantly slides off her respirator.

"We've found footprints and dirt throughout the facility. We need to get in there," she says, nodding at the chapel, "but it's pervasive. My guess is that we'll find the same results."

Wells touches the screen and the tablet lights up.

"What am I looking at here?"

"A chemical analysis of the soil samples. Indications of methane and hydrogen sulfide gases. Sand. Clay. Igneous rock and traces of crude oil."

"And what does that tell us?"

"It's the basic soil structure of Los Angeles. Not at street level. Underground."

Wells hands Sola back the tablet.

"Thank you. Carry on," he says. She turns away and slips her respirator back on. She opens the chapel doors and closes them again.

"I'm going to need help in there," she says, and heads back down the hall the way she came.

Wells looks at the Shonin.

"Did you ask him any more about the caverns?"

"I was getting around to it," the Shonin says. "You said

you saw caves within the fire when you were in Hobaica's mind. Do you remember anything more about them?"

I shake my head.

"Nothing more than I already said. I didn't get a good look."

Wells says, "There are old mines around the city. Tunnels where oil pipelines run. We're thinking of doing a search of the whole shebang. What do you think of that?"

I nod, not happy with where this is going.

"Sounds good. Sounds smart."

The Shonin says, "What happened in the chapel, this isn't the first time there's been a killing on a large scale. It's just the first time Saint Nick has been bold enough to do it in public. In the past he would have hidden it as bodies mutilated in bus or train accidents. Saint Nick needs a place where he can do more of these experiments in private. What better than somewhere underground that no one even knows exists?"

"When do you want to start?"

"In a day or two," says Wells. "We'll need to bring in some equipment from back east."

That's it then. I have a day to do something about the cavern. Back when zombies were running wild, I found tunnels under L.A. full of the city's dead. What's worse, they opened onto Mr. Muninn's private hidey-hole from when he lived here. He'd been under the city collecting bits and pieces of every human civilization since probably the beginning of time. He had trinkets from the heyday of Hollywood all the way back to kingdoms as big as Rome that existed ice ages ago. And a lot of what's in the cavern is magic and I don't want anyone, especially not the Vigil, getting their hands on it. I need to know what to do about it, but I can't figure it out on my own.

It's settled then.

I'm heading back to Hell. Candy will be so pleased.

AND SHE IS.

Back at home she says, "I'm coming with you."

"Yeah. When you're sick. What a great time to skip off to Hell."

"Fuck you. Why do you always want to leave me behind?"

We're in the little living room upstairs. I'm on the sofa and Candy is standing over me, arms crossed. Her face is red.

"What are you talking about?" I say. "I already took you to Hell once and you come with me all the time when I'm doing jobs for the Vigil."

She uncrosses her arms and rubs her temples.

"It feels wrong. Like you're not coming back. Like you're trying to ditch me again."

"I never tried to ditch you. I got stuck in Hell that one time. Mr. Muninn is in charge now. It won't happen again."

Candy goes into the bathroom. I think it's to keep me from seeing her cry, but a second later I hear her throwing up. She gargles and comes back out wiping her mouth on a hand towel.

I say, "Go see Allegra while I'm gone. Has she used those big chunks of divine glass on you yet? They helped heal me when I got shot."

Candy blows her nose into the towel and sits on the edge of the sofa just out of reach.

"Did you know that Kasabian has a date with my drummer?"

"Yeah, I heard. Hell of a thing, isn't it?"

"Okay," she says. "Maybe I'll go back to the clinic and volunteer with Allegra for a few days. At least until this clears up. I have to see her for my Jade methadone anyway. Maybe that's smarter than playing Dante with you right now."

I slide down the sofa a little and rub her back. She leans over and lets me.

"Tell Allegra I want a fucking diagnosis when I get back. Not just more drugs that make you feel better for maybe a day."

Candy sits up and slides back so she's leaning against the sofa. But she doesn't get any closer to me.

"Fine, asshole. Go play Dirty Harry. Just don't die without me. Okay?"

"Deal."

She rubs her temples. Her face is red, but I think this time it's just her trying not to cry.

I FEEL LIKE a heel for leaving her alone, but I do it anyway. I make sure she heads out for Allegra's before I take off.

Kasabian is downstairs working on his swami site while *The Devil's Rain* plays on his big screen.

"You heading back down to Dixie?" he says.

"It looks that way."

"You going to help me out with a client?"

"I can't this trip. Maybe some other time."

"Too bad. I already did a favor for you, so you're going to owe me one."

I already owe Muninn a favor. I don't like carrying debt around.

"What kind of favor?"

"I think I found your green-haired girl. What's her name?"

"Cindil Ashley."

"She used to work at Donut Universe?"

"That's her."

He swings his chair around to face me.

"Then it's her."

"Where is she?"

"Guess."

"The world's ending. Remember? I don't have time for this shit."

"A donut shop."

He leans back on his chair, lacing his fingers together over his stomach like the cat that ate the canary and a Buick for dessert.

"There's a donut shop in Hell?"

"Just one. The donuts don't look too good. I guess it's like gas station food. If you need tuna salad at four A.M. on the I-10 on your way to El Paso, you're only going to find it where you fill up."

"Where's the shop?"

"On the big boulevard about a block north of the palace. She was within a hundred yards of you the whole time you were Lucifer."

I check my pockets for weapons. Colt. My black blade. Na'at.

"I didn't get out much. Lucifer isn't a mingler."

"If you stop in on her, bring me back a Bavarian cream. I'll auction it off on eBay. Authentic Hellion snack food—the Satanists will love it."

"I don't think you can sell food on eBay."

"Then bring me back a baseball cap with a logo. Something."

"Sure."

I head for a shadow by the front door.

Kasabian says, "What's the magic word?"

"What?"

" 'Thank you.' That's what we say when someone does us a favor."

"Right. Thanks."

" 'Thank you' is the proper way to say it."

"I've still got pieces of people's guts on my boots. Thanks is as good as it gets."

"You're welcome."

He swings back around to watch his movie. Ernest Borgnine is turning into a goat.

I pull up the hoodie I put on under my coat and step into the shadow.

I SPENT ELEVEN years trapped Downtown and have been back plenty of times since, but it gets harder each time. I was only Lucifer for three months, but it left me wary of Hell in ways that even being a slave there didn't. I used to kill Hellions because I didn't have a choice. When I was Lucifer I killed them to stay alive and sometimes just to make a point. Part of the job description for Lucifer is "ruthless bastard," and even if I was a joke when it came to running Downtown, I was employee of the month when it came to saving my own skin. Sometimes in rotten ways. Like dragging a Hellion to death behind my motorcycle. I can't see Mr. Muninn playing

Lucifer the half-assed way I did. He's smarter than me, and for good or bad, he's nicer, even if he is part of the God that I swore I'd never trust again.

The inside of the Room of Thirteen Doors isn't much to look at. Just a circular chamber with a series of closed doors. To one side are a few books I brought to Father Traven while he was hiding here. I busted him out of Hell and it took a couple of days to get him to Blue Heaven, where he could hide from prying eyes. Across from the books are the Mithras and the Singularity.

The Mithras is the first fire in the universe. A tiny flickering flame in a glass jar right now. But if I ever let it out, it would burn all of creation to cinders.

The Singularity is sort of the opposite of the Mithras. If he made universes instead of orchards, it's what Johnny Appleseed would carry. Crack it open and you get a new Big Bang, followed by a brand-new spit-and-polish universe, ready to move into and suitable for children and pets. Of course, if I set it off outside the Room it would eat our universe and everyone in it to make way for the new one.

As long as the Mithras and Singularity are here, I feel safe. I'm the only one with a key to the Room and no one, not even God or Lucifer can get in here without me bringing them. And I'm not about to do that. They're exactly who I want to keep the Mithras and Singularity away from. Especially Ruach. He's crazier and a lot more dangerous than Aelita ever was.

Pandemonium, Hell's capital, is laid out like Hollywood, which puts Lucifer's palace in the Beverly Wilshire Hotel near Rodeo Drive. I could come out nearer, but I like to get the feel of the city when I go down. Big mistake this time.

Like Kasabian said, it's raining in Hell. Being Hell, it's raining blood. Good thing I put on the coat Candy Scotch-garded for me. Too bad I didn't put any of the stuff on my pants. The blood soaks into them, weighing down the leather. It drips through my hood too and runs into my eyes. I step into a doorway before I look like one of those poor slobs back at the chapel.

I'm on Hell's equivalent of Hollywood Boulevard. It looks about the same as the Hollywood back home. Pretty much deserted. But I can see lights on in some of the stores and bars, so someone is around. They're just smart enough to get in out of the blood. No way I'm walking to Beverly Hills from here. I find a shadow under the streetlight and step through. I do something I've never done before. I come out right in Mr. Muninn's—Lucifer's—penthouse at the hotel. He once said I could. Let's see if he's a devil of his word.

I come out by his private elevator. I lean into his living room, ready to duck out if he gets all wrathful.

"Mr. Muninn? Hello. It's Stark."

I take a tentative step into the room.

Muninn comes in from another room in a long crimson robe, a little shocked anyone would just walk into Lucifer's apartment. The room is dark. He squints until he can make me out.

"James. It's you," he says, and turns on a desk lamp. "And you've tracked blood all over my carpet."

I look down. He's exaggerating a little. I only have one foot on the carpet, but the blood dripping off my clothes has made a nice red stain there and on the tile floor by the elevator.

"Please step off the carpet and wait there," he says.

He walks out of the room and comes back a couple of minutes later with a bundle in his hands. There's a towel on top.

"You left some clothes here before you departed so quickly. Please clean up, change clothes, and meet me in the kitchen."

I just nod. Getting God and Lucifer pissed at you at the same time isn't a good way to start a visit.

I clean up and pile my dirty clothes on the tile floor. The clothes Muninn gave me were some of my better Lucifer gear. Gray creased linen pants with a pressed black shirt. I see myself reflected in one of Muninn's windows. My hair looks like it was combed by a five-year-old, but the rest of me is completely Playboy After Dark. I go down the hall to where I remember the kitchen is. Mr. Muninn is inside making coffee.

Making such a great entrance, I'm feeling a little tongue-tied.

"It's raining," I say.

"Is it? I hadn't noticed."

"It's raining in L.A. too."

"It will be raining everywhere soon," he says.

"But why blood down here?"

He points a finger upward.

"We can thank Ruach for that. Don't worry about the blood being contaminated with any of Hell's ills. It doesn't come from here. It's falling from Heaven."

"That doesn't sound good."

"It isn't. From what I gather, there's a new war brewing up there. Ruach's followers versus, well, I suppose mine and my brothers."

"I'm covered in angel blood?"

"I'm sure it's quite benign for you. It's just hell on my carpet."

"Sorry about that."

He looks back in the direction of the living room.

"The cleaners will be thrilled to have something to do. And in any case, it's good to see a friendly face."

He brings two cups of coffee to a marble-topped island in the middle of the kitchen. We sit down across from each other. He slides a cup to me. Hell might have the worst food in the universe, but the coffee, at least Lucifer's, isn't that bad. Still, I take a small first sip. Lucky me. I can still stomach the stuff.

"To what do I owe the honor of this very surprising visit? I have a feeling you didn't just appear here out of the blue to bring me good news from Earth."

"Not exactly. Angra sects are getting pretty hot and bothered back home. They're turning churches into meat markets and it looks like they might be storing their extra bodies in the underground tunnels where you used to look after the dead."

"And they open into my storeroom."

"Yeah."

Mr. Muninn nods and sips his coffee. He looks a lot older than when I saw him just a few weeks ago.

"If you don't mind my saying so, you look like shit, Mr. Muninn."

He smiles. No one down here normally talks to Lucifer like that.

"I suppose I don't. Things were going badly here, and with a new war in Heaven, we don't even need a threat from the Angra to feel a bit grim."

"It must feel funny to be on the side of the rebel angels this time."

"Don't think that hasn't occurred to me. But time and circumstances change."

"Do you think the rebels are going to win?"

"I honestly don't know. There isn't the great desire for suicide among Heaven angels as there is here, but there's plenty of bloodlust."

"I don't understand. If they're not part of Merihim and Deumos's suicide pact, what's the war about?"

"Us," he says. "The four remaining brothers. Brother Ruach wants the three of us dead and so do his followers. The rebel angels refuse to take part in our murder and so a war begins."

"Is there anything you can do to help?"

"Oh my. Why didn't I think of that?"

"Sorry. It's just, even though you're kind of broken, you're still a piece of God. You still have powers."

"Not like Ruach's. He's the part that broke away from the rest of us first, taking most of our power with him."

"Do you know where your missing brother is?"

Muninn fiddles with a spoon on the table.

"Chaya. He's right here. Asleep not fifty feet from us. Ruach was keeping him in Heaven hoping to draw the rest of us into a confrontation. Samael helped Chaya to escape and brought him here."

"Great. That's three of you. Can you do some kind of Voltron thing, put yourselves back together and kick Ruach's ass?"

"We tried to reunite and failed. If our brother Neshamah

wasn't dead, maybe the four of us could combine our strength and fight Ruach, but with just the three of us, it's doubtful. I don't know if the others want to try again."

I've never seen Mr. Muninn so down. And I'm the bastard who guilted him into becoming Lucifer.

"I'm guessing you're not working on repairing the city anymore."

"No one is left to do the work. Every sensible Hellion is at home hiding."

"Same thing in L.A. Some are running for the hills."

"I'm afraid there isn't anywhere for us to run."

"There won't be anywhere to run on Earth if the Angra keep making new little baby Angras."

He frowns every time I say their name.

I say, "You don't like talking about them, do you?"

"There is nothing but bad memories there. We—that is, I, when I was a single entity—flung the Angra from here and claimed this universe for myself. Not a noble gesture. But I was young and the young do all sorts of foolish and cruel things."

"And you were left with a universe you didn't quite know how to run."

"I did my best."

"That's what I told Mrs. McCarthy in fifth-grade Spanish. She still flunked me."

He sips his coffee and smiles.

"Yes. This is exactly like elementary school Spanish."

"I guess the idea I tossed out there the last time you were in L.A. isn't going to work. Shutting down Hell and letting everyone leave?"

He leans back, setting down his coffee.

"And let my angels go where? To a war in Heaven? To Earth, where the Angra are strongest and they'd have to hide from both them and mortals? Where should I send them? And then there are all the damned souls. What's to be done with them?"

"Send them to L.A. We could use the company."

"I'm sure."

We both drink our coffee, stuck in an uncomfortable silence. I was hoping for some kind of answers here. I can do gloomy all on my own back at Bamboo House of Dolls, where the drinks are better.

"Samael's kind of a hero these days, it sounds like."

"Yes," says Muninn. "I didn't expect it of the boy. He resented having two fathers around and now he has three. It can't be very fun for him."

Samael was the first Lucifer, but he quit and took back his original angelic name. He went back to Heaven before things went to shit. When they did, he hightailed it back to Hell with Mr. Muninn. Samael is the prick who stuck me with the job of playing Lucifer. But we kissed and made up. We have similar tastes in Dario Argento and Takashi Miike flicks.

"Our Angra sects are cutting up humans and making chop-shop people out of them. What do you think of that?"

"It sounds horrible. Do you know why they're doing it?"

"The theory going around is they're going to be vacation homes for Qliphoth. Sounds like fun, huh? What's going on with your Angra cheerleaders?"

He sighs.

"I wish I knew. I'm like Ruach when it comes to them—

mostly blind and half deaf. Deumos and Merihim have disappeared. I'm sure they're hiding somewhere in Pandemonium. They won't want to be far from the seat of power. But they have powerful allies and remain invisible to me."

"I got a phone call from Deumos."

"Did you? What did she say?"

"Nothing surprising. She wanted the 8 Ball. The Qomrama."

"No, not surprising at all. You're not giving it to her, I assume."

"She can have it right after she kisses my ass."

"Always the poet," says Muninn.

I wonder if he'd let me smoke a Malediction in here. I pat my pockets, then remember I'm not wearing my regular clothes. My cigarettes are back by the elevator, and probably soaked through.

"Let me have the Qomrama," says Muninn. "Bring it back to Hell, where it belongs."

"So Deumos and Merihim can grab it? I don't think so? They might have minions on Earth, but they don't have shit power yet. No. It's staying where it is."

Muninn says, "You owe me a favor, if you recall."

I knew sooner or later he was going to try and fuck me up with fairness and logic. Good thing I'm pretty much immune to those things.

"Do you know how to use it?"

He shakes his head.

"No."

"Then leave it with me. Believe it or not, I'm working with the Golden Vigil again. They've got this old Buddhist monk working on it. He seems pretty smart."

Muninn looks at me.

"A month ago you talked about Gnostics and called me the demiurge. Now you're spending your time with Buddhists. Your cosmological interests are broader than I thought, James."

"Strange times, strange company."

"Indeed."

Damn. Looking at this ragged old man I used to know and drink with, I feel an ugly wave of sincerity coming on.

"I'm sorry I stuck you with this job," I say. "I didn't think about what was coming. I just wanted not to be Lucifer anymore."

"Thank you," says Muninn. "I appreciate that. But as you've pointed out, you weren't very good at the job. I don't know that I've done much better, but I've held Pandemonium and the provinces together so far. It's better off this way."

"Let me know if there's anything I can do to help."

"Thank you. I will. In fact . . ." He gets up from the table and leaves the room. He comes back a minute later with a yellowish potion in a stoppered bottle.

"Take this with you," he says. "Just pour it across the ground at the entrance to my sanctuary and no mortal person or device will be able to detect it."

"I'm not sure the monk is exactly mortal. He's self-mummified. Died four hundred years ago and came back to leap tall buildings in a single bound, you know."

"Whatever powers he might possess won't be enough to see through this. It will be fine."

"Great."

"You still have the Singularity and the Mithras?"

"Safe and sound in the Room."

"Good. Don't remove them under any circumstances. If worst comes to worst, they might be our only hope."

It must be getting to him down here. I've never heard that kind of kamikaze talk coming from him before.

"I've got them. Don't sweat it."

He nods.

"Would you like to say hello to Samael while you're here? I could wake him up."

"Don't bother. I should get going. I didn't see Wild Bill last time I was here and I'm feeling kind of guilty about it."

"It's good to be close to family in times like these. Well, I'll see you out now. Keep those clothes, if you like. It's good to see you in something that doesn't make you look like a motorcycle delinquent."

"Thanks, Dad."

He comes around the table, takes my arm, and walks with me to the living room. He feels cold. God shouldn't feel cold, should he?

"These are the worst times we've faced, James. I had no right to do what I did to the Angra, but if they're allowed to come back now, they'll destroy everything."

"I know."

"It's going to take something drastic to stop them. I don't know what yet, but I have a feeling I'll be calling in that favor you owe me before this is over. Are you prepared to repay it?"

"Sure. Yeah."

"I think you hesitated."

"No. It's fine."

"Good. I just needed to know how loyal you'd be when the time comes."

When I get to the elevator, my wet clothes have left a red puddle on the floor.

"I'm there with you," I say. "Whatever you need."

He nods, looking tired.

"That's all I wanted to hear. I'll let you see yourself out. Good night, James."

"Good night, Mr. Muninn."

He turns around and goes out, a tired old man with the weight of three worlds on his shoulders.

I change out of my good clothes and put on my bloody ones. Roll and stuff the good ones in the special weapons pockets inside my coat. I don't know when I'll ever wear them, but Candy will like them. Too bad we missed Halloween. I could go as a grown-up.

There's a decent shadow around the edge of the elevator. I pull up my damp hoodie and step through, coming out in the blood rain on the boulevard near the palace. The street has been repaired, but there's no one on it. I walk north for a few blocks and there it is. Lit up and lonely, all *Nighthawks at the Diner*.

Donut Inferno.

There's only one person inside. She doesn't have funny bobbling antennae on like she did at Donut Universe. She's wearing plastic devil horns. But it's still her. I walk across the street and go inside. She's wiping down the counter and doesn't look up when I come in.

"Cindil," I say.

She stops wiping and stares at me. I push back the hoodie, wiping angel blood off my forehead.

"Remember me?"

She nods. Stands still, more or less stunned. Can't say I blame her.

I look around the place. The donuts are dry and sunken. Dusty. The coffee looks like fried sludge. The linoleum counter is cracked and half the stools are missing their seats. Donut Inferno looks like a wino crash pad fifty years past its prime.

I say, "You like it here?"

She shakes her head.

"No."

"You want to get out?"

"With you?"

"Yes. Right now."

She twists the dirty dishrag in her hands. Her face and arms are bruised, but her hair is still the same shade of green it was when she was alive.

She whispers, "I'll get in trouble."

"You're in Hell. How much worse can it get?"

"Lots. You haven't seen what I've seen."

I walk over and take the rag from her hand. Set it on the counter.

"I've seen what you've seen and lived what you've lived and I got away. I'm here to help you do the same."

"The last time I saw you I died."

"And I feel bad about that and I'm here to fix it."

"Why? You don't even know me."

"So what? I should have been able to help you before, but I didn't. Now I can. Come with me."

"Where?"

"To a friend's place. He's a hard old son of a bitch, but he'll take care of you."

Her eyes dart around the shop. She's confused. In panic mode.

I say, "Here's the deal. The whole universe might be ending soon. Do you want to spend the last few minutes of your existence here or do you want to take a chance on something better?"

"You came all the way to Hell to help me?"

"No. I was window-shopping for the holidays."

"Asshole," she says.

"Come with me and you can call me all the names you want."

It takes her a minute, but she unties her apron and tosses it on the counter. She starts around to my side, but I stop her.

"Before we leave, can I have one of those hats over the display case?"

She hands me one and comes around to my side. She looks out at the rain.

"I don't have a coat."

I take off mine and drape it around her shoulders. I'm already half soaked, why not finish the job?

"You ready?"

She's scared, but the first faint hint of a smile plays around her lips.

"Sure. Why not?"

It's too bright in Donut Inferno. I lead her out into the rain and find a shadow around the corner.

"Take my hand."

She does.

"Here we go."

WE COME OUT by Wild Bill's bar near the street market in Pandemonium's western hinterlands. Only the street market isn't there anymore. Just half-collapsed tents, overturned tables, and oil drums full of charred garbage. The sad red rain slicks over everything, turning the rows between the deserted stalls to mud.

Cindil drops my hand and takes a step back.

"What just happened?"

"We took a shortcut across town. It's just a trick I can do."

She looks at me, her hair matting down around her face.

"You're a weird guy, you know?"

"That's going to be my epitaph. You want to get out of this rain?"

I point to the bar. She heads over and we go inside.

I want to say that the place is usually crowded at this time of day, but I don't know what time it is in Hell or Earth. Still, there's usually some kind of crowd. Not tonight, today, whatever. A lone soldier from one of Hell's legions sits by himself nursing the Hellion equivalent of beer. He barely glances up as we come in.

Hank Williams is on the jukebox singing "The Devil's Train." The man smoking a cigar behind the counter is tall and lean, with shoulder-length hair and a serious mustache. His name is James Butler Hickok. Wild Bill Hickok to his friends and enemies. We're blood, separated by around seven generations. He looks up when he sees us. Puts out his hand when we get close to him. He and I shake. Bill isn't a hugging kind of guy. He takes a look at Cindil and gets a bottle from beneath a bar, sets down three glasses, and pours us all a drink of the good stuff. As good as it gets in Hell.

"I was beginning to think you'd forgotten about your grandpappy."

"Not with that mustache," I say.

He runs a knuckle under it, straightening it with pride.

We down our shots. Cindil has a hand around hers but hasn't picked it up.

"Who's your quiet friend?" says Wild Bill.

"I wanted to introduce you two."

I turn to her.

"Cindil Ashley, this is Wild Bill Hickok. Wild Bill, this is Cindil Ashley."

He puts a hand out to her. She takes it and they shake.

"Nice to make your acquaintance, young lady," he says.

She just looks at him.

"Wild Bill Hickok. Like in the movies?"

"One and the same," he says, not shy about his fame. "Born in Illinois. Sheriff, scout for the Union Army, shootist, gambler, and murdered dead as corn bread in Deadwood, South Dakota."

Cindil smiles a little.

"I make donuts," she says. "I used to paint and play bass, but not so much anymore."

"You play bass?" I say. "I wish you could meet my friend Candy. She needs a bass player."

"Is she down here too?"

"No. She's back on Earth. Still, with the crazy-ass way things are going, you might meet anyway. And I don't mean down here."

Wild Bill pours us more drinks. Cindil sips hers. I don't think she's tasted alcohol recently. I haven't tasted this Hellion swill in a while. I left a bottle of Aqua Regia with Bill once. Since he hasn't pulled it out, my guess is he's finished it off.

"What are you talking about, son?" he says.

I look back at the legionnaire. We could be playing badminton with a baked ham for all he cares. I keep my voice low anyway.

"This is just between the three of us. I'm hoping that Lucifer can square things away Hell-wise, but it's not looking good. If he can't, I'm taking you both out of here. Be ready to leave in a hot second if I give you the word."

"I'm ready right now," says Bill.

I shake my head.

"This isn't the right time. Be patient. And trust me."

Cindil finishes her drink and Bill pours her another.

"You can leave here?" she says.

"This one can go any damned place he likes. He just visits with us Hell-bound folks when he gets bored carousing with monsters and disreputable types back home."

"Back home on Earth," she says.

I toss back another drink. It tastes better as it numbs your taste buds.

"Yes. I can go back and forth."

"Why can't we come with you now?"

"It's like I said, it's not time. There are consequences for everyone when I steal a soul from Hell. I have to wait until the good outweighs the bad."

I stole Father Traven's soul from Hell a month before. Things haven't been the same between me and Mr. Muninn since.

"How will you know when it's the right time?"

"I'll know. Trust me. I have someone watching Hell. If things get bad, I'll be back for both of you," I say. Then to Bill, "Until then, meet your new barback."

Bill raises his eyes at that.

"Barback? I hardly get enough customers these days to justify my existence much less help's."

"Yeah, but you'll take her because I owe her. She's dead because of me."

Bill nods at that. Pointless death and the guilt that comes with it are things a gunfighter like him understands.

He looks Cindil over. She's drenched in bloody rain. Her hair hangs limp around her face. My coat is a couple of sizes too big and she's still wearing her devil horns.

"You ever tend bar before?" he says.

She looks at me, then back at him.

"At friends' parties sometimes."

"See? She's a natural," I say. "And she ran her own eating establishment down here for almost a year."

She frowns.

"It's only been a year? It seems a lot longer than that."

"I know. Time's funny when you're treading water in a river of shit."

Bill looks Cindil over.

"You can start by taking them things off," he says, pointing to her head with his drink. She reaches up and touches her horns. Smiles and takes them off. She sets them down and Bill sweeps them off onto the floor behind the bar.

"Enough of that insult to a friend of my great-grandson."

He nods and puffs his cigar.

"If the boy thinks you're all right that's good enough for me," he says. "Welcome to the best saloon in all the fiery Abyss. We don't get a lot of customers these days, but we have liquor and a little food from time to time and that decent music box the boy left behind."

"It's called a jukebox," I say.

"I know what it's called. It's a damned foolish word and I'm not about to use it, especially not in front of a lady who looks like she's endured enough foolishness."

Cindil looks around the bar. It's a ragged place, but back when I was Lucifer I had it built to look as much like Bamboo House of Dolls as possible.

"I can really stay here?" she says.

"Yes, you can," says Bill.

"What if someone comes to take me back to the donut shop?"

"The powers that be have a lot on their plate right now," I say. "I doubt anyone's going to notice you're gone. And if they do, they're going to have a hard time finding you. If anyone comes for you, don't worry. I'll know about it."

I look at Bill.

"You should have taken that gun I offered you back at the palace."

"That funny Glock thing where I couldn't even see the bullets? No thanks. Besides, with all the drunks and ne'er-do-wells that pass through here, I've got all the guns and ammunition I need. Under the floorboards back here."

He sets the cigar on the bar and picks up his drink.

"You think it's going to come to that?"

"No. But in strange times like this it's better having too many guns than too few."

"Amen to that," says Bill.

I cock my head at the legionnaire.

"Is he someone to worry about?"

"Him?" says Bill. He smiles.

"He's a deserter. That's pretty much all we get out here these days. Law enforcement or anyone in authority are the last folks he wants to see."

"Good to hear."

I look at Cindil.

"I'll say good-bye for now. Don't worry about anything. Bill will take good care of you."

"Thanks," says Cindil.

"Can I have my coat back?" I say.

She shrugs it off and hands it to me. When I take it she leans forward and gives me a quick hug. I think she's still a little shell-shocked.

"Take care, both of you. Look after her, Bill."

"That I will," he says.

I turn to the legionnaire. He's barely moved since we came in. My first instinct is to blow his head off just to make sure he won't talk to anyone. But Cindil is still skittish and has seen enough death, and the last thing I want to do is send her screaming into the night. I take out the black blade and go over. When the legionnaire looks up, I stick it under his throat.

"My name is Sandman Slim. I've killed more of you Hellion pig fuckers than I can count. You breathe one word about what's happened here today to anyone . . . well, you know what Tartarus is?"

Everyone in Hell knows what Tartarus is. It's the Hell below Hell. The resting place for the double dead.

The rummy nods.

I wrecked Tartarus once, but I had it rebuilt for just one man. Mason Faim, the mortal man I killed to become Lucifer. I hated him more than all the Hellions put together. He's the only soul in Tartarus these days.

"There's plenty of room in Tartarus for a dumb guy with a big mouth. Especially a deserter. No one would notice or care if you disappeared. So you didn't see anything today. And if anyone asks, that girl over there has been working here since the day the place opened. Got it?"

His eyes are wide. When he tries to nod he sticks himself on the tip of the knife.

"Ow."

"I'll take that for a yes."

I put the blade back under my coat and head for the nearest shadow.

"And you didn't see this either, fucker," I say, and step into the dark.

I COME OUT in Mr. Muninn's cavern under the Bradbury Building. The shelves are crammed with books, ancient weapons, and scientific instruments. Animal teeth and dinosaur bones. Paintings cover the walls and sculptures fill every empty corner. In the distance is a drive-in movie screen. Who knows what else? You could spend a couple of lifetimes down here trying to inventory the place.

I go to where Muninn's fortress of solitude opens onto the main tunnel that used to be home for L.A.'s dead. Kneeling, I pour the potion across the floor. A wall quietly assembles itself from the surrounding stones and fills the gap. It only takes a few seconds to form and it looks like it's been there since T. rexes used the Rockies as a skateboard ramp.

There's a new war in Heaven. Angels eating their own.

What a surprise. I don't have a good history with angels. They're bigger control freaks than Wells and crazier than manic-depressive cobras. Aelita, the loon. Rizoel, who made me take his arm when he tried to keep me out of Eden. That tricky bastard Lucifer. And my father. He was technically an archangel. Uriel. He went by the name Doc Kinski when I knew him and I didn't even know he was my father until after Aelita murdered him. The one good thing he ever did for me, that any angel ever did for me, was take care of Candy. He pulled her off the street and got her the Jade potion that keeps her from eating people. A couple of points for Doc Kinski, then. But the rest of them? I can't wait for the rain to break in L.A. because it will mean the blood has stopped in Hell, and that will mean there aren't any angels left in Heaven. Of course, we'll still have Ruach upstairs and the Angra knocking at the back door. Once again, the powers that be have completely fucked us. They play out their family traumas on a cosmic scale and we're caught in the middle, like we've always been. We're just bugs on God's windshield.

I try calling Candy to let her know that I'm back and everything is all right, but I can't get a signal this far underground.

I check on the new clothes that Muninn gave me, but Hell's red rain has soaked through my jacket and ruined them. I toss them on the ground and step through a shadow.

Come out on Hollywood Boulevard a few blocks from Max Overdrive. I walk the last five minutes home in the rain trying to wash as much of the blood off me as I can.

I'll have to remember to give Kasabian his hat.

In the morning, way too early in the goddamn morning, I'm back in a Vigil van moving through Hollywood. The streets are empty except for a couple of homeless people huddled asleep in the doorway of the wax museum near Highland. The traffic lights have stopped working, which doesn't matter since there's no traffic. Most stores are deserted, though a few places forgot to lock the door. Water sloshes up over the curb to soak their carpets. But the merchandise stays where it is. There's no one left even to loot the place.

An LAPD cruiser riverboats past us, too smart to slow or do anything but stare at our blacked-out caravan.

We pull over at the Hollywood and Vine underground metro stop. The place is locked down tight. There's a big "Closed for Maintenance, Sorry for the Inconvenience" sign on the gate blocking the stairs. Julie Sola jumps out of the second van, unlocks the gate, and pushes it out of the way. Just like at the funny farm, Wells's crew starts unloading personnel and forensic gear for our trip down the rails. The Shonin is back at headquarters, warm and dry. Mummies don't much like wading through ankle-deep water, and when we're downstairs, let's face it . . . the jerky on the guy's bones is going to attract rats. Best for everyone if he stays at the HQ sipping his poison book.

"Stark, stay close to me," says Wells.

"I didn't know you cared."

"I don't. I just don't want you making up your own mission and wandering off."

Someone gets the lights turned on below and we head down.

The Hollywood and Vine subway is a themed stop, a municipal tourist trap, trying to keep travelers out of their cars while they're in town. The concrete support columns below are tiled to resemble shiny palm trees. The ceiling is covered in empty film reels and along the walls of the tunnel are decorations that look like lengths of movie film.

The trains had been running less and less the last few weeks, and with no one left to ride them, they've stopped completely. A shallow channel of water flows from the surface all the way down to the platform and falls onto the tracks.

Around us, Wells's crew talks quietly as they calibrate their equipment. There's a few nervous laughs. A few brave ones and a couple that sound like I feel. Uncertain.

"Tell me why we're down here, Wells."

He drags his fingers along a map on a minitablet, enlarging the image. He doesn't look up while he studies photos that pop up as he moves his finger down the screen. I look over his shoulder. It's a subway map, but with more detail than the one commuters get, and with the tunnels between the stations laid out.

"Some of the lower tunnels run parallel with the cave system that held L.A.'s dead."

I look at him.

"You knew about them?"

He glances up at me then goes back to his screen.

"Of course. We're the Golden Vigil, we know everything about everything."

He raises his eyes again for a second.

"All your dirty little secrets."

"If you know my secrets then you know I'm not Saint Nick."

"You know what they say. Only a man with a guilty conscience keeps reminding you of how innocent he is."

"Okay, you got me. I *am* Saint Nick. And Mr. Bubbles. And the Easter Bunny."

Wells ignores me. The Vigil crew stops chattering, their gear pretty much squared away.

"If the Vigil knew about the corpse tunnels, why didn't you do anything about them?"

Wells slaps the cover shut on the tablet and puts it in his pocket.

"What was there to do? Move hundreds of thousands of bodies? To where?"

For a second he sounds like Mr. Muninn.

"Besides," he says, "before Jan and Koralin Geistwald came to town and turned the horde into a bunch of kill-crazy zombies, they weren't a problem. The Vigil has learned to let many of these things be and not to tamper with the balance of supernatural forces in the city, no matter how revolting and profane they might be."

A couple of the Vigil crew unfold portable staircases that extend from the platform to the tracks. Wells is the first person down. I follow him.

"You're not saying there's access to those dead tunnels from the subway, are you?"

"Don't be an idiot," he says. "I said they run parallel. There were never any stops in zombie country."

"Then why are we here?"

"We're looking for breaches."

"What does that mean?"

"You'll know it if we find one."

Sola walks over.

"We're ready to go anytime you are, sir."

Wells turns to the troops like General Patton.

"Let's move out."

Sola hands him a pair of night-vision goggles and puts on a pair herself. The rest of the crew does the same thing.

"Where's mine?" I say.

Wells takes something out of his pocket and hands it to me. A cheap plastic LED flashlight.

I say, "Gee. How does this work?" and shine it into his eyes for a second.

"What's wrong with you?" he says, his voice just a notch below rage. "This is no time for your playing."

"Sorry. I'm not used to this advanced Vigil technology."

As Wells starts down the tracks he says, "Stay behind me. But close behind. Marshal Sola, make sure our pixie doesn't flutter off."

"Yes, sir," she says.

Not far into the tunnels, the water rises to almost ankle depth. I guess monsoons weren't high on the worst-case-scenarios list when they built the place.

I play the light ahead into the tunnel. I can't see much of anything. The tops of the tracks. Bare concrete walls with occasional maintenance access doors. Long lines of metal conduits carrying power up and down the station.

"See anything interesting?" I say to Wells.

"Not much more than you, but we didn't expect to see anything out here. We're taking a spur line up ahead. Employees and maintenance personnel only. A line the public never sees."

"Great. If you spot any Angra roadside-attraction signs let me know. I'll pick up a pecan log and a belt buckle."

Wells ignores me.

Sola whispers, "Why do you do that?"

"What?"

"Go out of your way to aggravate Wells?"

"I have to do something. I can't bring my knitting along."

"No. Seriously."

"Wells agrees with Aelita a hundred percent about me. I'm an Abomination. A monster. So I give him what he wants."

"Why don't you try to show him you're more than that?"

"Try to convince him I'm a good guy? That would scare him more than if I showed up like Kali with ten arms and wearing a belt of severed heads."

Sola is quiet for a minute. Then she says, "I'm trying to see you as a serious person."

"What do you care? Are you spying for him?"

"No. I told you before. Maybe we can work together when this is over. I can restart my PI service. But I need to know you're someone I can depend on."

"When this is over." I never took Sola for that kind of optimist. But I guess anyone who goes out on her own and hangs out her detective shingle has to believe there'll be something down the road.

"How's this? I've saved this world more than once already. I have friends here and I'll kill anything that walks, crawls, flies, or oozes out of the ground if it hurts one of them. I know God and the Devil and their worst secrets. I know how to pull the plug on this whole rotten world and I don't do it. You know why?"

"Why?"

"I don't know either some days. But I don't do it and the only reason I think I'd ever do it would be to take down the Angra."

"You think."

"Yeah. I think."

I look at her.

"Serious enough for you?"

She nods.

"Enough," she says. Then, "Are you really getting a million dollars for working on the mission?"

"I wish. I got talked down to five-five."

"Fifty-five thousand?"

"Five hundred and fifty."

"Holy shit."

"I'm a special case. And I had the big weapon, the 8 Ball, so I told them I wanted to be paid like a defense contractor."

"Wow," says Sola. "No wonder Wells hates you."

"Imagine how much more he'll hate me when he has to hand me the check."

"Don't forget to get me those psych forms."

"Sure. I'll do them tonight."

"If you girls have finished gossiping it would be awfully nice if you joined the rest of us on the mission," says Wells.

Sola snaps to attention.

"Yes, sir. Sorry."

"Don't apologize," he says. "Just do your job. Go back with the others, Sola. It's obvious I can't leave you children alone together."

Sola goes back and disappears into the middle of the Vigil

crew. Lots of grins and quiet chuckles back there. Law enforcement. It's like high school with better guns.

"You don't have to do that to her," I say.

"Don't tell me how to run my people," Wells says.

"Aren't I one of your people now?"

"I'm not a hundred percent sure you are a person. Lots of things can walk on two legs. Monkeys. Dogs. Bears."

"You should have said parrots. Those others can't talk."

"I know. Just wishful thinking on my part."

We're well down the spur line now, heading to a dead end. There's nothing and no one down here.

Wells turns to his team.

"Anything, anyone? Life readings? Heat signatures? Any signs of Angra ritual marks or bodies?"

A few "No sirs" come from the back. Then a high-pitched whoop from somewhere. Like a howler monkey, but quiet. Then comes chattering, like a hundred people caught in the snow, their teeth tapping together. A scrabbling at the edges of the room. People look at their feet, checking for rats. I can hear breathing all around us.

"Take off your goggles," I say to Wells. "And tell them to do the same."

"Something's coming. I'm going to light this place up."

"Don't you dare," he says.

That's when the first person screams.

I say, "Wells!"

"Goggles off," he yells.

I don't wait to see who obeys the order. My hoodoo isn't subtle, but I figure that the tunnel is big enough to try it. I bark some Hellion and fire explodes across the ceiling. A lucky shot, as it turns out, since it knocks twenty or thirty of Saint Nick's chop-shop people off the roof of the tunnel down onto the tracks like sizzling lunch meat. After that, it's the O.K. Corral. The Vigil crew opens up with their weird angel tech guns, blowing bolts of purple light into Saint Nick's creations. But it barely slows them.

A couple of chop shops rush me. One is clacking his broken teeth together like he's gnawing his way through drywall. The other comes at me like a fucking velociraptor, his hands held out like claws, his legs pumping like pistons.

It's like a night back in the arena, where I fought for most of my time in Hell. By instinct, I pull out the na'at and snap it open like a spear with a curved sword on the end. Broken Teeth is closest, all fangs and milky red eyes. I slice the na'at through the air and off pops his head, rolling away in the subway tide pool. I start to do the same to the velociraptor when I get a stab of paranoia. If Wells really thinks I'm Saint Nick, what's tossing heads everywhere going to tell him?

I peg the velociraptor in the chest and angle the grip of the na'at up, forcing him to the ground. Then I pull the Colt and shoot him in the head. It's a relief when he stays down.

I glance at Wells's people. They're holding off the crazies and even have a few of them down on their backs, but each one takes a dozen or more shots.

I plug a couple more crazies between the eyes. It seems to put them down nicely. Too bad I don't have a hundred bullets.

More chop shops pour from the back of the tunnel. The Colt runs out of shots fast, but there's no time to reload. I put it in my waistband. There's no point pulling the black blade. I'd just start taking heads like with the na'at. That leaves one thing.

The flames at the top of the tunnel are burning down

and the place is growing dark again. I manifest my Gladius, my flaming angelic sword. Its bright white fire lights up the tunnel like a movie premiere downtown. Nothing on Earth can stand up to an angelic sword. I slice the nearest chop-shop killer nearly in half with one slash and wade into a crowd that's surrounded Sola and Wells. There's not a lot of strategy in this. No big battle plan. Just hunt and slash and keep the monsters off the nonmonsters for as long as I can.

Good thing these chop-shop types aren't big on brains. They're all either teeth or claws, which makes them pretty easy to take down. I put down a dozen fast and open a hole for Sola and Wells to run through. It doesn't smell good, all burned meat and fried hair.

One of the Broken Teeth lands on my back and sinks his choppers into my neck. It's not even like he's biting me. It's like he's trying to chew right through my spine. It reminds me of something, but that's not important right now because I can't reach the asshole with my sword and I can feel blood—my blood this time, not some Heavenly angel's from the sky—running down my back.

The biter twitches. Once. Twice and falls off. Wells and Sola keep firing into its body as it tries to get up. I wade into another crowd of them and slash away. It doesn't take long for whatever part of their brains still works to cop to the idea that fire is bad and running is good. The ones still alive and on their feet take off away from the spur track, down one of the other rail lines, and disappear, making those howler-monkey whoops, claws still out and teeth still grinding.

I keep the Gladius burning until I'm good and certain they're gone. Then let it go out. The night-vision gear is scattered all over the tunnel, so Wells's people pull out their flashlights. None of them say a word and most of the lights are on me. I guess they've never seen a Gladius before. Probably most of them never saw anything close to a real angel before. Must be a hell of time to see your first, even if he's only half an angel.

I say, "Mind getting those goddamn lights out of my eyes?"

A few of the flashlights move off me and flash around the tunnel, looking for stray crazies. There are a lot of them on the ground, and some of them still look alive.

I go over to Wells.

"What the hell is it with those guns? They didn't do shit."

He holsters his gun.

"Of course they do. My people took down more of them than you did with that flashy sword trick."

"Yeah, after you shot them fifty times. What kind of half-assed weapons are those?"

"Nonlethals," says Sola. "Keyed to stun the brain and muscular function of living organisms. I guess those things aren't quite technically alive. Not the way we normally define it."

I look at Wells.

"You brought nonlethals down here?"

He looks right back at me.

"We're not here to slaughter. We're looking for information and to capture anyone carrying out extranatural activities in the tunnels, whether it's Saint Nick or an Angra sect."

"Looks like you killed them pretty dead anyway."

"Yes. A lousy necessity," he says. He shouts down the tracks. "Does anyone have a live one?"

A voice comes down the tunnel.

"A couple over here, sir."

"Right. Bag them and get them back to Vigil headquarters right now. I want the Shonin to have a look at them."

"Want to hear a theory? Two really," I say.

"Make them fast," says Wells.

"The Shonin said the chop-shop bodies might be something to house Qliphoth. The way the crazies were moving, remind you of anything?"

"It was a little strange. What are you getting at?"

"Eaters and Diggers. Two of the most dangerous Qliphoth. They'd be good guard dogs if you wanted to keep something safe."

Wells watches his team wrap up the prisoners. They use some kind of expansion foam instead of cuffs on the arms and legs. Slide a harness with a rubber bit over each of their heads so they can't bite. Then zipper them into body bags with ventilation holes.

"You could be right. We'll let the Shonin decide."

They set the prisoners on hoodoo platforms like floating stretchers and glide them down the way we came, four agents holding on to the body and two riding shotgun.

"Want to hear the second theory?"

"Go on."

"We were ratted out."

Wells sighs. A few of his people continue to steal looks at me as they work.

"This again. You just said these things were guard dogs. You don't warn guard dogs. You just leave them in the junkyard for kids climbing over the fence."

"But what if they're not here all the time? What if they were here just for us?"

"That doesn't make sense."

"Maybe it does. A little, sir," says Sola. "This is a maintenance spur. Crews must work here all the time, but none of them have reported any trouble. Yet when we showed up, the creatures attacked without hesitation."

Wells looks up and down the track like he's trying to see into the dark and find something to shoot down the theory.

"Without further evidence I don't want either of you talking to anyone about this. Things are hard enough for these people without putting the idea of a traitor in their heads."

"Yes, sir," says Sola.

Before I can say anything, one of Wells's people shouts down the tunnel.

"We have something up here."

We move up to the marshals. One is staring at a video monitor. She guides a flexible line with a camera on the end into a hole in the wall. There isn't any dirt or dust on the debris around the hole. It's fresh. I know Wells notices it too because he gives me a "Don't say a word" look.

"You see anything?" he says to the marshal.

"No activity, but markings on the walls. There's a lot of debris. Some of it looks like bones. Some . . ." She stares into the monitor, studying the scene. "It could be more human remains, sir. Wait. Damn."

"Watch your language," says Wells. "What do you see?"

"I think it's a light switch. And wires. There's power in there."

"Who has functioning night vision?" Wells shouts.

A few seconds later a marshal comes over and hands Wells a set of goggles. He puts them on. I try to see past him into the dark.

"You're not going in there alone, are you? I just said there might be Diggers around."

"No," he says. "You're coming with me. If you're that het up about it, you can go first."

A marshal hands me a set of goggles.

"Thanks. But you can go in first. I have this thing about getting my head bitten off."

I reload the Colt and put on the goggles. The world goes green and flat and very bright.

"You ready?" says Wells.

"Hell no."

Wells gets down on his knees. The hole is only waist-high, like something crawled out of it. He goes through and I follow. The bite on my neck hurts like hell. The last time I got bit by a dead man bad things happened. Like I almost went zombie. This time I'm going to see Allegra before anything interesting happens.

The inside of the cave is extremely nondramatic in the sense that nothing comes out of the shadows to eat our faces. Wells finds the light switch and turns it on. The cave fills with light and we take our goggles off.

He was right. The subway line runs right next to one of the old walking-dead tunnels. The area where we're standing is about fifty feet across and stretches into darkness at both ends. The walls are hacked out of raw stone. The lighting fixtures are made of human bones. Skulls and other bones are cemented together on the walls, making elaborate shapes. Thirteen of them. Angra sigils, I'm guessing.

There are a couple of hospital gurneys on one side of the room along with the same kind of gory surgical scene like we saw at the hospital. Only this one is old. The blood on the instruments and ground is dry and dusty. The body parts are shriveled and so far gone they don't even smell bad.

"Still think I'm Saint Nick?" I say.

"Odds are you're not."

"What would be my motive?"

Wells looks around the tunnel.

"You're insane. The pressure of the Angra threat has pushed you over the edge, so you're acting out your murderous Hell fantasies."

"The Shonin doesn't think I'm Saint Nick."

"He doesn't know you like I do."

"I'm a bastard. I'm not insane. There's a difference."

"We'll see."

"Sir?"

It's Sola's voice.

"Is everything all right?"

"Send in the forensics team. I want this place examined down to the micron. Record the scene, then bag every single piece of evidence and bring it back with us."

"Yes, sir."

"Let's get out of their way," says Wells.

"Just a minute."

An old wooden box sits in a niche in the wall.

"I haven't seen one of those in an Angra scene before."

Wells follows me over.

"Don't touch it," he says.

"Okay."

I don't use my hand, but I flip the latch and push open the top of the case.

"Dammit," says Wells.

"Watch the language."

Inside is a skull on a deep blue velvet pillow. Its metal teeth glitter and it has lips and a nose made of hammered gold. Its eyes are like elaborate silver brooches, each set with a blue stone in the middle. Rubies flow down the top of the skull from an old head wound, each ruby smaller than the one before it, so they form a line of blood down to the eye sockets.

"Ever seen anything like it?" I say.

"No. And that's the last playing around you get to do today. Get out of the tunnel. Grown-ups have to work."

We crawl out of the hole and back into the subway. Wells stands and brushes dirt off his pants. The forensic team pushes past us, wrapped up in sterile white Tyvek suits. Julie Sola comes over to me.

"I guess no one's in there."

"No one's used that place in a while. Those chop-shop crazies sure weren't working in there. And they sure didn't make that skull."

"Whose skull?" says Sola.

"Good question."

"I'm disturbed," says Wells. "After the hospital, this isn't what I was expecting."

"This was probably their rehearsal space."

Wells shakes his head.

"No. It's more than that. Maybe forensics will tell us what. DNA. Dental records for the skull."

"Forget that. The teeth were gold too."

"That's disappointing."

"That's not what bugs me."

"What does?" says Sola.

"That the place was abandoned awhile ago. That means whatever the Angra groupies were doing in there—assuming it was them—they finished."

"I was thinking the same thing," says Wells.

He looks back at the hole.

"We need to seal off this whole part of the tunnel."

"You don't need me for that, right?"

I turn and show him the bite wound on my neck.

"I'd like to go and get fifty tetanus shots, so I'm taking off."

He looks at the wound, but doesn't say anything. Just nods.

"Be at headquarters early tomorrow. We'll have work to do."

"Sure."

Like today wasn't work.

I head back down the tracks and up onto the train platform. I wonder what the watercooler talk will be like tomorrow, now that people know all the gossip about me is true. That I'm not entirely human and I'm really good at killing things. Too bad I don't have a car. I bet I could get a really good parking space now.

I take a quick look around to make sure I'm alone and step into the shadow of one of the concrete palm trees.

I COME OUT of a shadow in the parking lot by Allegra's clinic. It's in a strip mall next to a nail salon and a pizza delivery joint. A sign on the clinic door says EXISTENTIAL HEALING. I knock on the glass. Fairuza opens up.

"Hey, Stark," she says. "Candy already went home."

"Good. I'm here to see Allegra."

I touch my neck and show her the blood. She just opens the door. Everyone here is pretty used to seeing me bleeding.

Allegra comes out of the examining room, wiping her hands on a towel. Her café au lait skin contrasts with the bright white medical lab coat.

She comes over and gives me a loose hug, trying to not get rain from my coat all over her.

"He's fucked up again," says Fairuza.

Allegra's brow furrows.

"What happened?"

"A dead man bit me. Sort of dead. Walking around dead, but not a zombie. I just figured I should get it cleaned out or something."

"Look at you being sensible for once. Come on in."

"Need any help?" says Fairuza.

"No. I've sewn this one back together more times than I can remember."

She has me take off my coat and shirt and sit on the exam table.

She cleans off my neck with Betadine. I hate the smell of hospitals and clinics. They make you feel like you should be sick just stepping inside.

"That hurts."

"Baby," says Allegra. "I'd ask how the new job was working out, but you walking in here voluntarily tells me everything I need to know."

"They make me get up early too," I say. "It's pure abuse."

"The good news is that there's a lot of blood, but the wound itself isn't bad. I have a salve that will help the healing."

"I'm good at healing all on my own. I just don't want rabies or lockjaw or diaper rash. Whatever a corpse bite can give you."

"I haven't had a lot of experience with this, so I'm going to take some blood and give you a wide-spectrum antibiotic."

"I hate needles."

"You really are a baby today," she says. "Which makes me think you're not just here because you scraped your knees. I've seen you hurt worse than this and you didn't come in."

"You got me, Perry Mason. I'm worried about Candy. What can you tell me?"

I can't see Allegra, but I hear her draw a long breath.

"Honestly, I don't know. I haven't worked on many Jades. I'm running some tests on her now. I should have something in a day or so."

"Call me when you do."

"You know, even though we're not a regular hospital, there's still this thing called doctor-patient confidentiality."

"I know. But call me anyway."

"We'll see."

"The clinic looks pretty quiet today."

"That's why Candy went home. We don't have that many patients these days. Still, we're doing better than the regular hospitals."

"What do you mean?"

"There are more Lurkers staying in town than people. Cedars-Sinai, big hospitals like that are pretty much empty. Even the doctors are gone. It's critical-care patients only with a skeleton staff."

"So, it really is only us funny people left."

"No, and that has me worried. I think people have been watching the clinic. There was a pickup truck in the parking lot across the street all day yesterday. A van the day before that."

"Who do you think it was?"

"I have no idea. It just makes me nervous."

"Are you sure it wasn't just people looking for a place to get out of the rain for a few hours?"

"Maybe. Maybe seeing the city like this is just making me skittish. I'm scared."

She puts some gauze on the wound and tapes it into place. I hate the feel of tape on my skin.

"If it happens again, call me. I'll check out whoever it is."

"Thanks. That makes me feel better. There. All done."

I put on my shirt and coat. Allegra sees the dirt on my pants and boots.

"Where the hell have you been?"

"Have you ever been in an ossuary?"

"I'm not sure I know what that is."

"They have one in Paris. Vidocq will tell you about it. It'll be great pillow talk."

"It's something gruesome, isn't it?"

"I'll let you be the judge."

"Go home," she says. "And stay in. Both of you."

"That's the plan."

I start out and stop.

"Candy is going to be okay, right?"

Allegra washes her hands.

"She'll be fine. I'm sure it's just a Jade-specific virus or something. I'm reading up on it now. Don't worry so much."

I nod and head out the front.

"Tell Kas I'll see him tonight," says Fairuza.

"Have him show you his new hat. And make him tell you where it came from."

I DON'T EXACTLY lie about who fixed up my neck when I get home, but when Candy guesses it was a Vigil medic, I don't correct her. It will bug her if she knows I've been talking to Allegra, and after her being sick and my discovering I'm a serial killer suspect, it would be nice to have a few hours free from drama.

I listen to Candy practicing guitar downstairs in the rehearsal room. Fairuza comes over around eight and disappears with Kasabian into his inner sanctum. Chinese delivery shows up soon after. I watch *Three Extremes* upstairs. It's all gloriously boring.

Candy comes up around eleven, bright-eyed and sweaty from practice. I haven't seen her this happy in days. The sofa is wobbly from when we broke the leg, so we head for the bedroom, where the furniture is sturdier. The only casualty is a bedside lamp shaped like the *Cowboy Bebop* spaceship. Personally, I'm not sorry to see it go.

"I think you did that on purpose," she says.

"I'd never do something that underhanded."

"Right. Don't worry. I intend to replace it with something more hideous and embarrassing."

"I hope it doesn't get broken too."

"You better. Each new lamp I have to get will be worse than the one before. Trust me. I know where to get more cute kittens, talking robots, and pink monsters than you can shake your ass at."

"Understood. I'll guard future lamps with my very life."

"Good boy," she says, then kisses me and lies down.

For a while, lying in the dark, it feels like nothing is wrong at all. Then I hear the rain battering the window and I remember that pretty much everything is wrong.

I don't remember falling asleep. I'm just lying beside Candy and then I'm somewhere else.

It's a strange mix of the Angra subway cavern and the scene at the hospital. The meat chapel is surrounded by rough, raw stone, the bone sigils bright red in the reflected blood light.

The thirteen crucified bodies writhe on their inverted crosses, crying and gasping for air like they aren't quite dead.

I look at the walls, but can't see the sigils. They jitter like liquid mercury, forming and re-forming themselves into new shapes. They don't hold any one long enough to make sense and then I understand that I'm not looking at their symbols, but at the Angra themselves.

From a spiral of skulls all shattered on one side steps a golden woman. Her skin is patterned like circuit boards and snake scales. On her head is a headdress with swept-back wings. Half of her face is missing. An empty eye socket above a nonexistent cheek and a jaw stripped of its golden flesh are all that's left on her right side. Though she's in pain, with half her skull revealed she's stuck in a perpetual half smile.

I say, "I remember you."

She nods.

"We met in the water, as the building fell into the ocean."

"Yeah. Kill City. You grabbed my leg. You tried to drown me," I say.

The other side of her face smiles. She folds her hands.

"That was before I knew how special you are."

"Are you the Flayed One or the Hand?"

"Neither," she says, drawing herself up. "Call me Ten Thousand Shadows. I hear all truths and lies, every whisper and secret told in the dark. There are no mysteries to me among mortals."

"Are you all torn up because that's all of you that can get through to this dimension or because you were always uglier than me?"

She turns her head giving me a good look at her wounds.

"The Terrible One did this to me when he threw us out of this universe and into chaos. Your God calls himself a God of love and mercy. See what his mercy looks like."

She steps closer. I back up. Even while she's trying to keep this form, she can't hold entirely still. Every time she moves, for a split second she blurs into something else. A bird skeleton. A crawling patch of furred fungus. A giant treelike thing, so twisted and knotted it looks like it grew in a hurricane.

"Trust me, lady. I know all about God's bad side. I've been on it most of my life."

"You are Abomination," she says. "As are we. You owe this God and his pitiful creations nothing."

"Yeah, but I like donuts, so what am I going to do?"

"Join us. Summon us to this realm and we'll raise you up to be Angra Om Ya. Stark, savior of the true rulers of the universe."

"And here I thought you liked me for my boyish charms."

"Call us. Bring us through and you can have anything in return."

She undoes a clasp on her golden gown and it falls to the

floor. She's beautiful. The half of her that's covered in skin. The rest looks like Thanksgiving leftovers a couple of days past their prime.

"Even if I wanted to help you, I don't know how to use the Qomrama."

She reaches out her almost meatless hand.

"Don't worry. We'll teach you."

"How?"

The golden woman fades away, replaced by the swirling skeleton-fungus-tree thing.

"We'll speak again."

"Goody."

She's gone.

I hear a sound and turn to the reliquary. The rubies on the skull are gone and blood pours from the hole in the forehead. It spills onto the floor and pools in the cracks. I turn to go down the tunnel, but there's no way out. Blood pours from the skull and the sigils on the wall, covering the floor. I climb onto the filthy gurney to get away from it. It dawns on me that this whole thing has been a trap. That the cavern is going to fill with blood and that I'm going to drown. I should have been nicer to Ten Thousand Shadows. Or maybe had less Aqua Regia with the movie last night. Either way, this is a hell of an end to a shitty day. I hold my breath and try to get as close to the ceiling as I can. In a few minutes it won't make any difference.

I come awake to Candy shaking me.

"Wake up, goddammit," she says.

I choke on my own spit and gasp for air.

"What's wrong with you? You're thrashing all over."

It takes me a couple of minutes to get my breath.

"I'm fine," I say. "Just weird dreams."

"What kind?"

I sit up. Rub a hand over my face.

"I was in a cave with the Angra. They were talking to me. One was. Ten Thousand Shadows. She wanted me to summon them."

"Who is she?"

"The one I saw in Kill City."

She pushes my hair back off my forehead.

"It was just a dream. How could the Angra be talking to you?"

"I've always had funny dreams that way. And that chopshop prick bit me. Maybe we made some kind of connection."

"Or maybe it was just a damned dream. You're all stressed out about work. You get hurt and you remember the one fragment of an Angra you ever saw."

"You're probably right."

"I'm always right."

Candy pushes me back down onto the bed and pulls the covers over me.

"Should I tell the Shonin about it?"

"Definitely not," she says. "You said Wells is trying to connect you and Saint Nick. All anyone over there needs to hear is that you're having pillow talk with an old God."

"Good point."

"I'll be back," she says, and gets out of bed. A minute later I hear her in the bathroom throwing up.

I'll call Allegra tomorrow about those goddamn tests.

IN THE MORNING, the bite is just bruises and a scab. There's no fieldwork or car chases scheduled for the Vigil today, so Candy heads off to help out at the clinic.

At Vigil headquarters, instead of the sneers and behind-the-back comments I usually hear, there's dead silence when I walk through. Julie Sola and Vidocq are coming out of the break room. Vidocq has a cup of tea and Sola is carrying a container of yogurt.

I say, "What's with the silent treatment around here? Did I suddenly get boring?"

"Just the opposite," says Vidocq.

Sola peels back the lip from the top of the yogurt and sticks in a spoon.

"Everyone knows about what you did yesterday. The flaming sword."

"The Gladius."

"You have to understand, even with all the fundamentalists around here, angels are still mostly an abstraction. To see something like that right in front of their eyes, well, you blew a few people's minds."

Vidocq says, "That silence you hear isn't boredom. It's awe."

"I don't like it."

Sola eats a spoonful of her yogurt.

"It's too late now. Even the old-timers only ever saw Aelita produce the Gladius, so they know you're at least as powerful as her. The younger ones, the ones who grew up with slasher movies and Ozzy, some of them think you're the Angel of Death."

It's funny how you get used to things and then when you

do them in front of other people it doesn't get exactly the effect you intended. I just want a paycheck from these people. The last thing I want is to be put in any category that Aelita is a part of.

"Maybe I need to shake their faith a little."

Sola puts the spoon back into the yogurt.

"How?"

"A good, long nose pick might be a good start. Really dig for the mother lode."

Vidocq laughs a little.

"Wait until I have gone home before you implement that strategy, please."

I look at Sola.

"How come you're not all dazzled by my Heavenly awesomeness?"

"The first time I met you, you had just abandoned the latest in your long line of stolen cars. Not too angelic, if you ask me."

"Good. The last thing I need are a bunch of Bible thumpers expecting me to walk on water or tell them what card they're thinking of."

Sola, stirring her yogurt, and Vidocq start away.

"Just be your usual charming self," she says. "The angel thing will wear off soon enough."

"Before you go, call me an asshole loud enough for people to hear."

She half shouts, "You always were an asshole, Stark."

I nod a thanks and put my hand on the scanner to get into the Shonin's room.

He's inside with one of yesterday's captured chop-shop

people strapped to a gurney. They're both over by the 8 Ball. The Shonin glances up when I come in.

"How was hunting yesterday, fatty? There's a rumor you got some new scars."

He doesn't have much in the way of lips left, so it's hard to tell if he's smiling.

"I heard one about someone using your skull as a bedpan."

The Shonin turns away in disgust.

"You have a dirty mind."

"Then stay out of it."

"At least show me your new trick."

"The Gladius? It's not new and it's not a trick and I'm not your dancing monkey."

He turns back to examining the body on the gurney.

"Too bad. For a few second there, you sounded almost interesting."

I watch the Shonin perform some kind of ritual over the chop-shop guy. He has incense burning and there are a dozen potion bottles open on a nearby table. He moves his hands in a slow, twisting pattern over the dead man's body, muttering spells. The guy on the table has a nice gash along his cheek, exposing his teeth. It reminds me of Ten Thousand Shadows, but I push her out of my head. He snarls and snaps at the Shonin's hands. He looks like one of yesterday's Eaters. Whatever the Shonin is trying to do, I don't think it's going well.

I settle down in a chair across the room and light a Malediction. Yeah, they smell like burning tires, but this place is so full of incense, I can barely breathe. One more layer of stench isn't going to hurt.

The Shonin works for a few more minutes, waving his hands like he's shooing away invisible flies and muttering old spells low in his throat, growling so much it's almost like he's speaking Hellion. Another five minutes go by and he drops his bony hands to his sides. Mr. Chop Shop snarls and spits. He'd like to make the Shonin into his personal chew toy.

The Shonin walks to the table with the potions and drops into a chair. He scribbles some notes on a piece of paper and sniffs the air. He looks at me and goes back to his notes, not bothering to tell me to put out my smoke. He's not being polite or giving in to my baser instincts. He just knows that whatever it was he was trying, the moment has passed and anything that happens now isn't going to make it worse.

I drop the last half inch of the Malediction into a cup full of cold tea.

"What exactly were you trying over there?"

"Anything," he says. "This is an Angra construct. I thought bringing it in close proximity to the Qomrama might have some effect on it."

"I didn't see anything happening."

"Neither did I."

"How long have you been trying?"

He glances up at a Naval Clock on the wall.

"All night apparently. Ever since the marshals brought the bodies back."

He leans back and pulls a loose strip of dried black skin from the back of his hand and drops it on the floor. It's not the only skin down there. I wonder if it's something to do with the poison book. First Candy and now him. Is everyone getting sick?

"What have you learned about the 8 Ball from your killer book?"

He flips through a notebook covered with long scribbled lines of kanji.

"Lots and lots. But the book is philosophical and theoretical. Not geared toward practicality. I can tell you the Qomrama's history, but not how to use it to attack or summon."

"Your book doesn't sound like it's worth a damn."

"It hasn't all been bad."

He looks at the 8 Ball rotating in the magnetic field.

"I got it to reverse direction for a few seconds once."

"I for one feel better knowing that you might have the power to make the Angra dizzy."

He flips through pages of his notebook.

"What am I not seeing?"

"That poison book is probably fucking with your mind. If it hasn't told you anything useful by now, why don't you stop drinking it?"

"Because what if it reveals something tomorrow? The answers we need might be in the next bottle. Or the one after that."

I walk over to the 8 Ball. Mr. Chop Shop bares his teeth at me. I want to knock them out.

"You keep drinking that stuff and the gristle holding you together is going to fall off. You know the old joke, a guy goes into his doctor's office and says, 'Doc, it hurts when I do this,' and the doctor says, 'So don't do that.' That's you. Stop doing that."

The Shonin sits up.

"That's your way," he says. "You can't conquer it with

your fists or your gun, you give up. I meditated in my tomb for centuries. I will find the answer."

"We don't have centuries, Jack Skellington. We need something now."

"Do you have any suggestions?"

I touch the glass chamber where the 8 Ball floats.

"You're trying to use all these potions and rituals, but the only time I saw the 8 Ball do anything is when someone was touching it."

The Shonin sets down his notebook.

"Yes, you told me about that. The Qomrama killed a group of soldiers in a market in Hell. Later, your Sub Rosa inquisitor used it to kill Aelita, an angel of considerable strength."

He shakes his head.

"What you're saying is it's too dangerous. No one is to touch the Qomrama until I understand it more thoroughly."

I take off my glove, revealing my Kissi hand. The Shonin stands up when he sees it. I wonder what the Vigil clowns outside would think if they got a look at it. Would they still think I'm an angel or something even worse?

The Kissi hand is like an insect appendage, but it's also like skeletal machinery. The Terminator's arm crossed with a praying mantis. I think it's the ugliest thing on the planet. Still, sometimes it comes in handy.

"I've never seen one of those before. Only block prints. I wasn't sure they were even real," says the Shonin. "You're more of a monster than I thought, fatty."

"That's nothing," I say. "Watch this."

I open the lock on the magnetic chamber. There's a whoosh as air rushes in to fill the vacuum.

"What are you doing?" shouts the Shonin. "Stop that."

I reach inside and pull the 8 Ball out of the field. It takes a couple of tries. The field doesn't want to let go. But with a little twisting, I work it out. And that's why the Kissi hand is so useful. In all the twisting and turning from a sphere covered in diamond plate to an egg covered in an intersecting pattern of serrated blades the 8 Ball doesn't do any damage. The Kissi hand is just too tough to cut and there's nothing to bleed.

"Put it back," says the Shonin. He backs away across the room.

I bring the saw-toothed 8 Ball over to Mr. Chop Shop. Instead of snarling and biting, he calms right down. The only sounds he makes are the ragged breaths through his torn mouth.

The Shonin slowly comes over to us.

"You're not entirely stupid after all," he says. "I don't know if it's of much value, but it's a little impressive."

"What do you mean it's not valuable? I calmed this fucker right down. That's more than you've done."

"It's a nice trick," he says, "but I caused the Qomrama to change rotation once. Is that any more useful than this?"

"Of course this is more useful. I'm controlling a Qliphoth. How is that not helpful?"

The Shonin looks at the 8 Ball and then at Mr. Chop Shop.

"All that power to control one little demon. I would think that with your experience you'd see the absurdity."

"You're just pissed because your holy books and snake oil got you nothing with a capital zero. Look. I can even touch the thing."

"Don't you dare," says the Shonin. "We don't know what might happen. Continue in this manner and I'll be forced to call Marshal Wells."

"That's right. Run home to daddy when things get a little intense. I thought you'd have bigger balls than that, *muertita,* or did those shrivel up and drop off too?"

"Put the Qomrama back in its chamber."

"When I'm done."

The 8 Ball jumps in my hand. Sprouts spider legs that wrap around my arm and hold on tight. It softens. Liquefies. Crawls over my sharp, skeletal claw of a hand, wrapping it in living silver. The 8 Ball jumps again, pulling my hand down onto Mr. Chop Shop's chest. The Shonin retreats back to his worktable, grabbing a fistful of talismans and charms and holding them up like a shield.

"Take it off," he shouts. "Take it off."

"I can't."

Mr. Chop Shop is back snarling and snapping his cracked teeth. His eyes are wide, the whites splotched with broken veins.

My Kissi hand closes on Chop Shop's chest, ripping into the skin. I have a bad feeling the hand is going to tear out his heart or lungs, but it only breaks the surface flesh. Chop Shop goes into convulsions, bucking and kicking against the gurney's straps. Rivets pop. I hear the restraints by his feet rip. I try to pull my hand away. I get it up an inch, then another. It feels like I'm being held to him by invisible chains. I lean back, using my weight to pull back my hand. Slowly, I come up off of him. But something comes with me.

The Qliphoth emerges from his flesh like a mist. A long

beaklike mouth. Concentric circles of cutting fangs and grinding molars. It's an Eater, but without a body. Just spiritual essence.

I plant my feet on the ground and pull, dragging the demon from Chop Shop's body.

Bad idea. It makes sense that a Qliphoth with no body wouldn't have any power. It makes sense, but it turns out it's not true.

The Eater twists and snaps at my face. I try to hold on, but it wriggles out of my hand and goes straight for the wall, attacking it with its massive choppers. In just a few seconds, it's almost through the concrete. I grab it with my Kissi hand and pull it back. Toss it across the room. It hits one of the lab tables by the door and bites right through it. Ripping through high-impact plastic and steel like it was cotton candy. It scrambles to its feet, pulling equipment off tables and the wall, cutting deep grooves into the floor, where it tears at them with its teeth. I throw a chair at the thing and its beak snaps it in two.

The Eater charges me. I pull the na'at and snap it open. It goes right through the Eater's mist body without slowing it.

Fuck me.

I'm reaching for my gun when the Eater hits me, driving me into the wall like a bull in a jet pack. The beak dives for my face.

And my Kissi hand closes on it. Holds it in place. Jerks up and snaps the beak like a Popsicle stick. It slides into the Eater's body to where its heart should be and closes on it. There's nothing in my hand but mist, but the Eater thrashes like I'm pulling its guts out. One more jerk, and the mist explodes, knocking me into the damaged wall. I scramble to my feet, my head spinning. I turn around in a quick circle, making sure the Eater isn't behind me. It isn't. It's gone. And the 8 Ball has changed. It's just a metallic ball in my left hand. I take it back to the magnetic chamber and put it inside. It hovers, spinning quietly.

I lean against the wall and slide down into a sitting position. Half the furniture in the room is broken. I hope the Vigil has homeowner's insurance.

"Do you think it's dead?"

The Shonin comes out from around his potion table. But he doesn't let go of his talismans.

"No doubt," he says.

"Admit it. That was fun, wasn't it?"

The Shonin looks around his wrecked lab.

"How did you remove it? And how did you kill it?"

"I have no idea. The damned thing acts a little different each time I use it. Every time anyone uses it."

"This is good. You made it work, fatso."

"I've made it work before, but I still don't know how. That's no help."

The Shonin walks around the room righting broken chairs, which fall back over. He tiptoes around scattered piles of herbs, dried lizards, caustic chemicals, and pickled animal hearts.

"The Qomrama likes your ugly hand."

"The Kissi were seriously fucked-up angels. Maybe they taste good or something. More goddamn theories aren't going to help."

The Shonin picks up a box of dried tarantulas.

"Wisdom comes from knowledge. Knowledge begins with theories."

"I don't want wisdom. I want a bazooka."

"We have other demon-possessed bodies. We can try more experiments."

I get up. My back aches where the demon drove me into the wall.

"How many experiments do we do? A hundred? A thousand? That means we have to catch more chop-shop assholes. Do we have that much time?"

The Shonin goes back to his table. Sets down the box and starts straightening things.

"Probably not. Do you have any ideas?"

I could use a drink about now. Getting monster-hugged by the 8 Ball and fighting a demon, it's more than I counted on. But I don't suppose the Shonin keeps Aqua Regia around here.

"You have any sake around here?"

"For rituals. Not for you to guzzle."

"Too bad. A drink would help me think better."

"Look what you did to my room. You think I want to see you drunk?"

He picks up and drops a shattered alembic.

"Some say I'm charming that way."

"Then you should go and work with them. I don't think I like your methods."

"I don't like anything about any of this," I say. "I don't know any more about the 8 Ball than when I came here. You people said you knew how it worked, but you were lying. As usual, the Vigil is full of shit."

"I don't know why I ever tried correcting your speech,"

says Wells, coming into the room. He stops by the door and looks around.

"What did you do to my laboratory?"

I drop the cup with the Malediction butt into a trash can before Wells can see.

"We pulled a Qliphoth out of one of Saint Nick's little Frankensteins. It kicked up a fuss about it."

Wells looks past me to the Shonin.

"Is that true?"

The Shonin nods and adjusts his conical hat, which is sliding off to one side.

"He extracted and dispelled it using the Qomrama Om Ya."

"That's a breakthrough then," says Wells.

I pick up a chair and sit down.

"It would be if we knew how we did it. I just picked up the 8 Ball and it did the rest. I wasn't in control at all."

Wells goes over to the magnetic chamber where the 8 Ball floats. He checks the lock on the chamber door.

"You took it out?"

"Yep."

"Knowing how dangerous it is."

"I just said yes."

"I could terminate you for that."

I pull the na'at from under my coat.

"You think any of your choir boys wants to come for me after what they saw me do yesterday?"

"Always looking for a fight, aren't you?" says Wells. "Put that away. I only meant terminate your employment."

I study him. His heartbeat is normal. Up a little, but that might be because I drew down on him. His eyes aren't dilated, another good indicator that he's telling the truth. I slip the na'at back under my coat.

"You're going to watch that kind of behavior for the next few hours," Wells says. "I'm pulling you off the Angra case for a while. You need to come with me."

"Am I getting detention?"

"You're going to want to watch that kind of thing too. Saragossa Blackburn is dead and someone is making accusations."

"Against me?"

"Yes. We need to deal with this."

"What happened to him?"

"Later. Shonin, I'll have some people come by to help you put your lab back together. Between that and the breakthrough with the demon, it sounds like you have enough work to keep you busy for a while."

"More than enough. You really think he killed Blackburn? I studied people a long time. He's a fool, not a murderer."

"We'll see," says Wells. He goes to the door and holds it open for me.

I turn to the Shonin.

"See you around, dead man."

"Keep your nose clean, dumb-ass."

IT'S A LONG walk to Wells's office. The silence is different this time. It's not the general silence of people going quiet as I pass. Now it's Wells's silence as he walks slightly ahead of me so he doesn't have to speak or look at me. This is truly fucked and potentially dangerous. But I have my na'at, my gun, and my blade. If things go bad for me, I'll make them worse for everybody else.

Wells's office is at the far end of the Vigil clubhouse. There's a plastic Christmas wreath on the door. Inside it's all wood paneling. A desk big enough you could rodeo on it. A Marshals Service seal and Vigil sigil on the wall behind. A cross on his desk. Everything you need to put the fear of God and Gitmo into anyone he drags in here. There's also something very loud in the room and it's in a really nice suit.

"Marshal, I want you to place this man under arrest right now," says Audsley Ishii.

Wells goes around his desk and sits in his leather executive chair. I'm betting he's not getting comfortable, but positioning himself so he's in reaching distance of his Glock.

"Based on what evidence?"

"Don't talk to me like you don't know Stark. Living in Hell. Playing the Devil. It's driven him insane. Don't forget that a few months ago he broke into the Augur's home and threatened him."

I look at Ishii.

"And I saved his wife and him from Aelita. How did he die?"

Ishii raises a righteous finger.

"Don't play detective, like you're investigating a crime you don't know about. It was a Saint Nick killing. You have a history of cutting people up, don't you? Story is, you cut off a friend's head and still have it in your house."

Wells picks up a pen and puts it back in the holder on the edge of his desk.

"We know all about his relationship with Aldous Kasabian. Do you have any actual evidence that Stark was at the murder scene?"

Ishii takes a plastic evidence bag from his pocket and drops it on the desk.

"We found this."

Wells has a look and hands it to me. It's the torn edge of a receipt from Max Overdrive. There's a mark on it like it was stuck to the bottom of someone's shoe. Or marked to look that way.

I say, "Seriously? You think I wouldn't check myself over before running off to kill the king of the Sub Rosa?"

"Blackburn told me that he was afraid for his family's safety," says Ishii. "He invited you over and a couple of days later he's dead and this is at the scene. You can't dismiss that."

I look at Wells. He's the sphinx. I don't get anything from him at all.

"I was there for him to offer me your job, asshole," I say, and wait for Wells to reprimand me. He's doesn't, which can't mean anything good. "What does Tuatha think? Does she think I'm Saint Nick?"

Ishii takes back his evidence bag.

"She's distraught. She doesn't know what to think."

"Meaning she doesn't think it was me. You've always had it in for me and now's your chance to prove you're the investigator to the stars."

Wells looks at me, then at Ishii.

"Is it true that Blackburn offered Stark a job?"

"According to him."

"Ask Tuatha," I say. "She was there."

"Where did the murder take place?" says Wells.

"In his office at home," Ishii says.

"What time?"

Ishii pulls out his phone and checks a note.

"The doctors say yesterday between eight and eleven. The necromancers say closer to ten."

Wells shakes his head. Leans back in his chair.

"Then it wasn't Stark. He was with my team on official Vigil business all morning. Sorry, Mr. Ishii, but you're looking at the wrong man."

Ishii closes in on Wells's desk, stabbing the top with his finger.

"No, I'm not. Saint Nick is clearly working with powerful magic forces. Stark is an accomplished magician. He could be fooling all of us. Played with time. Killed from a distance. Or possessed someone to kill for him."

Wells leans forward, glancing at the fingerprints Ishii left on his pristine desk.

"I have a dozen accomplished magicians on my staff. Not all of them are pleasant people. Personality defects seem endemic among the Sub Rosa. But it doesn't make them killers."

"Maybe it was you, Audsley," I say. "You knew your days with Blackburn were numbered, so you flipped out and killed him by mistake. Maybe you're the thing that was making him nervous for his safety. Then you go Jack the Ripper on the corpse to make it look like Saint Nick."

"That's an interesting point," says Wells. "Blackburn was a scryer. Why wouldn't he have seen who was coming after him or the time of the attack?"

Ishii gives me a look.

"More proof that it would take a very powerful magician to hide both his identity and his intentions from the Augur."

Wells nods.

"And you just said that Saint Nick was a powerful magician."

Now Ishii shoots Wells a death-beam look.

"I have the entire Sub Rosa board on my side. If you don't arrest Stark right now, I can't guarantee his safety."

Wells stands up and comes around his desk.

"You let me worry about his safety. And his criminal tendencies. Now, if you'll excuse us, we have a lot of work to do."

He goes to the door and holds it open. Ishii doesn't move.

"The chief of police is with us, Stark. There's nowhere you can hide in L.A."

I look at him for a minute.

"What size uniform do you wear? After your bang-up job protecting Blackburn, I'm picturing your next gig as a rent-a-cop guarding a Denny's in Fresno."

"That's it," says Wells. "Stark, you shut up. Mr. Ishii, thank you for the sad news about the Augur's passing and your concerns about his death. The Vigil will do whatever it can to aid in the investigation."

I know Ishii wants to say something more, but Wells looks like he's one deep breath from pepper-spraying the guy. Ishii turns and leaves.

Wells goes back to his desk. Takes out a handkerchief and wipes off Ishii's prints.

I say, "You finally convinced I'm not Saint Nick?"

"Not by that scene," Wells says.

He takes a print out from a manila envelope on his desk. It's a drawing. A crude map.

"Washington convinced me you're innocent. Their psychics are sure they've tracked down Saint Nick and he's not where you're standing."

"Where is he?"

Wells turns the drawing around. I was right. It's a map, probably drawn by one of the psychics. A long street dotted with what look like office towers.

"He's in the Pickman Building on Wilshire. They don't know if he's a guest or a prisoner, but they're sure he's there on the top floor."

He points to a building marked with a crude star, like something someone would draw while in a trance.

"You're going to go and get him," says Wells.

I look at the map. The mark looks like it's around the corner of Wilshire and South Robertson.

"Why me?"

"Because you're good at getting in and out of places. You're going to use that power for something useful and end this maniac's run once and for all."

"Do you have anything more than this map? It's pretty, but office buildings tend to have a lot of rooms in them."

Wells shows me another drawing with a room marked on the top floor of a ten-story building.

"We know right where he is. And you won't be going in alone. An agent from our special operations team will be going with you."

"I'm not Saint Nick, but you still don't trust me."

"You're right, I don't," he says. "But this isn't a matter of trust. It's a matter of skills, which the agent has. Also, it's a matter of judgment. Like what happened in the Shonin's room today."

I push the drawing back across the table.

"Do I get to meet Derek Flint before the job?"

"You already know her," says Wells. "Julie Sola. Why do

you think I wanted her back on the team? She was just a rookie in the service, but she was experienced in special operations for an agency you don't need to know about."

So that's why she was with Vidocq. Probably picking up a few last minutes of B&E tips.

"When do we leave?"

"Tonight. Marshal Sola has sketched out a good plan. She'll get you up to speed later."

"Shouldn't we go over things now?"

"She has work to do first. And nothing you're doing is complicated. You're just there to get her through any doors she can't breach herself."

"I can probably do this whole thing myself in ten minutes."

"Or blow it in one. The plan is already in motion. Be back here at midnight."

I leave Wells's office and walk around looking for Sola and Vidocq, but can't find them. Not a bad day all in all. I saw Ishii tossed out on his ass. I'm cleared of being Saint Nick. And I got to sucker-punch a demon.

Armed guards stand around the entrance to the Shonin's room as movers take out the wrecked furniture and bring in new. I've always been in such a hurry to get inside I never noticed that he's hung mistletoe over the door.

I RIDE THE Hellion hog home from the Vigil compound through wet, empty streets. The rain beats down hard today. Fat drops the size of quarters. I rev the engine and speed the hog down Hollywood Boulevard, sending mini-tidal waves onto the sidewalk.

Under a dead streetlight, someone has broken the front windows of a Gap store. A few kids run away with jeans and a couple of cops load armfuls of stuff into the back of their squad car. A whole deserted city for the taking and they're stealing Dockers.

I run the bike into the alley behind Max Overdrive and throw the cover on top, though I'm not sure why at this point. What's to keep dry anymore? We're living in an open-air aquarium. Everyone and everything is wet inside and out. Soon we'll grow gills and fins. We'll swim out into the California Current and let it carry us down to Baja, where we'll live off cheap cerveza and krill. Until someone decides our bones make good soup. Then we'll head out to sea, into the deep, deep water where transparent creatures, so long in the dark they're born blind, skulk along the ocean floor waiting for us to tire out or die or just give up. We'll drift down to the bottom of the world, food for things that have never dreamed of land or humans or the Angra. Will we be happy then? Primordial shit in a volcanic trench older than God's jodhpurs? I doubt it. We'll just get absorbed by something else and fed up the food chain again until we're back on land, food for the God or Gods that marooned us here in the first place. And we'll start the whole thing again. Our only consolation is that maybe in the new world, the studios will have more sense and no one will green-light *Battlefield Earth*. That would be worth coming back for.

I go in through the side door. I can feel the wrongness of the place even before I see it. Discs are scattered all over the floor. A display case is knocked over and another one is torn to pieces. Kasabian's door looks like it was ripped off its hinges. Screams come from his room.

The lights are off, but I can see someone on top of him. I grab whoever it is by the collar and throw them as hard as I can out the door. They slam into the floor, slide, and bang into the far wall hard enough to leave a dent.

It isn't until she gets to her knees that I recognize her. It's Candy. She's gone full Jade. I've never seen her so far gone before. Her skin has gone almost obsidian and her nails are curved back into claws. She growls, showing a mouthful of white shark teeth. Her eyes are red slits in black ice. She's sweating and blood drips from her mouth where she bit herself.

I shout, "Candy. It's me. Stop."

She charges and hits me square in the chest, knocking me onto my back. She's ridiculously strong in this form, and as vicious as an Eater. All teeth and madness. Candy's teeth are bad enough, but then she stretches her mouth open like a snake, exposing needle-thin fangs she uses to inject the Jades' necrotizing poison.

Candy's my girl, but I don't want to die and I don't want anyone drinking me when I do. But this isn't her fault. She's fucked up and I don't want to punch her out.

I bark some Hellion and she flies off me like ghosts playing horseshoes. She's up a second later and charging me again.

I grab her, wrapping my arms and legs around her. Still, it's all I can do to hold on. I bark a sleeping hex into her ear. She slows down. Her eyes close. Then I feel her body tense again as she fights her way through it, snarling and clawing at me again.

She braces her feet on the ground and pushes back against me, freeing one leg. It's enough to wriggle a leg, then a hand free. She drags her claws down my arm, shredding my coat and skin.

I yell, "Candy. Stop."

She bites my wrist down to the bone. I grab her again and shout more Hellion. Something harder and worse than sleep.

She lets go of my wrist, shaking violently. Every muscle in her body going rigid. Her eyes go wide and her lips draw back from her teeth in a painful grimace. She's having a seizure. A kind of hoodoo epilepsy. But even with every muscle in her body locked in place, she's still fighting. I push her off me, but hold on to her.

"Kasabian. You all right?"

He comes to his door like a groundhog afraid of the light.

"I'm okay. What the fuck is going on?"

"I'll tell you when I know."

I pick her up, slipping in some blood from my wrist. When I get my footing, I carry her through a shadow to the clinic.

The clinic is as empty as the streets. Fairuza sees us coming and yells for Allegra. She comes out of the exam room.

"My God. What's wrong?"

"Look at her. She's full Jade."

Allegra comes over and looks at Candy. Checks her forehead. Pushes up her eyelids.

"This doesn't make sense. I just gave her the potion."

I carry Candy into the exam room and put her on the table.

"Could something be wrong with it?"

"I made it myself."

"Check it anyway."

Allegra calls to Fairuza.

"Get me the skullcap sedative."

Fairuza opens a cabinet and paws through bottles. When she finds the sedative, she hands it to Allegra. I'll give Allegra points for brave. She sticks her hand into Candy's mouth and pries her jaws open enough to pour the potion into. It's green and smells of licorice like it has an absinthe base.

When Candy starts to relax, I speak Hellion to clear the hex. Her muscles unknot and her jaw drops open. In less than a minute, she's back to being Candy.

Allegra looks at me.

"We're going to have to restrain her until we know what's happened."

"I know. Try not to hurt her."

"I'll try to keep her unconscious until we figure out what's wrong."

She looks at my bloody wrist.

"You're bleeding. It's like the old days. You in here all the time covered in blood. Sit down. I'll get some gauze."

I do what I'm told simply because I don't want to argue. Allegra comes back a minute later with gauze and tape.

"I could stitch this up to stop the bleeding, but I know you'll say no."

"That's right."

"Why?"

"Because it's mine and I keep my scars."

She pushes up my sleeve, bandages my hand, and wraps gauze around it.

"Because you never want to let go of anything."

I look at Candy on the table. Fairuza puts straps around her feet and across her chest.

"I swear, if someone did this to her . . ."

"I know. But you have to prepare yourself for something worse."

"What?"

"That she might have developed a tolerance to the potion and it won't work anymore."

"Then you'll figure out another one, right?"

She finishes my wrist and sets the gauze and bandages on the counter.

"I'll do my best. I'm sure there will be something in one of Eugène's books."

"Find it. Whatever it is. I'll pay for it."

"We're getting ahead of ourselves. Let's take things one step at a time. The first step is you leaving."

"I don't want to leave her alone."

"She won't be alone and you're going to be in the way. If you want what's best for her, go home."

I look from her to Fairuza and back again. They don't want me here. All I do is bring them broken people. And maybe Allegra is right. I probably will be in the way.

"Thanks. Call me the moment you know anything. Middle of the night. Whenever."

"I know. Now go."

I STEP THROUGH a shadow and come out in Max Overdrive. Kasabian is kneeling on the floor with a spray bottle of cleaner and a roll of paper towels, wiping up my blood.

"Not exactly life at the Chateau Marmont," I say.

"If this was the Chateau, she still would have attacked me, but there'd be someone else to clean up the mess."

"I'll pick up the discs."

"Why don't you get down here and work on the blood?"

"You're doing a great job. I don't want to spoil your rhythm."

"Fuck you."

I pick up the DVDs and Blu-rays and stack them on the counter. They can fucking wait until tomorrow to go back on the shelves.

"She going to be all right?" says Kasabian.

"I don't know. I'm waiting to hear."

He doesn't say anything for a minute.

"Candy's all right," he says. "Recent events aside."

"Yeah. She is."

"Did you see Fairuza at the clinic?"

"Yeah."

"Did she say anything about me?"

I give him a look.

"Right. Wrong time."

He finishes up the floor and climbs creakily up on his mechanical legs.

"Thing is," he says. "Candy is a good influence on you. Around her you're almost like a person."

"I know."

He throws the bloody paper towels into the trash and puts the spray bottle back in the storeroom.

"You want a drink?" he says. "I've still got some Belgian beer Fairuza brought over."

I shake my head.

"Some other time."

I start upstairs.

"She'll be all right," says Kasabian. "Allegra knows what she's doing."

I don't say anything. I go upstairs and close the door. Find a bottle of Aqua Regia and don't bother with a glass. I fire up a movie on the big screen, but when I finish the bottle I realize I have no idea what I've been watching.

AT THREE A.M., Sola and I drive down Wilshire in an empty sixteen-wheeler. My head hurts—hell, my eyes hurt and I'd rather be at home waiting for a call about Candy, but maybe this is a little healthier. Getting a little action instead of sitting at home drowning myself in Aqua Regia. I put a glove on to match the one that covers my Kissi hand. It covers the gauze on my wrist and Sola will think I'm getting into the James Bond spirit of things. I'm not.

"Christ, if we're going to work together I wish you'd call me Julie instead of Sola," she says on the way over.

"Careful. You took the Lord's name in vain. Wells probably has the truck bugged."

"Not for long," she says.

She pushes the heavy truck through the gears like an expert and parks it on Wilshire a block away from Robertson. I start to help her drag our passenger into the driver's seat, but she waves me off. Our passenger is a corpse in a T-shirt and jeans. Apparently, the Vigil has an arrangement to pick up the occasional unclaimed body from federal prisons around the country. So much for respecting the dead. I get out while she wrestles the corpse into place behind the wheel. She does the dirty work cleanly and efficiently. I've never seen this side of her before.

"Julie," I say.

She looks at me.

"What?"

I shake my head.

"Nothing. Just practicing."

"Okay."

She smiles and hops down from the cab, slamming the door shut. We're both dressed in black coveralls, courtesy of the Vigil. Mine are too tight. Julie's are too loose. We look like a couple of idiot thrift-store ninjas. She slings a pack onto her shoulder and we cross the street, heading for our target.

Walking makes my head hurt, but sitting made it hurt too. The night rain is cool. It helps wake me up and get focused. No one at the Vigil knows anything about Candy. Rogue Lurkers are subject to immediate arrest, no questions asked. I'm not going to take a chance on that happening.

We walk to an empty store that used to sell high-end sound systems. We're near the corner and have a great view of the Pickman Building. Inside the store, power cords, stereo cables, and coax snake the floor and hang from the ceiling like jungle vines.

I say, "What were those three things again?"

Julie kneels and starts taking things out of the pack, laying them in a semicircle around her.

"Diversion, intrusion, and extraction."

"This is the first one."

"It will be in a minute."

She looks at me.

"You're not drunk, are you?"

"I toasted a friend's health tonight, yes. But I'm fine."

"Damn," she says. "I need you Johnny on the spot tonight. Can you handle that?"

"No problem."

"Screw this up and you can go back to calling me Sola. Marshal Sola."

"I'm fine. Just point me at whatever you want dead."

She plugs together several pieces of electronics, including a joystick and a small flat-screen monitor.

"With luck, dead won't enter into things tonight."

"That's not my experience with breaking into secure places, but fingers crossed."

The monitor comes on, displaying an image looking straight down Wilshire Boulevard.

"You ready?" Julie says.

"Not really. I can hoodoo us inside the building right onto the tenth floor, but I don't like doing that kind of thing. I like coming out places where I at least know the terrain. That way I avoid walking into deadfalls and snake pits."

"Here," she says, handing me another small tablet. "There's blueprints of the tenth floor, along with surveillance photos."

I flip through the shots.

"How many guards will there be?"

"If we're lucky, none. Most of the time no one is on the tenth floor but Saint Nick."

"But someone might come up for a smoke or a chat."

"If there's anyone there, let me handle them."

"Carrying another nonlethal, are you?"

She moves the joystick, getting a feel for it. The image on the monitor vibrates slightly. It takes me a minute to see that the image is looking out through the sixteen-wheeler's windshield.

"We always start with nonlethals," Julie says. "But we carry regular backup pistols."

"Fine. You're the one with shooting theories. I'm just the help. What's the stuff after diversion?"

"Intrusion and extraction."

"Yeah. Get in clean, then run away. Two of my favorite things, especially the last one."

She flips a switch on the box with the joystick. The camera jumps as the truck shifts into gear.

"You ready?"

I think about Candy strapped to the exam table in the clinic and I want someone to shoot at me just so I can strangle them.

"Ready."

She pushes the joystick forward and the truck moves out into the flooded street. Julie has the windshield wipers on full. The truck picks up speed and blasts through a red light at the corner. Then she floors it.

As the truck picks up speed, the wipers can't keep up with the rain, and the windshield shows nothing but splotches and colored lights. Without missing a beat, she thumbs a switch and the camera shifts to infrared. The scene is clear again, the building straight ahead.

Out the window, the truck barrels past us. Julie hits a button and the truck's air horn blows three times.

At the corner of Robertson, she hits the front brakes and the trailer starts to swing around, threatening to pull the cab over on its side. But she hits the accelerator and lets up on the brakes at just the right moment so that the truck slides across the intersection, up over the curb, and crashes into the front of the Pickman Building broadside.

Smashing through the glass and steel walls, the truck doesn't slow until most of it is resting comfortably in the lobby. Julie cuts the engine. This isn't the time for random fires. Just a distracting truck with a dead driver. How tragic.

"What about emergency response? We just set off a shit-load of alarms."

She hands me a box with one red button.

"Get ready," she says, shutting down her electronics. "Hit it."

I press the button. Nothing happens for a second. Then a dull thump echoes through the street. All the lights in the neighborhood go out.

"There's an EMP device in the trailer. We just blew their power and all their electronics. They'll come back up, but not until we're gone."

"You are diabolical."

"Coming from you, I'll take that as a compliment. Now get us inside."

"It's too dark. I need a shadow."

Across the street, guards are coming out of the Pickman Building, gazing up at the truck. Some fiddle with their walkie-talkies. Some are trying to use their phones. None look happy.

Julie leads me into a toilet in the back of the store and snaps a glow stick.

"Is this enough light?"

"Barely. But it'll work."

I push my arm into a shadow just to make sure. I hear Julie draw in a breath.

"You've never seen this trick before?"

"Not this close."

"You might want to close your eyes. It can be a little weird the first time."

She closes them and I take her hand.

"Ready?"

"Definitely."

I pull her into the shadow and out onto the tenth floor of the Pickman Building.

JULIE WAS RIGHT. There aren't any guards on the tenth floor. All that's there is a small room, a plastic cube in the center of the empty floor. This would be a cakewalk except that the floor is covered in magic circles. It was dumb luck that we came out between two of them.

"Don't move," I say. "This is why I don't like going into places I don't know. Step in any one of these circles and you're dead. Probably we're both dead and I'm not in the mood for that tonight."

"Damn. What do we do to get around them?"

"It's too dark for me to see them clearly, so I can't draw a countersign."

"I have climbing gear. We can go across the ceiling."

"Easy, Catwoman. That will probably be hexed too."

"What do we do?"

"If I knew what kind of hoodoo these were, I could answer that."

"These might help," she says, and pulls two sets of goggles from her pack.

I put mine on and find a button on the side. The room blazes with the light, showing every nook and cranny protected by hoodoo power. The only thing glowing brighter than the circles is Saint Nick himself in the plastic cube. I guess that answers Wells's question. I get the feeling he's locked up tight. Nick is no guest.

"Well?" says Julie. "Can you get us through?"

"Give me a minute."

I kneel and examine the first circle. Shit. I don't recognize it. Probably some Angra bullshit. If only Father Traven was here. A good guy who deserved to live a lot longer, he'd read these signs like a cookie recipe and we'd scoot right through. But he's dead, I can't read these, and we're stuck.

"Anything?" says Julie. I don't want to tell her that we've come this far and can't go on. There has to be something. There's always something.

"Ever hear of a potion called Spiritus Dei?"

"Sure. It's one of the most powerful potions around. Supposed to ward off any supernatural being. Do you have some?"

"No."

She lets out a breath.

"But I always dip my bullets in it. We can jump the small circles and there are only two big ones between us and Saint Nick's door."

"You're going to shoot them?"

"Unless you have a better idea."

She looks up and down the room like she's hoping a cab will pull up and take her away from the crazy man. Finally, she shrugs.

"Magic is your end. Do what you think is best."

I pull out the Colt.

"This is going to be loud. Cover your ears," I say.

She does. I aim with one hand and put the other over one ear. No point in going completely deaf.

I cock the hammer on the Colt and fire into the first circle. The hoodoo light through the goggles flickers. The circle pulses like broken neon and goes out. I pull the trigger again and the second circle flickers off.

"Is it safe now?" says Julie.

"Only one way to find out."

I jump the small circles and the place where the first big circle glowed just a few seconds earlier. Nothing happens.

"Don't touch anything," I say. "There might be hoodoo the goggles can't see."

"Thanks."

"You know I'm stealing them, right? I mean, when this is over, these goggles are coming home with me."

Julie shakes her head.

"Just come up with a good story for the report. I didn't see anything."

We make it to Saint Nick's door. He's sitting in a plastic kitchen chair staring at us. Not hostile, but not looking like he's thrilled about being rescued. They might keep him drugged. Or he might be so crazy he doesn't know what's happening. That's the Saint Nick I'm hoping we don't have to deal with.

Julie flicks on a small flashlight, holds it between her teeth, and examines the cube's lock. It looks like some combination of a keypad and a physical lock. She pulls a small silver box from her pack and fits it over the mechanism. It glows and something whirs inside. Julie looks at her watch.

"The building has shielded generators. The power will be back on in the next three minutes. We need to move."

Through the goggles I can see a sigil burning on Saint Nick's door. It's a circle with designs I don't know. Tentacles and tree trunks and human limbs. At the bottom of the outer circle in letters like something off a beer-hall menu it says

DER ZORN GÖTTER. Of course. Pickman Investments. Heavy money. Heavy power. We've just blown the Angra's Vatican bank. Yes, we need to be out of here as fast as we can.

The lock pops and Julie slides open the door. I look around for hidden hoodoo or trip wires. There's nothing. These people are pretty confident that their power and magic will protect them. I guess they have for all the years it's taken to put the Angra's return plan together. Personally, I don't want to meet them or their Gods in anything bordering on a fair fight.

Saint Nick stands up with his arms at his side. He looks like he's in his mid- to late thirties. A nondescript guy. Brown hair and eyes. Flat nose and thin lips. No one you'd ever notice on the street, but isn't that how it is with serial killers? They're the most boring people in the world until cops dig up the basement and the news vans show up. *"He was always so quiet and polite. I would never have guessed . . ."*

He isn't cuffed or shackled. There's nothing in the cube with him, not even water or a slop bucket or any sign he's ever had them. That means he isn't locked in all the time. Does that mean he's not a prisoner? This isn't the time to worry about that.

Julie approaches him slowly and takes his arm. He lets her, and when she pulls him, he follows her out of the cube. She nods at me.

"Okay," she says. "Take us out of here."

"You have another glow stick?"

She lets go of Saint Nick's arm. He sways, looks around like he's never seen the place before. And steps into a circle.

Lights come on all around us. In the ceiling, the walls, and the floor. Julie and I pull our goggles off. I shove mine in my pocket. Saint Nick looks around. Points to the far side of the room.

Qliphoth claw their way out of an altar built into the wall. A Digger comes first. It gets out and slams into the far side of the cube, clearly not getting the difficult concept of transparency. More Qliphoth crawl out behind it.

"What do we do?" says Julie.

"It's too light. There are no shadows. How far to the roof?"

"It's right above us."

"Come on."

I get down on one knee, lay the Colt's barrel flat on the floor, and pull the trigger. The bullet cuts a groove in the plastic tiles all the way to the door at the end of the room.

"Come on."

"What about the circles?" says Julie.

"I hope the bullet broke them. Otherwise we're dead."

That makes Saint Nick giggle.

I grab Julie and she grabs Saint Nick. We run for the door. Nothing comes out of the floor to bite off our legs, but the Qliphoth across the room are finding their way around the cube.

The door is locked. I start to blast it open, but if I do that, the Qliphoth will be able to follow us through. Julie doesn't need me to tell her that. She has another lock-picking device out and attaches it to the door.

The Qliphoth are coming at us fast. I manifest the Gladius and slice it through the air. The front ones come up short and the rest bunch up behind them. They growl and grab at us, but none want to chance becoming Gladius meat. Then it hits me. They don't have to rush us. They can just keep us here until guards find us or some Diggers tunnel through the floor and come up behind us.

"Any time now, Julie."

"Working on it."

Then:

"Got it."

When the door opens I concentrate, flaring the Gladius to star bright. I have to cover my eyes, and the Qliphoth shrink back from the light. I go backward through the door and slam it shut, praying that it's demon-proof. Just to make things more interesting, I run the Gladius around the edge of the door, welding it to the frame.

Saint Nick is standing in the stairwell smiling at nothing. I flash on Candy in the hospital and want to smash his face.

"Stark!" Julie yells. "Guards are coming upstairs. What's up on the roof?" she says.

"Shadows. I hope."

We run up a fight of stairs to a locked door. I kick it open and we're on the roof. Where it's pitch fucking black. The city lights haven't come back on yet. Probably no one left downtown to hit the reset button.

Julie breaks a glow stick and holds it up.

"Forget it. It's too open. There's not enough light up here."

"I didn't want to do this," she says.

She pulls out a phone and punches in a code.

I say, "Why isn't that fried?"

"It's shielded from the EMP."

"Calling us a cab?"

"Better. A chopper."

I can already hear it in the distance. As much as I hate the Vigil, I'm suddenly thrilled with them and Uncle Sam for blowing all that money on a helicopter and the fuel it's going to take to rescue my sorry ass from a bunch of demonic accountants.

We move to a clear area near the street where the chopper can get in close. Julie sets off a blinking light and drops it at our feet. The chopper circles around, finally coming back to the building and hovering over us.

The thing about helicopters is they're very loud. Loud enough for a metric ton of security guards in night camo to sneak up on the roof behind us and open fire.

Someone gets a lucky shot and hits the tail rotor. The chopper spins in a wild circle. It tilts away from the building like it's looking for somewhere to land, but it's way too out of control for that. It swings back around, the guards still firing, and crashes into the roof, punching through and into the floor below. There's a small explosion, smoke, and the stink of burning rubber and fuel.

Now that the chopper is down, some of the guards are looking lean and hungry in our direction. I seriously do not have time for more bullshit tonight. I bark some Hellion and use a version of the hex I used on Candy earlier tonight. The one that knocked her off me. Only I don't hold back and rip the hex as hard and long as I can.

It's like a giant bowling ball blown by a hurricane. It knocks over the twenty or so duckpin guards, tossing some off the roof and others into the hole where the chopper went down.

But we still need a shadow. There's only one good light source in the area and only one wall that's going to have shadows.

I grab Julie and Saint Nick and bring them to the edge of the hole where the chopper went through. The fire is at the rear of the copter. Its fuselage throws a nice fat shadow on the wall. Julie sees it too. I lead her and Saint Nick a few yards away from the hole.

"The chopper blocked the stairs," Julie says. "How are we going to get down there?"

"Do you believe you can fly, Wendy?"

Her eyes narrow. Saint Nick snickers.

"What?"

I grab them both and run like a son of a bitch, jumping at the last second, hoping really, really hard that carrying two lumps of meat with me hasn't fucked up my aim.

Turns out it did a little, but not enough to kill us. Saint Nick catches the edge of the wall with his forehead. We come out of the shadow rolling like someone threw three Raggedy Anns from a car at a NASCAR race.

Eventually, we stop, and lie there on the cold Vigil floor like the lunch meat we are.

I push myself up on one elbow.

"You okay?"

One of the Vigil guards pulls Julie to her feet. She wobbles but with help stays up.

"Saint Nick is bleeding," she says.

I look over at our cargo. Ten Vigil guards stand over him with nonlethals while a couple more squirt restraint foam over his hands and ankles. Nick has a nice gash on his forehead, but he's blinking and looking around, lucid enough to know he's out of the cube and with people who probably aren't much friendlier than *Der Zorn Götter*.

"Damn," he says. "That's the most fun I've had in a long time."

He rolls over and grins at me and Julie. His face is covered in scars and sutures.

"Look at you. The Lone Ranger and Tonto. Saviors of the little people."

I kick him in the ribs.

"Don't talk to me like you know me."

He rolls up into a ball, hurting and laughing.

"Don't be a killjoy, Jimmy. Come over here and give me a hug."

It's like someone opened me up and emptied me out. I'm cold and hot at the same time. I want to throw up. I look down at Saint Nick. His face is different, but I recognize the voice.

It's Mason Faim.

ONCE UPON A time I was a regular jackass living a regular jackass life. I was part of a Magic Circle. There were six other people in the circle. All of them are dead now because I killed most of them, including and especially Mason Faim. Why? Good question. Because he was the prick who sent me to Hell and the others were the assholes who stood by and watched.

But that wasn't enough. Mason had my girlfriend Alice killed. That was just one little thing too much. I escaped Hell and came back gunning for everyone in the circle, Mason most of all.

Like any Sir Galahad asshole, I went for the worst revenge I could think of—I sent him to Hell alive to live among the slickest, sickest Hellion torturers in the universe. Only fairy tales are full of lies and Mason is the best liar I know. He just wouldn't take his punishment like a well-behaved villain. Mason cut deals, cut throats, and used his considerable hoodoo to try and become the new Lucifer. Did I mention that he stole Alice's soul from Heaven and dragged it to Hell? So I had to go after him all over again. It was during that little barn dance that I lost my left arm.

I killed him once and for all in a rigged game of Russian roulette. Watched him blow his brains out, and felt just fine about it. After that, I made sure Mason's soul was exiled in Tartarus, the Hell below Hell, where he was going to spend the rest of eternity alone in darkness.

And I lived happily ever after.

The end.

Okay, the happily-ever-after thing didn't exactly work out, but the one thing I knew I could count on was never seeing Mason Faim alive again. And now here he is. The universe has a fucked-up sense of humor.

Of course, the lump of meat squirming on the floor isn't entirely Mason. His real body is long gone in Hell—I made sure of that—so all that existed of him was his soul in Tartarus. It took some massive hoodoo to bust him out and plant the worm in one of the chop-shop bodies. I should have looked closer at Saint Nick's eyes when we snatched him. Even if the body is all wrong, I can see Mason clear as day, staring at me from his mismatched brown and green peepers.

Still, there's only one good thing about this moment.

I pull the Colt and point it at his hand.

I get to kill him all over again.

"Stand down, Stark," shouts Wells.

He pushes my arm out of the way and gets between Mason and me.

"Your presence here is no longer required. Get out of here until we sort this out. You can give me your report in the morning."

I stand there, just breathing. Mason lies on the floor looking around at the assembled Vigil morons who don't have a clue about what's happening but know that it's really, really bad. Worst of all, no matter what happens after this, Mason knows he's won the war we've been waging for eleven years. Just making it back to Earth and into a skin suit puts him one up on every civilian, Sub Rosa, and angel that's ever lived. Which doesn't mean I'm giving up. I sent him Downtown once before and I can do it again. And this time I won't get fancy with Tartarus or anything else. I'll kill his body and destroy his soul, wiping him out of existence.

"Stark," says Julie. "Did you hear Marshal Wells?"

I look at him. He's still in reach. I could toss him across the room and kill Mason before anyone could stop me and he knows it, but he stays put. Slowly, it sinks in that maybe there's more to all this than Mason and me. There's a dozen bodies in a meat locker and around ninety more in an asylum. And how many more that we don't know about yet? And it's all tied up with the Angra. Kill Mason so we can't get any answers and it might be the biggest favor I can do for the end of the world.

I put the Colt away.

Wells nods to his crew.

"Get this thing out of here. Max lockdown. No one talks to him but me."

They haul Mason to his feet and hustle him away to the cells at the far end of the clubhouse. He hums "Onward, Christian Soldiers" until I can't hear him anymore.

"Marshal Sola, see Stark out of here, please. When you're done I'll take your report in my office."

"Yes, sir."

Julie leads me behind some storage crates where there are a lot of deep shadows to leave through.

"Are you going to be all right?" she says.

"I just need to get out of here awhile and think."

"I'll probably be here all night, so I can brief you on anything that happens tomorrow. Okay?"

"Yeah. Sure."

I'm about to step into a shadow when my phone rings. I check the caller ID. It's Allegra. I hit the talk button.

"How is she?"

I don't her anything for a minute.

"Allegra? How is she?"

"I don't know what to say. I was only gone a minute."

"What's happened?"

"Candy hadn't moved, hadn't changed since you left. I went to the closet for some supplies."

"Is she alive?"

I must have shouted, because I startle Julie.

"I think so. I'm so sorry. I heard a noise while I was out of the room. When I came back, Fairuza was on the floor and a window was broken. She's gone, Stark. She's gone."

I hang up.

"What's wrong?" says Julie.

My mind is going a million miles an hour.

"He did this."

"Saint Nick? What did he do?"

I push past her, pulling the Colt. Julie gets in front of me.

"Stop. Talk to me. What's happened?"

"Candy is missing, and I know that motherfucker had something to do with it."

"Then what good is it killing him? Think about it."

I do. I start for the cells again.

"Stop," says Julie. "What's your plan? Kill Saint Nick? Tear up the city looking for Candy so you'll feel in control? The Vigil has resources you wouldn't believe. We can find anyone. What do you have besides anger? Be smart for once. Let me handle this. You go home. I'll call you when we find her."

I look at her. Is this more Vigil bullshit? Is she on their side or mine?

"Please," she says. "If you kill him, there's no coming back. You'll have the Marshals Service, Homeland Security, and the Vigil after you."

In my mind I can see Mason's head exploding. It feels even better than the first time.

Julie says, "I promise you I'll find her. Give me twelve hours."

I get out my phone and set a timer.

"Twelve hours. After that, he's mine and I'll hurt anyone who gets in my way."

Julie nods.

"Okay. Let me go talk to Wells and tell him what's happened."

I nod and start for a shadow.

"Twelve hours."

"Don't come back unless I call you," she says.

I GO HOME, fire up the Hellion hog, and head out again. But I don't need a bike. I need a goddamn ark to get around. On some of the side streets off Hollywood and Sunset, the water comes up to the hubs. Even a Hellion bike starts getting pissed off after a while at that kind of thing. The Hellion hog was built for Hell's heat, not L.A.'s *Titanic*-on-its-last-legs act. The bike coughs and threatens to tap out a couple of times, but it keeps going. I lose track of time in the empty streets.

Here and there, stop lights work. A single streetlamp glows. Every now and then I see another vehicle in the street. Whenever I do, it veers off onto another street. Looters probably, afraid I'm out scouting for LAPD. Take it all, you soggy bastards. I'd love to know who you're going to fence it to. There's something almost comforting in the fact that even at the end of the world, there's always going to be one guy ready to pick your pocket.

I go by Bamboo House of Dolls first. Then Vidocq and Allegra's place. Nothing. I call Brigitte. She hasn't heard from Candy. Where else would she have gone? Maybe to be with other Jades? Do I know any other Jades? Just Rinko, Candy's ex-girlfriend. I'm the last person on the planet she wants to hear from and the last she'd tell anything to. What an idiot scene this is. Me driving in circles in a monsoon like the Flying fucking Dutchman hoping to spot one lone girl on a million square miles of Southern California roads. It's my fault and a little Candy's, I guess. We're both so closemouthed about our pasts. I keep waiting for her to tell me about the Jade world when she's ready and she wants me to talk about Doc and that whole mess. Tonight's lesson, class, is—assuming we live through this—to ask more questions. Man, I hate the sound of that. I just want to go back to the Chateau Marmont, order room service, get drunk together, and break all the furniture in the master bedroom. Is that too much to ask?

After the bike finally stalls a couple of times and the rain is coming down so hard I can't see more than five feet ahead of me, I turn back for Max Overdrive.

I'm putting on dry clothes when the phone rings. It's Julie.

"Have you found Candy?"

"Not yet, but we're following up on leads."

"Why did you call?"

"Wells wants you to come in. It's about Saint Nick."

"Stop calling him that. His name is Mason Faim."

"How do you know?"

"Because back when he was a person I killed him."

"You know a lot of dead people."

"What does Wells want?"

"Saint Nick, Mason Faim, whoever, won't talk to him. He wants to talk to you."

"I'll be right there."

I get a dry coat and a gun. I step through a shadow.

THEY HAVE MASON in a cell with walls thick enough to stop a meteor. They're covered from end to end, top to bottom, in a hasty scrawl of protective wards and crosses. It's like they let a gang of junior high taggers go at the cell with a copy of *The Little Wizard's Handbook of Scary-Looking Shit*.

Inside, Mason is seated at a metal table bolted to the floor. The walls are covered in binding hexes. Mason is cuffed hand and foot with cold iron shackles and dressed in orange coveralls. The zipper on the front of his jailbird suit is pulled down low enough that everyone can see the sutures holding his chop-shop body together. All that and his mismatched eyes make him look like a garage-sale-love-doll-at-Hammer Studios Frankenstein movie.

There are guards outside, but the room is empty. Julie follows me in. I pull up a chair and sit down across from Mason.

"Where's Candy?"

"It's good to see you too, Jimmy."

"Where's Candy?"

He shrugs.

"You're the one with the sweet tooth. I always preferred my snacks salty."

"Don't be cute. I can kill you before anyone here can stop me."

Mason leans on the table.

"You already did, remember? That's what I wanted to talk to you about. You cheated."

"I sure did."

"You told me not to use magic and then you went ahead and used it yourself."

"My game. My rules."

"That's exactly what I was going to say to you."

"I'm not playing games with you. I'm going to ask questions and you're going to answer them."

He leans back in his chair, looking relaxed.

"And what if I don't? You'll kill me? How did that work out last time? You ended up stuck in Hell playing Lucifer. Badly. Your lover left you. Heaven, Hell, and L.A. suffered all sorts of calamities. And through it all, the Angra grew stronger. No, killing me just made things worse for everybody. Besides, you think I can't find my way into a new body? You could fill a stadium with all the bodies my friends and I have created. And all I need is one. You can't win playing your old games, Jimmy."

"Where's Candy?"

"In the cut-glass bowl on Grandma's coffee table."

Before he or Julie can move, I lean across the table and punch him. He shakes it off and looks at me.

"In a caravan to Timbuktu."

I hit him again.

"On the Matterhorn ride at Disneyland."

I start to hit him again when I hear Julie.

"Stark! Stop it."

Mason spits blood on the floor.

"Tell you what, Jimbo. You like games. Play a game with me and I'll tell you everything I know about your squeeze."

"What kind of game?"

He turns to Julie.

"Do you have any playing cards around here?"

"We have a few games in the break room," she says. "I'll check."

"Hurry back, darling."

Mason turns back and raises an eyebrow at me. His chop-shop face is almost as scarred as mine.

"One of yours?" he says.

"You don't need to know anything about her. Or anyone else here. I'm the only one you need to worry about."

"How is it?"

"How's what?"

He opens his hands, rattling the shackles.

"The Qomrama. Having fun with it? Teaching it to do tricks. Fetch? Roll over."

"We're doing great with it. The Shonin practically has it sussed."

"The Shonin. I've heard about him."

"From who?"

"A little demon told me."

"Where's Candy?"

Mason looks down at the table. Purses his lips.

"Every time you say something stupid or break a rule you lose a turn."

"We aren't playing yet."

"Yes we are."

The door opens and Julie comes back into the room. She sets a deck of cards on the table between us.

"What happens now?"

"Shuffle them," Says Mason.

I shuffle them a couple of times. Set them back down between us.

Mason turns to Julie.

"Would you cut the cards for me, dear? I'm a bit encumbered."

Julie glances at me. She comes over and cuts the cards. I look at Mason.

"What are we playing?"

"In my time in the dark I learned that there's only one game worth playing and it takes many forms. One form is cards."

"What's the game?"

"Chaos. Entropy. Catastrophe. Infinity."

"I don't know how to play that."

He sits up straight, his eyes on the cards.

"It's your whole life, Jimmy. You're an expert. You just don't know it."

I look at the time on my phone and then at Julie.

"Shouldn't you be out looking for someone?"

"I have a team on it."

"Ready?" says Mason.

"What are we playing?"

"Simple draw poker. You can handle that, can't you?"

"You don't have anything to bet."

"We have the whole world to bet."

"If I win you'll tell me about Candy."

"Everything. Deal."

I deal out five cards, each facedown. I get two threes, a queen of diamonds, a ten of clubs, and an ace of hearts.

Mason nods at his cards to Julie.

"Would you hold my cards up for me, dear?"

"Don't call me that again. I'm Marshal Sola."

"Would you hold my cards for me, Marshal Sola?"

She does it.

"Higher, please."

She raises the cards a little.

"Thank you."

I set my cards down and pick up the deck.

"How many do you want?"

"Four," he says.

"What's wrong with you? That's how a six-year-old plays."

"I'd like four."

I deal him out four facedown. He points to the card he wants to keep. Julie lays down the others and picks up the new cards.

"Dealer takes two."

I get an ace of diamonds and a two of spades.

"We're not betting, so I guess we just show our cards."

"Yours first," says Mason.

I lay down two pairs, threes, and aces.

Julie puts down Mason's hand. He has a three, a six, a four, a ten, and a jack. None of the suits match.

Mason says, "Alphabet soup as dear old Dad used to say."

"I win. You answer my question."

"Of course."

"Where's Candy?"

"I honestly have no idea."

"Stark," says Julie, a warning tone in her voice. I don't get up and I don't try to hit Mason.

"You had something to do with her getting sick."

"Me? No. Possibly some of my associates."

"Why?"

Mason slams down his fists.

"Because fuck you, that's why. Because you cheated, and putting a bullet in my head really hurt. And because in the Infinite Game there are no rules and there are infinite rules. That's why it's so fun."

"If anything happens to her . . ."

"What? You'll kill me? Stop it. We both know if you were going to kill me you'd have done it already. No. You're still here because you want to play the game."

"Why would I want to do that?"

"Because unlike that gabby mummy no doubt listening to

us right now—hello, Mr. Shonin—I know exactly how the Qomrama works and I'll teach you. But you have to play my games and, of course, you have to win."

"The Vigil has all kinds of funny technology. I bet they have some kind of brain sucker around here. What's to keep them from hooking you up and downloading you into a Tamagotchi?"

Mason's face brightens.

"You have one of those? Neat. I'd love to see it."

"You didn't answer the question."

He drums his fingers on the table a couple of times.

"If the machine exists it wouldn't work on me for the same reason it wouldn't work on you. We wouldn't let it. Do you really think these Keystone Cops have anything that could hurt people like us? You ruled the Underworld. I escaped Tartarus. Their magic can't touch ours."

"You didn't escape Tartarus. Someone broke you out. Merihim and Deumos or some of their people."

"They cracked open the door but I'm the one who did the heavy lifting, like when you first made it out of Hell."

"So this is how we figure out the fate of the universe? Poker?"

"Of course not. That was nothing. That wasn't even the appetizer before dinner. It was just to see if I should invite you for a full meal."

"Should you?"

"Do you want to know how the Qomrama works?"

"The Shonin will figure it out."

"Not in time."

"How do I know you know anything?"

Mason closes his eyes. A minute later I hear the door to the cell open and the Shonin comes in.

"What did you do?" he says.

Mason laughs when he sees the Shonin.

"This is mankind's savior? You're like third prize at a backwoods Halloween fair."

The Shonin says, "What did you do?"

"I proved I know how the Qomrama works."

The Shonin starts to say something, but I hold up my hand and he quiets down.

I say, "What did he do?"

"The Qomrama opened the magnetic chamber and left it," the Shonin says. "It's floating in the center of the room, a ball of fire and ice. Boiling the room one minute and freezing it the next."

I look at Mason's beaming face. "Why should I believe you'll teach us anything?"

"You have my word," says Mason. "Every time you win a game I'll tell you something about the Qomrama. I want you to learn it. I want to see you use it. And I want to see you fail so that in the end, you'll know that I was always the better magician."

"If I said I'd play, how would it work?"

"Simple. I call the games and we play. Every time you win, I tell you a secret."

"And when you win?"

"I get to hurt you."

"What does that mean?"

"Anything I want."

"This is just between you and me. You can't hurt anybody else."

"I can do anything I like."

"Don't take the bait," says Julie. "He's crazy and he'll never tell you the truth."

"She's right. I'll continue my work," says the Shonin.

Mason looks at him.

"Do you know the Epistle of Saint Paul to the Romans?"

"I know many spiritual books."

"Chapter four, verse seven. Recite it."

The Shonin thinks for a minute.

" 'Blessed are they whose iniquities are forgiven: and whose sins are covered.' "

"Very good. Now, recite that backward in Hellion and you can make the Qomrama do the little trick I did a moment ago. You can also use it to return it to its original resting spot."

"That can't be all," says the Shonin. "A spell of that power would require meditation on a sacred object. A mandala or angelic sigil."

Mason holds up his hands from the table. Using the sharp edge on one of his cuffs, he's cut an inverted cross in a hex circle into his right palm.

I put my hand in my pocket around the Colt. Then let go and take my hand out. I turn to Julie.

"You have two hours to find Candy or I'm killing this guy, 8 Ball or no 8 Ball."

She checks her phone.

"I have a message. I'll see how the search is going."

She leaves and the Shonin goes to Mason's side of the table.

"You're been a very bad boy from what I hear."

Mason gives him a bland, condescending smile.

"I know that in your quaint foreign land what you did to yourself is considered a holy act, but here it would get you 5150'd. You're going to have to forgive me if I'm unimpressed with the elaborate way you chose to sublimate your masochistic tendencies."

The Shonin wags a finger at Mason.

"We had boys like you at the monastery. Big power. Little brains."

"You didn't have anyone like me. Tell him, Jimmy."

I don't say anything.

Mason's scarred face clouds over.

"Tell him."

I look at the Shonin.

"I doubt you ever had anyone like him."

"Or him," says Mason, pointing to me.

The Shonin throws up his hands.

"Fatty and Big Balls, a mutual admiration society. I'm going back to work."

As the Shonin heads for the door, Mason calls after him.

"Be careful with the Qomrama. If you get the recitation wrong she has a nasty bite."

The Shonin goes out, and before the door closes, Julie comes back in.

"We found her," she says.

I get up.

"Where is she?"

Julie puts up her hands.

"Wait. You need to know something. She's under arrest."

"For what?"

"She attacked a homeless man and almost killed him.

They're both lucky we have a serum that reverses the effects of Jade venom. The man will live."

"I want to see her."

"She's being processed. You can see her when she's done."

"No. Now."

Julie gets right in my face.

"Shut up and listen to me. I just did you a favor. Washington has classified Saint Nick's revived bodies as Lurkers, and under a new statute, any dangerous Lurker can be killed or detained indefinitely. My team had every legal right to kill a Jade attacking a civilian, but I gave them orders to bring her in. So you can fucking back off and wait until things cool down. And stop barking orders at me."

Julie turns and goes out, slamming the door behind her.

I want to follow her and make her take me to Candy, but if what she said about the new law is true? Then she really did do me and Candy a favor, and there aren't many people who would do that.

"You sure like the feisty ones, don't you," says Mason. "How's Alice these days? Heard from her recently? I hear that things aren't going too well in Heaven. I hope she's all right."

I knock on the door to be let out and head straight for an exit. Out in the parking lot I put my fist through the window on the side of a Vigil van.

Ow.

I forgot they use bulletproof glass. When I pull my hand back, I've peeled all the skin off my knuckles. I lean against the van, pull out a Malediction, and light it up. Out in the gloom across the drowning grass, a couple of Vigil cops play golf under a big umbrella.

I WAIT TWO goddamn hours, fidgeting and burning through the rest of the Maledictions. Outside, even the other smokers don't want to be around me and the tire-fire smell. My bloody knuckles don't help any chance of meaningful social interaction. I'm tempted to spook these dainty fucks by lighting my last smoke off the Gladius, but I'm in too foul a mood for that kind of fun.

I check the time on my phone. It's close to what should be dawn. A gust of wind blows rain all over us, sending the Vigil agents back inside. Most of the good boys and girls are off to bed, leaving just a skeleton crew. If I need to go *Wild Bunch* on them, this would be a good time. But for now, I'll wait and play by the rules like a good dog.

Around seven A.M., Julie comes outside.

"You can see her now," she says, and heads back into the clubhouse. I follow her down to the Alcatraz end of the place, passing Mason's cell on the way. I know he can't see me, but I have the feeling the fucker is watching me somehow. I need to find out more about how he got out of Tartarus. What's going on Downtown. And who I should snuff first, Merihim or Deumos.

Julie lets me into a small cellblock that holds a series of ordinary-looking jail cells. A sink. A cot bolted to the wall. Bars to keep the prisoners in, like any county lockup. All the cells are empty except for the one on the end. It's wrapped in strong Kevlar netting so that whoever is inside can't get their claws through it.

Candy has her back to me when I reach the cell. She paces back and forth like a caged animal. Her hair is in tangles. Some of her nails are broken off at the quick. When she turns to face me one of her cheeks is swollen, like she took a rifle butt to the face. She's mostly out of Jade mode. Mostly human-looking, but her eyes are still black, her pupils red pinpoints. I go up and grab a fistful of the net.

"You all right?"

She comes closer, but stops a few feet from the bars.

"I'm fine. Never better."

"You look like hell."

"Go peek in a mirror and then tell me how bad I look."

She starts to pace again.

"They say you tried to kill a civilian."

She puts a hand on her chest and opens her eyes all wide and innocent.

"I wasn't trying to kill anybody. I was just hungry."

I glance over to Julie. She has one hand resting gently on her gun.

I say, "This isn't your fault. Something went wrong with the potion. Allegra will figure it out and you'll be all right again."

Candy stops pacing and comes right up to the bars.

"Fuck Allegra. Fuck the potion. And fuck you. You want me to feel all right? I feel great. Like I'm myself for the first time in years."

"Like hell you do. Doc Kinski took you out of the killing life so something just like this wouldn't happen."

"Fuck Doc too."

That's new. I've never heard her talk that way about Kinski.

"You can't run around taking down random people and you know it."

She flicks the bars with one of her broken nails.

"Listen to you. All you do is kill, but no one else is allowed or you won't feel special anymore."

"I don't kill random civilians in the street."

"No. You kill other creeps no one cares about. I'll have to remember that for next time."

She smiles and tugs at the net. Julie comes closer to the cell, ready to pull her gun.

"You always did think you were better than me, didn't you?" says Candy. "I was your pet monster. Something you could take home and feed and fuck so you could show your friends the wild girl you tamed."

"If you really think that, why are we even talking?"

Candy goes over and sits on the cot.

"Go and rescue someone, hero. I don't need you condescending to me anymore."

She stretches out and rolls over so she's facing the wall. I wait a minute to see if she's going to say anything, wanting to say something else myself, but having no idea what.

"Come on," says Julie, and leads me to the jailhouse door.

Before we go out I turn around.

"You might have gone crazy, but I didn't. I'm going to figure a way out of this."

From the cell I hear, "Go away, please. Just go away."

Outside, Julie says, "She's been like that since we brought her in."

"Yeah." Then, "Sorry about yelling at you. Thanks for what you did for Candy."

"You're welcome. See how easy it is to be nice?"

"I'm always nice. It just comes out funny sometimes."

"Most of the time."

"I know."

Julie leads me to the break room. I spot Vidocq, nursing a cup of tea.

"What are you doing here?"

"Marshal Sola called me when Candy was arrested. She thought you might need someone to talk to."

"I need someone to punch."

His eyes go to my knuckles.

"It looks like you already found that."

I look at my hand. The bleeding has stopped and a scab is forming. Still, it's pretty ugly to look at. I pull a paper towel off the roll and wrap it around my hand.

"I've never seen her like this before, and I've seen her turn Jade plenty of times."

"You've never seen it because she's never been this way before. She's been poisoned."

I sit down across from him.

"Keep talking."

"I tested the rest of the Jade potion Allegra had on hand. Not only has it been watered down, but there's a toxin in it I can't identify. I'm sure it's responsible for her behavior."

"Now all we have to do is convince the Vigil and the entire federal government that a murderous Jade didn't mean it and is really sorry."

"It's a problem, I admit."

I go over to the counter and pour myself some coffee. I want Aqua Regia, but this isn't the time for a fuzzy head.

"If you make more of the real Jade potion, will the Vigil let you give it to her?"

He shrugs. Sips his tea.

"I have no idea, but giving it to her now would probably be pointless. Whatever she was given was meant to hurt her, not kill her. We need to wait until it clears her system before giving her anything else."

I swallow some coffee. It's some kind of sweet caramel blend that's been burning all night, so it tastes like a candy bar someone left on an engine block. I push the cup out of the way.

"I can see someone poisoning me, but why her?"

"A distraction perhaps? You're working on very important matters. There are people allied with the Angra who would love to see you not in a proper state of mind."

"Between Mason and Candy, I guess they pretty much succeeded."

Vidocq leans forward and whispers.

"Then it's true? Saint Nick is Mason Faim?"

I nod.

"Don't go telling anyone. I want to keep this quiet as long as I can."

"I can understand why he would want to leave Tartarus, but why come back here?"

"That's what I want to know. It's sure as hell not to teach me the ABC's of the 8 Ball."

"Curiouser and curiouser," says Vidocq.

"Yeah, that."

I look around to see if there's any normal coffee. I can't find any.

"You know, if it comes down to it, I could walk Candy out of here through a shadow."

"It's pointless to think like that. Right now she needs rest and medication more than she needs you."

"She said something like that too, only louder."

"Go home," says Vidocq. "You must be exhausted. Waiting here like this benefits no one."

I rub a knot of muscles at the base of my neck.

"Maybe you're right. I need to talk to Mason again later and I want a clear head for that."

"I'll stay here. If anything changes, I'll call you."

"Thanks," I say. Then, "How's Allegra doing with all this?"

"Not well. She feels responsible for both the poisoned potion and Candy's escape."

"I still think there's an Angra mole in the Vigil. Could there be one at the clinic?"

"The only people who work there regularly are Allegra, Fairuza, Rinko, and sometimes Candy. But patients go in and out all day. I suppose one of them could have done it."

"We're not going to figure anything out tonight. I'm getting out of here."

"Rest easy, my friend."

"Next lifetime."

Later, when I'm asleep, I don't dream about Candy. I dream about the Angra. I'm back in the cavern, but it's not like the last time. Ten Thousand Shadows doesn't talk to me. I just see the meat chapel and hear something faint and faraway, like noise from an old sitcom. The sound of someone laughing at me.

I'M TEMPTED TO go and see Mason early in the day, but I want him to stew for a while, so I stay in bed and don't go in until nearly two. Kasabian has his door propped up over the entrance to his rooms. He's built a little barricade around it with boxes of discs. A nine-year-old could get through it, but I guess it makes him feel better, so I don't say anything.

I step through a shadow and come out in Vigil headquarters and head straight for Mason's cell.

This time, before letting me in, a guard goes over me with a metal detector. It must be some special Vigil tech because not only do they find the Colt, but they spot the black bone blade. I don't want to waste time arguing, so I hand over my weapons. It's not like I can't snap Mason's neck with my hands, but it feels weird. I've hardly been without a weapon for going on twelve years. I feel a tad underdressed. Heading inside to see Mason, I'm feeling already a little fucked with.

He's at the table again. This time he's cuffed, but his hands aren't bolted down. People know I'm here to play games with the psycho.

I look back at the door and see Wells watching us. No pressure, kids.

Mason smiles at me, but doesn't speak. I pull up a chair and sit down across from him.

"What's the game today? Old Maid? Crazy Eights?"

"It's still the Infinite Game. If you keep thinking we're playing different games, you're going to lose."

"You never said where you learned the Infinite Game."

He looks away, like he's thinking.

"You'd be surprised what you hear when you're alone long enough in Tartarus. I knew I was going to be rescued before it happened because they told me."

"The Angra?"

"Yes."

"I don't believe you."

"Someone in Hell sent them to me because they knew I could help their cause."

"Stop. I can't deal with your bullshit without a drink. What's today's game?"

"Billy Flinch."

Billy Flinch is a favorite game among the highly intoxicated and the clinically insane. It's William Tell, only you play it by yourself. Take potshots at the far wall and try to ricochet a bullet so that it breaks the glass on your head. Most people only play Billy Flinch once. It doesn't have an Old-Timers League.

"They took away my gun, so forget it."

"That's disappointing," he says.

As hard as Mason is to read, this time his pupils constrict a millimeter or two, so I know he's lying. He wants to play something else.

Two upside-down plastic cups sit on his side of the table. He pushes them into the middle and lifts them. A couple of scorpions make a break for it, but he corrals them back under the cups, laughing as he does it.

I look at him.

"Where the hell did you get scorpions?"

"What's the scarier answer? That I had them all along or that someone snuck them in to me?"

Neither one's a comfort, but this is Mason. Nothing about him is comfortable.

"What are we playing?"

"Lady Sonqah's Wedding Night. Have you heard of it? The Luderes can't get enough of it."

"I've seen them playing at Bamboo House of Dolls. I don't know how it works."

"Give me your hand."

I put out my right hand. Mason bites off part of the scab over the sigil he cut into his hand yesterday. He squeezes his palm so that a few drops of blood fall onto my fingers.

"I'm glad this isn't our first date," I say. "What's the blood for?"

"It excites the scorpions."

"There's still time to switch to Candy Land. I'll even let you go first."

"Maybe next time."

Mason doesn't wipe the blood off his own hand, so if the game is what he says it is, at least so far he's playing fair.

He lifts one of the cups, but before the scorpion can run out, he recites some hoodoo and it freezes in place.

"As you see, I've tied a slip of paper to this scorpion's tail. The other one has a similar note. Your job is to get the note off your scorpion without getting stung. Each time you're stung you get a point. At the end, we add up the points. Low score wins."

Mason snaps his fingers, releasing the scorpion from the hex. He puts the cup down over the bug and pushes it to my side of the table. I tap the cup with my finger, listening to the scorpion scrabble around inside.

"What if I just squash the damned thing and take the note when it's dead?"

"That's an automatic loss and I get to hurt you."

"Who poisoned Candy?"

"Shouldn't you be asking about the Angra instead of trying to fix your love life?"

When I don't make to pick up the cup, Mason reaches across the table and raises it.

"You might want to concentrate on the game."

The scorpion sits there for a minute, looking as pissed as I feel.

"You made her crazy and almost got some poor street slob killed for nothing."

"I got a lot more than nothing out of it. I got you to play with me. Just like old times. Your little friend is moving. Play or forfeit."

Now that the scorpion has decided to move, it's all over the place. Darting in one direction, then another. I try to follow it, but it never goes in a straight line for very long. Finally, I catch the rhythm of its turns. Get my hand hovering right over its stinger. I'm fast when I want to be. I snap my hand down to the bug, then back again before it can sting me. But I miss the paper. I do it again. And miss again. The third time I come really close, but still miss.

I see the problem. While I'm fast enough to outrun the scorpion, if I go full speed I'm going too fast to grab the paper. The trick is to slow down. Feel the bug's rhythm and move in at just the right moment.

Which is exactly what I don't do. The fucker stings me on my first try. I always heard that scorpion stings feel like bee stings. Whoever said that never met this particular scorpion because this thing stings like a hornet with a blowtorch.

I pull back my hand and try to shake some of the pain out of my fingers.

"Will Candy recover?"

"Jades are sturdy beasts," says Mason. "I'm sure she'll be fine."

I go for another try. And get stung again. I slow my breathing. I'm rushing things. Mason didn't say anything about a time limit on the game. I'm going to follow the scorpion and wait for just the right moment.

"Still, attempted murder," he says. "That's the kind of thing that sticks to a person. Even if the Vigil ever releases her, which they won't, there won't be many places she'll be able to show her face in L.A."

I get stung again.

"Maybe you two can get a little cabin in the woods. Take up a trade. Pig farming. She can cook biscuits and you can learn to whittle."

Okay. I admit it. My concentration really is shot. I'm worried about Candy and so fucking mad at having to be here I want to get my knife and take out Mason's tongue and feed it to him.

I get stung three more times before I get the goddamned paper off the goddamn bug and corral the thing back under its cup. Welts are coming up all over my fingers. Mason didn't say it, but I have a feeling that healing hoodoo is against the rules, and I'm not about to ask and admit that his little pincered fucker hurt me.

I think when I cut off Mason's head I'll put it in a bowling bag and drop him back in Tartarus. Maybe collapse the joint on top of him so no one will ever find him. Let him talk to ghosts all he wants down there.

"So, who poisoned her?"

"Now it's my turn," Mason says.

With his cuffed hands, he knocks over his cup and lets his scorpion loose. Like mine, it looks confused and after a few seconds starts running randomly across the table.

He waits, tracking the scorpion's moves, trying to figure out the best moment to strike. He takes his sweet fucking time about it.

"Before Christmas, please."

When he moves, it's fast. He pins the scorpion's tail with the cuffs, and before it can rear back and get him with its pincers, he grabs the paper. Then slams the cup down on top of it.

"What the fuck, man? You cheated."

He sets the paper down between us.

"What was it you said when I complained about you putting a bullet in my head? My game. My rules."

"We're even now, asshole."

"Not even close."

He reaches for his paper, but I put my hand over it.

"Before we count up the points, tell me this. Whose skull is that in the cavern?"

"Mine, of course."

"I burned your body after I chucked your soul into Tartarus, so unless there's a rewind button on your bones, that skull isn't yours."

I lift up my hand and he slides the paper back to his side of the table.

"It's metaphorically mine. Putting it there was just a bit of fun. Give you a clue as to who Saint Nick might be."

"It's fucking hysterical. Who did you shoot in the head to make your joke?"

"No one. The skull is sugar, like one of those Día de los Muertos candy skulls. *Der Zorn Götter* had some local artisan make it and then put it in that lovely reliquary."

"Just to fuck with us?"

"Just to fuck with you."

"And to make you out as a saint."

He moves his hands in the sign of the cross.

"Santa Muerte."

"You're having such a good time."

"I am. Shall we add up the scores?"

I hold up my brutalized hands.

"Why bother? You didn't get stung once. You've already won."

"Not necessarily. A black dot on the paper is an automatic loss. Who knows what I drew?"

Mason opens his paper. Printed on it is the number ten.

"See? Ten points," he says. "You were only stung, what, six times? You're in the lead."

I unfold my paper. It's a black dot. Mason tsks.

"You lost even before the first sting. What a shame."

"Fuck you."

I can feel my pulse in my swollen fingers.

Mason says, "We're just about done for today. You don't get any information. Ready for your spanking?"

"You already got me half stung to death. You going to set my hair on fire too?"

"Don't give me ideas. Here's what you get for losing: the poison Candy drank has a side effect. Like liquor, it's a disinhibitor, meaning people will say and do things on it they wouldn't normally do when they're in control. You understand what I'm getting at?"

I lean back and cross my arms.

"You mean that whatever Candy says through the poison is the truth. I don't believe you."

"I don't have to lie. You talked to her. Did she seem woozy or drugged? You know I'm not lying. Like your hand, it stings, doesn't it?"

"Let's play another game."

"When you win you can decide when we play, but you lost, so go away until tomorrow."

I slam my fist down on the table hard enough that I knock over the cups. They're empty. The scorpions are gone.

"There's no time to fuck around like this."

Mason stacks one cup inside the other and pushes them to the side of the table.

"Fucking around is part of the game, or haven't you figured that out by now?"

"Who poisoned Candy's medicine?"

"You're being boring, James. Keep it up and I'll hurt you again. Do it twice and there won't be any game at all tomorrow."

Were the scorpions phantoms? A hoodoo hallucination? I look at my hand. Whatever just happened in here, my fingers really are swollen and they really hurt. I go over and knock on the cell door. It opens and a guard lets me out.

"Where's my gear?" I say.

He hands me the Colt and my knife.

"I unloaded the pistol. It's an unauthorized weapon. Rules."

I put it in the waistband at my back and put the blade in my coat.

"I want to see Candy."

"I'm not authorized to let anybody into those cells."

I look at him. His heartbeat goes up. I'm tempted to lean on him. Or I can go into the cellblock through a shadow. But they'll have surveillance in there. If I go breaking the rules it could mean they'll move Candy somewhere I can't find her. I could try taking her out of here, but with the mood she's in, who knows if she'd go with me?

Wells comes out of an office and walks over to me. He's the last person I want to talk to.

I say, "Where did you go?"

"I had to deal with a phone call from Washington. How did it go in there?"

I hold up my swollen hand.

"We played. I lost. He didn't tell me a goddamn thing."

"Language. What happened to your hand?"

"Scorpions. I think. You might want to be careful who deals with Mason. He had two of them. Or maybe I just imagined it."

"What does that mean?"

"It means I lost and I have to come back and do this all again tomorrow."

"Didn't he tell you anything?"

"Yeah."

"What?"

"It's good to be king."

I go straight home. In the end, it doesn't matter if those scorpions were real or not. I just had my ass handed to me on a silver platter. A wasted day means I brought the Angra one step closer to Earth. I look out the window. I swear the rain is coming down harder than ever.

I TRY SOME healing hoodoo from the arena days, but I've always been better at breaking things than fixing them, so my improvised spells don't work. Between the swelling from the scorpion and the last ragged remains of the scab from where I punched out the van window, my hand looks like I stuck it in a wood chipper and set it on frappé. I go downstairs to see if Kasabian has any aspirin.

He and Fairuza are sitting on some of the boxes outside his room, sipping beers. She sets hers down when she sees me.

"How's Candy?"

I shake my head.

"Everything's fucked. Candy's crazy and I'm playing Chinese checkers with a psycho. Oh, Kas, you'll be amused to know. Mason Faim is back from Hell."

His beer goes down the wrong way. He coughs and it takes him a minute to catch his breath.

"Mason? I thought you buried him under the floorboards."

"He's a roach. He got out."

Kasabian gets up and starts for his room.

"Bye."

"Who's Mason Faim?" says Fairuza.

"I'll tell you about him from my fallout shelter."

"Calm down," I say.

Kasabian points his beer at me.

"I've got some good news for you too. Someone just took a potshot at one of the God brothers."

"Muninn?"

"No. One of the others. I can't remember which is which."

"Is he alive?"

"The rain's messed up all kinds of stuff down there. I can't see everything."

"I might have to go Downtown. Maybe Muninn will have some ideas on dealing with Mason."

Kasabian disappears into his room.

"Good luck with that. If you don't see me for a while, I'll be in here having a stroke."

"You could come to my place," says Fairuza.

I shake my head.

"No, he can't. And don't let anyone know you're hanging around with Prince Valiant over there. If Mason finds out, he might send someone after you."

"Who the hell is Mason Faim?" says Fairuza.

"You know all that stuff I told you about Stark?" says Kasabian. "Mason is worse. One time when he was still in school he used magic to blow the top off a mountain in Thailand, all to get back at a magic man that did him wrong. He killed a whole village. All the men, women, and kiddies and didn't blink an eye. That's who Mason is. And on a personal note, Mason is the guy who killed me."

"I thought Stark cut your head off."

"Yeah, but that was just my head. He didn't, like, kill me. That was Mason."

Fairuza picks up her bag and gets her raincoat off the peg by the door.

"I'm sorry. I'm leaving."

"No. Wait," says Kasabian.

She holds up a silencing finger.

"Listen. I could maybe deal with the robot thing, but more crazy killers from Hell? Forget it. Sorry, Kas. I'll see you around."

She goes out into the rain. The wind slams the door behind her.

"You happy?" says Kasabian. "Fairuza was as close to a love life as I was ever going to have."

"Relax. She's just freaked out. Give her some time to calm down."

"You just told her not to have anything to do with me."

"Until things settle down. Then go and bring her flowers and chocolates or drumsticks and scorpions, whatever it is she'd like. It'll work itself out."

"Nothing's going to work itself out as long as Mason is back. And what the hell happened to your hand?"

"Nothing. It's just a paper cut."

"Mason did it. Oh shit. How fucked are we?"

"Get a grip. The Vigil has him. He can't pull any heavy hoodoo in a prison protected by angelic tech."

"I hope you're right."

I don't tell him about the scorpions disappearing. I don't want to think about it myself.

Kasabian says, "Not to sound selfish or anything, but do you think he's going to come after me?"

"Probably. But he has a pretty busy schedule fucking with me right now, so I wouldn't worry about it."

"Okay. Thanks. Sorry."

"Don't worry about it."

"I'm going to go inside and lie in a fetal position for a while. Call me if the world doesn't end."

"You're top of the list."

He goes into his room, pulling the boxes back into place, leaning the door against them. It's a sad, small gesture, but I understand it. I'd like to hibernate for a few years myself, but I'm stuck in the middle of this thing. I need to see Mr. Muninn, but Hell is the last place I want to go right now.

ONCE AGAIN I have to ask myself, Do I just show up at the worst time at the worst places or am I a shit magnet dragging all this horror down on everyone? Once again, I have no answer.

I used to curse God for deserting me when I was in Hell, and, oh yeah, deserting the world the rest of the time. Now I know him and, okay, I might have a little sympathy for his situation. But what does that get me? Me or anyone else? We're still stuck in this second-rate carnival where the rides that don't rip off a limb will sure as shit kill you. I'm not saying that the Angra would have built a better Earth or smarter or kinder people, but if Muninn and his brothers hadn't butted in, maybe things would at least make sense. Like teeth. Whose idea was it to stick us with little porcelain mouth bones that chip, rot, and fall out? That's not intelligent design. That's your-boss's-dumb-ass-nephew-intern-smoking-a-bowl-the-Friday-before-spring-break design. And there's aneurysms, shopping malls, lawn furniture, cancer, Mickey Mouse, clinical depression, jellyfish, the Vigil, the Kissi, ambitious Hellions, all angels, and tofu.

Could the Angra have done worse? Yes, technically. They could have. But would they? We'll never know because a grabby little shitbird shanghaied the entire damned universe. We get to live with all of his mistakes. Hell, we *are* his mistakes. The idiot dropped a glass sphere full of divine light on one of his half-formed worlds and life just sort of happened. We're not God's stepchildren. We're the cigarette burns in the living room carpet.

And with all that, I'm inclined to cut the fucker some slack because he knows exactly how badly he's fucked up. We've got that much in common. He thought he locked out the Angra and I thought I buried Mason. Maybe Muninn and I can go halfsies on a few sessions with a life coach. Learn to set goals. Visualize our success. Take over a Denny's franchise in Fresno. Cash in on the hungry truckers. Easy money and no one gets hurt.

Who am I kidding? A month of that and I'd burn down the place for the insurance money. Hit the road with Candy and not look back. Like Doc and Carol McCoy in a cartoon version of *The Getaway.*

Only that's not going to happen. And the Angra aren't coming back to fix things. And the God brothers aren't going to square anything with them or us. We'll be lucky if we get out of this with any skin left, because whether it's Muninn or Ruach or Zhuyigdanatha or Lamia, we don't count. No matter which God is in charge, we're bugs on his windshield. Always were. Always will be. Amen.

I step through a shadow and come out in Hell.

I don't want to come out in Mr. Muninn's room after tracking the place up last time, so I step out into the palace lobby. The blood rain pounds down on the windows, as heavy as ever.

The first thing I want to know is if he and his brothers are all right. The second thing I want to know is how to deal with Mason. I get part of the answer to my first question without moving an inch.

There's blood everywhere, and not the kind tracked in from outside.

The lobby is cordoned off with iron grates, like cop crime-scene tape.

In the center of the lobby is a dried patch of rust-colored blood maybe four feet across. Crimson streaks around it from where his attackers stepped in his blood. I can picture the scene. Roman-style mayhem. A bunch of Hellions taking down a Caesar. They surround him from all sides when he comes into the lobby. The sap is one of the God brothers, which makes him Lucifer's kin. Unreachable. Untouchable. Only he's not. How many Hellions with knives would you need to take down a piece of God? A lot, from the look of things. Dotted round the lobby are ten, maybe fifteen explosions of black Hellion blood and gristle like shotgun Rorschach blots. Whoever killed him is as dead as he is.

I go to the elevator and touch the brass plate. Nothing happens. I'm not Lucifer anymore. Why should it? I take out the black blade and slip it under the edge of the plate. Feel around inside for contacts or hamsters in a cage. Something that runs the lift. After a few seconds I see a spark and hear something sizzle. The elevator door slides open and I get inside. I do the same trick to the brass plate inside the car and up we go to the penthouse.

I'm twitchy with that hyper adrenaline feeling like right before a fight or when you see the surgeon coming out of the operating room frowning. My fingers tingle and I want to hit something to calm down, but after seeing those exploded bodies in the lobby, I curb that quick. Still, I don't know who or what is waiting for me upstairs, so I slip the na'at out of my coat and get it ready to spring open.

When the car reaches the penthouse, the door slides open. I listen and sniff the air for a second before stepping into the room.

"Mr. Muninn?"

When no one answers I say it again.

Footsteps click down the hall, coming my way. Then nothing. Silence for maybe thirty seconds.

"Are you going to hide in the elevator all night or are you going to come have a drink with me and Father?"

It's Samael. At least his voice. I step out of the elevator with the na'at held high. Move around the corner until I can see the whole living room.

Samael is there. His suit isn't quite as sharp as usual. His smile is faint and gone in a second, like he was as uncertain about me as I was about him. I put the na'at back in my coat. There are stains on his shirt and trouser cuffs. Black blood.

"Come to comfort the bereaved? What a softie you've become. Everyone is in the library."

Samael starts down the hall.

"Which brother was it?"

He doesn't turn around.

"Nefesh."

I follow him down the hall.

This stinks. I'm the one who wanted Nefesh to come down to Hell in the first place. I told him he'd be safe here with Muninn. We met when he was hiding in a Roman bath at the bottom of the Kill City mall. Who knows how long he'd been there, hiding in noncorporeal form? Pretending he was nothing more than a mad old ghost. Then I came along with some friends and got him to tell us where Aelita had hidden the 8 Ball. I told him to give up the ghost game. Grow a pair and head Downtown for some face time with his brother and, most of all, safety. Things were bad enough back then that a piece of God took advice from me. Things must be even worse now if all it took were a few legionnaires to bring him down.

I follow Samael into Lucifer's enormous library. Muninn is sitting on one end of a long velvet couch I used to sleep on. At the other end of the couch is his twin, only instead of being black like Muninn, he's blue. Everything. Clothes. Skin. Hair. The works.

"James," says Muninn. "What a nice, if ill-timed, surprise. Let me introduce my brother Chaya."

It's Muninn's house, so I want to be polite. I put out my hand. Chaya doesn't move. In the arena, I had Hellions, beasts, and other lost souls look at me with hate in their eyes, but none of them comes close to Blue Boy. I pull back my hand.

"So this is him," says Chaya. "The monster who kills monsters."

"Be nice, Chaya," says Muninn. "James is a guest."

"I don't remember inviting him. And I know it wasn't you. Was it you, Samael?"

"No, Father," he says.

Chaya looks at me.

"That's not a guest. That's an interloper."

"James knew Nefesh," Samael says. "Perhaps he's here to pay his respects."

"Yes. That," I say. But no one is buying it. "Okay. Truth is, I didn't know which one of you it was that got hurt—"

"Killed," says Chaya.

"Right. Killed. I wanted to check in and see what the situation is."

Chaya says, "He wanted to know if we're all right. What a sweet murderer you are."

"Truth is, I was really checking on these other two. You I don't know from a hellhound's asshole."

Chaya's face turns kind of a dark fucked-up purple, which I guess is him turning red.

"Listen to him, Muninn. You let a mortal speak to you like that?"

"In case you haven't noticed," I say, "I'm not exactly a mortal."

"No. You're Abomination. Why didn't we kill you as an infant?"

"Maybe because you spent a billion years trying to find your ass with two hands and a sextant? I mean, you can't even keep your own angels in line. What chance did you have of finding one little kid?"

Chaya doesn't say a word and I'm pretty sure he's working up to a good smiting when Samael tugs on my arm.

"Why don't you take James to the kitchen," says Muninn. "I'll be along in a few minutes."

Samael heads out of the library, dragging me by the arm like a dog that just shit on the *Pietà*.

I half expect him to chew me out, when he lets go of my arm and says, "Thank you. I couldn't take one more minute of that old maid's squawking. He hasn't shut up since he got here."

"Sure. It was all part of my plan."

"Of course it was."

In the kitchen, Samael finds an open bottle of wine and pours us both a drink. He raises his glass in a brief toast and downs it. I sniff mine. Hellion wine. If Aqua Regia is battery acid, the local Cabernet tastes like the runoff at a Hellion slaughterhouse. I take a polite sip, but that's as far as I'm willing to go.

"Having three fathers here was bad enough," Samael says. "Then one gets killed and it's the wrong one."

"Sorry."

Samael pours himself another drink.

"At least you're here to be Chaya's punching bag for a while. Ever since he got here he's been going at me the way he went after you tonight. He'll never forgive me for rebelling."

"Fathers can be like that."

"I seem to remember you having some kind of father drama."

"Yeah. He tried to kill me. Good thing he was a lousy shot."

Samael sits down at the kitchen counter.

"I remember. And he still got into Heaven. That's got to sting. Now imagine having to sit next to him while he lists off all your faults for everyone to hear over and over and over for eternity. That's my life."

"I guess we both got lucky escaping to Hell."

"As you can see, even Hell isn't an escape anymore."

Samael shakes his head, gets up, and prowls the kitchen looking for more wine. I swirl mine in my glass like I'm contemplating its enticing bouquet. The reek just about makes my eyes water.

"So, what happened to Nefesh?"

"Exactly what it looks like. He was approached by what he thought were loyal soldiers. But they were part of Merihim and Deumos's suicide cabal. They were all over him. He didn't stand a chance."

"I don't understand. Aelita needed the 8 Ball when she killed the first brother, Neshamah. How could a bunch of grunts kill Nefesh with a few knives?"

"Ah," says Samael, taking down a bottle from the top shelf of a cupboard. He brings it to the table and takes a corkscrew from a drawer. When he gets the cork out of the bottle and pours himself a glass, he looks at me.

"The longer my fathers are separate entities, the weaker they get. No one can know, but Nefesh's death proves that you don't need—what's the Angra name for the Qomrama?"

"Godeater."

"Yes. You don't need the Godeater to kill a God anymore."

"All the blood and body parts in the lobby. Was that you?"

He takes a sip of wine and shakes his head.

"That was all Muninn. The only other time I've seen him like that was when he knocked me out of Heaven with a thunderbolt. He blew those traitors to bits with a wave of his hand. Good for you, Father."

He clinks his glass against mine and I have to sip more of the Hellion swill.

"Good for which one of us and for what?" says Muninn, coming into the room. He sees the open bottle of wine and gets himself a glass. Samael fills it for him.

"Your righteous wrath," says Samael.

"Oh. You mean the lobby. It was certainly wrathful, and I don't apologize for it. But I'm not so sure about righteous."

"Righteous enough," says Samael. "Those pissants got exactly what they deserved."

"Perhaps. I don't really want to talk about it."

"I'm sorry about your brother," I say.

"Which one?" says Muninn. "The one who died or the one who lived? They're each a different problem."

"Both?"

"Good boy," says Samael.

"My secret shame is that I would have preferred that Nefesh be the one who lived. Sometimes I think I'm no better than Ruach."

"You didn't look to kill either of your brothers," I say. "I'd say that puts you ahead of Ruach in the asshole department."

"Thank you," says Muninn.

"Samael told me that the longer you're in pieces, the weaker you become. What happens when parts of you start dying?"

"Exactly what happens to any organism when it loses limb after limb. I get weaker faster."

"That means Ruach is getting weaker too."

"Yes, but not so much that Chaya and I can take Heaven from him, if that's what you mean."

"I'm surprised Chaya can feed himself," says Samael.

"Enough of that," says Muninn.

He looks at me.

"Now you know the sorry situation down here. And as much as I appreciate you stopping by to check on us, I think Chaya and I need to be alone for a while to mourn our brother."

"I understand. But I need to ask you something before I go."

"What's that?"

"Don't ask me how, but Mason Faim is back on Earth. He has information I need to operate the 8 Ball, but to get it I have to play something he calls the Infinite Game."

Muninn puts his hands flat on the counter.

"Mason Faim," he says. "I hoped I'd never hear that name again."

He takes a long breath.

"I'll tell you right now that you have no chance of winning that game against someone like Mason Faim."

"Can't you teach me?"

"The Infinite Game is like its name. Infinite. It has no boundaries. The rules are impossible to explain and harder to learn. It's life, with all its complexities and contradictions. It takes longer than a human life-span to become proficient at it. If Mason has become adept at it in the few months he was in Tartarus, he had help."

"Deumos or Merihim or one of their Angra toadies," says Samael.

"Where did they learn it?"

"If they're in contact with the Angra they could have learned from them."

"If I killed both of them, would this thing be over?"

Muninn shakes his head.

"I wish it were that simple. But I can't say I'd object to seeing them gone."

Chaya stops by the kitchen door and looks us over.

"What's this thing still doing here? I thought you were sending him back to wherever it is he wallows."

"I wallow in L.A. And yeah, it can smell funny on a hot day, but at least it's not raining fucking blood."

"This is what happens when you don't discipline earthly trash regularly. That was supposed to be your job. Wasn't it, Muninn? But you hid in your cave, playing with your toys while mortal vermin ran wild over the world."

"Calm down," says Muninn.

"I won't. Nefesh is dead because of you. You doted on humans and coddled an Abomination. Nefesh is dead and Ruach will finish us all."

Muninn gets up. I've seen this kind of family square dance before. One parent tries to talk the other one down and it just makes the batshit one even crazier.

Muninn says, "Let's talk this over in private."

"Look at you. Taking this monster's side over your own brother's. Maybe I should have stayed with Ruach. Maybe I should go back. He'd gladly accept me as an ally against you, the family traitor."

Light flares up in the room. I have to cover my eyes, and when I take my hand away, Samael is standing in front of Chaya with his Gladius blazing.

"Do you recognize this, old man?" he says. "It almost laid you low once. You're not half the power you were in the old days. Should we test that with a rematch?"

"Samael," says Muninn. "Stop it."

Samael keeps the Gladius blazing for a few seconds before letting it go out. Chaya leaves without saying a word.

"You should go and apologize," says Muninn.

"Among the many things I should do, that's at the bottom of the list."

Muninn runs a hand through his hair.

"The two of you are making me old faster than Ruach and Chaya combined."

"Listen," I say. "I'm sorry to stomp into the middle of this Hatfields and McCoys thing you have going with yourself, but you were saying something about how I could play the game with Mason."

Muninn looks at me like he doesn't know what I'm talking about. I can't tell if he's distracted by the fight or getting slow as he gets weak. Then his eyes focus and he nods.

"You can't beat Mason, but maybe you can play him to a draw. Win a few small victories here and there. With that, you might get enough information that you won't need it all. Bring me whatever you find and we'll see what we can do with it."

"And how am I supposed to win these small victories?"

"Don't fight him. Play with him, not at him. When you don't understand what's happening—"

"That's all the time."

"Mimic him. Move the way he does. Move for move, if you like. He'll catch on but he won't be able to stop you because to get you to play badly he'll have to play badly himself and risk losing."

"That's not exactly the plans for D-Day."

Muninn looks at the kitchen door like he's expecting Chaya to come back and apologize.

"I'm sorry," he says. "As you can see, there are a few things going on here too. I've given you all I can for now."

"Thanks. It's more than I had when I got here."

"Now I really think it would be a good idea if you left. I'm going to see if I can calm Chaya down."

"I'll see you around, Mr. Muninn. Sorry again about Nefesh."

He walks out like he didn't even hear me.

"Let him go," says Samael. "Neither one of us can help him fight himself. I hate all this talk about brothers. It just covers up the fact that Father is slowly killing himself."

"You think he's going to make it?"

"I don't know. I just hope that a piece survives and that it's not Chaya."

"Maybe I should get out of here before he changes his mind and reincarnates me as a tapeworm or something."

"Don't be so glum."

"What should I be? Candy's in jail. Muninn is coming apart. The Shonin is poisoning himself. Wells is busy corralling chop-shop corpses. And Mason has me thumb-wrestling scorpions. In case you haven't noticed, I'm losing. We're all losing. Muninn and you and all the good little angels in Hell and Heaven."

"Take a walk with me," says Samael. "You haven't seen much of the palace since you gave up the throne. The hellhounds miss you."

He goes to the elevator and I follow him.

"I think I could use some hellhounds in L.A. before all this is over."

The elevator doors open and we get in. He touches the brass plate and we start down.

"Take a few," Samael says. "Take them all. You taught them to love you. They'll follow you anywhere."

The elevator shudders to a halt underground. The door opens to the unmistakable machine-lube-and-raw-meat smell of the kennels. But there's a faint trace of something else too.

Hellhounds are clockwork dire-wolf-size war dogs, run by a brain suspended in a glass globe where their heads should be. They're smart and deadly and, like all dogs, loyal to their master, which they still think is me. I roofied them a few months back when some of Hell's legions were seriously contemplating my demise. The addled dogs imprinted on me and even those hard-core Hellion soldiers backed off when I strolled out of the palace surrounded by my mechanical hounds. It looks like the imprinting stayed strong. When the hounds smell me they move to the front of their cages and press their heads to the bars so I can pet them as we walk past.

Samael would never admit it, but I know he's eating his heart out seeing his hounds so loyal to me. It's his fault for leaving me in Hell on my own way back when. How long ago was it? Just a few months. This year, ever since I escaped from Hell, time has been like a carnival midway. Loud, twisting, and confusing. Full of dead ends and dark, empty places. I look at Samael for a second. Does he know what I'm thinking? Maybe. Not much I can do about it, off kilter like this. Anyway, pride isn't the issue here. But I don't think it's hounds either.

"What are we doing here? It's nice to see the pups, but I don't have time to skip down memory lane."

Samael says, "Of course you do. It just depends on what you're skipping to."

He leads me around a corner of the kennel to where a man is shackled to the floor. The slave collar around his neck is attached to chains with links as large as a man's arm. They're so heavy, the man is slumped on the floor. Samael walks over and kicks him in the ass. The man's head jerks up like maybe he was asleep.

"Up, pest. You have company."

The man slowly rises to his feet, the heavy chains clanging against each other. He staggers a bit when he's up, trying to get his balance. His clothes are shredded and he's filthy, but I'd never forget that face. It's Merihim.

"How did you find him?"

Samael takes a Malediction from a silver case and offers me one. I take it. I get out Mason's lighter and spark our cigarettes.

"I'm the bad angel, remember? I hurt people until someone told me where he was," Samael replies.

"Welcome back, Lord Lucifer," says Merihim.

I get closer and blow smoke in his face.

"You know, I didn't like the 'Lord' thing when I was Lucifer, but now it's growing on me. How's destroying the universe going? It looks like you started with your clothes."

He closes his eyes for a long few seconds, then opens them again.

"I thought you were better than this one," says Merihim, glancing at Samael. "But you're just alike. Naughty children. You once mistook your mischief for rebellion. Now you mistake it for bravery. Stand with this fool and you're going to die, Stark. The longer you fight us, the worse your death will be."

"Let's have a show of hands. Who isn't chained to the floor?"

Samael and I both raise our hands. Merihim rattles his chains.

"That's exactly the kind of empty gesture I was talking about. You run off to Earth, fight a ghost here, a demon there, and you think you've saved the world. This one tracks me down and thinks he's saving his dear addled father. Neither of you can admit that what's coming cannot be stopped."

"I'll stop the Angra," I say.

"No you won't and you know it. The game is too far along.

Death is coming. We're all going to die at the hands of the old Gods. The only question is how your death will come. Those of us who brought them home will die quickly and easily. While those who fought on the side of the beast in Heaven will die over aeons in unimaginable pain."

"You watched *The Exorcist* a lot when you were a kid, didn't you? You've got the whole spooky 'hail, Satan' patter down cold."

"Don't talk like a fool," Merihim shouts, rattling his chains loud enough to get the hellhounds growling. "You sound like Samael, the spoiled son, when you do that. Listen to me, Stark. You don't have to play the brave soldier anymore. That time is over. You're more on my side than his. You always have been. I know you have the Mithras hidden away. You could have burned the universe on your own, and you came close a few times, didn't you? Admit it. You hate this place. This universe that calls you Abomination. But you're not the Abomination. It's God. All the pain there ever was he started by exiling the Angra. He invented our doom that day. And he compounded the torment for creatures like you and me and even Samael, the fool, by exiling us in Hell. You owe angels and mad Gods nothing. The Angra will embrace you as a brother."

"And then they'll kill me."

"Death is our only release."

"I was just thinking about that. You know the one good thing about Mason Faim being back on Earth?"

"What?"

"There's a vacancy in Tartarus."

I pull out the Colt and shoot Merihim right between his

bloodshot eyes. The Spiritus Dei–coated bullet blows the back of his stupid Hellion head apart. The hellhounds howl and paw the floor with their metal claws, tearing up stone and mortar.

"Did that feel good?" says Samael.

"Yeah. It did. Why don't you come back to L.A. with me? There's lots more people to shoot and I could use the help."

Samael smiles and crushes his cigarette with the toe of his perfect shoe.

"Before tonight I would have said yes. But with Nefesh's murder and Chaya's impending breakdown, I need to stay here and protect Father."

"You mean Muninn, right? 'Cause I think we could get along without the other one."

Samael lets out a long breath.

"That's the problem. They're both my father. And people say stupid things when they're scared. But I won't let Ruach or Angra scum win. Do you want my advice on dealing with Mason Faim?"

"Anything you've got."

"When you see him, just be your usual charming self."

I nod, thinking it over. I toss the rest of my Malediction in Merihim's black blood.

"Do you mind if I do something with the body?"

"It might make more of an impression if we do it together."

Samael unlocks Merihim's chains and we drag his body through the kennel and out into the rain. The hellhounds follow us, fanning out in a protective ring. The legions guarding the palace watch us silently as we two ex-Lucifers hoist Merihim's carcass into a gibbet and lock him in. Samael gives it a push and the cage swings back and forth like the pendulum in a grandfather clock. And I think about time again. But not for very long.

I have to shout to be heard over the downpour.

"Anyone who touches this body gets to be his roommate in Tartarus."

Samael goes back into the palace with the hellhounds and I step through a shadow.

Right into Mason's cell, where's he's asleep. I bark some hoodoo that should blow out all the surveillance cameras in the Vigil compound. Grab a fistful of Mason's jailbird jumpsuit and toss him across the cell into the steel door. That wakes him up in time for me to grab him again and toss him into a wall. Not too hard, just hard enough to keep him interested in the situation. I pull the black blade and hold it to his scarred throat.

"Prove to me that you'll teach me about the 8 Ball."

Mason looks up at me. What else is he going to do? I'm kneeling on his chest.

"What is it you want?" he wheezes, trying to get a breath.

I pull a quarter from my pocket.

"Call it in the air."

I toss the coin.

"Tails," he says.

I catch it and check. Show him the coin. It's heads.

I get up off his chest. He takes in a big lungful of air and I grab his hand. Bend his pinkie back, holding the blade tight against the top knuckle.

"Tell me something right now. Every time you lie I get to hurt you."

Mason looks at me calmly.

"The Qomrama is alive. You want to give it orders. But that's not how it functions. You have to work together."

"How does a summoning work?"

"You've practically done it yourself. A summoning and using it as a weapon are almost the same thing. You're not summoning the Gods or using the Qomrama as a shotgun. What you're summoning is power. It's how you direct the power that's the key."

I drag the blade across Mason's fingers, drawing a bead of blood. He winces.

"It can't be that simple or either Deumos or Merihim would have done it already."

"You're right. It isn't. But you'll have to play me and you'll have to win to find out more."

"Why the hell are you doing this?"

Mason pulls his hand away from me and I let him.

"Spend some time in Tartarus and you'll do all sorts of funny things. You'll make deals with anyone to get out. You'll kill anyone. And you'll die before you'll go back. Maybe along the way, you'll get to prove to a smug Robin Hood who's the better magician."

Electronic beeps come through the door. Someone is using the keypad to get into Mason's cell. I bark some Hellion. It twists the door hinges just enough that it will take whoever is outside a minute to get the door open.

I pick Mason up and set him on his bunk. He licks the finger where I cut him.

"See you tomorrow," I say.

"I can't wait, Sunshine."

Bloody Hellion rain drips off me and covers the floor of Mason's cell. With my finger, I make up a scary-looking nonsense hoodoo circle and shove Mason into it. He slips and falls in the center just as Wells and the guards burst into the room. I'm out through a shadow by then. They'll find the circle and blame Mason for screwing the door and the cameras. One small consolation at the end of a shitty night.

I CAN'T STAND the idea of going home and listening to Kasabian whimper downstairs, so I head to Bamboo House of Dolls. I stand outside for a minute, letting the L.A. monsoon wash the last of the bloody Hellion rain out of my clothes.

Nothing but a skeleton crew in the bar. Carlos and a dozen or so hard-core drinkers. All Lurkers and Sub Rosa. Except for one.

"Jimmy," she says. "I was wondering if I'd see you here."

Brigitte comes over and kisses me on the cheek. She feels warm after being out in the rain and smells good after being Downtown. For a second, it's like something normal. Two friends running into each other at a favorite bar. But nothing is normal now and we both know it, though neither of us says anything.

"Nice to see you too. Buy you another martini?"

She empties her glass and sets it down on the bar.

"You must. I am bereft of drink."

Carlos comes over and takes a couple of light-beer bottles off the bar.

"The evening rush," he says, raising a hand to the nearly empty room. "I'm grateful for the few brave souls, but all anyone wants is beer and shots. If this kind lady hadn't ordered an actual drink, I would have drowned myself in the maraschino cherries."

"You have cherries and I didn't get one?" says Brigitte.

"You don't put cherries in a martini."

"I do."

He shrugs.

"The customer is always right, even if what they want is wrong."

He looks at me.

"The usual for you?"

"Some of the red stuff, yeah. I need to wash the taste of Hellion wine out of my mouth."

Carlos comes back in a minute with Brigitte's junior high martini and pours me a shot of Aqua Regia.

"I'm sorry to tell you, but this is my last bottle. Can you get any more?"

First floods and now no booze. Another bad omen. I can't go drinkless at the apocalypse, but why bother raiding some Hellion's liquor cabinet if we only have a couple of days to live?

I say, "I'll look into it."

Carlos mixes himself a manhattan and we all drink together.

Brigitte stares at her drink for a minute.

"You've been to Hell again, I take it?"

"Just got back."

Carlos says, "The way you talk about it. Like taking the bus to Westwood."

"I'd rather go to Hell than ride the bus."

"I don't suppose you saw him?" Brigitte says.

She means Father Traven, ex-priest, part-time sin eater, and a surprisingly brave guy. He and Brigitte had a brief thing together. Brief because Traven died killing Medea Bava and basically saving a lot of people's lives, including mine and Brigitte's.

"No, I didn't."

Traven was handed a first-class ticket Downtown when the Church excommunicated him for translating a forbidden book about the Angra. As far as most people know, Hell is where he went and Hell is where he stayed. I never wanted to tell Brigitte anything different because even though I stole Traven's soul out of Hell, he's still dead and I thought it was best for her to let him go. But with everything hanging by a thread, I'm not so sure anymore.

"I didn't see Traven because he's not in Hell."

Brigitte gives me a look. It's not quite surprise. More like confusion with just a little bit of hope.

"What does that mean? Where is he?"

"He was in Hell and it wasn't fair, so I did something about it."

"What?"

"I can't tell you everything, but I can tell you this much. He isn't stuck in Hell."

Her hand closes on my arm.

"Where is he?"

I don't want to tell her about taking him to Blue Heaven, a strange place outside of normal time. She might want to go there. I'm not willing to take her to a dead man she can't be with anymore.

"Listen. I dealt with it. He's in a better place. That's all I can tell you."

Getting Traven out of Hell cost me. I don't think Muninn

has ever quite forgiven me for stealing a damned soul from right under his nose. Now I owe him a favor. Anything he wants. I don't want to think about what a piece of God might ask for.

"You're telling me the truth, yes?" she says.

She's upset. Her accent is coming back and it would be hard to understand her if I didn't already know what she was going to ask.

"Yeah. It's the truth." As much of it as she needs to know.

"Dìkuji," she says. "Thank you so much."

She puts her arms around me.

"Glad to. Next time you can get the drinks."

She lets go, wiping a few tears from her eyes. It's strange to see a stone killer like Brigitte cry. I wonder what I would do if something happened to Candy. I drink my Aqua Regia and put that thought out of my head real quick.

"You've both known me for a while. You've seen me fucked up and not entirely fucked up."

"Emphasis on the first," says Carlos. "You've been various degrees of fucked up ever since you walked into my bar last Christmas. That's why it's always nice to see you in those brief moments when you've got your head on straight."

"That's what I'm getting at."

I already feel stupid for starting the conversation, but I can't really stop it now.

"I'm a bastard. I know that. But am I a bastard bastard?"

"Does that sentence come in English?" says Carlos.

"I'm not sure I understand either," Brigitte says.

Is there anything worse in the world than having to explain yourself? Serves me right for starting this.

"Am I an unforgivable asshole? Unfair? Do I use people? Did I ever use either of you?"

"Used for what?" says Carlos. "If this is about the drinks and food, don't sweat it. You'll always eat and drink free as long as I run the place."

Brigitte says, "I don't think he's talking about that. I think he's talking about love."

That fucking word.

"Never mind," I say.

"Oh, Jimmy, I was only teasing."

"I know, and it's not about that. It's that whether I'm fucked up or not is beside the point. What's important is that the other person thinks I'm maybe too fucked up."

Brigitte shakes her head.

"That's not it at all. If someone unfairly accuses you of bad behavior or neglect, you are entitled to be upset, even angry about it."

I hate this. I can't deal with this angst bullshit. This is when I dream of Hell. Of the arena, where everything was simple and the closest thing to a next day was a knife in the belly or a club in the eye. Give me blood all the livelong day. What I can't take is all this being-human-and-being-responsible craziness. I want to tear my own head off. I want to go and snap Mason's neck. Chaya was right. I hate this place. Let the world burn and me with it.

"Never mind. Stupid question. Let's drop it."

Carlos picks up our glasses.

"For what it's worth, you're all right by me. I'll get us all another round."

He moves off to get our drinks, but I think what he's really doing is leaving me alone with Brigitte.

"I understand that these things are hard for you, but we're both alike. Killing is easier than being with someone. But it's not impossible. And you can always talk to me about it."

I look past her at the band posters on the wall. I feel ridiculous. Helpless under the weight of all this emotional garbage.

"Thanks. It's never going to happen, but thanks anyway."

She laughs a little like she knew what I was going to say. And she looks away. She's thinking about Traven. She wants to ask me more about him, but she knows I won't tell her so she lets it go.

She says, "In this world of blame and accusations, I do have one piece of news that might make you feel better."

"What's that?"

"I saw Tuatha yesterday, to give her my condolences on Saragossa's passing. She knows that Audsley Ishii has accused you of being involved in his death."

"Is she getting a necktie party ready for me? Should I catch the first stage out of Dodge?"

Please say yes. I could use a fight right now.

"No. She wants you to know that she doesn't believe a word of it. And she's ordered Audsley to leave you alone."

"Good luck with that."

"Do you think he'll disobey her?"

"He needs someone to blame and we've never gotten along. I'm John Dillinger to him and no one is going to talk him out of it."

"You don't sound sorry."

"In my current placid frame of mind, I'd love someone to come at me."

"Don't look for trouble."

"Don't worry. I've got plenty on my plate. Till then, Ishii can piss his sorrows in a teapot and brew himself a hot cup of fuck off."

Carlos comes back with our drinks.

"What should we drink to?"

"To love," says Brigitte.

"To the few loyal customers I have left," says Carlos.

I have to think for a minute.

"To the dead. Let's think of them always, but not join them too soon."

Everyone in the bar drinks to that.

JULIE CALLS EARLY the next morning.

"Wells and the other bigwigs are at a meeting downtown. If you get over here right now, I can get you in to see Candy."

Lucky for me, I fell asleep in my clothes last night. I run a comb through my hair so I don't look like I escaped from Greendale House and go out through a shadow.

Julie is waiting for me when I come in and pulls me into an empty office.

She says, "As far as anyone knows, you're here to talk to her about Saint Nick. Got it?"

"Got it."

"Good. Now give me all your weapons."

"You too?"

She puts out her hand impatiently.

"It's procedure. And if any of the higher-ups come back early, it has to look like everything is by the book."

I hand her the Colt, the black blade, and my na'at. She puts them in an attaché case sitting on the desk.

277

"Can we go now?"

She looks at me hard.

"You're going to behave, right? I'm sticking my neck out for you."

"I know. Yeah, I'll be a good boy."

She picks up the attaché case.

"By the way, before you come back you might consider a shave and a shower. You smell like a brewery and look—"

"Like Steve McQueen in *Wanted: Dead or Alive*?"

"Like a vagrant. Let's go."

I follow her through the Vigil's country club. They've knocked down walls and raised ceilings so they could bring in bigger equipment. Helicopters and armored vehicles like they're going to invade Santa Monica by way of Kabul because that's how you fight transdimensional gods. Like they're pot farmers in the Central Valley. I'm glad to see that, as usual, Homeland Security is thinking outside the box.

A guard opens the door to the lockup. I go to Candy's cell. She's curled up asleep on her bunk. She hears me come in and turns over. Stands when she recognizes me. Her face is still swollen where someone rifle-butted her. She's pale, with dark circles under her eyes. When she comes over, she slumps against the bars, looking a head shorter than usual.

"I was wondering when you were going to come and see me. Where have you been?"

"I saw you right after they brought you in."

"Really? That's nice, but I don't remember."

"It's okay. You look a lot better today."

"I feel like something floated up out of the sewer. They say I tried to kill someone."

"That's what they say."

"Is it true?"

She nervously twines her fingers in the netting threaded around the cell bars.

"I don't know. I didn't see the guy or anything, but Julie Sola told me about it and I trust her."

Candy looks at the cellblock door.

"They're never going to let me out of here, are they?"

"Why do you say that?"

"I hear the guards talking. They're not big fans of Jades. Or any Lurkers."

"Point them out and I'll have a word with them."

She shakes her head. Her shaggy hair is a mess, tangled and pressed down on one side.

"Don't do that. I don't want any more trouble. I just want to know what happened."

"You were poisoned. Someone spiked your Jade potion. You had a relapse and it affected your mind."

She looks at her twining fingers.

"Relapse. That's a funny word."

"What do you mean?"

"Relapse for me means going back to my true nature. Like you think who I am is a disease."

"Yeah. You said something like that when they brought you in, only louder."

"Did I? It's all such a blur."

She lets go of the net and takes a small step backward. Looks up at me.

"Is that what you think?" she says quietly. "That I'm just some kind of disease?"

I take a breath. This is why I drank too much last night. To blot out all of this. Shit like this moment.

"I shouldn't have said 'relapse.' That was stupid. I just mean people like us, we're always fighting some part of our own nature. You don't think I want to kill every one of the fuckers who roughed you up? Or that lots of days I wouldn't mind seeing the whole world go up in flames? When I got back from Hell, all I could think about was hurting as many people and destroying as much of this place as I could. I still have to fight that feeling sometimes. I always will. We're not like the people running this place. We're monsters to them. That's all we'll ever be and I'm okay with that."

"But you're out there and I'm in here."

"I'll get you out. I'll make a deal with Wells. He needs me to work the 8 Ball. I'll blackmail him to Hell and back if I have to, to get you out."

She smiles faintly.

"That's sweet."

I want to ask her about some of the other things she said the other night. Cursing Doc. Cursing me. But I don't want to hear any of it again right now. We're having a not-totally-fucked-up moment and it feels so fragile. One wrong word could blow it away and I don't want to do that.

"I'm going to figure this out."

"I heard someone say Mason Faim is back."

"Ain't life grand?"

"At least he's locked up too. I'd be a little distressed if I was in a cell and they'd put him up in our room at the Chateau Marmont."

She comes back to the bars.

"Well, he doesn't look so good right now. He tripped and fell into a wall a couple of times."

She smiles and wraps her arms around herself.

"Did I say something wrong the other night? I can't remember and you're acting funny. What happened?"

I shake my head.

"You didn't say anything. I'm just worried is all."

"If I said anything to hurt you, I didn't mean it."

"I know."

"You forgive me?"

"There's nothing to forgive."

"You're lying, but that's okay. Us jailbirds need the occasional hopeful lie."

She puts her hand up against the net and holds it there. I reach out for her.

The cellblock door slides open and I pull my hand back.

"Stark," says Julie. "It's time to go."

"Thanks for coming to see me," says Candy.

"I'll be back soon."

"If I'm not out by Christmas, bake me a gingerbread man with a file in it."

"Baby, I'll bake you a neutron bomb."

She stands at the bars watching until the door closes.

I walk with Julie back to the empty office.

"Thanks for letting me see her."

"Just remember. If anyone asks, you were talking to her about Mason."

"They really think she's working with Mason?"

"All Lurkers are suspect right now. If you're not human, you might as well be an Angra."

"If any of those fuckers tries to hurt her . . ."

"They're all too scared of you and Wells to do that, but I won't lie to you. Her chances of getting out of here get worse every day. Homeland Security is talking about renditioning captured Lurkers to camps out in the deep desert. The only way they won't come for her is if I can make it look like she's part of your work."

"I won't forget this."

"I won't let you forget. You're going to owe me plenty before this is over."

"I already do."

"Just remember that when I reopen my detective agency."

She opens the attaché case and hands me my gun and other toys.

Would someone be stupid enough to try and rendition Candy? No. That's not going to happen. I'll let the Angra in myself before that happens and I'll go Saint Nick on anyone who gets in my way.

As Julie and I come out of the office, Wells is going by with a gaggle of his pencil pushers. He stops when he sees us.

"Don't you have somewhere to be, Marshal Sola?"

"Yes, sir," she says, and disappears like she never saw me.

"How about you, Stark? Shouldn't you be with Mason doing your job?"

"I was just going in to see him."

"Did you hear what happened last night?"

"Do tell."

He hands a thick manila envelope to one of his lackeys.

"It looks like Mason tried to pull some pixie magic. Shut down our surveillance for almost an hour and locked himself in his cell."

"That naughty boy."

"That he is. There's just one thing."

"What's that?"

"He wrote a spell in blood, but the only cut we could find on him was a scratch on his little finger. And he had a black eye and some bruised ribs. You wouldn't know anything about that, would you?"

"Maybe he fell off his bunk."

Wells purses his lips like he's thinking.

"That's what he said. I guess accidents happen. We just need to make sure they never happen again or we'll have to transfer all the other prisoners out of this facility. You understand?"

"Yeah. I get it."

"Are we done here?"

"I was done five minutes ago."

Wells takes my arm and leads me aside.

"Go in there and win today. The Shonin isn't looking so good. He's drinking that lousy poison book because you're not coming up with the goods. Get something useful today."

"I'm working on it."

"Don't work on it. Do it."

He lets go and moves off with his suits. I'll give him one thing. He's got quite a grip.

EVERY TIME I walk into Mason's cell I half expect to see one of the meat cathedrals. Pink light glowing off his smug face. Flayed guards hung upside down in narrow naves. It's almost disappointing when the door opens and it's the same flat fluorescent light as always. I think I'd prefer an Angra butcher shop. We'd be somewhere real, where the consequences of our games—the ones on the table and the ones we're playing in each other's head—are laid out, bare and raw, on cards made of skin and chips carved from bones. But no, we're in a dismal cell, playing Old Maid like we have all the time in the world.

Mason is at his table, handcuffs secured to the top again. He doesn't seem to mind. He looks up and smiles when he sees me.

Wells was telling the truth. Mason's eye is black and the sclera is red from a broken blood vessel. He moves from his shoulders, like he has a stiff back. Well, my hand still itches a little from where I punched out the car window, so in my book we're even.

There's a deck of cards on the table.

"More poker?" I say. "I already beat you at that. Wait. I forgot. It's all the Infinite Game. I'll have to infinitely beat you again."

"These cards aren't exactly what we should be playing with, but we can make them work," he says. Then his voice goes raspy and guttural. "The game is called Take and Give."

Mason is speaking Hellion. I forgot that he could do that. Hearing it come out of his mouth brings back bad memories of him running Hell, me chasing Alice's soul, and losing my arm.

I speak Hellion back to him. Whoever is monitoring the room is scrambling for dictionaries and flipping on supercomputers for voice analysis, but they're going to be shit out of luck.

"A Hellion game? I never heard of it."

"Aristocrats played it, but you killed off most of the people who might've taught it to you."

"How does it work?"

Mason cuts the cards, breaks the deck, and slides half the cards to me.

"I take something from you and then I give you something. A card in this case. Hellion cards are more interesting, but we'll just have to make do. You take something from me and give me something. The one with the most at the end wins."

"What am I giving and taking?"

"Anything."

"That doesn't make sense."

"You'll get the hang of it. I'll go first so you'll see how it works."

He lays his hand on his cards.

"I take your heart and give you . . ."

He draws a card.

"A three of spades. Your turn."

"That's it? That doesn't tell me anything."

"Just try it."

I keep waiting for him to laugh in my face and explain the real game, but he just sits there. I draw a card.

"I take your lace doily and give you . . ."

I throw down the card.

"A two of diamonds."

"See? It's easy. I take your eyes and . . ."

He draws a card.

"Give you an ace of clubs."

I take a card.

"I take your bullshit and give you a nine of hearts."

"Fun, isn't it?"

"It's fucking ridiculous."

"I take your arrogance and give you a jack of hearts."

"How do we know who's won? How do we add up the points?"

"I'll show you when we get through the deck. By the way, the winner gets to take one of the loser's fingers. Your stunt last night is what reminded me of the game."

"The guards won't let us have knives."

"Then the winner will just have to gnaw off his prize."

We play a few more hands and the game doesn't make any more sense than when we started. I can't find a pattern in the taking or giving. Mason is tossing out numbers, body parts, places, and animals. There's nothing I can do but follow his lead.

"I don't know what the hell I'm doing."

"Did you always know what you were doing in the arena? Just keep going."

I draw a card.

"I don't believe you about Candy, by the way."

"Believe what you want. You heard what she said."

"Whatever you drugged her with, it scrambled her brain. That wasn't truth coming out. It was paranoid hallucinations or something."

"She's a creature that needs shelter. Her doctor friend, Kinski, died. You were convenient. Don't mistake refuge for love."

"I take you trying to mind-fuck me and give you a six of clubs."

"You should take this more seriously. Remember sweet

Alice? Thinking about her let me beat you once before. All these little people you think you care about now are ruining your concentration. Don't make the same mistake you made eleven years ago."

We run through a few more nonsense hands. I'm not going to win. I have to salvage something from this.

"Tell me about Blackburn."

"The late great. What about him?"

"Why did you kill him?"

"Did I?"

He takes my soul and throws a five.

"Saint Nick sure did. And I know there's not another Saint Nick because you have too big an ego for that."

"The reason for killing Blackburn should be obvious. Without the Augur, the Sub Rosas will panic and split into factions, attacking each other. Of course, I've been busy. How do you know it wasn't my friends who killed Blackburn?"

"*Der Zorn Götter?* Forget it. I've seen their hoodoo and it would take more than that to get to the Augur."

"If anyone needed to get to him."

"An inside job? Ishii is an asshole, but he's better at his job than that."

"Play," he says.

"I take your sense of satisfaction and give you a queen of spades."

"Now you're talking," says Mason. "Of course, what if Ishii was Saint Nick? For a few minutes, I mean."

"Possession? I don't buy it. One of his people would have noticed if he showed up for lunch with a chain saw and twenty feet of intestines."

"I was just throwing out hypotheticals. No. Ishii isn't a good candidate at all. No. You'd want someone who can come and go and get as close to Blackburn as they want."

"Tuatha?"

Mason rests his hand on his cards for a minute before moving. His heart is beating faster.

"Poor dear. Having your soul ripped out the way Aelita did to her, well, you're never quite right in the head again."

"You made Tuatha kill her own husband?"

"I take your disbelief and give you a four of diamonds."

He throws down the card.

"I didn't say Tuatha was made to do anything. We were just speculating on the best subject for a possession. Besides, the key is in Hell."

"But you know who has it. And you could get a message to them."

"If you say so."

"If Tuatha did it, where's the body?"

"You're not playing."

"I take your lies and give you a ten of hearts."

"The Blackburns have a lovely mansion," he says. "You'd be surprised how well these modern garbage disposals deal with bones."

I look at Mason, trying to read him. The light is shitty in here and I can't get a good look at his eyes. But his heartbeat is up and he's not sweating. It's not fear that's getting him excited.

I say, "What are the chances she'd ever remember doing something like that?"

He draws a breath. Moves his wrists in the cuffs where they're rubbing the skin raw.

"Who knows? Besides, now that I think about it, it was probably me. I've killed so many they tend to blur together."

"You're really having fun, aren't you?"

"The time of my life. You know, in Tartarus I was adrift. Truly going mad. All I wanted was some sense of control. And now I have it and it feels great."

He draws a card.

"Now that I think about it, yes, I did kill Blackburn. I'm sure of it. Still, you might want to ask Tuatha about the clogged kitchen plumbing. Terrible timing too. While she's planning her husband's funeral and all."

"All these lies. They're obvious and boring."

"Is our biblical flood boring?"

"You're not claiming credit for the rain, are you?"

"No. That's the Angra. Just their approach brings calamity. Can you imagine what it will be like when they arrive?"

"It's like you've got Tourette's. All the shit that comes out of your mouth."

"I take your fear and give you the king of spades."

"I take your never seeing daylight again and give you a deuce of clubs."

"Tell the lovely Ms. Fortune to count her nightgowns. I bet she'll find one missing. Covered in blood and down the drain with her hubby's guts. Your turn."

I don't want to believe him, but he seems to be telling the truth. Maybe he meant what he said. Tartarus made him even crazier than when I put him in. He talks like a suicidal Hellion. Does he want me to kill him or does he want to kill himself? I'll tell Wells to put more guards on him.

"You think you're coming on like the Devil, but you sound more like a bawling brat."

"That's something else you took from me," Mason says. "My chance to become Lucifer and move my legions against Heaven."

"Heaven would have destroyed you. I saved your life."

"Thanks oodles. I take your humanity and give you a four of spades."

I keep trying to make sense of it all, the game and Mason. What does he really want? My brain vapor locks. I can't think of what to bet.

"You're not doing very well today," he says.

"You said there weren't any rules in this infinite crap."

"Like life, there are always rules. They are just not necessarily logical. But you're even less logical than usual."

"I think you just made up this game as payback for last night."

"Does that mean you forfeit?"

The cell door opens and the Shonin shuffles in. If a skeleton can look more skeletal, that's how he looks. Blackened skin flakes off his face. His hands tremble and he has trouble walking in a straight line. He stops and leans against the wall. I go over to him.

"What are you doing here?"

"You need to stop this foolishness. Your personal feelings for the girl and your past with Mason are making you unfit for work. You should go. Let me play him."

"Even if you're right, he won't play you. This whole thing is to show me up."

"I'll play him," says Mason.

The fucker always did have good hearing.

"I mean, if you're incapacitated. Besides, the game is almost over. There's just a few more hands."

"Let me finish," says the Shonin.

He takes a step toward the table and his legs give out. I grab him by the shoulders and lift him up. He's just bones and robes. He weighs nothing. By the time I have him up, the cell door is open and guards are coming in, their guns drawn.

The Shonin punches me in the shoulder. It's so feeble I wouldn't have known it happened if I hadn't seen it.

"Put me down."

I set him on his feet.

"I'll finish with the book," he says. "I'm learning great things. But you must play the game. I can't do both."

"Go and lie down, old man. Let me handle this."

The guards help the Shonin out, locking the door behind him.

"That was dramatic," says Mason. "He's even more pathetic than you and Muninn. Always running to help the older gents. Those daddy issues run deep."

"You know if you call the Angra, they'll kill you too."

"All those L.A. good vibes you've picked up have made you afraid of death. But death is what you and I do."

There's only one thing I haven't tried.

"Forget it. I quit. You win."

Mason cocks his head like he's waiting for me to say something else. He sighs and pushes his cards away.

"I admit. That's the last thing I expected from you."

"Then I did win after all."

He smiles.

"No, but you fooled me. And you played horribly, even

for you," he says. "I tell you what. I'll give you something anyway."

"You'll give me something even though I lost? Why?"

"Because I want you to come back and play some more."

"Okay. What will you give me?"

Mason thinks for a minute.

"You already controlled the Qomrama when you used it to remove the demon from one of my bodies. But you don't know how you did it?"

"No."

"The Qomrama likes you. It wants to please you. But remember that it's transdimensional. Your desires for it must also be transdimensional."

"What does that mean?"

He leans back in his chair.

"It means if you can't play the game, you can't control the Qomrama."

"If you know how to use it why haven't you?"

"Because you have it."

I sit back down at the table.

"I took it so the 8 Ball is mine. Possession is the key to controlling it, isn't it?"

He nods.

"That's why Aelita had it hidden in the palace."

"All I have to do is play with it long enough and I'll figure it out without you."

"The world is falling apart, Jimbo, and it's going to get worse. By the time you get the keys in the ignition, there might not be much left to save."

I look back at the cell door. I know Wells is on the other

side shitting fried green tomatoes, waiting for me to get more information, but I'm lucky Mason gave me this much.

"Thanks for the freebie."

Mason nods.

"Of course, I'm still going to hurt you."

I put my Kissi hand on the table and take off the glove.

"I owe you a finger. Take it."

He looks at it like a chef would look at rat shit in a Dumpster.

"I don't think I want it anymore. I'll have to hurt you some other way."

"I'm ready."

He shakes his head.

"Later. We're done for now. Come back around dinnertime for tomorrow's game. I have some preparations to make."

I put the glove back on, happy my hand was too ugly for even Mason to want it.

"Tomorrow then?" he says.

I think for a minute.

"Forget the Infinite Game. I'll play you Russian roulette again. This time by your rules."

He looks right through me.

"I'll watch, but that's your game. I want to play mine."

He gathers up the cards from the table.

"Send in the guards on the way out. I want to get started on the new game right away."

After checking on the Shonin and translating as much as I can remember of the conversation in Mason's cell into English, I head home. Vidocq calls about an hour later.

"I thought you'd want to know. They burned the clinic."

"Allegra's? Who did it?"

"Men have been hanging around for the last few days. They park across the street or up the block. Nothing has happened until tonight."

"Did you call the cops?"

There's a pause.

"A few came. They say harboring Lurkers is now a crime in Los Angeles. They arrested poor Fairuza."

I know what this is. I should have let him take my finger. Instead I gave Mason the perfect opening to hurt me through someone else. I practically handed Mason Allegra and Fairuza on a platter.

I go to Vidocq and Allegra's apartment. Not through a shadow. I ride the Hellion hog so I can feel the rain for a while. Vidocq stays with Allegra as she cries in the bedroom. I spend the night, listening for sounds at the door. I have a lot of guns with me.

During the night, I go out through a shadow to see the clinic. The whole mall is gone. Just burned timbers, broken glass, and collapsed roofs. I don't mention it to either one of them.

There are bottles and packages scattered over Vidocq's worktable. It's too haphazard to be his stuff. I pick up a small bundle of yellow herbs and give it a sniff. They stink of smoke. These few things are what Allegra managed to grab from the clinic before she had to run. Bottles of rare potions and plants. A couple of old handwritten books. Probably Doc Kinski's personal medical notes. A chunk of blue amber. Some red mercury. Carefully wrapped in silk are the two pieces of divine light glass that heal most injuries. There are a couple of small vials on the end that I don't recognize.

"They're potions for Candy. Allegra made them fresh herself, so there's no chance of them being poisoned," says Vidocq.

I didn't hear him come in.

"How's Allegra doing?"

He shrugs.

"Badly. But it could be worse. Thank you for coming over."

"Anytime. What else can I do?"

He drops down onto the old couch. Rubs his eyes.

"Nothing. She's asleep now. I think when she wakes she'd like to be alone for a while to collect her thoughts."

"Sure. I'll take off."

"I don't mean to throw you out."

"Don't worry about it. But there's one thing," I say.

I set down a Desert Eagle .50 that some Satanists gave me a while back.

"That will shoot through a wall and still kill anything on the other side. Don't be shy about using it."

Vidocq picks up the gun and weighs it in his hand. Sights down the barrel. He nods.

"I don't like these things, but times like this force us to reconsider our prejudices."

"Call me if you need anything."

"Thank you."

"I know it will sound lame, but tell Allegra I'm sorry and I'll try to find out who did it."

"I'll tell her."

I ride the hog home. It's morning, but no brighter than it

was the night before. I change my route when I see a couple of patrol cars in the distance. A big vehicle—maybe one of the Vigil's ASVs—shoots across Hollywood near Western.

I park the bike next to Max Overdrive and go in the side door.

Kasabian is hiding in his room. Delivery food boxes and beer bottles are piled up outside his door. Money is the magic anyone can do, and Kasabian always has a little stashed away no matter how broke he claims to be. Only he could find someone still delivering food. I wonder how much a burger costs these days.

When Howard Hughes went crazy, he locked himself in a room and watched *Ice Station Zebra* on a loop. With Candy it's *Spirited Away*. Kasabian has the original *Dawn of the Dead* going in his room. The jagged Goblin sound track fills the whole first floor. I go upstairs and close the door.

I wonder about the cops that watched Allegra's clinic burn. Was that official policy or hillbilly street justice? Maybe the cops and the arsonists were working together to take out a Lurker safe haven. That's just with the city needs. A bunch of righteous vigilantes.

I suppose the existence of Lurkers couldn't be a secret forever. It was hard enough for the Sub Rosa plants in the police department to keep them off the books. Now that everything's falling apart, the few assholes in power who knew something or suspected something are free to shake whatever tree they like and see what falls out. How long before someone pays a visit to Bamboo House of Dolls? It's a good thing the city is deserted. What Lurkers don't need is having all of L.A. going ballistic when they find out that monsters have been living among them since forever.

I walk around the apartment. Look at Candy's things and wonder if I found something that might make her feel better, would Wells let me give it to her? I doubt it. He doesn't want to look like he's doing me any more favors than he's already done.

I keep hoping for a call that Mason wants me to come in early so we can get things over with. After yesterday's crash-and-burn, I don't want to lose my cool again. He's going to try another one of his nonsense games and I can't let it get to me. Follow Muninn's advice. Go with whatever Mason wants. Don't fight back. Watch him. Go total Zen on the little prick and see what happens.

Sometime in the night Kasabian stuffed towels around the bottom of the front door when water started leaking in. They're soaked through. I go down and replace them. There. That used up a whole two minutes. I keep checking the time.

Kasabian watches the news sometimes. I should ask him if things are this crazy in the rest of the world. But do I really want to know?

My phone rings. I grab it without bothering to check the number.

"You didn't think I was going to leave him to the vultures, did you?" says Deumos.

"Vultures. Worms. Hellhounds. It's all the same to me, as long as he's dead."

"You could've joined us, but that moment has passed."

"I guess so. Anything else on your mind?"

"Enjoy what's coming."

"Nothing is coming. I'm going to stop it and you're going to live a good long miserable life in Hell with all your idiot followers. Assuming they don't lynch you."

"When will your friends turn on you? Your lover is in jail. Your friend's hospital is burned. Your benefactors at the Golden Vigil are losing faith in you. You'll long for Hell and then oblivion before this is over."

"What kind of cell contract do you have? Are these calls from Hell expensive or do you have a good roaming plan?"

"Enjoy the games."

I pick up a Malediction and light it.

"Enjoy watching your precious Angra eat shit and die."

The line goes dead.

Kasabian pushes my door open.

"Who was that?"

"No one."

"It sure sounded like someone. Like someone from Downtown. You don't get calls from there, do you? That could have helped my swami business. When I had one. That's as dead as the store."

"You can't blame me for that."

"Maybe. But it makes me feel better to do it."

I tap some ash from the Malediction into an empty wineglass with Candy's lipstick on the rim.

"What do you want? If you came up here to panic, I'm not in the mood."

He comes into the room and leans against the wall, crossing his metal arms and legs. He looks like a nervous lawn ornament.

"I was flipping by the news. There was a fire last night. From the shots it looked like Allegra's place."

"We still have local news? How about that?"

"Was it the clinic?"

"Yeah."

"Is Fairuza all right?"

"I don't know."

"What do you know?"

"Go downstairs and watch your movie. There's nothing you can do."

He comes over, looking like a tin toy John Wayne.

"Where is she?"

"LAPD and the feds are rounding up Lurkers."

"What's going to happen to her?"

"I don't know. They still have Candy at Vigil headquarters, so maybe they're just holding everyone until Washington decides what it wants."

"You're not going to let them hurt her, are you?"

"I don't even know where she is."

He takes a beer from the fridge, but he doesn't open it. Just stands there holding it.

"I have some of her stuff. We could do a locator spell."

I nod and smoke.

"Tell you what. You do it and tell me what you find. I'll see what I can do after that."

"Can't you help? You're the better magician."

"Am I? I'm not feeling so good hoodoo-wise right now."

"Mason's really getting to you, isn't he?"

"No. I just can't get these soup stains out of the drapes."

"You want some advice?"

"Not even a little."

"Kill him. He beat you once and sent you to Hell. He's going to beat you again and it'll be worse for everyone this time."

"I can't. He has information I need."

"He'll never give it to you."

"I know."

"Then why are you doing it?"

" 'Cause these are my last cigarettes and there's nothing good on TV."

Kasabian shakes his head and looks out the window.

"Don't talk like that. Even if you're kidding."

"I told you. I'm not in a comforting mood right now."

"Kill him. The moment you see him."

I crush out the Malediction.

"I need a drink. Do you need a drink?"

He sets down the beer.

"No. And neither do you. Have some coffee. Spend the day with a clear head for once."

"That sounds incredibly boring."

"Sit there. I'll put on a pot."

He goes to the little kitchen. Starts running water and pawing through the cupboards looking for coffee and mugs.

"When did you learn to do anything, Susie Homemaker?"

"I could do a lot of things before some asshole cut off my head."

He fills the coffeepot with water. Pours it and some coffee into the top of the maker, then does something mysterious with buttons that turns a red light on. I can survive Hell, but most of the coffee I drink is instant.

"I'm not going to work for a while. Want to watch something?"

"What?"

I pick up a DVD box.

"Candy and I were watching *Baron Prásil*, that Czech Baron Munchausen movie she borrowed from Brigitte."

"Is Brigitte in it?"

"No."

"Is there any nudity?"

"Not so far."

"Put it on and let's cross our fingers."

I WALK INTO Mason's cell a little after eight. He looks the same as usual. Sitting at his table in a prison jumpsuit, a cat-that-ate-the-canary grin on his face, and his handcuffs secured to the table. There's a little more slack in the cuffs today. The reason why is spread out in front of me, so big that the sides hang off the ends of the table.

It looks like Mason raided the Vigil's break room and didn't leave anything behind. Six or eight game boards—right off, I recognize Monopoly, Go, Risk, and backgammon—are duct-taped together to form a stripped-down version of Metatron's Cube, the mystical symbol that's part of the ritual I used to track down the meat-locker asshole, Joseph Hobaica, on his way to Hell. The Cube is a power symbol I used a lot back when Mason and I were in the same Magic Circle. Points to you, Mason, for remembering that.

The game boards are in the shape of a six-pointed star with a circle in the middle containing playing pieces. At the point of each star is another circle. Straight lines cut from a chessboard connect each of these outer circles. I don't bother asking how he got the boards apart or how he put them back together again because he'll lie and I don't need to start off aggravated.

"Did the trash fairy shit on your table for Christmas?"

Mason taps his fingers on the collection of game boards.

"Don't tell me you don't appreciate my work. It took me all night and all day to put this together."

"It's very pretty in a better-up-the-voltage-on-my-electroshock kind of way. So what's this mess called?"

He moves his hands forward to touch the edge of the board.

"This is where you truly meet the infinite part of the Infinite Game. And being infinite, it's also extremely simple. All you have to do is move each of your pieces onto every single space on the board. You can move them in any order and go in any direction. Here's where things get really interesting. The rules change with each move and how they change depends on the previous move."

"I can tell I'm going to love this. How do I know what the new rules are?"

"I'll tell you."

"How do I know you're telling the truth?"

"That's the beauty of the Infinite Game. Lying doesn't matter. With the rules changing every move, the lie I tell you now could be the truth that lets you win later. And I have some other good news for you."

"They're muzzling you before we play?"

"If you win tonight, I'll tell you everything you want to know about the Qomrama."

I know he wants me to bring up Allegra's clinic and how he hurt me by going through a friend. I won't give him the satisfaction. Nothing that's already happened can be fixed. Concentrate on today and hope the fucker keeps his word when I beat him.

"There's still time to forget this shit."

Mason looks over the boards.

"You're being boring. Do it again and I'll hurt another one of your friends. Now play."

The longer I look at the board, the less sense it makes. It's hypnotic. Like heat dancing off the asphalt in the desert. I get woozy staring at the twisted thing and soon I don't care about saving the world. I want to leave. I don't want to be in this room with this lunatic. I can't breathe. I can't think straight. The harder I try to understand the board, the dizzier I feel. Finally, I have to look away. And Mason sees all of it. All my weakness and doubt. Nothing I can do about it now. Hell, maybe feeling sick is part of the Infinite Game too. Maybe if I throw up on the board I'll get a free turn.

We start with thirteen pieces in the middle. Mason tosses a coin and I call it.

"Heads."

It's tails.

"You lose," he says. "You have to move seven pieces around the board to win. I only have to move six."

Naturally. I was losing before I walked in the room.

"One more thing. After each move we say . . ." He pronounces a Hellion word. It literally means "power to you," but is really a sarcastic version of "good luck." Something you say when you want to see someone face-plant.

Head games within head games.

Mason makes the first move. He closes his eyes and picks up a few Go stones.

Three black and two white.

"Three times two," he says. "I move six."

There's a three-inch-tall metal Empire State Building with the game pieces. He moves it six spaces along a piece of a Candy Land board. Then he growls, "Power to you."

It's my turn. I reach for the Go stones. He shakes his head.

"The rules change, remember? Try spinning the wheel."

I spin a flat plastic wheel from another game. It's numbered one to twelve. I get a seven.

Mason says, "Good. The number of your players and it's a prime. Move two of your pieces, splitting the seven. Four and three. Five and two. Six and one. You get the idea."

I move two pieces.

"What's the magic word?" he says.

I stare at him for a minute. Then remember. I bark a Hellion "power to you." He grins and throws a set of poker dice. He gets a full house and moves the Scottie dog from a Monopoly set in the opposite direction of the Empire State.

How do I describe the next few hours? It's not a game. It's some kind of stoner Dadaist performance art. The rules shift and turn back on themselves, sometimes in the middle of a move. Mason spins a dreidel. Rolls one of the dice. Or two. Or all of them at once. He moves three of his pieces, all in different directions across the board, always careful to follow the move with "power to you" because sometimes if you forget, you have to start over and I might blow my brains out if this goes on much longer.

I make the same moves as Mason, or as close I can imitate him. I pick cards. I toss stones and dice. I move my pieces forward, or backward when Mason says I lost a round. After an hour I get bored and knock one of his pieces off the board like we're playing marbles.

He applauds.

"Bravo! That's the first original thing you've done since we started. It's good to see you getting into the spirit of the game. I was getting worried."

We play a couple of more rounds. Dice. Stones. Sometimes rock-paper-scissors.

The game goes on for another two hours. I know that somewhere Wells and the Shonin are watching us. I'd love to know what they're thinking right now. Especially the Shonin. Does he have any more of a clue about the game than I do?

Mason says, "Feel free to keep imitating my moves if it makes you feel better. With the rules changing, the move that hurts me might bring you luck."

He deserves a "fuck you," but I give him a "power to you" instead and he gives it right back to me.

The things we do to stay alive for another year. Another day. Another hour. The deals we make with the universe and ourselves. You start to feel dirty. I made plenty of deals Downtown. Found tricks to kill my way out of most of them. Why not? What's a deal with a Hellion worth? It's like a joke the Irish used to tell.

"What do you call a dead Englishman?"

"What?"

"A good start."

Where has all the killing and all the deals left me? Worse off than ever. I stopped Mason's Hellion war with Heaven, but looking back, maybe I should have let them go ahead with their attack. Let Ruach and his angels slaughter the legions from their golden fortress. The Hellions would have satisfied their suicide fetish and maybe that would have been enough to stop this apocalyptic freak show before it got rolling.

But I also stopped the war for my own selfish reasons. I wanted to get hold of Mason and kill him myself. Then I abandoned Hell to come home when I could have stayed and maybe stopped Merihim and Deumos and their Angra games before they came to Earth. When I left, I made a deal with myself. I didn't want to die Downtown. I'd go to Earth and see Candy. Restart my life, then go back to rescue all the lost souls from the big bad Angra cult. Only I never did it. The moment I set foot in L.A. I knew I'd never go back. And it gave Merihim and Deumos all the time they needed to invent Saint Nick and bring dead-as-a-doornail Mason back to life. That means I'm the one responsible for Mason coming home so he could goad me into replaying our Russian roulette game by his rules.

It would make me laugh if it wasn't all so pathetic. I've wasted this whole year. I even started thinking I was some kind of good guy. A one-man *Seven Samurai* out to save the innocent rice farmers from the marauding bandits. I should have stayed in Hell and done my job. My father, Doc Kinski, laid it out for me one night, simple and clear. I'm a natural-born killer and nothing more. If I'd have killed everyone in Hell that needed killing, this Angra horror show wouldn't be happening. I won't make that mistake again. Mason coughs up the information we need or he dies and I follow him Downtown. Babysit him at the entrance to Tartarus and personally make sure he never gets out until the end of time. Maybe I'll see if Candy wants a summer home on the River Styx. The weather isn't any worse than L.A. these days. Maybe she and Cindil can work at Wild Bill's bar. I've heard worse retirement plans.

But first there's the game. I walked away from Mason before, but not again.

"Earth to Jimbo. You in there somewhere?" says Mason.

Beautiful. I got lost in my head and he saw. Not a good start to my dramatic comeback.

"Is it my turn?"

"There's just the two of us."

"I don't know what to do."

"It's an easy round. Draw a card. Move that many spaces. Eleven for a face card. Twelve for an ace."

I draw a five. I move a white checker across five countries on a Risk board. I don't know if the move is legit, but Mason doesn't say anything.

"Don't forget," he says.

I growl, "Power to you."

"Good boy," he says, eyeing his next move.

He spins the number wheel and moves a Go stone.

"Now that we've been playing for a while, are you figuring out the game?"

"I've got it down. I'm going to write a goddamn book about it."

"I'm not sure I entirely believe you."

"Why's that?"

"Because I just won."

I look over the board. He's moved each of his six pieces into one of the six circles on the tips of the star.

"But you didn't touch all the spaces on the board."

He gives an exaggerated sigh.

"You didn't really think I'd play something that tedious, did you? I told you I might lie as part of the game. I'm just sad you weren't paying more attention."

"I'll fucking kill you."

"Too late, Sandman Slim."

He slams his right hand down on the metal Empire State Building. It goes all the way through. Blood splatters the board, pooling under his palm.

He shouts, "Power to you!"

The building jolts in one direction and back the other way, like the aftershock following a big quake. I hear shouts from outside. Something massive scrapes and crashes with a twisting metallic sound.

I look at Mason.

"What have you done?"

He drags his hand off the Empire State. Bone and torn muscle peek out of the hole between his knuckles.

"You locked me away in the Abyss and took away everything I ever had or ever wanted. I'm just returning the favor."

Please no. Tell me I'm not that stupid. I wait for what I'm afraid is coming next.

There's an explosion at the far end of the cell. Steel shards and concrete from the wall pepper the room and my arms as I cover my face. I look and the Qomrama Om Ya is hanging over the table. It spins, glowing like a ruby with a black sun captured inside. The black nonlight shoots out of the faceted sides in sharp rays, like the spokes of a wheel. I get up and move away from the table.

"What's happening?"

"The ritual is almost complete. I told you the Qomrama isn't that complicated to use. Break down the process into parts. You catching me and bringing me to it was one part. The game was the other. There's only one part left."

He said it right to my face. The 8 Ball is transdimensional. *Your desires for it must also be transdimensional.* These nonsense games were what a transdimensional summoning ritual looks like to three-dimensional assholes. "Power to you." That wasn't a dig at me. We were mainlining speed into the Angra for the whole game. Mason needed me because I control the Qomrama. He used me because I'm an idiot.

I shout, "Stop it. Or I'll make you stop."

"I told you I'd rather die than go back to Tartarus. You let these people and their rules muddle your head. You could have killed me when you found me, but you didn't. More fool you."

Gunshots crack against the cell door. More shots as the guards return fire. Then it stops. The door opens. Wells comes in.

"Wells. He started the ritual. We have to stop it."

"You can't stop it," says Mason. "I'm the only one who knows how. That's why I'm the end of the ritual."

Mason closes his eyes.

Wells brings up his Glock and empties the clip into Mason's head. Keeps pulling the trigger even after the last bullet is gone.

I knock the gun out of his hand and shoulder-butt him. He hits the steel wall, but he doesn't go down.

This isn't over. I still have time to use the Metatron's Cube ritual to find Mason before he goes to Hell. I'll crack his arms and legs until he tells me how to stop the summoning.

Like everything else today, that plan doesn't work out so well.

I grab the 8 Ball, hoping that will slow down the summoning. It responds like it did when the Shonin and I used it on the chop-shop body. First, it wraps itself lovingly around my Kissi hand. Then it draws Mason's soul out of his goddamn corpse. I swear the fucker is smiling as it happens. And just like it did with the Qliphoth, it eats Mason's soul.

The last of the ritual. The Angra's stooge sets off the summoning, then sacrifices himself so that no one can stop it. A hell of a fail-safe. And Mason's last laugh at me.

The building lurches again, harder this time. A steady

rumble builds under us. The walls shake and buckle. A hairline fracture rips across the ceiling and rain pours in.

Wells is still standing against the wall where I tossed him. I get a good look at his eyes. He's possessed. Someone is having a grand old time playing with the Vigil tonight.

"Enjoy what's coming," said Deumos. I'm not enjoying it one tiny bit.

Now that it's eaten Mason's soul, the 8 Ball isn't putting out the black light anymore. I sprint back to the Shonin's lab.

A good part of the ceiling is down. I crawl over beams and broken furniture to the magnetic chamber. The door is blown open, but it looks like it's basically intact.

I run through the calming breath rituals I used before a fight in the arena, trying to relax my mind. Gradually, the 8 Ball slips off my hand. I close the chamber and lock it.

I need to get to Candy. I start out of the lab when a hand closes on my ankle. It's the Shonin. He's trapped under a wooden beam. I crouch and slide it off of him. His chest has caved in and one of his arms has snapped in half and dangles by some dry cartilage. I pull him upright and lean him against the wall.

"You calmed the Qomrama. How?"

"I'm not sure. I did the only thing I could think of."

He grabs my shoulder with his good hand.

"I know why it likes you. The book told me. You're not human and you're not angel. To it you're the closet thing alive to an Angra."

"It thinks I'm its mother?"

"Maybe an uncle, which will have to be enough to control it."

Wells come into the lab. His eyes are clear. He's back to himself again. I don't think he's noticed the blood on his nice suit where he shot the Vigil agents as he broke into Mason's cell.

"Stark," he says. "What happened to the Shonin? Did you move the Qomrama? Why?"

"I was trying to save the world again. More than you've been doing."

"Mason is dead in there. Did you kill him?"

"Guess again. You did it."

Wells loses his balance on the wreckage. Takes a couple of steps back.

"That's ridiculous. You smuggled in a gun."

He turns to the door.

"Guards. Get in here. Arrest this man."

"They have you on surveillance putting a bullet into Mason's skull. You're fucked. Welcome to my world."

"Quiet," he says. "You're unstable. It was a mistake to ever try to work with you."

"You might want to start running, Richard Kimble."

A group of agents comes in, led by Julie Sola.

"Marshal Sola, arrest this man for the murder of Mason Faim."

"I can't do that, sir."

"Why not?"

She takes out her handcuffs.

"Because you shot him. Along with four other agents standing guard. Chief Deputy Marshal Larson Wells, I'm placing you under arrest for murder."

He looks at them, then at me.

"It's true, Wells. But it wasn't your fault."

I turn to Julie.

"He was possessed at the time. I'll testify to it."

Wells gets up. Tries to look commanding. Dignity is all he has left right now. I'll tell everyone that it wasn't his fault, but I doubt that's going to carry much weight with a bunch of Washington suits who think magic is Grandpa telling them to pull his finger.

"What happened in there, Stark?" he says.

"Mason started the summoning ritual, but I got the 8 Ball, so I think I stopped it before it finished. But the gate was open for a few seconds."

The agents lead Wells away.

"Do something," he shouts. "Fix this. Mason was your job, so it's your responsibility."

I hear it, but I don't care. I'm already running to another part of the compound.

The door to Candy's cellblock is jammed. I have to kick three, four times before the lock breaks.

She's pressed against the bars trying to see who's huffed and puffed and blown her door down.

"Stark?"

"It's me," I say, and go to her cell.

She grabs me when I get there and kisses me through the netting.

"What going on out there?"

"Just a party. These button-down types get wild at Christmas."

She wraps her fingers around mine.

"They're putting something in my Jade potion. Doping me. I can't think. I can barely stay awake. Take me out of here, please?"

"There's no going back if I do this."

"The world is ending. Who's going to come after us?"

"The Vigil will. And it won't be an arrest. They'll shoot you like Old Yeller."

"I don't care."

I slip into her cell through a shadow and she throws her arms around me. Not like it's great to see me. More like she wants to make sure I'm not a drug illusion. She feels weak and drunk in my arms. She is definitely on something. I bring her to a shadow.

"Last chance to not be a fugitive forever."

"Take me home."

"I have to come back and talk to the Shonin."

"I'll bake an apple pie to pass the time."

I kiss her and we step through the Room and out again into Max Overdrive.

Kasabian is eating microwave chow mein when he sees us. He blinks at Candy.

"I thought you were under arrest."

"It wasn't any fun. And I missed you," she says.

I have to hold up her upright.

"Get over here," I say.

"Is she safe?" he says.

"She's fine. Don't be such a jellyfish and get over here."

He puts down the chow mein and comes over. I put her arm around his shoulders. Candy smiles at us.

"Do-si-do, boys."

I aim them at the stairs.

"Take her to our room. She'll show you where my guns are. If anyone but me tries to get in, shoot them."

Kasabian says, "I don't know anything about guns."

"You point the hole at the bad guys," says Candy.

"Just take her upstairs and stay with her."

Candy blows me a kiss as I head out.

"Bring me some ice cream when you come back."

"L.A. is closed, dear. There isn't any ice cream."

"Then bring me a kitten."

"Kittens aren't ice cream."

"Oh. Then bring me some ice cream."

"You got it."

Kasabian steers her up the stairs.

BACK AT VIGIL headquarters things are settling down. Agents are cleaning up the wreckage from the earthquake. Rain still pours through the hole in the roof. It's gotten worse since I was gone.

I head for the Shonin's lab.

The door is off the hinges and a couple of agents stand guard. They stop me when I try to go in.

"Shonin. It's Stark."

"Is your belly too big to fit through the door, tubby? Come in here."

The agents give me a look that tells me I won't get on the group insurance plan anytime soon. I go into the lab.

The Shonin is looking a little better than when I first found him. He's sitting upright in a desk chair holding a cup of tea. He sets it down when he sees me.

"Your friend. The young Jade. She's gone, isn't she?"

"Must have escaped in all the excitement."

"Marshal Wells won't be pleased."

"He's got his own problems."

"Like me," he says, waving around his crushed arm.

"A little while ago, you told me I was the 8 Ball's uncle. Is there some way we can use that?"

He picks up the teacup and studies it.

"You have something that the Angra need. And I don't mean the Qomrama."

"I have a gun, a knife, and a video store. What the hell do they want with me?"

He sips the tea.

"Tell me about your old Hellion master, Azazel."

"He bought and paid for me when I was still in the arena. I still had to fight sometimes, but from then on I also had to play slave boy to one of the most powerful Hellions Downtown."

"You were his assassin."

"Yeah. Mainly other upper-crust Hellions. Anyone with pull. Anyone who pissed him off or got in his way."

"His political enemies."

"Right."

"He told you this?"

"No. But it was obvious. I was only killing off other generals and blue bloods. Hellions that had Lucifer's ear. Hellions are like Sub Rosas. Heavy into social status. Azazel wanted to be number one. Right behind the boss himself."

"And all the years you were killing for him you had the key to the Room of Thirteen Doors inside you. You could have escaped Hell at any time."

"He told me that my old girlfriend Alice was safe as long as I stayed. Then she was dead and I knew he'd been lying. So

I killed him, came home, and went after Mason. What's this got to do with anything?"

He tries to pick up the tea, but his hand is shaky. He bumps it and the cup lands on the floor.

"Shit," he says.

"Don't cling to things," I say. "That's Buddhism 101."

"Fuck you, fatty. Talk to me about clinging when the last of your tea is gone."

"Why do you care about Azazel?"

"The universe is a very big place," he says. "Even Gods need roads to cross it. Do you understand?"

"What? The Angras need a good deal on a rental car? Let them join AAA."

The Shonin tries to pick up his broken teacup. I get it for him.

He says, "Think about it. Thirteen Angra. Thirteen roads. Thirteen entrances and exits. Now does it make sense?"

"The Room of Thirteen Doors? The Angra want it?"

"The book implies that it was the Angra who built it. It's their crossroads. They lost control of the key when God, your friend Muninn and his ilk, banished them. In the long aeons since, the key ended up in Hell."

"And then it ended up in me."

The Shonin wipes his cup on his torn robes.

"I wonder if Azazel knew what the key really was."

Things are falling into place. My whole past.

"I wouldn't be surprised. Hell, he might have started the whole Angra cult in Hell. He put the key in me to keep it from his enemies. Used to me to kill off all the Hellions who fought him on his plan to commit mass suicide."

The Shonin looks at me with his big empty eye sockets.

"He invented you. He invented Sandman Slim to destroy the universe."

I feel a little queasy inside, like when I was looking at Mason's game board.

"It would probably have worked if Mason hadn't killed Alice."

"Now Mason has brought down the Angra to destroy us all. And he used you to do it. Quite a revenge."

"Mason was right all along. He was the better magician."

"That's all you have to say, fatty? No bluster? Nothing clever?"

"How do I stop it?"

He sets the teacup on the desk. There's a fine crack running from the lip to the base.

"Lock yourself in the Room and blow your brains out so no one else can use it. You can't stop the Angra from coming, but you can stop them from spreading across the universe."

"As long as I can burn all of creation with the Mithras, I'm not offing myself."

I look up at the rain coming down through the ceiling. The clouds open to reveal the stars beyond. The twinkly bastards look kind of ominous to me right now.

"On the other hand, your stupid idea gives me a good one."

"Tell me," says the Shonin.

"Later. If you eat all your vegetables. Right now I need all the protective wards and sealing charms you have."

The Shonin waves a bony hand at me.

"Idiot. You can't seal the Room. You need it to fight the

Angra. Or are you going to barricade yourself in and let the rest of us die?"

"Crawl back in your tomb, Imhotep. As long as Candy is alive, you assholes get to live. But I need something else now that Mason is dead."

"What?"

"I stopped the 8 Ball from letting all the Angra in. That was a mistake. The only way to beat them is to get them here. How do I do it?"

"I won't help you do something that insane."

I reach across him to the vials sitting on his desk.

"Fine. I'll drink the rest of your damned book. I hope it doesn't kill me before I find what I need."

The Shonin reaches for the potions.

"Tell me your plan and maybe I'll help."

I hold the bottles out of his reach.

"First you tell me: Who are you working for? The Vigil or the world?"

He looks at me.

"I didn't sit in a tomb for four hundred years to be a dog for bureaucrats. I work for the world."

I give him back the vials and tell him my idea. He isn't happy, but he doesn't say no.

Another tremor shakes the building. People scream. Rubble shifts. I have to grab the Shonin and the book to keep them from falling on the floor. The lights go out.

I look up at the cracked ceiling. Lightning rips across the dark and something huge tears the sky open. Stars flutter and wink out. The sky around the rip is pitch black. It doesn't last long, but something like smoke and bones slips out of the breach before it reseals itself.

The lights come back on.

"You're with me on this?"

"Go. Do what you need to do," says the Shonin.

With all the rubble around, there are plenty of nice shadows. I step through one and head Downtown.

I COME OUT by the elevators in Mr. Muninn's penthouse. Lucifer's penthouse. I'll always have a hard time thinking of him as the Devil. I should never have guilted him into taking the job. He's not cut out for it and now I might have to ask him to do something worse.

Chaya is by the big picture window watching the red rain fall. I clear my throat and he turns my way.

"How dare you break in here?"

"I didn't break in. Mr. Muninn said I could come in whenever I wanted."

"Muninn. You don't even know his real name."

"He goes by Muninn and that's good enough for me."

"Not for me."

Chaya sweeps his hand across the room and I'm Peter Pan doing a clumsy air pirouette, before slamming into the far wall and hanging there like a mounted moose head.

"I'd say this is what all you ungrateful mortals deserve, but you're not a mortal, are you? Still, you're good practice."

My throat closes up. I try to get some air. Can't. The world shrinks to a very small dot and I can't believe that after all I've been through I'm going to die because some metaphysical buzzkill is having a tantrum.

I hear Muninn's voice.

"What's all the commotion?" Then, "Chaya. Put him down now."

"I've had it with this one. Don't you see? Sooner or later he'll turn the Godeater on us."

"Let him go."

I know what's going on. I'm right on the edge of fainting, but Chaya wants me to enjoy every minute of this game, so he won't let me. Even when he crushes my windpipe and all the air goes, I'm still awake and pinned to the wall like a greasy garage pinup.

Muninn steps in front of his brother and slaps him. Chaya is surprised enough to drop my sorry bones on the carpet. Muninn makes a small gesture at me and air floods into my lungs. I take a long, cool breath of it. Even stinking Hellion air tastes good right now.

Chaya rubs his cheek, glaring at Muninn. If looks could kill, the Angra would have once less piece of God to deal with.

Muninn says, "Stark has had more than ample opportunity to turn on us and he hasn't done so."

"He's a killer."

"He's my friend."

"Don't talk like that. It's disgusting and demeans us all."

Muninn comes over and helps me get on my feet.

"Are you all right?"

"I could use a drink."

Muninn pours me something from a decanter on the coffee table. I sniff the stuff. It smells good. Muninn must have snuck back to Earth and raided the cavern with all his hidden treasures. I can't blame him for being homesick. That's Hell all over. I swallow the drink. It tastes like good whiskey and honey and burns like an August wildfire all the way down my mangled throat.

"Feeling better?"

"Yeah. Thanks."

Samael comes in wearing a silk bathrobe, like Cary Grant looking for Katharine Hepburn.

"I heard noise. Did I miss anything fun?"

I give him the finger. He looks at me slumped on the couch and Chaya's red face.

"I did. Damn."

"Shut your mouth, child," says Chaya to Samael. "You never did know your place."

"My place? I'm quite comfortable in Hell, Father. You're the one who looks like a peacock in the Sahara."

"Enough, you two," says Muninn.

He takes the empty glass from my hand and sits down across from me.

"Why are you here, James?"

I cough a couple of times, trying to get my voice back.

"The Angra are on their way. Mason did the summoning ritual. I stopped it before he was done, but something still got through."

Muninn turns and looks out the window.

"It had to happen. It was just a matter of time. Still, if we had a little longer maybe there's something else . . . I don't know. We'd be so much stronger if we could reunite with Ruach."

"He'd rather die and see us dead first," says Chaya.

I set down my glass.

"I might have a way to beat them, but it's going to cost someone big."

"What's your idea?" Muninn says.

"The Angra want you dead and they want the Room. I can give them the second thing. Herd them in and seal it forever. The trick is getting them inside."

"How will you do that?"

"Not me. One of you two. The Angra hate you. They'll follow you anywhere. One of you leads them into the Room and I seal it so no one gets out."

That quiets everybody down. Samael looks at me. He isn't happy. I just told him that one of his dads has to die and he knows I'm right. I think the only other time I shut him up was that time I stabbed him. That was fun.

"You're asking us to commit suicide," says Muninn.

"Technically, just one of you."

"See?" Chaya says. "It's exactly what I told you. He wants us dead."

"It's not what I want. If one of you big brains can figure out a better way to guarantee the Angra get in the Room, please tell me."

"There might be an alternative," says Samael.

"What's that?" says Muninn.

"Reunite. You fell apart because you couldn't bear the weight of all creation. Reunite now to save it."

Muninn looks at Chaya and Chaya looks at Muninn. They can't stand each other.

"We would be stronger reunited, Chaya," Muninn says. "Perhaps strong enough to convince Ruach to join us. Even force him if we have to."

"We'll still be incomplete. Nefesh and Neshamah are dead."

"The alternative is for one of us to die and we'd be weaker still."

"I don't trust the Abomination. He is made of lies."

"We should try."

"I won't do it."

"Yes. You will."

Muninn lunges at his brother. Grabs him by the shoulders and pushes him into the wall hard enough that they leave a dent. Chaya grabs Muninn's arms and spins him around. Now he's against the wall and Chaya tries to push him away, but only succeeds in driving him farther into the drywall. Muninn hugs his brother, pulling Chaya's body onto his. Their bodies blur, like a camera going out of focus, then sharpening again. They're drained of color. Just a couple of round gray men settling a family squabble that's been festering for aeons. Muninn lays his hands on Chaya's face, and when he pulls them back, Chaya's skin comes with him, stretching like warm taffy. Chaya pushes away, but Muninn leans in like he wants to head-butt his brother. Everywhere Muninn touches Chaya, they sink into each other. Chaya fights back, pulling away from Muninn so their half-melted flesh rips and snaps. But each time he does, Muninn moves in again, and they sink into each other. They fall on the floor, a writhing gray mass of furious protoplasm.

Then it stops. The mass breaks apart. The two brothers lie sprawled on the carpet, each regaining his color. Muninn sits up first. He tries to talk, but he's out of breath.

"It won't work. Chaya is too resistant and I'm too weak."

Samael says, "Forget Stark's idea. There has to be a better way."

Muninn shakes his head.

"No. We tried it your way and it didn't work. And Chaya is right. Even if we two came together, we wouldn't have the strength to hold off the Angra for long. They would destroy Heaven, Hell, and Earth. And who knows how much of the rest of the universe?"

Chaya stands up and goes across the room, trying to put some distance between himself and his brother.

"You're a fool to volunteer."

He looks at Samael.

"And you're a fool to let him."

He looks at me.

"You. Get out. Now."

Samael helps Muninn up off the floor.

He says, "Chaya is right. There are things we have to take care of. When do you think you'll want to do this?"

"Soon. Tonight."

Muninn looks at the bottle on the table. He goes over and pours himself a stiff one.

"All right. I'll be ready."

I get up and go over to Samael.

"Take a walk with me?"

"Of course."

He turns to his fathers and for a second I see how strange this whole thing must be for him. The only father I knew was a bastard who tried to shoot me. Samael has to balance two versions of the same father simultaneously. Muninn, all compassion, but who's spent most of his existence pretending not to be a deity. And Chaya, dog shit in a tight suit, but one who'll never give up. He'll fight forever to stay alive.

Samael and I get in the elevator and go down to the basement and the kennels.

"Do me a favor and make sure the hounds are hungry and ready to go. I have a feeling we'll need them before the night is over."

He looks around at the beasts pawing at their cages.

"I'll make sure. And I'll join you in Los Angeles when Father settles on how he wants to handle things."

"We should talk about that."

"How so?"

"Later. When you come to town. For now work on the dogs. I need to make a stop before going home."

"I'd give you one of the cars, but you don't want to be seen in the streets. Neither do I. Not after what we did to Merihim."

"You sorry about that?"

"Not in the slightest."

"Good. See you Uptown."

"Don't destroy the world without me."

I step into a shadow and come out by the deserted market across from Wild Bill's bar.

PANDEMONIUM IS AS waterlogged as L.A. and just as deserted. Are all the little Hellions huddled in their grimy Hobbit holes or, like L.A.'s scaredy cats, on the run, hoping to find a haven less obviously doomed?

I walk through the bloody downpour and push open the door to the bar.

In all the time I've been coming here I remember very few moments without noise from the jukebox, from arguments, from laughter, and from deals and schemes being hatched. But tonight it's quieter than a Texas graveyard on Super Bowl Sunday. Bill and Cindil are seated at a table on the far side of the room. Each has a glass in front of them, but neither is drinking.

"Is business so grim you don't even go behind the bar anymore?"

Bill's eyes flicker to something over my shoulder. I reach for the Colt but get a whiff of the room and listen for the scraping of boots. I don't bother with the gun then because I know I'm surrounded. One of them moves around in front of me. I look left and right. Four more Hellion legionnaires. Lucky me. It's not a whole platoon, just some hotshots looking for a bounty. I put my hands up.

The solder in front of me gets his Glock right up in my face and reaches under my coat, feeling around for my gun. When he locates something solid, the idiot tries to snatch it, but ends up screaming. What he got hold of was my knife and now his fingers are bloody bratwurst cut down to the bone. I punch him in the throat and, while he's gagging, pull the Colt, shoving the pistol under his chin.

Unfortunately, I miscounted the number of creeps in the room. One must have been crouched nearby under the tables. Before I can turn, he coldcocks me. I stumble, trip over a chair, and land on a table still holding on to Mr. Sausage Fingers. The clumsy landing knocks the Colt out of my hand and it slides across the room, too far for me to dive for.

I shove the maimed Hellion away and slump over a chair, looking a lot more hurt than I really am. I wish I could reach my gun, but I can't, so I pull the na'at. I feign a fall, and as the cold-cocker moves in to hit me again, I swing the na'at, extending it into a barbed spear. It goes deep into the soldier's gut, and when I pull it back, a fair amount of insides comes with it. The sight freezes his buddies long enough for me to get out the black blade and toss it through the eye of a soldier by the jukebox.

A legionnaire by the bar pops off a few shots. Seeing his friends go down so fast must have spooked him because he fires wildly, murdering furniture and the floor. I move in on him as he finally remembers he's a soldier and raises his gun. He hits me twice in the chest and I go down face-first.

I'm beginning to think no one in Hell likes me.

I try to sit up and meet a gun barrel halfway there. Mr. Sausage Fingers has his Glock pointed at my head. He squeezes the trigger and there isn't a goddamned thing I can do about it.

A gun goes off and the first thing I notice is how extremely not dead I am and how Mr. Sausage Fingers has a fist-size hole in his chest. I look over and there's Cindil, shaky-legged, her mouth open like she's either going to puke or sing "America the Beautiful," holding my Colt. She shoots again and Mr. Sausage Fingers hits the deck.

Cue all hell breaking loose. The three remaining legionnaires open up on the room, some shooting at me and some at the others. I roll behind Sausage Fingers' body, find his dropped Glock, and fire back. My hand is unsteady enough that I hit absolutely nothing of interest.

Cindil keeps firing my Colt, even while Bill drags her behind the bar. I don't know if she hits any of the soldiers, but she looks fierce enough to give them something to worry about.

A moment later Bill pops up from behind the bar with the pistol I gave him earlier. I stop firing and make myself very small. What else am I going to do? I'm good with a gun, but Wild Bill was the greatest shootist in the west, and even if he's past his prime he's better than me nursing a couple of slugs in my chest.

The shooting doesn't last long. When it's over Sausage Fingers has a few more holes in him, but I don't. The rest of the soldiers lie splayed around the room. Bill comes from around the bar and puts one more bullet in each of their heads. Technically it's to make sure they're really out, but there's also a small measure of payback for the century of misery he's spent under the heel of Hellions.

I pull myself up and onto a chair.

Cindil comes around in front of me. She opens my coat and makes a face.

"You're shot."

"It's not the first time. And I've been hit worse. Let me just sit here a minute."

She crosses her arms and looks down at me.

"You walk into Hell to find me and you blow it off when you get shot. What exactly are you?"

"Just hard to kill is all."

When I first went to Max Overdrive after escaping Hell, Kasabian shot me six times. I'm pretty sure I only took two bullets tonight, but they hurt like six banshees with seven machetes. The bullets will have to come out eventually, but not tonight. Tonight I get to rattle around like a pinball machine.

Bill brings me a glass of Hellion rotgut. I take a long pull. Bill pulls up a chair and sits down.

"You can't stay here and you can't come back. More soldiers will come looking for their friends."

"You can't stay either. You're both coming with me."

"Where to?" says Cindil.

"To meet Lucifer. Well, retired Lucifer. He'll explain it."

By the time I finish the drink my head feels like it's back on straight again. I get up and head for a shadow.

"You two coming?"

They follow me over and I lead them through the Room and out again into the hellhound kennel.

Samael is still there, smoking a Malediction and drinking from a silver flask. He raises his eyebrows at us.

"That was quick," he says. Then eyes my shirt. "But you took the time to hurt yourself again. If only you were this productive when you ran Hell."

Cindil looks at me.

"You ran Hell?"

"I was more of a summer intern. Samael will explain everything."

I point to each of them in turn.

"This is Cindil and this is Wild Bill. Take care of them, will you?"

Samael graciously offers his flask to his guests. Both decline.

"Of course I will. And then I'll wash your car, shall I?"

"You know I ride a bike these days. But it could use some detailing."

I nod toward the cages.

"You three might want to get out of here. I'm letting the hounds out."

Samael leads Bill and Cindil to the elevator.

As the doors close Samael says, "Love you in red, James."

ONCE THE HOUNDS are happily prowling around the kennels, I head back for Vigil HQ.

Shot and bloody, I need a moment to myself, so I come out into the parking lot with a lovely view of the golf course. It's flooded now, so they've given up playing games. Abandoned golf carts still loaded with clubs sit out in the rain with water up past their wheels. I wade out into the deep and steal a club. I always wondered what those things feel like. The weight is strange. All on the end, like a morning star. Maybe we could have used these in the arena. Play a quick round of eighteen holes and the winner beats the loser to death with a putter. I take a swing and the bullets in my chest grind against bone.

Ow. That was stupid.

But the pain pulls me back into myself and I toss the club out into the rain. When I turn to go inside I happen to notice that I'm standing next to a God.

He's in an ordinary chop-shop body, but it's obvious he's not an ordinary demon. He's naked. Rain pools and trickles down the thick scars where his mismatched limbs go together. A blue-eyed blond head perched on an olive-skinned chest, one muscular nut-brown leg and the other white and flabby with the Addams Family tattooed down the calf. His form isn't entirely solid, but transdimensional like Ten Thousand Shadows. With the slightest movement, like when he looks up into the night sky, his body morphs from male to female, to something like a sea anemone with eyes on the ends of its stingers, to an ice-blue light encased in a living glass cage shaped like one of Mason's polyhedral dice.

The rain stops. It doesn't end. It just stops. Drops suspended in the air like a million Christmas lights.

"It is good to finally meet, Sandman Slim. I heard so much about you from Aswangana."

"How is Lamia? She looked better in a party dress."

"You could have killed her when she was in such a vulnerable form. Why did you hesitate?"

"I guess I felt sorry for her. Fucked over once by God and again by the people controlling her earthly form."

The God cocks his head. It goes from the blond man to a bird's skull to something dark and gelatinous.

"Sympathy for a fallen God," he says. "That is why we respect you. You have a better sense of us than most. That is why I'm here. The nephilim and Angra are outcasts together. Join us and be an outcast no more."

"What's your name?"

He looks at me like it's a strange question.

"I do not have a name. My name is the sound of the trembling void between the stars."

"Listen, Shaky, some of your friends already tried the sales pitch. I told them no and I'll tell you no. I understand how pissed off you are. I've felt it too. It isn't easy being the only one of me in a universe where everyone hates you. But I can't let you destroy the place. All my friends are here, and so's my stuff. I mean, I just got *Bullet for the General* on Blu-ray."

"I know you cannot use the Qomrama Om Ya. Give it to me. Only a portion of me came through the rift. I will summon myself and then the other Angra. You will see. It will be glorious."

"It's not just me, you know. The Vigil will fight you. The Sub Rosa too."

He laughs and I get a little hint of what he means by the void between the stars. The sound is deep, lonely, and cold.

"The Sub Rosa will come to us when the moment is right. They are part of us. Why do you think their portion of humanity is more powerful than the rest? Able to manipulate the forces of nature? What you call magic."

"They ate all their vegetables when they were kids?"

"It is because like all demons, the Sub Rosa are simply another form of Qliphoth. The most sophisticated form, which means that when the time comes they will recognize us as their progenitors and return home to us."

Holy shit. The Sub Rosa are just skin flakes from the Angra's backside. Brainy, complicated Qliphoth, but in the big scheme of things no better than a Digger or an Eater. Wait until the gals around the watercooler hear about this.

"If I told you yes, you'd know I was lying, so I'm not going to bother. The answer was no before and it's no now."

He raises his hand, claw, tentacle.

"I could kill you right here, on this spot."

I take a step back.

"I have the Qomrama, so I'm not sure I believe you. I'm not great at using it, but it's killed for me before. Want to see if it will kill again?"

"If you can kill me why don't you?"

"I don't want to kill you. I just want you to fuck off and leave us alone."

Shaky takes a step, closing the distance between us.

"You can't kill me. The Qomrama won't let you."

"I told you. I don't want to kill you."

I pull the black blade and slash his throat, cutting through the vertebrae and muscle at the back so his head pops off and slops onto the wet ground. Shaky kneels down and picks it up.

"Let's see if you can put yourself together before I figure out the 8 Ball."

Shaky sets his head onto his shoulders and walks away into the dark.

Rain begins to fall again.

So, to sum up. Tonight I had my throat crushed. I was tossed around like a beanbag. I was beaten with a gun butt. I was shot. And now another God hates me. I want a smoke, but when I cough I taste blood. Maybe some bullet fragments in a lung. I put the Maledictions back in my pocket.

It's nights like this that make me want to give up the glamorous work of world saving and take up woodworking or needlepoint. Something soothing and without quite so much ass kicking aimed in my direction.

I wipe the blood off my mouth and head inside.

THE PLACE IS still a mess. Marshals clear away wreckage and try to salvage equipment. They're dispatching patrols to make sure the rest of the city didn't fall down. Rain pours in through the roof, making the floor slick and dangerous. No one pays the slightest attention to me.

The Shonin's lab is still a wreck, but a pathway has been cleared from the door to his worktable. He's picking through the wreckage, looking for books and manuscripts he might be able to save. When he hears me he drops into his chair, cradling his broken arm in his good one.

"So, did you mess everything up, fatso?"

"They're going to do it. Mr. Muninn is. Oh, and I met Zeus on the way in here."

He sits up a little straighter.

"One of the Angra?"

"*The* Angra. The head cheese. Seems like a sweet guy, but a little pissed off."

"You're going to need the Qomrama."

"You're not going to rat me out, are you?"

"At the monastery, the only people punished more than rule breakers were tattletales."

I help him up and we slowly pick our way over downed beams, crushed furniture, and ceiling tiles. He's so full of poison he can barely lift his feet. It takes minutes getting across the room and I can feel every second ticking away.

Once we get to the magnetic chamber, he shuts it down and opens the door. I pull off my glove and take out the 8 Ball with my Kissi hand. The Shonin gives me the box Father Traven made to hold the Qomrama. I put it inside and drop it into my coat pocket.

"There," he says. "If anyone is watching us, we are both complicit."

"Thanks, old man."

I help him back to his chair. He sits and scratches his head with his good hand.

"What time is it?" he says.

I get out my phone.

"A little past eight-thirty."

He doesn't say anything and doesn't move when I go over to him. That's it then. Four hundred years hanging around this rock and it ends in a broken-down Beverly Hills country club. A funny end to a strange life. But he came through when he had to, and that's more than I can say for most people.

I straighten him upright in the chair and lay his hands in his lap in the Dhyana mudra, the only bit of dilettante L.A. Buddhism I can remember.

Someone is at the door. I look up and see Julie. She stops and grimaces.

"You're shot."

"Yeah. I'm hard on clothes."

"Where have you been?"

"I just got my ass kicked in Hell. How are you?"

She comes in and looks around the room.

"I never know what to believe when you open your mouth."

"Want to meet the Devil?" I put out my hand. "Just say the word."

"I'll pass."

I try to angle myself between her and the magnetic chamber, hoping she won't notice that it is gone. But she isn't looking at me. She's spotted the Shonin and goes over to him.

"My God. What happened?"

"I think the book finally finished him. Will you take care of his body?"

She shakes her head.

"I can't. We have a report of a mob of Saint Nick's corpses around Hollywood Forever Cemetery. They're starting to move into the streets, destroying everything in the way. Believe it or not, there are still civilians in the city."

Hollywood Forever. I can't get away from the place. When I die for the last time, dump me in the ocean or a landfill or chop me up and serve me as corn dogs at the state fair. Just don't bury me in Hollywood Forever.

"Let me handle it."

"By yourself?" she says.

"I'll have backup, but your agents won't want to meet them. Give me an hour before you send anyone in."

"Listen. After everything that's happened, these cowboys want to get out and shoot something. I don't know how long I can keep them here."

"Think of something. I'm just asking for an hour. It'll save some of your people's lives."

She thinks for a minute.

"Half an hour."

"Good enough."

I start out, but stop.

"You mind if I take some body armor?"

She looks at my bloody shirt.

"You look like you need it."

"Yeah. I kind of do."

"Let's go find you something."

"One more thing. I want you to do me a favor."

Her eyes narrow.

"Why should I?"

"Because afterward you'll own me."

"Keep talking."

WHEN I'M FITTED up with a vest, I take a shadow to Max Overdrive, fire up the Hellion hog, and head Downtown. Not to see Muninn or Samael or anyone else who can talk. I come straight out into the kennels, where a hundred-plus hellhounds wander restlessly. I'm in and out fast in case anyone wanders down here. I only have a half hour and I don't want to spend it explaining anything to anyone.

As soon as I corral the last hounds I lead them into a shadow at the far end of the place. Their growls and the grinding of their gears fill the air. Their claws tear up the concrete. It's beautiful.

We come out right in front of Hollywood Forever.

Julie said there were chop shops here and she wasn't exaggerating. Only they're not in the cemetery anymore.

It's like New Year's fucking Eve outside the gates. Wall-to-wall, shoulder-to-shoulder Qliphoth morons claw their way onto Santa Monica Boulevard. When the street opens up enough that they have room, they head off in different directions, splashing like happy monster pups off to gnaw on what's left of L.A.'s soggy carcass.

I don't have to tell the hellhounds what to do. They sense it the moment they get a look at Mason's berserkers and rip into the mob without a word from me. The chop shops fight back, but they're just stitched together meat salads and no match for a hyped-up mob of mechanical hellspawn. In just a minute, it's like a holiday sale at Ed Gein's butcher shop. Arms and legs in the half-price bin. Bones and livers on special, two for one.

I can't say the carnage is pretty, but it is satisfying. Mason got the better of me with the games, but I can take back a little from him by flattening his street muscle.

The hounds are well trained. They don't hang around playing with the dead chop shops. Groups of them peel off and follow the rest of the mob through the storm into town.

I rev the bike and head that way too. Mason's goons will be on Hollywood Boulevard eventually, which means they could make it to Max Overdrive. I have to make that sure that Candy and, yeah, even Kasabian are all right.

I head up Gower from the cemetery. Notice a couple of cop cars a street over, but mostly keep my eyes on the road. It's hard to hold the bike steady in the flooded streets.

There isn't a light on anywhere and the clouds have closed in, so even the stars are gone. I stop and put on the night-vision goggles Julie gave me. The city glows a faint green, just bright enough that I can navigate.

I make it across Fountain and Sunset, but at Selma Avenue the streets light up like I've gone over the rim of a volcano. I pull the goggles off and squint my eyes as two LAPD squad cars pull up nose to nose, blocking the road.

Normally in a situation like this I'd be quite disinclined to stick around. I'd zip around the cars on the sidewalk or turn tail and head south. But I still have my Vigil ID. Protection from on high and legit as greenbacks. I button my coat so they won't see the bullet holes and ask stupid questions, then step off the bike.

"Hands over your head," one of the cops calls.

I yell back.

"I'm with the Marshal Service. The Golden Vigil."

"Hands over your head."

I can tell this guy isn't going to take my word for anything, including that I'm a biped from planet Earth. I put my hands up like the nice man said. The pain in my chest heats up again when I get my hands over my head.

"Turn around and walk backward toward us."

"Come on, guys. We're wasting time. Let me just show you my ID."

"If you do not comply we are authorized to use deadly force."

I should have seen that coming. Martial-law bullshit. Shoot looters on sight and harass stragglers while you're at it.

I walk backward to the men in blue. It's not as easy as it sounds in ankle-deep water with your hands over your head throwing off your balance. But I make it out of Dixie and into the promised land of the cops' headlights.

"The ID is in my back pocket if you want to get it out yourselves."

I hear someone splash up behind me.

"Don't even breathe," he says.

He sounds like the nervous type, so I keep my hands up and my mouth shut while he spelunks in my jeans.

"What's this?" he says, pulling the Colt from behind my back.

"That's my gun. Like I've been saying, I'm with the Golden Vigil."

He reaches into my back pocket and comes out with something. It's quiet behind me for a while. Maybe reading wasn't his strongest area back at the academy. I'm sure he has other redeeming qualities.

"Stark," he says. "James Stark."

"That's me."

"The Golden goddamn Vigil."

"Can I put my hands down now?"

"Hey, boys," he says, calling to the other cops. "Want to meet a real live Vigil agent?"

The sound of splashing coming up behind me. No one

gives me permission, but I lower my hands and turn around anyway.

Four of LAPD's finest are going over my credentials under a flashlight. One by one they look at the ID and up at me like they've never seen a photo before and are wondering how I got that tiny doppelgänger onto the card.

A different cop says, "You're James Stark."

"I thought we'd kind of established that."

"Just double-checking," he says.

A second later I'm on the ground. I've never been Tasered before and I can't say I enjoy my first taste of it. Still, just to make sure I get the full effect, another cop lights me up. I want to get up and clock someone, but my body would rather stay down and twitch in the gutter, so that's what it does.

When they let up on the juice, one of the cops rolls me onto my back and shines a light in my eyes. I think he wants to make sure I'm still breathing because when he sees that I'm basically intact, he kicks me a good one in the ribs. Then his friends join in. I'm beginning to think this isn't a by-the-book group. They might even be the vigilantes who helped burn Allegra's clinic.

I try to fight back, but seeing as how I already have a couple of bullets in my chest, I'm less Bruce Lee and more Donald Duck. The body armor takes a lot of the punishment, but these are experienced boys and they know how to make it hurt.

Eventually they get bored or tired or hungry and the kicking stops. One of them, I think it's the one who first took my ID, pulls me upright.

"Audsley Ishii says hello."

All of a sudden this makes more sense.

The cop rolls me over and wrenches my arm around to my

back. I hear the rattle of cuffs and know that if the bastard ever gets them on me I'm dead.

I push back with one hand and buck the cop off. Then I have the other three on top of me and I can't move. Someone else gets their cuffs out. I feel one close on my wrist. Even though I know I'm going to lose, I'm not going to make killing me easy. I kick back and launch one of them off me and get a swift knee to the back of my head. It forces me all the way down under the filthy street water. I have to hold my breath to keep from drowning. I can't even fight anymore.

At first, the sound of screams is muffled by the water. It churns around me as one by one the cops disappear off my back. I sit up and gulp in a lungful of air.

Hellhounds are outlined in the squad-car headlights. One gnaws on a downed cop's leg and the others are off chasing the rest. I hear gunshots, but can't see out into the dark. I don't have to because I know what's happening. The cops are losing. Hellhounds are bad one-on-one. When they're in a pack, there isn't much that can stop them. Sure as hell not a few cop sidearms.

I crawl over to the downed cop and feel around his belt. Find his keys and unlock the handcuff snapped around my wrist. I get up and look around the scene for my gun and ID. I find both by one of the squad cars. The gun is all right, but the ID is a little waterlogged. I slip it into my pocket and put the Colt in the waistband behind my back. Candy has been on me to get a holster. She says my not using one is part of my just-passing-through mentality and that I should get over it. Maybe she's right. Not necessarily about the holster, but about the passing-through thing. Here I am half drowned and with bullets in my chest trying to fucking save this piece-of-shit world. Again. Maybe that doesn't qualify as just passing through anymore. Hell. Maybe I really am sticking around. But I'm still not folding towels.

By the time I'm on my feet, the rest of the hounds have run off after the cops or gone back to chasing down the chop shops. I find my goggles and get back on the bike. Slowly. Every move aches. The body armor might have kept the beatdown from cracking more of my insides, but my ribs took a pounding and the bullets danced a jig all over my insides. I sit still for a minute pulling myself together.

I try to kick-start the bike, but my body has had about as much as it can take tonight. On the third try, I get lucky. The engine rumbles to life and I take off. My half-hour lead time is probably up by now, but the hounds have cleared out of Hollywood Forever by now. I'll let them clean up the last of the chop shops for a while before herding them back Downtown.

I take off on the bike, but as I swing onto Hollywood Boulevard another cop car makes the turn with me, its blinking light bar turning the empty street into the world's saddest rave. But I'm not about to let any more vigilantes get their hands on me and there's no way I'm leading them to Max Overdrive.

I gun the bike, blowing by Musso & Frank's and the Egyptian Theatre. Wouldn't you know it, right at the corner of Hollywood and North Highland there's a familiar naked guy in the street. I try to go around Shaky. As I swing past he looks like a granite monolith, a tangle of thorns, a pulsing black hole. Just as I'm about to pass him, the bike sputters, coughs, and stops. The asshole did it. The asshole killed my bike. I put down the kickstand and head for him.

"Just who the fuck do you think you are?"

"The wronged returned for retribution," he says.

The squad car fishtails to a stop fifty feet from us. The cops get out and hunker down behind the doors. They don't bother with pistols. One has a shotgun and the other an HK rifle.

"Put your hands on your head," shouts the woman cop.

Shaky looks at me. I shrug.

"I'm not doing it. But you can do what you want."

He looks at the cops and says, "Die, God's favorites."

The cops evaporate, like ice dropped into boiling water.

"I could have used that trick five minutes ago."

Shaky turns back to me.

"Give me the Qomrama. I won't ask again."

"No."

"Do you doubt who I am?"

"I know who you are, but it's in my best interest not to give a damn."

Shaky walks to the corner, by the old Hollywood First National Bank Building. Like a lot of L.A. buildings, it can't decide what it wants to be when it grows up. A weird mix of Gothic, Art Deco, with a little Spanish thrown in, it's the perfect place for Shaky to duck into—an empty eleven-story hulk, way past its sell-by date. Just like him.

Only he doesn't duck inside. Shaky strolls into a wall, softens, spreads out like mist, and merges with the concrete.

I hear his voice in my head.

"Perhaps my godly power will not hurt you as long as you possess the Qomrama, but that does not mean you cannot be hurt."

The building shakes like we're having another quake, but the street stays perfectly still. It's just the bank that's moving.

The sidewalk around it cracks and splits open. Water pipes burst. Parked cars roll over on their sides. Buildings all up and down the block shatter and collapse.

Slowly, the bank rises up off its foundations. It twists, like an animal shaking a pest off its fur. Then it stands. Yes, the building can stand because it has a kind of human shape now. A grimy concrete, steel, and plate-glass body. I-beam and ductwork limbs. On top is a billboard for a new reality-TV series featuring five freakishly attractive teens. Their ten vacant eyes blink in unison as Shaky surveys his domain.

His voice whispers in my head.

"Die, God's Abomination."

Shaky swings his massive body, slamming a concrete and rebar fist into the street just a few feet from me. For about two seconds I consider standing my ground and throwing some hoodoo back at him. Instead my ribs throb and I cough a little blood into my mouth and remember that running away is also a good strategy.

I run across the street, and when I turn I see the only thing that might be stranger than a building ready to stomp me into apple butter. It's Mr. Muninn, standing in the middle of the intersection calmly looking up at Shaky like he sees sentient buildings every day of the week.

Only this isn't a Muninn I've seen before. He's yellow, and a little trimmer than the Muninn I know. His face is badly scarred, and when he scans the street with his dead eyes I know who it is.

Fuck this guy. Of course Ruach would show up now that Shaky is going GG Allin all over Hollywood. Better to wreck L.A. than muddy Heaven's golden streets. And lucky me, I'm right in the middle of it all.

Ruach cocks his head this way and that. Blind, he's listening for Shaky, but Muninn said he's half deaf too, so his moves are slow and tentative. But that doesn't mean he's helpless.

Shaky reaches for him and the whole street rumbles and shakes. Ruach swings his arms in Shaky's direction and lets go with a thunderbolt that leaves me blind for a few seconds. When I can see again, Shaky is flat on his back. He slams his concrete-and-steel fists into the street, crushing cars and knocking over streetlights, hauling himself back onto his feet. He roars, blowing out windows up and down the boulevard. I put my hands over my ears and watch him lunge at the small figure of Ruach.

The God brother doesn't move as the bank lands on top of him, leaving a deep crater in the intersection. Shaky stands with Ruach in his giant mitt. He raises his arm and slams Ruach into the crater.

For a moment there's only the sound of the rain. Then another thunderbolt explodes from the crater, hitting Shaky full on, shattering the windows in his chest. Plate glass cascades like a shower of diamonds into the street.

This fight has been a long time coming. How long has it been since Ruach and Shaky have seen each other? A few billion years ago when God was still in one piece and he gave the Angras the bum rush out of town. That's a long time to nurse a grudge. It must be the way I feel about Sylvester Stallone after he remade *Get Carter*.

Shaky staggers as Ruach steps out of the crater. He makes a sweeping gesture and the crushed cars and trucks all along one side of Hollywood Boulevard rapid-fire launch themselves at the bank. Concrete shatters. Steel snaps. But Shaky is still standing, batting away the last few cars with the back of his hand.

He wrenches a huge slab of asphalt from the street and slams it down on Ruach. Stomps it down with his huge foot, buckling the boulevard for a block in each direction.

This could go on all night and wreck half the city. Two partial Gods, duking it out and neither quite strong enough to take the other. Maybe I can do something. Maybe no one needs to sacrifice himself tonight.

I pull Traven's box from my pocket and get out the 8 Ball. The Shonin said it wants to please me, and it's killed for me before. I stare at it, trying to will it to do something, but it just sits there in my hand.

Then shit gets extra interesting.

I don't know if the 8 Ball has a smell or a glow or does a little dance that only Gods can see, but whatever it is, it gets Shaky's attention. He takes a step in my direction. When he does, the ground opens up under him and Ruach pulls him down. He crashes into the street, his body crumbling down one side. Ruach looks like he's heading in for the kill when he stops. The bastard must have picked up the 8 Ball's scent because now he heads my way. But Shaky grabs him and drags him back. I head back up the street, hoping that with them distracted, I can get the bike started again.

A woman staggers up the street in my direction. What's a goddamn civilian doing around here? I head for her, ready to grab her and throw her on the back of the hog.

I get hold of one of her arms and yell, "Come with me."

She bites me. I push her away and she comes back harder this time, shattered teeth chattering like I'm the last drumstick at Thanksgiving.

If I wasn't trying to dodge a couple of angry Gods, I might have looked her over before I got too close. The Eater in her chop-shop body doesn't appreciate my dime-store chivalry and lets me know by trying to gnaw my arm off.

I'm hurt and I don't have time for this noise. I shove the 8 Ball in her face. The moment it touches her she screams. I pull the Qomrama back, drawing the Eater out of her body. As it dies, the woman face-plants in the street.

I head back for the bike, but Ruach is headed there too. I'd bet that, even blind, he saw the 8 Ball light up like a flare and he knows exactly where to find me. He runs toward me, his scarred yellow body glowing into holy fire. I hold up the 8 Ball and it just seems to make him angrier. There's nowhere for me to run.

"Father."

Ruach slows and looks around.

"Father, what are you doing wasting time with this mortal? Your enemy is behind you."

Samael walks calmly across the shattered boulevard to stand beside me.

Ruach points.

"He used the Godeater."

"Not on you."

Ruach starts to say something else when a concrete hand the size of a truck grabs him and pulls him away.

"This might be a good moment to leave," says Samael.

"Hold on a second. I have an idea."

I grab the Hellion hog and roll it off the street, hiding it in a flooded restaurant, between the broken furniture and the islands of rotting arugula.

"Come on," I say. "And grab her."

Samael frowns.

"Where are we going and who is this?"

"Just grab her."

I head for where the cops went down. There's no trace of them and no keys in the car. I pull out the black blade and jam it into the ignition. Turn it hard. The engine revs loud and strong.

Samael trots to the car with the woman's body in his arms. I open the passenger door.

"I don't have a key to the backseat."

"Please," he says, a little disgusted.

He touches the door and it pops open. Right. Locks. An easy trick for angels. He tosses the chop-shop body into the back and settles on the passenger seat.

"This is fun," he says. "Are we on a scavenger hunt?"

I throw the car into reverse and floor it. Water geysers on both sides as I twist the car into the clumsiest one-eighty in the history of car theft, pop it into drive, and head back across town. Ruach and Shaky are still throwing *kaiju* kung fu in the rearview mirror as I break every speed law in L.A. county.

"Are you going to tell me where we're going?" says Samael.

"You're about to save the world. But give me a minute, I have to make a call."

I get out my phone and thumb Candy's number.

"Hey. Where are you?" she says.

"How are you feeling?"

"A lot better. Is anything wrong? You sound out of breath."

"Everything's fine. I just wanted to check in on you."

"That's sweet. Do you have my ice cream?"

"Not exactly. But I have a corpse and a few hundred hell-hounds. And I stole a cop car."

"That's fun. Pick me up. We'll toss a coin to see who gets the handcuffs first. A car will be harder to break than furni-ture, but maybe more fun."

"Sounds great, but I'm sort of busy right now. I did men-tion the corpse and hellhounds, right?"

"Fine. Be a drag. But come home soon. I don't want to spend my last hours on Earth drinking peppermint tea with Kasabian."

"Peppermint tea?"

"I'm still a little dizzy. Peppermint helps."

"I'm living with a hippie."

"Shut up, thief. For once don't forget to wipe your prints off the car before you ditch it."

"Anything else, dear?"

"Seriously, if it looks like things aren't going to work out, come home."

"They're going to work out."

"But if they don't."

"I'll be there."

"What's the corpse for?"

"A long shot. Got to go."

"Don't forget the handcuffs."

"I know. And ice cream."

I hang up. I don't have the heart to tell her that the hand-cuffs disappeared with the cops.

I DITCH THE car across from Vidocq and Allegra's apartment, remembering to wipe down the steering wheel on the off chance that the world doesn't end.

"Let's go," I say.

"Where to?"

"The Room of Thirteen Doors."

I leave the headlights on and take Samael in through a shadow.

He takes a long look around the place.

"Thirteen doors. How charmingly literal. But it's a bit dreary, don't you think? I thought you might have brought in a carpet or at least a table with some flowers on it by now."

"When you fêng-shui Hell, I'll call you for decorating advice."

He points to something near the Door of Drunken Eternity.

"What are those?"

"Those are mine."

He walks over and peers down at them.

"One is the Singularity, isn't it? I don't recognize the other."

"It's the Mithras."

He nods, impressed.

"So that's where it went. Planning on having a cookout?"

"Only if I have to."

"I'm glad all our fates are in the hands of someone whose decisions are so nuanced and well thought out."

Samael walks around the entire room, touching each door as he goes.

I say, "You know how you opened the cop-car door? I

need you to do the opposite here. Seal these doors. Use whatever powers you have to lock them tight so they can never be opened again."

He raps on the last door with his knuckles.

"This one is already sealed."

"That's the Door to Nothing. I sealed it, but I didn't know what I was doing. I need it done right."

"Why?"

"It's where the Kissi lived."

He makes a face.

"You did us all a favor locking them out. What's that door?"

"The Door to Fire. Listen, we don't have time for a full tour."

"This is probably the last chance I'll get to see the place."

"Me too, so stop whining."

I check the time on my phone. It's nine thirty.

"Make sure you bring Mr. Muninn and Chaya to Pershing Square by ten."

"Why there and why then?"

"It's a nice open space. I want to keep clear of big buildings. And I want to make this happen soon. The longer we fuck around, the more Shaky and Ruach are going to trash the city."

"And the world."

"That too."

"Ten o'clock then."

"When Shaky gets there be ready. Things are going to happen fast."

"Of course."

"And let me handle the big stuff. If I need help, you'll know it."

"I enjoy doing the least possible in these situations, so it sounds like a grand old time."

I stand there for a minute overwhelmed and probably looking stupid.

"I don't know if I have this thing entirely figured out."

"You're trying to see the future. That's a mistake. Even Father can't do that. If he could, we wouldn't be in this position in the first place."

I go to the door.

"When you get there, keep an eye on Chaya. I don't want any freak-outs or surprises. But I want the whole family there when it happens."

"If you want this done by ten I should get started."

"I'll leave one door open so you can get back Downtown."

On the way out I say "Thanks," but he's already working on sealing hoodoo and doesn't hear me or pretends he doesn't.

I put the Singularity and Mithras in my pocket and leave Samael in the Room. Any other time I'm not sure if I would leave him in there alone. He'd do something cute, even if it was to get under my skin. But I have to trust him now. And anyway, his skin is on the line too.

I go back to the squad car, then head up to Allegra and Vidocq's apartment. It used to be my apartment when I lived with Alice. Before Mason killed her. Vidocq put a hex on the place when he moved in. Basically, only Sub Rosa and other hoodoo types can see it. It's invisible to civilians. Everyone forgot about the place. Vidocq was never big on paying rent.

I knock on the door and he answers. I leave my package behind some garbage cans in the hall.

"Good to see you. Please come in," he says.

I go in and look around for Allegra, but I don't see her.

"How is she?"

He shrugs.

"Comme ci comme ça."

"I'm fine."

It's Allegra's voice, coming from the kitchen. She walks in with coffee for her and Vidocq. She offers me her cup. I shake my head.

"I'm okay," she says. "It's the clinic that's ruined."

"I'm really sorry."

She sits on the sofa, clutching the cup in her hands.

"I don't suppose it could have lasted forever. Sooner or later someone would find the place and shut it down. The cops. The Board of Health. Someone. I was just hoping it would last a little longer."

Vidocq sits down and puts his arm around her. She rests her head on his shoulder. Lifts it off a moment later and looks at me.

"Are you hurt again?"

I pull my coat closed.

"I tripped on a chocolate bunny."

"I have enough supplies to fix you, you know. And I could use the distraction," she says.

I shake my head.

"Thanks. Tomorrow."

"You look worried. Can we help with something?" says Vidocq.

I listen to the door for a minute in case someone walks down the hall. I don't hear anything.

"I know you lost a lot of gear in the clinic, but remember

when Brigitte got bit by the zombie that time and you put her in a kind of coma. What was that?"

"You mean the Winter Garden?" says Vidocq. "You want to put someone to sleep?"

"She's already kind of asleep."

"What does that mean?" says Allegra.

I get the chop-shop woman from the hall and bring her inside. Allegra raises a hand to her mouth when she gets a look at her.

"What happened to her?"

"Yeah, she isn't pretty, is she?"

She puts her hand on the body's forehead.

"James, she's already dead."

I set the body down on a chair.

"I don't think so. I think she's just empty. The body is fine, but there's no one inside."

Vidocq and Allegra look at each other for a moment.

Allegra opens the chop shop's eyes and peers at them. They're still clear.

"It's not like I have anything else to do right now. I still think she's dead, but I can keep her from getting any deader."

"Thanks. When you're done, just stick her in a corner somewhere. She won't be here long. I have to go."

"Do you need any help?" says Vidocq.

"Lots. But I have a plan. I think. Maybe. I hope. If not, maybe we'll all get lucky and Hell will survive and I'll see you there."

"Why do you think we're going to Hell?" says Allegra.

"Because you're my friends."

It's 9:50. I head out through a shadow for the Nickel— Fifth Street and Pershing Square.

THE SQUARE IS above street level, so it's fairly clear of the flooding. There are trees and benches and not much else around us for a giant to crush me with. The monsoons have backed off a little and the rain has gone from pounding to merely drenching.

After everything that's happened and everything the Shonin told me, I still don't feel like the thing that came along to destroy the universe. Not that I'd know what that felt like. But I have to believe it would feel like something. Not evil or anger or anything like that. Maybe hunger. A deep-down gnawing hunger that won't be filled until it swallows all of creation. What do you chase the universe with? Beer or a cold Coke?

I wonder what oblivion will be like? Let's face it. The chances of everything working out the way I want, the chances of anything I plan working out, are dim at best. Still. What else is there to do? I have a lot to make up for, I guess, even if I never intended to murder everything. Yeah. I thought about it, but I never did it and now I find out I was doing it all along. Funny, the things you find out about yourself. Maybe I should get my aura read or try going macrobiotic. That should take the edge off being a universe killer, right?

I don't know what to think anymore. If I can't trust my own past, what can I trust? And don't say the future because one, there might not be one, and two, how do I know I'm not something else nefarious? A jaywalker or a sleepwalking flimflam man?

I guess I'm supposed to be okay with everything dying. Marcus Aurelius, a guy I read when I was stuck in Hell and finished all the coloring books said, "Death, like birth, is a secret of nature." Only with birth you get a blanket and a bottle. You get a blanket with death too, but they call it a shroud and everyone else gets the bottle. How am I supposed to be okay with that?

The future is a mess, the past is a wreck, and I'm center stage at the shit storm of the century. I guess I can take comfort in knowing that if it all goes balls up tonight, I'll be among the first to die and won't have to see everything gobbled down like an all-you-can-eat buffet.

It's 9:55.

I take the 8 Ball out of my pocket, toss it up into the air, and catch it a couple of times in my Kissi hand. As it falls, it changes shape too quickly for me to see. I want to look anyway because it's the last time I'll see it. I keep tossing it and waiting.

The light in the square goes up a couple of notches. The trees blur and the air turns red. A vault slowly emerges in the air above the treetops. It's red and wet. Not with rain, but blood. The flesh cathedral encloses half the park, like a Grand Guignol band shell. I don't know how many bodies hang inside it. The naves stretch back as far as I can see. It's all of Saint Nick's victims, plus the Angra worshipers who offed themselves.

Weaving through the suspended bodies are two chop shops. The guy is Shaky. I don't recognize the scarred woman.

She says, "I told you you should have joined us. All this pain. All this fighting and here we are, just where I told you we'd be."

I know the voice from our phone chats.

"Deumos? Is that you? Your look finally matches your personality."

She shakes her head. Her face is split nearly down the

middle. Her eyes and lips don't quite line up right. Her face is a mass of wrong angles.

"I won't engage with you, Stark. You're just stalling and you know it's futile. Just give us the Qomrama."

Shaky looks a little bruised after his fight with Ruach.

"Don't waste any more of my time or I'll kill all of your loved ones and make you watch," he says.

I toss the 8 Ball one more time.

"You know, I think I can pull Deumos out with this thing. I wonder if I can do any other tricks?"

I touch it to Deumos's body. The ball glows for a second and stops.

"You see?" she says. "Nothing."

"I'm not so sure. I think you're stuck in that body now."

"What difference does that make?"

"You won't die like an angel. You'll die like meat. Like a mortal."

I check my phone. It's ten o'clock.

Shaky puts out his hand.

"Now, Abomination. Give it to me or see the young Jade die."

"Okay."

I toss it to him. The 8 Ball bounces off his chest and he catches it. Stares at it for a second like he doesn't quite believe it's real. Then he smiles, a wild, ecstatic thing. A smile that's been coming for a billion years.

Shaky holds up the 8 Ball and it sort of unfolds, becomes a hundred different shapes at once. Some alive and some inert. It writhes, spins, flaps, swims, burns, melts. Grows wings, eyes, spines like icebergs, and limbs like dead trees. It does all this at once. I can't look. It hurts my eyes. It hurts my head, trying to take it all in. But I can see the sky. Lightning flashes and the rift opens again. The rip blacks out stars. Something comes through, and this time it's not just smoke and bones. It's fully formed things that are as wild, unidentifiable, and painful to look at as the thrashing 8 Ball. It hurts, but I keep looking.

Shaky takes off like a rocket to meet his asshole buddies. Something huge and yellow streaks after him. It's Ruach, blown up as big as Shaky was when he was a building. But it doesn't do him any good. By the time Ruach catches up, Shaky's friends are close enough to grab him. The twelve of them go wild with their first taste of God-flesh gumbo. They take their time ripping him apart. The Angra's squeals of delight and Ruach's screams of pain are like overlapping claps of thunder.

Nearby, Muninn appears, flanked by Samael and Chaya. I go over to them, wishing Ruach hadn't pulled his little stunt. It's not going to make this any easier.

I open the one remaining door to the Room.

We don't say anything to each other. Just watch.

Deumos loves it. I bet she was a big fan of the arena in Hell, even if she hid it well. I take out the Colt and shoot her in both legs. I don't want her dead just yet. While she's still stunned in her new body, I carry her to the door and toss her in.

"Ladies first," I say.

She just lies there looking around the Room, amazed at how much having a body can hurt. I go back to the carnage in the sky.

By the time I get back, the Angra have finished with Ruach. L.A. becomes Hell for a minute as Ruach's holy blood mixes with the rain, staining the streets red. Where drops touch the flesh cathedral, it and the hanging bodies shrivel up and disappear.

Watching his brother being killed, Muninn walks forward so the Angra can see him. He's a brave son of a bitch. Samael keeps a hand on Muninn's shoulder and Muninn doesn't seem to mind. Chaya looks like he'd like a one-way ticket to Zanzibar or wherever the farthest place from Pershing Square is.

The Angra spread out across the sky.

Shaky looks down at us, his lunatic smile smeared with God blood. It's easy to tell when he spots Muninn because he lets out a shriek that deafens every bird and sets off every car alarm from L.A. to downtown Tokyo.

All thirteen of the Angra Om Ya, pissed, crazy, sporting vengeance hard-ons the size of Mount Rushmore, dive for Pershing Square.

Muninn moves closer to the door. He can't let them get him. He has to draw them inside for this to work.

It's hard to figure out the exact timing on everything. Staring up through the rain at flying elder Gods, it's not easy to get a sense of scale and distance. We're going to have to do this free jazz. Try to find a melody and a beat in the cacophony, and improvise our way to the end.

Samael walks Muninn closer to the door.

I go to Chaya.

"Aren't you going to say good-bye to your brother, you chickenshit?"

He looks like he wants to strangle me again, but he's too freaked out to do it. I shove him and he lets me. But he looks at me hard.

"Tread lightly, monster. I'll be the God of this universe soon."

I look over at Muninn, then up at the sky. The Angra are almost down on us.

Samael puts his arms around his father.

The Angra can't be more than a hundred feet above us.

I gut-punch Chaya. He doubles up, then chokes when I take something from my pocket and shove it down his throat.

Samael lifts Muninn into the air as I shove Chaya as hard as I can into the Room.

Samael throws Muninn on the ground and I hit the deck as the Angra fly overhead, chasing the only God brother they can see into their precious Room. Then I close the door.

And wait for the universe to explode.

But it doesn't.

There's just a soft thud and a mild earthquake, like a nuke going off a hundred miles underground. Then all I can hear or feel is the rain. And the pain in my chest because throwing your dumb ass on the ground with bullets in your chest is a poor escape plan. By the time I push myself back up to my feet, Muninn is heading my way. If he was another kind of God, he'd be spitting fire and locusts at me.

"Was it your plan all along to sacrifice Chaya?" he shouts. "You made a promise to me and you didn't keep it."

I hold up my hands in case he thought of the locusts on the way over.

"The universe needs you more than it does your idiot brother."

He turns on Samael.

"And you," says Muninn. "You were in on this together."

"No," says Samael. "But to be fair, Father, if Stark hadn't done it, I would have."

Muninn sits on a bench, his hands balled into fists.

"You've given them the Room. You've unleashed the Angra on all of creation."

I pull the Mithras out of my pocket and show it to him.

"Relax. Chaya bravely volunteered to swallow the Singularity. With all the doors locked, the Angra either died in the Big Bang when it went off or they have a whole new universe to play with. Whichever it was, they're stuck in the Room and they're not coming back."

Muninn looks at me.

"You killed my brother. You killed part of me."

"With all due respect, Mr. Muninn. You killed off all those other parts of yourself when you stole the universe and started this fight. I just made sure you were the last man standing."

Muninn puts his hands flat on his knees.

"You understand that you can never use the Room again."

"Maybe we can chip in and get him a bus pass," says Samael.

I look over at him.

"If your stupid brother hasn't killed my bike completely, I'll be fine."

Muninn stands up, looking into the sky, blinking against the rain.

"I have to go and think about things."

He vanishes.

Samael and I look at each other. He follows me under a tree and I light a Malediction.

"I'm kind of fucked, aren't I?"

He furrows his eyebrows.

"You he might just kill. I have to go home and live with the man. Which one of us is truly the fucked one?"

I puff the cigarette like it might be my last, because it might.

"I can't take the hellhounds back now. You'll have to do it."
Samael nods.

"Another mess I have to clean up for you."

"Probably the last."

I offer Samael a cigarette and he takes it. I give him mine and he lights his off it.

"With the Room gone, I suppose we won't be seeing each other very much anymore," he says.

"Good riddance. You never returned your videos anyway."

"And I never rewound in the VHS days."

We don't talk as we finish our smokes.

When we're done I say, "Think you can give me a ride home? My bike's in Hollywood and I can't shadow-walk anymore."

He rolls his eyes.

"Come along, Abomination," he says.

I stand next to him. And in the next instant I'm alone in front of Max Overdrive. I go in the side door and straight upstairs.

Candy is asleep in the bedroom. Kasabian is under a blanket on the sofa. *Destroy All Monsters* plays silently on the big screen. I turn it off, strip naked, and slide into bed.

I wake up a few hours later when I hear something strange. Silence.

I go to the window. The rain has stopped. The war in Heaven is over. Muninn is taking charge there and in Hell.

I go back to bed. Muninn has it in for me and the bullets are still in my chest. I'll either wake up dead or I won't.

I COME AWAKE with someone shaking me. I expect Candy, but when I open my eyes I see Samael. He hands me my clothes and puts a finger to his mouth telling me to be quiet.

We go out into the living room and I close the bedroom door.

"What are you doing here?"

"I got you a black shirt to hide your wounds."

I take the shirt and start dressing.

"Did Mr. Muninn send you here to kill me?"

He looks out the widow and doesn't say anything for a minute.

"How does it feel to be stuck in one place at a time with no shadows to stroll through?"

"It's only been a night. Ask me in a week."

"You'll be begging Father for wings."

"Wings are for you angel types. Maybe I'll ask for a jet pack."

"I wouldn't ask for anything for a while."

He takes my arm, and in the time it takes to blink, we're in Muninn's penthouse in Hell.

Muninn is at his desk in the library signing and organizing papers.

"Hello, Mr. Muninn."

He doesn't say anything. He doesn't turn around. He just starts talking.

"However well intentioned your actions were last night, the fact remains that you broke our agreement. When I owed you a favor I complied. When you owed me a favor you couldn't fulfill the commitment."

"I'm sorry you feel that way, but I stand by what I said.

The universe is in bad enough shape. It doesn't need to get worse and it would have with Chaya in charge."

He finally turns around. He's frowning.

"That's not the point."

"For me it is. I know that makes me an arrogant asshole, but so's your kid. He agrees with me."

Samael puts up his hands.

"I'm a neutral third party in this discussion."

"Coward."

"Yes."

Muninn shakes his head. Sets down his pen on the desk.

"Everything is different now. Everything is changed."

"That's a good thing, isn't it?"

"You're the cause of much of it, but if I asked your opinion you'd point out that I was the original instigator. Isn't that right?"

"Who cares how we feel about things? The universe is safe now. That's all that matters."

Muninn gets up and walks to a set of bookshelves, not like he's looking for anything. He just wants time to gather his thoughts.

"I've been thinking about some of our earlier conversations. Samael and I have been talking them over."

I lean on the sofa.

"Did you bring me here to kill me? I could have stayed in bed for that."

He scratches his chin.

"I thought about it. I had to ask myself if your continued existence was more of an asset or a liability for the universe."

"And?"

"I've put off a final decision for the time being."

"Thanks, I guess. I mean all us nondeities are born with

a gun to our heads and someday it'll go off. At least I know I'm not immortal. The laundry bills would have killed me."

Muninn goes out into the hall and we follow. He walks us down to the main room by the big picture windows.

"The real reason I wanted to bring you here was to remind you of the state Hell was in when you left."

I get a bad feeling in my gut.

"You're not going to make me Lucifer again, are you?"

"No. That would be cruel to the damned. But I wanted you to have a last look at the place. As I said before, everything is different now."

"Are you making Samael Lucifer again?"

Muninn seems lost in his thoughts again. Like he's still trying to find the words.

"There won't be any more Lucifers," he says. "And no more Hell. At least not in its present form."

"I'm not getting you."

"We talked once . . . well, you harangued and I politely listened, about opening the gates of Hell. Dismantling it in a sense. Opening Heaven to whoever among the fallen can make their way there and who choose to stay. Hell will remain as it is. With a few repairs to make it more hospitable. Any angel or soul that chooses to remain here can do so."

"That's great news. Really."

He nods, but doesn't look happy.

"Now that things have changed, we must change with them."

"You're going home now to run Heaven, I guess."

He shakes his head.

"No. I'm old and worn out and need a rest. Samael will rule in Heaven."

Samael smiles like it's his birthday and he got a free Grand Slam breakfast at Denny's. I give him a couple of seconds of applause.

"Lucifer finally gets to make Heaven the way he wants it. What will the tabloids say?"

"That I'm a reformed devil. Don't forget to mention that when they call you for a quote."

"He won't be entirely in charge, of course," says Muninn. "More of a regent taking care of things day-to-day in my place."

Samael shrugs.

"I tried to get him to retire, but he won't give up the family business."

I look at Muninn.

"Where are you going?"

"Where I wanted to be all along. Back to my cavern under Los Angeles. Maybe I'll even reopen my shop in the Bradbury Building."

"That sounds great. I'll stop by and say hi."

"Yes. You should," he says. "But not for a while."

"Understood."

He takes a battered piece of metal from his pocket. It looks like an old skeleton key, but one that he saved from a garbage disposal.

"I thought about adding this to my collection, but since you gave me the Mithras I thought you might like it."

He hands it to me.

"The possession key?"

Muninn nods. He walks down the hall and we have to follow again. He goes into the kitchen and starts making a cup of tea.

"You have some bad history with the key. I thought you might like to see that no one else had it. Even me."

"Is this another test? Like when you gave me the Mithras?"

He spoons leaves into a tea ball.

"I'm letting you test yourself."

I weigh the mangled key in my hand.

"I might actually have a use for this."

He looks up, surprised.

"You're going to use it, then?"

"Just once. And with her permission."

He puts a kettle on to boil.

"I'm too tired to care about your schemes. Do what you want as long as the other person agrees."

"Thanks."

He goes to the refrigerator and looks around for milk. Samael taps me on the shoulder.

"Time to go," he says.

"Bye, Mr. Muninn. I'll see you around. But not for a while."

"But not forever either."

"Don't say a word," says Samael. "For once, leave while you're still ahead."

We go down a few floors in the elevator.

"Your friends have adjoining rooms at the end of the hall on the right. I'm on the floor just below Father's. Take your time. Come get me when you're done and I'll take you home."

"Thanks."

He nods and goes back upstairs.

I walk down the hall and knock on a door. A man's voice says, "Come on in."

Standing in the middle of the room in a hotel robe as fine as a terry-cloth Cadillac, and with a glass of whiskey in his hand, is Wild Bill. He turns around once to show me his good fortune.

"Hi, Bill. How are you doing?"

He comes over and shakes my hand.

"I've been worse. The grub in this place is par-damn-excellence."

"Fancy talk for a gunslinger."

"I'm no dandy, but a feller could get used to this."

"Or maybe something better. You heard about the changes happening around here?"

He sips his drink.

"'Bout opening up the place? Yeah. I heard. I can't say I entirely hold with letting all those murderers and bushwhackers out of here."

"I guess it's a philosophical thing. Can even busted-up souls be saved or redeemed or something?"

He looks at me.

"What do you think?"

"I wanted to kill everyone in the world, but I got over it. Maybe some of these other idiots can too."

He nods like he's thinking it over.

"I hear they're leaving the place open for folks who don't want to go."

"You're thinking about staying?"

"Hell no. I'm no fool. But I can't say what Heaven's about. I'll go, but I'm keeping the saloon in case the place isn't to my liking."

"Sounds like a good idea."

"What about you? Where are you headed?"

"When I came down here I thought maybe it was going to be permanent. But it doesn't look that way, so I'll be heading home to Earth."

He comes closer. Taps his finger on my chest. It hurts.

"Be good to your gal. I could've done a lot better in that department. Maybe I'll get a chance to make up for some things like that."

I nod so he'll stop poking me.

"Listen, Bill, something happened last night and I won't be able to come Downtown again or up to Heaven."

He puts his hands behind his back and looks at me.

"The old man finally clipped your wings?"

"Something like that."

"Well, it's been a hell of a time getting to know you. I owe you a lot, not a thing I say lightly."

"You don't owe me anything, Bill. Take care of yourself. We'll see each other again down the road."

"Make it a good long time."

"That's the plan."

He pours me a whiskey and we have a drink together.

"That little Cindil gal's been asking about you. You should go and see her."

"I will. Bye, Bill."

"Take care, son."

I go out into the hall and knock on the next door.

Cindil opens it.

"I thought I heard you in with Bill. I'm glad you're all right."

"I'm fine."

She pulls me inside the room. Touches my shirt and takes a step back.

"You're still hurt."

"I've got a friend who can fix me up, but I wanted to see you first."

"Why?"

"You heard about how everyone can leave now, right?"

She nods.

"Yeah. Everyone is excited."

"That's what I wanted to talk to you about. I still feel bad about what happened to you back home."

"You saved me down here. And now I get to see Heaven. That's not so bad."

"How would you like to come back to the world?"

When she speaks, her voice goes up a little.

"What? How?"

"There's a woman back on Earth and there's nobody inside her. No soul. No mind. Nothing. I can give you her body."

She sits on the bed.

"I can come home?"

"Understand, this isn't an ordinary body. It's kind of a mess. If you come back you won't have any past or any ID. You won't be pretty, but you won't be any worse than me. And you'll be alive."

"Yes," she says. "Please. How will you do it?"

I take out the key and show it to her.

"It doesn't look like much, but I can use it to kind of possess you into the body."

"I can't believe it."

"I'll see you in L.A. soon."

I go back upstairs and Samael takes me to where I left the Hellion hog in Hollywood. I just want to go home, but I have to go and see Julie. We have a lot to talk about.

I SLEEP THE whole next day with Candy curled beside me. When I dream it's about stars and churning clouds of gas and things moving through the void, shaping the new universe as they go. Sometimes I dream about the arena and how I'll never see it again, and in a strange way it makes me sad. But mostly, I don't dream at all and it feels good.

When I wake up, I open the curtains. The rain hasn't come back. The sky is still mostly clouds, but they're starting to break up. Patches of boring, flat blue L.A. sky flash by every now and then, looking great. The street in front of Max Overdrive is still wet, but the floodwaters are gone and it doesn't feel like we're riding steerage in Noah's ark anymore.

By the time I make it downstairs, Kasabian has cleared up his mountain of delivery- and frozen-food boxes and deposited them outside in the overflowing Dumpster. We don't talk to each other, just nod because it's too strange to talk and risk that this is a dream and that it's still pouring outside and talking will wake us. I take the wet towels away from the bottom of the door, bring them upstairs, and hang them over the shower rod. At some point, all this silence is going to get old, but for now it suits me just fine.

A half hour later, Candy comes sleepily out of the bedroom in one of the silk shirts left over from when I was Lucifer. I'm on the couch. She sits on my lap and wraps her arms around me like she's going to fall asleep again. We stay that way for a few minutes, but I have to break the clinch when the pressure of her on my chest grinds bullets against bone.

She gets off me and says, "You should go see Allegra."

"Yeah."

"Today."

"Sure."

She goes into the little kitchen and does whatever magic people do to make the coffeemaker work. I suppose learning how to use it is one of the things she meant by not acting like I'm just passing through. I'm probably going to have to learn a lot of new things now that I don't have the Room anymore. At least the bike worked when Samael brought me back to Earth. It was a relief to be back and away from Mr. Muninn. I kept waiting for him to change his mind and smite me good, but I guess he's tied up organizing bus schedules to ferry a few billion souls and angels north. Good. A busy God is a happy God and it means I'm not on his mind. I'm going to give him a lot of space when he gets back to L.A. Maybe I'll send him a card next Christmas and see if I get a lump of coal back.

It's sometime in the late afternoon when Candy and I manage to get dressed. I pick up my clothes I dropped when I got back from Downtown. Put the body armor, the na'at, the Colt, and the black blade on top of the dresser. I don't know what I'm going to do with them now. I'm not fighting Qliphoth or elder gods or Hellions or High Plains Drifters anymore. What am I supposed to do with myself? Am I really just going to be a schmuck running a video store? At least the government money should be coming in soon. I solved their little end-of-the-world problem. I should have asked for a half million in pennies so Candy and I could go surfing on it. But I'll happily take a check. Oh shit. I'm going to have to get a bank account. I hadn't thought of that. I wonder if my

Vigil ID will be enough for a bank to believe I'm true blue or if I'll have to get one of Vidocq's crooked friends to set me up with a new identity. I should ask him anyway. Cindil will need one.

I check my watch. It's going to be a long day and I'm not looking forward to it.

There's a knock on the downstairs door around three. The sky is closing up again but it doesn't look like rain. I go downstairs and open the door. It's Julie and a whole football team of Vigil agents.

"Agent Sola. I thought it was a snow day and I could pick up my homework tomorrow."

She doesn't crack a smile.

"This isn't about you, Stark. It's about Candace Jade. Remember her? The prisoner you helped escape? Don't tell me she isn't here because I know she is. Go and get her or I'll have her extracted by force."

I look over her stone-faced Pinkertons.

"You're fucking kidding me. I do your job for you, clear out the chop shops myself and stop the goddamn Angra, and you pull this?"

"She's an escaped prisoner. There are rules."

"The Shonin wouldn't be happy with any of you right now. And he was a fucking monk. A holy man."

"Stop stalling."

"I asked him once if he worked for the Vigil or the world. He gave me the right answer. You loafer-wearing shitbirds don't have a clue what the right answer is."

Julie unbuttons her jacket. Puts a hand on her Glock.

"Now, Stark."

The video-shop door slams open. Candy comes running

out in one of my coats. It's too big and she looks ridiculous. She has my Colt in her hand.

She yells, "Fuck," but before she gets "you" out, Julie pulls her gun and puts six shots into her.

Candy drops the Colt and doesn't move. Blood pools under her. A lot of it. It drips over the curb and into the street. Flows away with the rainwater down into the sewer. Julie takes a couple of steps toward the body. I get in front and stick a finger in her face.

"Not if you want to live," I shout. "Don't touch her. None of you."

For thirty seconds it's a *High Noon* standoff. The Vigil punks try to stare me down, but none of them make a move.

Finally, Julie puts her pistol back in its holster and says to one of the agents, "You have video?"

"Yes, ma'am," says the Pinkerton with the camera.

Julie waves to her posse.

"Back on the trucks. The tape will do. Washington doesn't need any more pixie corpses contaminating the facilities."

Julie leads her agents to an ASV parked down the street. The asshole with the camera lingers for a few seconds. Gets some good footage of me crouched over Candy's body like a dumb animal.

When they're gone, I call Allegra. She says she and Vidocq will be right over.

Kasabian is back hiding in his room again.

AND THEN IT'S Christmas. I'm at Bamboo House of Dolls and I'm drunk. The bar is as close to crowded as it's been in weeks. Vigilantes burned a lot of the other Lurker bars in town, or they flooded, so Carlos has a whole new clientele.

How many days has it been since the scene outside the store? I'm a little blurry on the matter. Anyway, it's the jolly time of year, right? And in a couple of days it will be exactly a year since I escaped from Hell, a place that, by now, might not exist anymore.

I'm back drinking Jack Daniel's. It's not bad, but it's not Aqua Regia and I can't go Downtown to get more. I'm down to my last carton of Maledictions. The world is closing in fast and I don't like it one bit.

People tried talking to me earlier, but I'm not in the mood, so now they're mostly leaving me alone. Except for Carlos. For once he's not tending bar. He hired Fairuza for the holidays. Turns out she can pour beer and whiskey in glasses as well as anyone, and she even knows how to make a couple of cocktails. Kasabian hangs around the end of the bar chatting her up at every opportunity. She even smiles back at him. I guess she's gotten over the Mason-is-coming-to-swallow-our-souls thing. Carlos is still pouring drinks, but I'm his only customer at the moment. I'm happy that the Sub Rosa stepped in and got the Lurkers released, but I don't want drinks from Fairuza because it makes me think about Candy's band and I don't want to go there right now.

Carlos and I are hunkered down at a table in the back corner of the bar, a bottle of Jack between us and two shot glasses. On the jukebox, Martin Denny is playing a tiki version of "White Christmas."

"You are one morose fuck, you know that?" says Carlos. "You're literally sucking the entire concept of happiness from my body."

"I've got a lot on my mind."

"I know. I'm just saying that you're a holly jolly black hole and I thought you ought to know that."

"Your advice is much appreciated."

"That wasn't advice. That was an observation. If you want advice, it's to have another drink."

"Thank you, Doctor. I concur."

Carlos pours us both shots.

Vidocq and Allegra are at a table by the door. Cindil is with them. She doesn't look like Cindil anymore, but she doesn't look like the chop-shop train wreck I put her in. Allegra has been using the divine light stones and other medical hoodoo to fix up Cindil's face and erase the scars. She's dyed her hair magenta. It looks good on her.

Manimal Mike, the Tick Tock Man, is at the end of the bar deep in discussion with Tykho, the head of the Dark Eternal vampire gang. Most vampires don't do Christmas, but here she is. I guess we all need our secret vices.

I packed up the last of Candy's things and put them in the storage room this morning. I put her guitar in last.

It's a good thing Carlos is having this sort of reopening party. Kasabian and I don't have enough cash to throw our own party. Even after saving this sorry rock one more time, the government welshed on paying me because I never did turn in those psych evaluation forms. A technicality, but isn't that what bureaucrats exist for? Max Overdrive needs money and I've lined up work. It might be a huge mistake, but it's one more favor I owe.

Carlos pours us another round and goes off to make sure that in all the merriment Fairuza is remembering to charge people for drinks.

I wonder if I should get rid of all the sheets and pillowcases too. Candy brought them with her when she moved in.

Word is that the Vigil is cleaning up the last *Der Zorn Götter* cells around L.A. What do you charge people with for trying to murder the world? I'm sure the Vigil will come up with something suitably creative and vindictive. I hope so.

I'm learning to use the coffeemaker. Turns out there are manuals for that kind of thing. I hope the wash-and-fold place opens again soon. I need to clean the blood out of a few delicates.

The Sub Rosa is doing double shifts this holiday season, springing Lurkers like Fairuza from federal pens and covering up for dying Gods, walking buildings, and all the other catastrophic hoodoo that's been going down in L.A. The Augur might be gone, but the Sub Rosa still have friends in high-and-mighty places. Tuatha is running things temporarily while the board of directors searches for a new scryer. Lots of luck. If any Sub Rosas come around looking for trouble, I won't hit them. I'll tell them the one thing that they won't want to hear. That they're Qliphoth. Just Eaters, Diggers, and Gluttons in designer shoes.

Brigitte comes in with a blonde. She waves to me. The blonde raises her hand to wave, but Brigitte gets between us and steers her to the bar.

On the plus side of things, Audsley Ishii has disappeared. I'll probably have to kill him sometime, but not tonight. Tonight is eggnog and reindeer games. Ho ho ho.

I pour another shot.

When I look up, Julie is standing by the table.

"Can I sit down?"

"You own me. Why not?"

"Don't complain to me. You're the one who wanted a favor."

"According to Carlos, I'm the Krampus. A total Christmas sinkhole."

"Is it because of Candy or because of me?"

"I lost a girlfriend and gained a boss. You tell me."

"You didn't lose her. You just lost a version of her. I bet she's here right now. Isn't she?"

"You tell me."

I owe Julie a lot. So does Candy. More than either of us can ever repay, but I guess I'll try playing second fiddle now that she's reopened her detective agency.

"I don't see her."

"Good. That's the idea."

She pours herself a drink in Carlos's glass.

"I hear through the grapevine that Wells might not go to prison after all. I put in my report about possession and mind control and someone back east believed me. They'll want your report too. To corroborate mine."

"To help Wells?"

"You said you would."

"I say a lot of stupid things."

She holds up her glass. I clink mine against hers.

"I'll do it this week."

"Tomorrow."

"Yes, boss."

The best-dressed man in L.A. bellies up to the bar and asks Fairuza a question. She points to where I'm sitting and he heads in our direction.

I lean over to Julie.

"You can stay for this or you can leave. If you stay, it'll be weird. If you go, you'll be sorry."

Julie squints at me.

"I hope you aren't going to write your reports in riddles like that."

Samael reaches our table.

"Too late now," I say.

"Too late for what?" says Samael.

"For her to avoid you. Now that you're here, please be nice."

He beams down at Julie and puts out his hand.

"Hello. I'm Samael."

"Another one-name guy. Like Stark."

He pulls up a chair and sits down.

"We do share that affectation, I'm afraid."

I point at him.

"For me it's an affectation. For him it's just his name. He doesn't have a last name."

"Everyone has a last name," says Julie.

"Not angels."

She looks at me, then Samael.

"Is this another one of your tall tales? Going to Hell? Hanging around with God?"

"This is your new employer?" says Samael. "She doesn't seems to have a lot of faith in you."

"What we are and what we do is hard for sane people to accept."

"You're serious," says Julie. "This man is an angel."

"Why is that so surprising?" he says. "It's Christmas. L.A. must be full of angels."

Samael reaches into his coat and pulls out a bottle of Aqua Regia and sets it on the table.

"You are a God," I say.

"No. But I'll do in his stead."

Julie looks at us.

"You two are so full of shit."

Samael says, "This man fights monsters for you. He fought a serial killer who couldn't possibly be a mere human. He killed ancient evils and is sitting here right now with bullets in his chest, and you can't take his word for it that I'm an angel?"

Julie blinks.

"No one's ever asked me a question like that before."

Samael gives her his ten-thousand-watt smile.

"Of course we're joking, my dear. There's no such thing as angels. They're an old folktale, like leprechauns and virgins."

He gets up from the table. Puts his finger on top of the Aqua Regia bottle.

"I've left a case of this and some Maledictions at home for you."

"Merry Christmas, Samael."

"And to you. Nice meeting you, Julie."

"How do you know my name?"

"It's just a trick I can do."

"Stark said that to me when we first met."

"I guess all us angelic frauds know the same jokes."

He turns, weaves his way through the crowd, and heads out, slowing for just a second to look at the blonde with Brigitte.

"Will Samael be coming around the office when we're working together?" says Julie. "He's kind of cute, in a vaguely sinister way."

"And that's your type?"

She looks at me.

"Unfortunately, it is."

I start to get up and walk to the bathroom when I notice Brigitte heading our way. She comes over and hugs me.

"Merry Christmas, James."

"Merry Christmas to you."

She points to the blonde. She's Japanese. Young, in a shaggy pink fake-fur coat.

"Have you two met?"

"Hi," she says. "I'm Chihiro."

She puts out her hand and I shake it.

"Like the girl in *Spirited Away*."

"What's that?" she says.

"It's a movie."

She smiles crookedly.

"I'll have to watch it sometime."

"I think you'd like it."

"May we join you?" says Brigitte.

"Of course."

Brigitte brings over a chair. She sits next to Julie and Chihiro sits where Samael was, next to me.

Julie does a small wave.

"Hi. I'm Julie."

I can't take my eyes off Chihiro.

"Sorry. This is Julie. My new boss."

"New boss? What kind of work do you do?" says Chihiro.

"I used to work for the government. But now I run a detective agency."

Chihiro nods.

"This is a good town for it. Things go missing all the time."

"It's our job to bring them back home again," I say.

"You any good at it?" says Chihiro.

"We'll just have to wait and see."

"Don't wait too long. It might get away."

"Then I wasn't supposed to find it in the first place."

Chihiro raises her eyebrows.

"You're a philosopher."

"No. Just drunk."

"That sounds like a very good idea," says Brigitte. "Let's all have too many drinks. I'll get us more glasses."

Chihiro presses her leg against mine under the table. I want to kiss her and I know she wants to kiss me too, but we'll have to take it slow. Let the idea of Candy being dead settle into everyone's mind.

She has a new name and she's blonde now. To the ones who can't see past the glamour. Having Julie here was a good test. She didn't spot Candy at all. It took my hoodoo, Vidocq's alchemy, and Allegra's herbs and potions to come up with a glamour strong enough to fool even most Sub Rosa. I don't know how long it will last, but we have the formula now, so we can reapply it when we have to. Too bad we're the only ones who can ever know about the stuff. We could make a fortune selling it.

"What do you do for a living, Chihiro?" says Julie.

"I'm a guitarist."

"Are you in a band? Would I have heard of you?"

"We broke up, unfortunately. But I'm putting a new one together."

"Good luck," says Julie.

"Thanks."

Chihiro looks at me.

"Aren't you going to say good luck?"

"I don't think I have to. By the way, I have a guitar at home that no one is using. It's red . . ."

"Sold," she says. "When can I come by and see it?"

"Tomorrow. Around one?"

"A late riser? Me too. I'll be there on the dot."

Brigitte comes back with glasses and a bottle of vodka.

"I know the whiskey and I've heard of the vodka," says Julie.

She picks up the Aqua Regia.

"But what's this?"

"It's not from around here. And it's kind of strong. You wouldn't like it."

She sits back in her chair.

"That sounds like a challenge."

"It isn't. Trust me. Only very bad people drink this swill."

"You talked me into it."

Julie downs her Jack Daniel's and points to the empty glass.

"Hit me."

"Okay. But first I have to piss. Don't touch the stuff until I get back."

I give the bottle to Chihiro.

"You're in charge. Keep this away from her. If she's going to taste it, I want to be here to see."

She salutes me.

"I'm on it, sir," she says. "None shall pass."

I head to the bathroom in the back of the bar.

Okay. We met. But that's it for now. It will take awhile

to get used to calling her a new name, but I should have guessed that if she had to pick a disguise she'd go for a *kogal* pinup.

Tomorrow I'll give her the guitar. That will have to be it for a while. Then, sometime after New Year's, we can accidently run into each other at the bar and buy each other drinks. Of course, Chihiro won't be able to use any of Candy's stuff. She'll need everything new. Clothes. Music. Lots of Hello Kitty, robot, and anime tchotchkes. It will all cost money. The last thing I want to be is a half-baked Mike Hammer, but until I pay off my debt to Julie for helping me fake Candy's death, it's what I'll do.

I wait until the last guy clears out of the bathroom and shove the trash can under the doorknob, blocking it. I need a moment to myself.

I go into one of the stalls and close the door.

It hurt seeing Candy even playing dead. It's nothing I ever want to see again. I'm just glad none of the Vigil assholes got close enough to tell that what she was bleeding was blood from my chest wounds cut with some Karo syrup, all taped to the body armor under her coat. It was all so close to falling apart. Mason. The Angra. Tossing Chaya and Deumos. Killing Candy. One wrong move could have brought the whole thing down on top of us. But we got away with everything. For once.

I want to live small for a while. No Gods, good or bad. No angels or Hellions. No ghosts or zombies. Just divorcées and insurance scams. That sounds like paradise. Like two weeks back at the Chateau Marmont with twenty-four-hour room service.

I light a Malediction and draw the smoke slowly into my lungs. It hurts so good.

There's a light knock on the stall door. Great. The place wasn't clear after all.

"Go away. Sorry I blocked the door. Just move the can."

He knocks again, so light it's almost inaudible.

"Please go away."

No one says anything. I wait to hear the sounds of the trash can being moved.

"Mr. Stark?"

"Yeah?"

"May I speak to you for a moment?"

"No. It's Christmas. Go away."

"I can't."

"Sure you can. Aim your feet. First right, then left. Try it."

He knocks again.

"What?"

"Mr. Stark. I understand you do investigations."

"No. That's my boss. She's outside. In the back with a drunk Czech and a hot blonde. You can't miss them."

He knocks.

"Please, Mr. Stark. I'd rather deal with you. My case is unique."

"How unique?"

The guy who pushes the stall door open looks like yesterday's lunch, eaten and thrown back up again. A gray, patchy beard. Hair a terminal thicket of cowlicks. A trench coat that might have been tan once, but is now the color of cold grease and rhino shit.

"Please, Mr. Stark," he says. "It has to be you."

"Why?"

He opens his coat. He isn't wearing a shirt. His chest is a mass of torn muscle and cracked bones. There's a gaping hole where his heart should be.

"Mr. Stark, I need your help with an investigation. My name is Death. And I appear to have been murdered."

I hate this job already.

ABOUT THE AUTHOR

New York Times bestselling author Richard Kadrey has published nine novels, including *Sandman Slim, Kill the Dead, Aloha from Hell, Devil Said Bang, Kill City Blues, Butcher Bird,* and *Metrophage,* and more than fifty stories. He has been immortalized as an action figure, his short story "Goodbye Houston Street, Goodbye" was nominated for a British Science Fiction Association Award, and his novel *Butcher Bird* was nominated for the Prix Elbakin in France. The bestselling and acclaimed writer and photographer lives in San Francisco, California.

I BREAK HIS wrists so I don't have to break his neck.

He falls to his knees, but I don't think it's the pain, though I make sure there's plenty of that. It's the sound. The crack of bones as they shatter. A sound that lets you know they're never going to heal quite right and you're going to spend the rest of eternity drinking your ambrosia slushies with two hands.

I'm surprised to see an angel down here right now, considering all the cleanup going on in Heaven after the recent unpleasantness. Still, there are sore losers and bad winners in every bunch. I don't know which one this guy is, but I caught him spray-painting GODKILLER on the front of Maximum Overdrive, the video store where I live. I might have let him off easy if all he wanted to do was kill me. I'm used to that by now. But this fucker was ruining my windows. Do these winged pricks think I'm made of money? I'm about broke, and here's this high-and-mighty halo polisher setting me up for a trip to the hardware store to buy paint remover. I give his wrists an extra twist for that. He gulps in air and makes a gagging sound like he might throw up. I take a couple of steps back and look around. No one on the street. It's just after New Year's, the floods have receded, and people are just beginning to drift back into L.A.

"What exactly is your problem?" I ask the angel. "Why come down here and fuck with me?"

He rests his crippled hands on his thighs and shifts around on his knees until he's facing me.

"You had no right. You killed him."

"I didn't kill God and you know it. He's Uptown right now putting out new lace doilies in Heaven."

What really happened is a long story. Truth is, I did fuck over Chaya, a weasely fragment of God who, if he'd lived, would have ruined the universe. But I also left one good God part, Mr. Muninn, fat and happy and back in Heaven. But that's the problem with angels. They're absolutists. I clipped a tiny bit off their boss and now I'm the bad guy. Once angels get an idea in their head, there's no arguing with them.

Like cops and people who listen to reggae.

The angel narrows his eyes at me.

"Yes, a part of the father yet remains. But you didn't have the right to kill *any* of him, Abomination."

Damn. This old song.

"See, when you start calling me names, it really undercuts your argument. You're not mad because I got rid of Chaya. You're mad because you know *you* should have done it, but you didn't. And what happened was a mangy nephilim had to step up and do the deed for you."

The angel staggers to his feet and sticks his hands out in front of him, pressing his mangled wrists together.

"You must pay for what you've done, unclean thing."

"Go home, angel. My store is a mess, and looking at the big picture, I'm more afraid of Netflix than I am of you."

To my surprise, the crippled creep is able to manifest his Gladius, an angelic sword of fire. He has to hold it with both hands, but he can move it around by swinging his shoulders back and forth. Maybe this guy is more trouble than I gave him credit for. A badass will try to break your bones, but someone crazy, who knows what they'll do? Mostly, though, I'm glad the neighbors aren't around so I have to explain the gimp with the lightsaber in my driveway.

The angel comes at me hard and fast, all *Seven Samurai*, ready to send me to asshole Heaven. In his present condition, he's still quick, but far off his game. I sidestep the Gladius and punch him in the throat. He falls. The Gladius turns the pavement molten where it touches. As the angel goes down, I snap up a knee and break his nose. He falls over backward and the Gladius goes out.

I walk around behind him and push him upright. His eyes have rolled back in his head. He's completely out. I take out a flask full of Aqua Regia, everyone's favorite drink in Hell, and pour some down his throat. The angel gasps and his eyes snap open. He looks up at me and sputters.

"You're trying to poison me."

"You were unconscious. If I wanted you dead, I could have drilled a hole in your skull and tea-bagged your brain. Now shut up and go home."

The angel crawls away and lurches to his feet. He's covered in blood and booze and his hands are sticking out at funny angles, like he just fell out of a Picasso. He takes a breath and hauls himself upright, trying for a last little bit of dignity. I walk away.

"This isn't over," he yells.

I open the door to Max Overdrive.

"Yeah it is. See? I'm going inside. Bye."

I close the door and wait a second. When I open it again, the angel is gone. But he left blood and mucus all over the front steps. Something else to clean up.

Inside, Kasabian is behind the counter. He looks at me as I come in.

"What was that? I heard shouting."

I wave it away with my hand.

"Nothing. Some idiot rented *Bio-Dome* and wanted his money back."

Kasabian shakes his head.

"Fuck him. We're not paying for some schmuck's bad taste."

"That's pretty much what I said."

"Did you say it with your knees? You've got blood on them."

I look down. He's right. I'm hard on clothes.

"I'm going upstairs to change."

Here's the thing. Most angels aren't like the idiot outside. They're annoying, but a necessary evil, like black holes or vegans. Most angels are gray-suit-yes-sir-no-sir-fill-it-out-in-triplicate company men. Someone you wouldn't remember if they shot themselves out of a cannon dressed like Glinda, the good witch. A few angels, not many, go rogue and have to be put down like dogs. No tears shed for them. Still, as annoying as angels are, they keep air in the tires and gas in the tank so the universe can go on dumbly spinning. The only angels anyone is happy to see take a powder are Death and the Devil, one of whom is currently asleep in the storage room at Max Overdrive.

But I'll get to that later.

So, the angels are fucking off and God's away on business. What do the mice do when the cat's not looking? They drink. And if they're smart they do it at Bamboo House of Dolls. Candy and me, we're mice with PhDs. I'll meet up with her at the bar.

Chihiro, I mean. Not Candy. I have to remember that. *Chihiro*. Candy is dead. So to speak. Dead enough that the feds and the cops aren't looking for her, and that's all that counts. Now she's Chihiro, with a different face and name and, well, everything. Everything we can think of. I just hope it's enough. I'm sure we've missed a few things. I hope not so many that anyone is going to notice. I might have to kill them.

I change and go back downstairs, my na'at, knife, and Colt under my coat.

"I'm going to Bamboo House. Want to get a drink?"

Kasabian shakes his head, carefully putting discs in clear plastic cases with the tips of his mechanical fingers.

"Nah. I'm waiting for Maria. She's coming by with a new delivery."

"Anything good?"

He looks up and shakes his head.

"Don't know. She said it's a western."

"Fingers crossed it brings some goddamn customers into this tomb."

"Patience, grasshopper. This new deal with Maria is our stairway to Heaven."

"It better be. There won't be room for you, me, and Candy in a refrigerator box if this place closes."

"Chihiro," he says.

"Fuck. Chihiro."

"Later, Mr. Wizard," he says.

"Yeah. Later."

Outside, I wonder if I can scrape GODKILLER off the windows with the black blade instead of spending money on paint remover.

A week ago I saved the whole goddamn universe from extinction and now I can't afford the hardware store. I need to have a serious talk with my life coach.